Derivative Lives

Biofiction Studies

Biofiction is literature that names its protagonist after an actual historical figure, and it has become a dominant literary form over the last thirty years, resulting in publications from global luminaries as varied as Gabriel García Márquez, J.M. Coetzee, Margaret Atwood, Joyce Carol Oates, Mario Vargas Llosa, Laurent Binet, Peter Carey, Olga Tokarczuk, and Hilary Mantel. **Biofiction Studies** explores the history, rise, evolution, and nature of biofiction. Because it raises questions about the nature of the subject, of selfhood, on the ethics, politics, and psychology of representations, on the relationships between what is perceived or constructed as factual and fictional, **Biofiction Studies** will be of interest to students and scholars in numerous fields, including philosophy, ethics, literary, and genre theory.

Derivative Lives

Biofiction, Uncertainty, and Speculative Risk in Contemporary Spanish Narrative

Virginia Newhall Rademacher

BLOOMSBURY ACADEMIC
NEW YORK • LONDON • OXFORD • NEW DELHI • SYDNEY

BLOOMSBURY ACADEMIC
Bloomsbury Publishing Inc
1385 Broadway, New York, NY 10018, USA
50 Bedford Square, London, WC1B 3DP, UK
29 Earlsfort Terrace, Dublin 2, Ireland

BLOOMSBURY, BLOOMSBURY ACADEMIC and the Diana logo are trademarks of Bloomsbury Publishing Plc

First published in the United States of America 2022
This paperback edition published 2024

Cover design by Eleanor Rose
Cover image © Getty Images

Library of Congress Cataloguing-in-Publication Data
Names: Rademacher, Virginia Newhall, author.
Title: Derivative lives: biofiction, uncertainty, and speculative risk in contemporary Spanish narrative / Virginia Newhall Rademacher.
Description: New York: Bloomsbury Academic, 2022. |
Series: Biofiction studies | Includes bibliographical references and index. |
Summary: "Considers the surge in biographical fiction (biofiction) as a paradigm shift in our understanding of real-life narratives, relating literary expression to theories of risk and uncertainty"– Provided by publisher.
Identifiers: LCCN 2022006077 (print) | LCCN 2022006078 (ebook) |
ISBN 9781501386909 (hardback) | ISBN 9781501386947 (paperback) |
ISBN 9781501386916 (epub) | ISBN 9781501386923 (pdf) | ISBN 9781501386930
Subjects: LCSH: Biographical fiction, Spanish–History and criticism. |
Spanish fiction–21st century–History and criticism. | LCGFT: Literary criticism.
Classification: LCC PQ6147.B57 R33 2022 (print) |
LCC PQ6147.B57 (ebook) | DDC 863/.0820907–dc23/eng/20220513
LC record available at https://lccn.loc.gov/2022006077
LC ebook record available at https://lccn.loc.gov/2022006078

ISBN: HB: 978-1-5013-8690-9
PB: 978-1-5013-8694-7
ePDF: 978-1-5013-8692-3
eBook: 978-1-5013-8691-6

Series: Biofiction Studies

Typeset by Integra Software Services Pvt. Ltd.

To find out more about our authors and books visit www.bloomsbury.com and sign up for our newsletters.

For Richard, for always believing in me

And for my daughters—Emily, Susanna, Grace, and Lily,
who give me four wonderful reasons to believe

CONTENTS

ACKNOWLEDGMENTS

Writing can often feel like a very solitary endeavor, but it is always a conversation. So many people contributed to this book, even in those moments when I felt alone with my ideas. When I first met four years ago with my Bloomsbury editor, Haaris Naqvi, at a conference in Utrecht, Netherlands, I thought, "This book will be done in a year or two, at most." Now, four years later, it is complete—or as complete as any conversation ever is. In the time it took to start and finish, the world closed amid a global contagion, and is tentatively, hopefully, reopening even as the pandemic lingers. Daughters graduated, and another is about to embark on college. One began, and is now about to finish medical school. Life goes on, amid uncertainty and risk—as this book explores—and we imaginatively draw from others' biographical lives to chart new possibilities for how to live and create, and the collaborative risks and responsibilities we share as human beings striving for meaning and purpose on this planet.

I am thankful to the many colleagues, friends, and family who have helped me along the way, and who have made this book better. I am blessed with wonderful colleagues at Babson College. My dear friend, poet Mary Pinard, offered insights on one of the chapters and gave an interview that markedly deepened another. Julie Levinson, my departmental chair, has also provided support throughout. As someone who enjoys exploring new places as much as I do, I am looking forward to further intrepid travels together, and the opportunity to share this work widely. All of my "Caravan of Care" (you know who you are!) friends in Arts and Humanities have been sources of cheer as the ideas and pages accumulated. I have also benefited from numerous grants from the Babson Faculty Research Fund (BFRF), including support for my interview in Spain of writer Javier Cercas.

In that regard, I am deeply indebted to Javier Cercas and Rosa Montero, both of whom graciously met with me and provided rich interviews that have added not only to this book, but also to new understandings of approaches to biofiction more broadly. Those interviews appear in another Bloomsbury publication, *Conversations with Biographical Novelists: Truthful Fictions across the Globe.*

Within the expanding field of Biofiction Studies, the editor of the above volume of interviews, Michael Lackey, has been not only a leading scholar, but an always-generous colleague, reader, and collaborator. He has been instrumental in generatively drawing together a community of global scholars in diverse areas of biofiction research. Through this community, I have been lucky to collaborate with terrific scholars such as Laura Cernat, Bethany Layne, and Todd Avery, who have organized conferences, edited volumes, and been willing to read and comment kindly on one of this book's chapters, even after a long day of teaching. I am especially grateful to the editors for this new Bloomsbury series on biofiction: Michael Lackey, Monica Latham, and Lucia Boldrini. Their confidence in this project throughout and incisive suggestions have energized my thinking and enriched this book. The care and alacrity with which they have approached their roles as editors should be a model for academic publishing everywhere.

One of the greatest joys of this project has been sharing my work with my beloved daughters, whose intelligent and deeply perceptive commentary on this book and its ideas has been an extraordinary gift. I am awed at the brilliant young adults they are. I am ever grateful to my family for their support, and especially to Richard, whose love and encouragement have always sustained me, and who has always "read" me best.

Introduction: Derivative Lives: Biofiction, Uncertainty, and Speculative Risk in Contemporary Spanish Narrative

The title of this book alludes to the challenge of finding one's way within the contemporary market of virtually limitless information and claims to veracity. Amid this profusion of options, it is easy to feel lost in spaces of uncertainty where biographical truth teeters between the real and the imaginative. The title thus also points to the prolific market of biographical novels that openly play in the speculative space between the ostensibly real and the fictional. Whether we choose to see it as a timely shift or a newly dominant literary form, the past few decades have produced a boom in a wide variety of biographical fictions, which Alain Buisine conceptualized with the term "biofiction" in 1991.[1] As fiction that names its protagonist or other high-profile characters after real-life individuals, biofictions consciously reference a specific historical subject and then open that life narrative to imaginative possibility. What motivates the proliferation of literature that fictionalizes the lives of real people, and why now? Are changing perceptions of the fixity of biographical identity or the centrality of uncertainty and flux in our lives driving so many writers and readers to this mode? How do these works employ postmodern strategies while at the same time expressing a tension with relativism and a desire to reconnect to real lives and issues beyond the text? Moreover, to what extent is this area of literary experimentation reflective of questioning that extends across multiple geographies? Alongside exploration of these initial inquiries, this

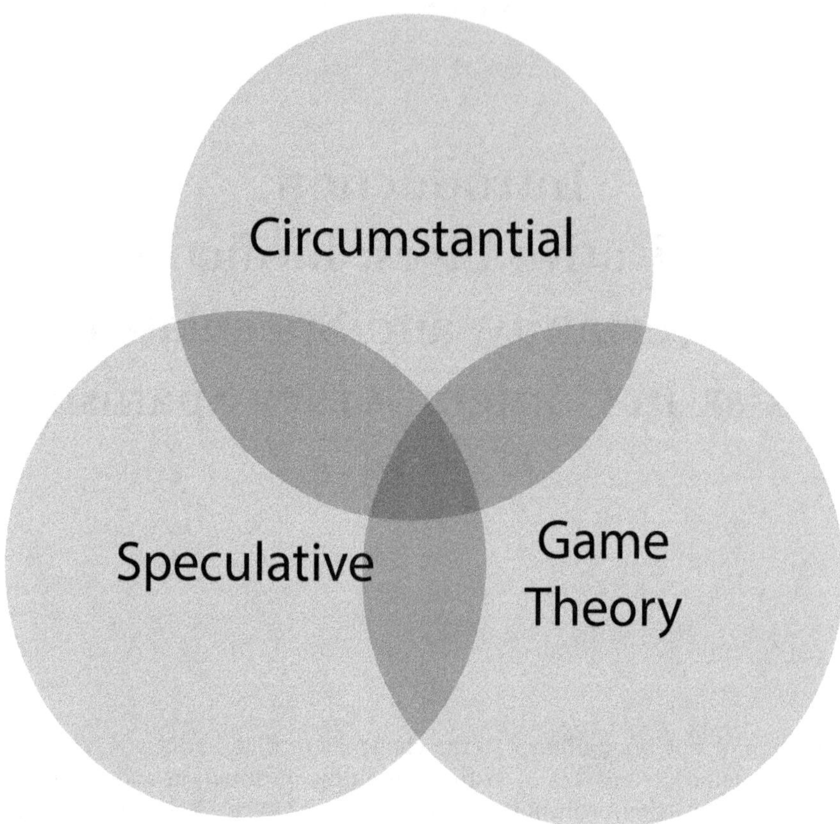

FIGURE 0.1 *Circumstantial, speculative, and game theory models.*

book argues that biofictions provide thresholds for experimenting with what we think we know, negotiating between realities of the human condition and fiction's capacity to shape their reassessment.

A growing number of Spanish writers have written prominent and popular biographical novels. Drawing on theories of risk and uncertainty, this book considers the surge in the biographical novel in Spain and globally as part of a broader paradigm shift that deepens, diversifies, and disrupts options for imagining and investing in real-life narratives, relating literary expression to concepts such as circumstantiality, derivatives, speculation, and game studies. Despite a diversity of approaches to the biographical novel, these writers collectively reflect consciousness of the insecurity of any singular biographical truth. At the same time, they express that instability not only to more accurately reflect reality or a contested past, but also to invoke new ways of seeing in the present. As a result, they are less interested in the fact versus fiction ontology so often associated with discussions of biographical fiction than in the creation of novels that openly examine how to live and to create in this context. As writer Rosa Montero observed in an interview, "life has always been uncertain, but now we are much more conscious of that uncertainty."[2] Montero suggests that biographical novels both expose the existential uncertainty of our lives and contend with the consequences of this insecurity by creating "emergency map[s] to navigate a confusing world. [...] One doesn't write a novel to simply illuminate through images or illustrations, let's say, the biography of another person, but to try to better understand the world, to search for the meaning of existence."[3]

The word "risk," for example, derives from the early Italian *risicare*, to dare. In *Against the Gods: The Remarkable Story of Risk*, Peter Bernstein argues that in this sense, "risk is a choice rather than a fate. The actions we dare to take, which depend upon how free we are to make choices, are what the story of risk is all about. And that story helps define what it is to be a human being."[4] Notably, the surge that we see in the contemporary biographical novel reflects a consciousness both of the uncertainties associated with immersion in a context of constant options over what to believe and acknowledgment that tension among these choices shapes not only literary lives but also the human experience more essentially. Accordingly, what I refer to—seemingly paradoxically—as the speculative realism of biofiction reflects a desire to chart differing pathways of how we navigate a world in which truth is often questioned and fiction may achieve an honesty that more purportedly "truthful" narratives fail to convey.

Because I situate these works within critical conversations beyond biofiction, I draw from varied scholarship not directly related to literary studies. Connecting themes of uncertainty, identity, and risk, contemporary social theorist Anthony Giddens has argued that "modernity is a risk culture" in which we are constantly revising our biographical narratives amid a "puzzling diversity of options and possibilities."[5] Ulrich Beck has also written extensively on the concept of contemporary life as a risk society, especially with respect to the risks that human choices and creations have themselves produced. Changes wrought by technology that have in many ways eased communication have also produced new uncertainties, just as one might argue that the subversion of master narratives posited by postmodernism has simultaneously created new challenges for how we understand truth. Other scholars such as Christopher Lasch and Zygmunt Bauman have focused on the contemporary impact of mobility and flux to identity, and the challenge of managing this rootlessness with respect to one's own self and relationships with others. Connecting these issues further to literary shifts and changes in genre, theorists such as Alison Gibbons have proposed that the literary cosmos is rearranging itself amid the perception that the Western world "feels like a more precarious and volatile place." Within the dominant cultural logic that is forming, our connectedness to one another is being built increasingly with fictional characters as representations of ourselves.[6]

In response to the precariousness of truth and the permeability of the potentially fictional, I consider the expansion of biographical fiction as a literary approach that engages directly with how we manage such risks—not to eliminate them, but to incorporate them as part of the essential construction and formation of our lives and their narration. Since questions that writers explore are not isolated from other areas of thought, *Derivative Lives* relates changes in literary strategy and shifts in cultural logic, reflecting on approaches in other fields and disciplines such as law, finance, and economics that similarly contend with competing claims to truth and value. Through intersecting approaches—what I have termed the *circumstantial*, *speculative*, and *game theory* models—this book explores the work of eight Spanish authors (across eleven texts) who present alternative ways of conceptualizing the biographical novel. [See Figure 0.1] These writers' varied approaches draw unexpected connections between changes in genre and strategies in other fields that broach the real and the possible, collectively commenting on the epistemological challenges of contemporary life.

Overview of the Circumstantial, Speculative, and Game Theory Models

The *circumstantial* model emphasizes the contingent, competing nature of evidentiary information, which on its own is simply a collection of discrete details that are later composed into a convincing thread. While many biofictions carefully document the historical record, they also build from the conception that the accumulation of biographical details can never add up sufficiently to resolve the identities and motivations of real individuals who form part of contested, conflictive historical moments. In the law, a circumstantial case is one in which, lacking direct observation of the events in question, an argument must be crafted from disparate traces. One of the ways we can better understand the intentions of the biographical novel is to examine more closely the novelist's freedom to renegotiate and contest narrative claims regarding what the evidence of a life tells or fails to tell us. In so doing, writers of biofictions see themselves as free to interrogate the individual choices involved in complex histories and to liberate the interpretation of facts to new conceptions. Writer Javier Cercas has argued, for example, that contingent moments are so important in his books because they are "so important in life. It's possible that recent history, through any number of circumstances, has given a great deal of importance to social, collective phenomena, and has overlooked the importance of individual decisions."[7]

We may wonder what arguably has changed to make this trend more predominant among writers and more persuasive to readers. In many ways, the experience of contemporary life has become increasingly circumstantial. The speed, profusion, and anonymity of images and information that inundate our pages and screens make it difficult to determine either origin or firm identity, and suggest the capacity to continuously reinvent oneself and others is enormously powerful. Rather than direct observation, we interact and make decisions about others—the verity or believability of their stories and histories—based on increasingly disembedded information and images. In response to what Jonathan Sturgeon has referred to as this "vitality of self in excess of systems—of control, capital, information, whatever"—the biographical novel reveals and opens to challenge how the writer chooses to discern, distill, and make sense of profuse and ever-evolving details in the crafting of biographical meaning.[8] This process shows how any life narrative is a "living hypothesis" or, as Ben Lerner has argued, "how we live fictions, how fictions have real effects, become facts in that sense, and how our experience of the world changes depending on its arrangement into one narrative or another."[9]

The *speculative* model focuses attention on how biofictional writers shape investment in the biographical subject as a source of fictional experimentation and creative potential. This sense of the speculative underscores contradictions of contemporary life, in which the immediacy and profusion of information may be perceived as destabilizing and fragmenting or, alternatively, as liberating and connecting. One may choose to hedge against unexpected shifts in meaning and value, as traditional biography does by adhering closely to documented fact, or instead—as many writers of biofiction do—to apply creative invention in ways that capitalize on variability and the risk of conjecture.

Economic theorists such as Peter Bernstein, Robert Tally ("Meta-Capital: Culture and Financial Derivatives"), Dick Bryan and Michael Rafferty (*Capitalism with Derivatives*), Stephen Nelson and Peter Katzenstein ("Uncertainty, Risk, and the Financial Crisis of 2008"), and Mark Taylor (*Confidence Games*), among others, have written compellingly about theories of speculation and risk in contemporary culture. These discussions spark connections to the literary experimentation we see in biofiction. The concept of the speculative is associated in a financial context with "connotations of risk, lack of firm evidence, and uncertainty."[10] We can also relate biographical risk, the ambiguities, and absences of information with respect to another self and the certainty or confidence we have in our interpretations, with other approaches to addressing uncertainty with respect to value and meaning. According to Judith Merril, speculative fiction consists of "stories whose objective is to explore, to *learn* by modes of projection, extrapolation, analogue, hypothesis, and paper experimentation something about the nature of the universe, of man, or reality."[11] While such narratives can be future driven, they can also explore "what if …" with respect to how things may have played out in the past. In this sense, the effort to speculate on and project contemporary visions on a real past can also be a mechanism to better understand the present.

Colm Toíbín has referred to the "anchored imagination" that fuels biofiction.[12] This convergence between the "anchored" real and its imagined derivatives invokes connections with the theory and growth of financial derivatives, which also depend upon a foundational asset but then become sources of investment and exchange in their own right. In the financial markets, derivatives refer to options whose value derives from an underlying asset. We can also conceive of these options in literary terms as narratives *derived from* the real. Yet, as in the financial context, all the varied derivative identities we create (literary selves, biofictional characters, social media identities, etc.) can become their own sources of investment and exchange, and thus detached from the "real" lives from which they originated. Robert Tally has argued that "there is clearly something strange going on when the derivative instrument, so named because it's supposed to *derive* from the underlying asset, actually becomes the measure of value for the underlying asset."[13] The biographical novels I consider both conjure and challenge the idea that the fictionalized derivation of a life story can actually become more real and more defining than the original biographies from which they deviate. The creation of new derivative options in the market strives to protect against variability in value or alternately capitalizes on this variance. We can view the growth in biofiction similarly in relation to the discovery and application of new instruments for addressing uncertainty and risk as other strategies become exhausted.

The interactive, multiple formats by which we represent versions of identity, creating and discarding images of a life, and through which we "follow" and intervene in the representations of others, have changed dramatically in the last few decades. The question of trust is embedded in the nature of any fiction, but especially so in biographical fiction. The process of writing a life, even a fictionalized version, is often framed as a struggle for authorship ("authority"/"authorized" versions) or control over information. Just as digital identities can be deleted, retouched, reposted, or retransmitted by whomever, whenever, biofictions acknowledge that our biographical lives are also in transit. Amid increasingly networked relationships, the capacity to intervene in the construction of identity is mutable and played out through dynamic multiplayer interactions among authors, readers, critics, and other (potentially hidden or unknown) stakeholders invested in the outcome of these representations.

In turn, the *game theory* model considers biofictions as narrative games that openly reveal and reconfigure the networks of relationships invested in the representation of a life story. As a paradigm that indicates the true source of uncertainty derives from the intentions of other players, game theory provides a useful mechanism to conceive of new forms of biographical fictions as simulations through which the writer, real-life subject, biofictional "avatar," and others become embedded in the vast, multiplayer game of narrating a life. For example, Spanish writer Lucía Etxebarria actively shifts the biographical novelist's role from external creator or operator of the simulation to one knowingly immersed in the game, competing for control of the narrative with the biographical subject and other players. Notably, in contrast to postmodern games that self-consciously draw attention to their own fictionality to undermine the truth value of the narrative enterprise, such writers frequently use ludic games of fictionalized truth to evoke and play out political, ethical, and other real problems beyond the text.

Rather than focusing on the confluence of fact and fiction or bemoaning this slipperiness, many writers of biofiction explore a different type of risk—the risk of ignoring the responsibility that we have to truthfulness within the postmodern paradigm that we have created. Colum McCann, for example, contends that a central responsibility of biofiction is to challenge the universality or domination of any one representation or "authorized" version: "This manipulation of what is true and untrue is what the contemporary novelist is flaring up against. [...] And you have to work out of a reckless inner need to challenge and interrogate the notion of what is true and what you can trust."[14] Postmodernism had an important role in biofiction's emergence as a dominant form, as it granted writers permission to reimagine and reconstruct their own versions of biographical lives. Yet, while postmodernism created openings for us to question and contest dominant narratives, the fact that meaning may be interpreted differently and across differing times does not let us off the hook with respect to the truth claims of the narratives we create or mean that all representations are equally valid. We also bear an obligation to our involvement and imaginative intervention in others' biographies. Against the view of the writer as simple transmitter of narrative or the reader as passive receiver, these works invoke our own responsibility to be active participants of networked realities in ferreting out biographical truths amid competing versions.

Chapter Organization

This book's three sections reflect the models I have described. While these approaches often overlap and are not mutually exclusive, they provide an important way of framing the connections I explore regarding the growth and popularity of biofictional works and strategies in other fields. With the exception of the first, each additional chapter includes discussions of two biofictional works, and, in a number of instances, the novels of different authors paired within a single chapter. The aim of this structure is to put these texts concertedly in conversation with one another, while continuing to link their ideas to the through-line of the book as a whole. Given my emphasis on the literary experimentation of biofictions and approaches in other fields of inquiry, I have purposefully selected a number of works that might be categorized as hybrid or even borderline biofictions. By this, I mean that these examples incorporate biofiction with other modes of narrating and fictionalizing our auto/biographical lives. While my focus is on biofictional aspects, this blending with auto/biographical and autofictional aspects in various works is reflective of the complicated intermingling of these forms in contemporary life—the often fragile borders and complex relationships among biographical, fictional, and authorial subjectivities that we navigate in reality and not only in these texts.[15] Consistent throughout my selections is the effort by these authors to make the fictionalized biographical subject a central character and interlocutor, even as they may also incorporate a fictional version of themselves.

Part One, *The Circumstantial Case: Chasing Criminals/Tracing Traumatic Histories,* examines the intentional confluence of carefully documented evidence and invention in novels that are framed as both biographical searches and investigations into traumatic crimes and histories. Chapter 1, "Making the Circumstantial Case: Reasonable Doubt and Moral Certainty in Javier Cercas' *Soldiers of Salamis*," explores a central issue in many biographical novels: the discretionary power we have within a context marked by the simultaneous insufficiency and multiplicity of information and wide participation in its formation. Rather than resolving a crime or traumatic history and putting it to rest, Cercas uses fiction to reimagine individual motives and choices involved in complex histories and to liberate the interpretation of facts to new conceptions. Especially at this cultural moment, when public discourse is fixated on notions of truth or its abrogation, biofictions challenge master narratives that consecrate one dominant perspective and disempower many others. The publication of Cercas' *Soldiers of Salamis* marks an important shift both in his work and in the development of the biographical novel in Spain. By incorporating elements of a personal interview with Cercas, this chapter helps to foreground many of the theoretic discussions that follow.

Antonio Muñoz Molina's *Like a Fading Shadow* and Gabriela Ybarra's *The Dinner Guest* are the subjects of Chapter 2 ("Fugitive Biofictions"). In the former, Muñoz Molina combines a methodical retracing and imaginative reconstruction of the two months that Martin Luther King Jr.'s assassin, James Earl Ray, spent as a fugitive, focusing especially on the ten days he spent in Lisbon. Muñoz Molina's impressionistic novel strays far from fact in the often surreal story of a chase that comments on the elusive process of pursuing and capturing the fugitive biographical subject. In the latter, Ybarra imaginatively reconstructs the story of the kidnapping and murder of her grandfather by Basque terrorists, events that took place six years before she was born. In postulating her version of the story, she also imaginatively retraces and reclaims the story of her mother's death to cancer in 2011. In both, hints and provocations of the biofiction reveal the tension between reimagining another life and the autobiographical freedom or compulsion to escape and rewrite one's own.

Part Two, *Speculative Truths and Derivative Fictions*, examines how we have come to depend more heavily upon speculation and derivative instruments such as biographical fictions. Just as the concept behind financial derivatives is not new—people have hedged and capitalized on unexpected changes throughout history—novels that protagonize the life of a real-life individual have long existed. What has changed or intensified is the prevalence and complexity of these practices within the contemporary context. Chapter 3, "Entertaining the What-Ifs in Rosa Montero's *The Madwoman of the House* and *The Ridiculous Idea of Never Seeing You Again*," contributes to further thinking about biofiction as a literary response to managing uncertainty. By playing out a multiplicity of options, Montero contends that biofictions constitute models that explore alternative ways to navigate the ambiguity and flux of contemporary life. While Montero's works present the volatility and viability of options as destabilizing, this variance is also a source of invention and creative possibility.

Employing an alternative conception of the speculative, Chapter 4, "Fraudulent Pasts and Fictional Futures in Javier Cercas' *The Impostor* and Adolfo García Ortega's *The Birthday Buyer*," examines the construction of derivative fictions in these two novels from the differing outlooks of false and real victims of historical trauma. In reimagining the biographies of both criminals and innocents, these works openly acknowledge their use of fiction, challenging facile, distorting narratives that lay claim to singular truth.

Part Three, *Critical Play in Biofictional Games*, considers new forms of biographical fiction as narrative games that play out and upon the uncertainty of the motivations and identities of various stakeholders involved in the dynamic process of narrating a life story. Chapter 5, "Playing for Real: Simulated Games of Identity in Lucía Etxebarria's *Courtney and I* and *Truth Is Nothing but a Moment of Falsehood*," explores the creation of biofictions as interactive processes that upend the traditional subject of the biography as the center of the narrative, demonstrating the intersubjectivity of networked lives that intersect in unpredictable ways. Incorporating strategies from other games of simulation where individuals play an active and intervening role in the construction of fictionalized narrative identities or avatars, I consider the use of technology and various media to stretch the limits of narrative representation through the lens of what Henry Jenkins and others call transmedia storytelling.

The sixth and final chapter, "Literary Afterlives and Paratextual Play: Elvira Navarro's *The Last Days of Adelaida García Morales* and

Antonio Orejudo's *The Famous Five and Me*," considers novels that use diverging techniques of co-creation, paratextual games, and the "spinoff" to play into and imaginatively recreate the interconnections between writers' creations and their literary afterlives. As with other "game theoretic" strategies, these works demonstrate the interaction between creation and reception and the tension between the claim to sole authorship and the reality of more dispersive adaptations. Through the dual temporal approaches of biofiction, playing a simulated character "in" the narrative and as an outside player operating from a distance, these authors comment satirically and critically on the past and present of their own generations, then and now.

Why Spain? Spanish Biofictions and the Biographical Novel Globally

Considering the concept of the market as a metaphor for the confluence of apparent agency and innumerable choices, it is notable that many contemporary writers of Spanish biofictions came of age or were young adults during the transition from dictatorship. If these writers perceived themselves as freed up from authoritarian models and mores of narrowly defined social and gender roles, of monolithic Catholicism, they also leapt into a climate of vast technological change in which the authority and control we assert over our narrative lives are more open and uncertain. While this immersive system of options creates obstacles for the endurance of any singular biographical narrative, it also creates space for biofictions to disrupt dominant histories and to pose alternative conceptions that re-contextualize and revalorize meaning.

In the early years of transition following end of the Franco dictatorship in 1975, it is perhaps not surprising that many writers turned to historical fiction or historiographic metafiction to reveal versions of history that had long been silenced. However, in the past few decades, a burgeoning number of Spain's most innovative and prominent novels have been works of biofiction. This recent turn to the biographical novel in Spain coincides with the rising production and popularity of this form among writers in other parts of the globe, as evidenced by the work of J.M. Coetzee, Margaret Atwood, Joyce Carol Oates, Colum McCann, Laurent Binet, Michael Cunningham, Anchee Min, Colm Toíbín, Olga Tokarczuk, and many, many others. Michael Lackey has observed that an impetus among some biographical novelists has been to escape the overemphasis on the role of history in shaping and determining identity and to consider more fully the importance of human autonomy. In Spain, for example, Javier Cercas has emphasized how an important shift in his work was exploring the contingent, individual decisions that have influenced history and that escape documentation. With authoritarian power, as in Franco's Spain, there was only one truth. In a more open society, as with a more pluralistic approach to biographical truth, writers are free to examine the past outside of specific social, historical, and cultural constraints, or to use fiction to allow us to examine those from alternative perspectives and to see them anew. Moreover, as Rosa Montero has contended, biographical novels "make us conscious of reassessing our reality. [...] We live in a world that's so insecure, and so the narrative has to be uncertain as well."[16] In this sense, then, the lives of the biographical characters in these works become "enormous screens," as she describes them, onto which we can project possibilities.[17] This combination of a more circumstantial reality open to speculation reinforces our own responsibility as writers and readers, because it is a choice rather than a fate how much risk we are willing to take on—how open we are to exposing and engaging with life's uncertainties.

By focusing on contemporary Spanish biographical novels, this work strives to address the gap in the understudied area of Hispanic biofictions while simultaneously contending that these examples are reflective of literary experimentation and questioning that is pertinent across multiple domains. In turn, this book builds out the growing scholarship on the contemporary biographical novel and biofiction, including the work of leading scholars such as Lucia Boldrini, Marie-Luise Kohlke, Michael Lackey, Monica Latham, Bethany Layne, Martin Middeke, and Julia Novak, among others, whose work has inspired new areas of exploration in this field. Notably, my approach relating uncertainty, speculation, and game studies takes a unique and unexpected perspective that straddles the risks and rewards of the ambiguous borders between the certain and the credible, the real and the imaginative. This book speaks to the belief that the questions explored in literature extend beyond disciplinary boundaries to reflect, inform, and challenge conceptions of the human experience.

PART ONE

The Circumstantial Case: Chasing Criminals/Tracing Traumatic Histories

1

Making the Circumstantial Case: Reasonable Doubt and Moral Certainty in Javier Cercas' *Soldiers of Salamis*

"The past is never dead. It's not even past."
(WILLIAM FAULKNER, *REQUIEM FOR A NUN*)

Javier Cercas refers to the "dictatorship of the present" as the current tendency to intensify the dominion of the immediate present and to neglect versions and voices of the past that inhabit and continue to act on our reality. This perspective illuminates some important motivations propelling the growth in biofiction. Cercas states that beginning with *Soldiers of Salamis* (2001), his books "took on a battle with this impoverished present and in support of one that is more complete, complex, and that draws more fully from the past."[1] Since *Soldiers of Salamis*, he contends, "all of my books are really about this ongoing dialogue between past and present. Before that, my books only lived in the immediate present. That's why I believe I used to be a postmodern writer" (up to, he suggests, the third part of *Soldiers of Salamis*) "and maybe now, I'm a post-postmodern writer."[2] What is it about this third section of Cercas' biofictional novel that he believes communicates this marked shift? Are we experiencing a wider epistemological and ethical crisis that biofictions reveal and potentially help navigate? Can Cercas' novel help us with that taxonomy and better understanding of its implications?

This chapter combines elements of conversations with Javier Cercas with the analysis of *Soldiers of Salamis* as a text that marks a seminal turn in the expansion of the biographical novel in Spain and that conveys a burgeoning tension with postmodern narrative.[3] I frame this approach as a heightened awareness of and resistance to the circumstantial nature of our lives. The accumulation of constantly circulating information and images fails to solve the more complex, often contentious questions and claims to truth that clutter our minds and inboxes. In turn, many writers of biofiction emphasize the ethical and discretionary power we have within a context of simultaneous insufficiency and multiplicity of information. How do we access something real while acknowledging its provisionality? How do we engage with competing biographical and historical truths that lie scattered and fragmented, without declaring it all relative? As Christopher Schaberg has pointedly posed, "If everyone's stories are valid, who is to say that Klan members cannot march, that white supremacists aren't right, just *in their own way*"[4] (emphasis mine). Cercas has observed that with *Soldiers of Salamis* he doesn't abandon postmodernism altogether, but that new tools and interests come to light. "And there appears," he adds, "a strong moral inquiry that was there before, but was more subdued, much less evident."[5] In turn, he suggests this shift stems from a desire to expose the holes of relativity and ambiguity, the absence of real connection, in pursuit of a deeper hermeneutic engagement in which the expansion of the biographical novel plays a part.

Framed around this overarching concept of the circumstantial, this chapter looks specifically at how changing conceptions of "reasonable" doubt and the ethics of uncertainty can illuminate new ways of thinking about the uses of biographical truth in fiction. If, as Cercas says, new "tools and interests come to light" alongside a heightened moral inquiry, why is this? Moreover, how might these new biofictional tools and interests reflect, as Mary Holland has contended, "that changing concepts of reality and real advances in technology change literary technique and form as they strive to more accurately reflect that reality, in turn reshaping the real world?"[6] I begin by considering current efforts to define and locate the shifts we are seeing in literary outlook, both in Spain and more comprehensively. Centering on *Soldiers of Salamis* as a novel that prominently demonstrates these emergent trends in Spanish fiction, I consider how Cercas' self-conscious reflection on biographical uncertainty and human responsibility to the truths of another life examines critical tensions implicit to many contemporary biofictions. And finally, I examine how attention to essential, humanistic questions of our time may help to explain the sustained growth in this form.

While people often refer to Cercas' novels as historical novels, he resists that label: "I write novels in which history has a role, but they are not historical novels."[7] Why does he deny that categorization so pointedly? Michael Lackey has argued that the turn from the historical to the biographical novel is not merely aesthetic, but reflects shifting theories of consciousness and history that contest interpretations of the individual biographical subject as shaped primarily by social and collective forces.[8] A circumstantial reality is one in which information comes to us indirectly, so that we must be inferential judges not only of its validity or truth, but also of the place of seemingly discrete circumstances within a larger narrative. While postmodernism liberated us from metanarratives that lay claim to singular truth, it also opens to other complexities of responsibility for interpretation and intellectual judgment. Russell Banks has noted how the qualities that have loosened history and biography from claims to objectivity have also revised the freedom with which fiction writers can draw creatively from these sources to reveal differing truths. As Banks describes, "the novelist can humanize a historical figure by inhabiting the character in a way that a biographer and a historian can't. But that's in the interest of humanity, extending our interest as human beings, not history."[9] In this vein, Cercas argues that the emphasis on external, collective influences overlooks the very real importance of individual decisions and the powerful roles of contingency and uncertainty in shaping human agency. As he claims, "individual decisions, at times risky ones that depend largely on chance, are absolutely crucial in our lives. They're not myths in my novels; they're essential realities of people's lives."[10]

The rearrangements in cultural logic that we observe in approaches to biographical risk are not limited to literary outlook, but extend to other fields of thought that draw upon real sources to engage with truth, conjecture, and ethical inquiry. Referencing transformations in the literary use of circumstantial evidence, legal scholar Barbara Shapiro emphasizes the important intersections of law, literature, and other aspects of culture that strive to represent and distinguish "reality" and the "verisimilar." She contends that "neither law nor literature is an isolated phenomenon" and both should be understood in broader and more integrated contexts than they have traditionally been treated.[11] Among others, scholars such as George Fisher, James Franklin, Richard Greenstein, and James Whitman have written about evolving and uneven interpretations of circumstantial evidence and "reasonable doubt" in the law and approaches to uncertainty in other fields. As Franklin sees it, the history of reasonable doubt "does not by any means belong exclusively to the law. It belongs to a much larger history of the search for certainty, a search that preoccupied scientists, theologians, and philosophers as much as it did lawyers."[12] For Shapiro, the rule is only part of this grand modern effort to understand the sufficiency of certainty as a practical matter, what the law refers to as "moral certainty." The continued challenges of the courts to interpret or consistently apply concepts of "beyond reasonable doubt" and moral certainty evoke larger epistemological shifts, exposing fractures in evidentiary rules intended to "probe the complexities of ambiguous human transactions" and that literary texts expose to further scrutiny.[13] As Michael Wood reinforces, engaging with questions that seem to speak to the essence of biofiction,

> How much doubt is reasonable doubt, and how far does one have to go towards a dissolution of community before notions of shared

> reasonableness becomes a problem? [...] How do we alleviate our panic about knowing too little (about another person, for example) or too much (about the multifarious details of the world)?[14]

By revealing our biographical lives as contested sites, biofictions are perhaps the perfect metaphor or vehicle for negotiating our contemporary human condition. In *Supplanting the Postmodern*, Nicholas Stavris relates the re-emergence of the real in literature to a twenty-first century engulfed by a climate of anxiety and uncertainty regarding identity and selfhood. Rather than postmodern displacement, he notes a transition towards a "realigned focus on truth" and a "positive desire on the part of the subject to reclaim wholeness and selfhood in a globalized culture that is clouded in uncertainty."[15] In *Metamodernism: Historicity, Affect and Depth after Postmodernism*, van den Akker, Gibbons, and Vermeulen attempt to periodize this shifting paradigm, beginning with the decade of 2000 as a critical point of inflection. Citing the host of new modes in which the real "insistently infiltrates the fiction to assert its epistemic imperative," Alison Gibbons observes how contemporary crises such as the 2001 terrorist attacks and the global financial crisis have reinforced our perception of a "fragile and fragmentary reality" in which the self reasserts itself through personal, situated experience and human connection.[16] Writer Jose Ovejero encapsulates this further as a nostalgia for the real. He notes that while it might be easy to minimize or ridicule this anxiety, such nostalgia—as the testimony of a lack—should not be devalued. Rather, like a ghost pain, it reminds us that we are missing a necessary element of our lives.[17] From the point of view of biofiction, I see this "truthful tension" (to use Mary Holland's term) as acknowledgment of a desire for a humanizing realness, particularity, and connection that we perceive to have lost, but also with the awareness that we cannot recover these innocently or confidently.[18]

The period after 2000 marks a similar shift in Spain, especially with respect to the novels of memory that deal with reconstructing and reimagining the buried histories of the Spanish Civil War (1936–9) and its aftermath in the almost forty-year Franco dictatorship. While many of the novels of the 1980s and 1990s are largely concerned with binary versions of the past suppressed and distorted under Francoism, the post-2000 memory novel presents a more multi-perspective view in which conflict with the past is often expressed within individual identity and through an auto/biographical lens. Hans Hansen has observed that against the "weak or erased postmodern subject," these works feature the return of the author as a figure in the text. Defying "postmodernism's ontological questioning, these texts insist on the reality of the past and the authenticity of its representation," whether in the forms of realist description and/or the inclusion of signs such as photos, copies of letters, and other archival evidence. At the same time, many of these novels "maintain postmodern questioning of how to obtain knowledge about this past, and about the criteria of historical truth."[19]

Soldiers of Salamis signifies an important example of these changed interests and strategies. However, within what I characterize as the turn to the *circumstantial* mode, postmodern tools persist amid growing resistance to relativism and a heightened desire to connect to real lives and issues beyond the text. Cercas' novel shares, for example, the aims of historiographic metafiction to question the selection and composition of evidentiary facts as well as *whose truth gets told*. Yet, while Linda Hutcheon contends that postmodernism "never offers answers that are anything but provisional and contextually determined (and limited)," beginning with *Soldiers of Salamis*, Cercas searches for truths that speak more enduringly to the human condition.[20] He uses the meticulously researched details of a specific historical moment, while also attempting to surpass its contingency—to project a creative, symbolic vision and to affirm its relevance to the making of present and future realities. "This novel," he claims in an interview, "doesn't only want to find historical truth but wants to go beyond that to find say, a literary and moral truth that is universal truth."[21]

All evidence tells stories, and the construction of these stories, along with judgments about their relationship to the truth, necessarily depends upon inferential reasoning and imagined connections. As Richard Greenstein has argued, "just as we understand the narratives of our own lives as having both a past and a future, so the narratives we use to understand our experiences generally are both backward and forward thinking." He observes that while we think about evidentiary facts as anchored in the past, it turns out that "recapturing the past always implicates the future and always expresses a moral perspective. When factfinders determine 'what happened', they simultaneously pronounce how the world should be."[22] Cercas applies similar logic through fictional means; biofictions allow us to imagine a future as much as they reflect on a past. These works are concerned with the hermeneutic process of the biographical subject to navigate and shape a world of incomplete evidence. From this viewpoint, openly revealing the subject's reasonable doubts gets at a more truthful expression of lived experience and simultaneously creates a vision of the world. As Cercas has claimed, "It's not even just an act of honesty to bare the mechanisms of the book and show them to the reader. It's also a tool to set out the central problems of life."[23]

Opening Argument: *Soldiers of Salamis* and Biofiction as Moral Inquiry

Since its publication in 2001, *Soldiers of Salamis* has become an international best seller, translated into more than thirty languages, and received multiple literary prizes. Its "surprise mass market triumph," as Nathan Richardson describes, ushered in a new period in which "remembering became not simply a trend but *the* trend."[24] The novel traces the narrator's efforts (a journalist and novelist also named Javier Cercas) to investigate and write the "true tale" of fascist leader Rafael Sánchez Mazas, who remarkably escaped from a Republican firing squad towards the end of the Spanish Civil War. While attempting to hide, Sánchez Mazas is reportedly discovered by a Republican soldier who points his gun at him, looks him in the eyes, and then inexplicably walks away. This circumstance becomes the impetus for the biographical quests that drive the novel.

The novel is composed of three sections. The first part emphasizes the narrator's efforts to resolve the circumstantial, contingent, and often competing details of Sánchez Mazas' story and to come up with the "true tale" of what happened. The second part is the product of trying to pull into coherence these "fleeting allusions," "memories and recounting of memories," "contradictions and ambiguities" based on "reasonable conjectures."[25] Yet, when the narrator reads through this "sort of biography," his elation at finishing quickly turns to disappointment: "The book wasn't bad, but insufficient, like a mechanism that was whole, yet incapable of performing the function for which it was devised because it was missing a part."[26] Unable to conclude the story satisfactorily with the biography of Sánchez Mazas, the third part of the novel shifts to the search for the missing piece: the unknown soldier who may have spared Sánchez Mazas' life.

Numerous scholars have written thoughtful analyses of this novel, and it is not my intention to reiterate what has already been done.[27] Existing scholarship has tended to focus on the metafictive, historical, and autofictional aspects of *Soldiers of Salamis*, overlooking its original and generative function as a biographical novel. Addressing that gap, my analysis centers on the use of biofiction as a narrative tool of "moral inquiry," especially as this builds to the comments Cercas has made about the third part of the novel. Through an analysis of the three different sections of the novel, I explore how the first two parts of the novel contribute through evidence formation and presentation to building the circumstantial case for the biofictional discoveries in the third section. In so doing, I relate legal and literary approaches to managing uncertainty, and examine how the risks and responsibilities of reaching a decision regarding biographical truth speak to our current reality.

Part I: The Evidentiary Functions of "Circumstance"

All biographies and histories are circumstantial and composed of competing narratives. Whatever happened in the past can only become intelligible and coherent in retrospect, as a decision among alternative sets of narrative possibility. Moreover, with more dispersive authority over meaning and one's own biography, the transition from institutional power to an emphasis on individual choice accelerates, and the discretionary responsibility for how we decide the truths of these narratives and their relationship to our own lives deepens. As part of a generation that did not experience it directly, the narrator begins his investigation by acknowledging that the Spanish Civil War is as distant and unreal to him as the battle of Salamis in 480 BC—stories nothing more than "excuses for old men's nostalgia and fuel for the imagination of unimaginative novelists."[28] In addition to the narrator's reference to using real events as a mode of evading the difficulties of invention, Cercas as author also treats ironically the narrator's reflexivity and immediacy, in which even recent history seems outmoded and disconnected from his reality. In an interview, Cercas has commented,

> My impression is that, naturally, all of us tend to think that the past doesn't have anything to do with us, with our real lives and current interests, but is instead something distant and archival. [...] This is completely false: this illusion that I call the dictatorship of the present. Rather, the past—as recorded by memories and witnesses, these differing versions that inform my books—also forms part of the present. It is a piece and dimension of this reality, without which the present would be completely incomprehensible.[29]

That the narrator begins from a siloed perspective of the present is essential to the novel's discovery of how traces of the past intrude and act upon his reality, and how he chooses to make sense of these seemingly isolated and incomplete points within the unfolding narrative. Cercas' use of the term "dictatorship of the present" is not casual.

> As he observes, "the less authoritarian or the more democratic power is, there is more competition over meaning; there are different stories about the past and the present. But with more authoritarian power, as in Franco's Spain, there was only one truth. So what literature does [...] is to fight against the story imposed by power. It's trying to tell the truths that power is concealing."[30]

Julian Baggini has referred to the abundance of truth claims in the contemporary context as a "crisis of trust." Rather than a crisis of truth, which he contends we still value, he argues that what has become uncertain is what "counts as a reliable *source* of truth. [...] This leaves us having to pick our own experts or simply to trust our guts."[31] The novel reveals both the discovery of these more polyvalent clues and the narrator's struggles to discern who or what to believe (or to trust). These questions begin with the search for physical proof and eventually turn to more metaphysical questions: How much doubt is reasonable? What determines which version of an event, or which individual stories to believe, and how might these differ from those that have been officially recorded as fact? Without a collective determination or verdict, what sort of truth is possible? How do we make sense of what has been lost?

A central tension that Cercas establishes from the start of the novel is the pursuit of evidence-based information, or "proof" to explain a confusing reality, while simultaneously exploring the limits or possibilities of fiction in that same regard. The narrator looks for answers that will not only explain the contradictions in Sánchez Mazas' biography but also give clarity to his own. Reinforcing this relationship is the metaphoric connection between the wilderness that serves as the locus of the biographical mystery and the absences and uncertainties that complicate the narrator's personal and professional life. Against these ambiguities, he explains that he will write a "true tale [...] cut from the cloth of reality, concocted out of true events and characters, a tale centered on Sánchez Mazas and the firing squad and the circumstances leading up to and following it."[32] If anchoring his narrative to factual evidence seems to provide refuge from his own biographical uncertainties and the risks of imagination, the narrator declares that he also intended for this evidence to resolve a vaster history.

> [This] entailed writing a *sort of biography* of Sánchez Mazas which, focusing on an apparently anecdotal but perhaps essential episode in his life—his botched execution at Collell—would propose an interpretation of his character and, by extension, of the nature of Falangism; or more precisely, of the motives that induced the handful of cultivated and refined men who founded the Falange to pitch the country into a furious bloodbath.[33]

So, from the start, Cercas clues the reader that the guise of trying to solve the smaller mystery, the obscure and essentially forgotten story of Sánchez Mazas' survival, is an attempt to unravel more complicated moral questions.

The first section of the novel relates the narrator's process of investigation in his effort to create a coherent and convincing narrative from the divergent evidentiary details, absences, and dead ends related to the story of Sánchez Mazas' survival and escape. Nathan Richardson has referred to this shaping of the novel's content as a "narrative form that 'wants to know'."[34] Yet, this focus on knowledge and information acquisition is at least equally an examination of doubt, or rather how the narrator manages his doubts regarding the evidence he accumulates and its ability to prove the truth of the story. It becomes in this sense a meta-examination of the narrator's ability to overcome his own postmodern skepticism. Throughout, Cercas displays the narrator's striving for direct and seemingly conclusive evidence that could resolve his uncertainties regarding the validity of the story and reveal the "essential secret" that eludes him. The accumulation and distillation of information act as a kind of wilderness in his investigation; one way he navigates this complexity is by envisioning the archival evidence as a repository of answers, so that he has only to find the direct source, the document, the missing object. However, rather than a first-hand story, the narrator has doubts that all he may be discovering is reconstructed narrative, a story that has gained validity from its own retelling. When he is finally able to speak to Jaume Figueras, one of the sons of the "friends of the forest" (the witnesses who helped Sánchez Mazas survive while in hiding), he has the sense of coming to a "real" connection to the story. Yet, even when Jaume provides the narrator with a key piece of evidence, a diary he says his father had with him in the forest, this element of proof is also incomplete, containing fragmented notes and a number of torn-out pages. Other irregularities seem to challenge whether the witnesses' testimony might be true. On the one hand, the three witnesses seem to corroborate each other's stories. On the other, if the telling of the story is too consistent, it seems false, as when the narrator reviews Sánchez Mazas' filmed testimony and it seems he is simply performing or reading a script.[35]

Why does Cercas include all of these excessive details of the narrator's evidentiary search? Not only in *Soldiers of Salamis*, but in many biofictions, there's a great deal of attention to the historical record, to tangible documentary evidence that can be rescued: pictures, documents, and journals, and also to what goes missing, what has been destroyed, lost, falsified, or left in fragments. Nancy Miller's *Pieces of a Jewish Past* refers to "splines," which is a dual metaphor referring to both the "part of a window that holds the frame together" and, in science, imagined connections between isolated points.[36] These splines form the scaffolding of the biographical narrative, making visible the intricate connections between documentary evidence, memory, and narration. Cercas has referred to these as "*pecios*," the remains of a shipwreck of time. And he contends that there is a desperate effort to reconstruct our stories based upon these fragments: "a conversation with a witness, a paper that surfaces at just the right time." What narrative does, Cercas suggests, "is to gather all of these remains from the wreck to give them meaning, to search for what they might mean [...] in an effort to salvage something of a life, at the last moment, when everything is about to disappear."[37] There are a number of relevant points here. One is to consider the simultaneous importance of these circumstantial findings while recognizing the frailty of such proof on its own to ever contain or comprehend human experience. Such linkages to the real require an imaginative narrative framework. While this is true in both the law and in literature, a key difference is the kind of truths one hopes to discover.

Alexander Welsh has written about the function of "circumstance" in literature and specifically the relationship of theories of proof in law to representations in modern narrative. He argues that the use of circumstantial evidence, what he calls "strong representations—making facts speak for themselves," became the most prominent form of narrative in England in the later eighteenth and nineteenth centuries.[38] In his paradigmatic example of Fielding's *Tom Jones*, the protagonist is first framed by false but believable testimony, and then successfully defended by the circumstantial evidence presented by the narrator. As John Loftis has summarized Welsh's characterization of the cultural logic of the time, "Witnesses can lie, be biased or just wrong, but facts never lie, so inferences drawn systematically from facts are more reliable than direct testimony."[39] Welsh's study further examines the reassertion of the preference for testimony and personal experience later in the nineteenth century in the novels of Robert Browning, Wilkie Collins, and Henry James. Barbara Shapiro asserts that unlike the earlier form of the novel, however, "testimony is not merely reported, but investigated, and authors devise multiple narratives, provide a larger role for the unconscious, and combine testimony and managed indirect evidence." She adds that "literary texts, which often invoked legal models to generate a sense of the 'real,' were [and I contend still are] particularly sensitive to these changes and oscillations in evidentiary paradigms."[40] Shapiro, James Whitman, and others have related transformations in legal approaches to reasonable doubt to broader questions regarding the management of skepticism and uncertainty. These linkages between approaches to evidence in the law and literature reinforce the relationship between epistemological changes and transformations in cultural logic, and suggest the place of fictional narration in mediating a circumstantial, discontinuous reality.[41]

What becomes important is understanding both why Cercas spends so much time emphasizing the narrator's desire for "strong representations" that would speak for themselves, and why he then undermines that confidence to expose the narrator's increasing awareness of the insufficiency of the biographical or historical evidence on its own to complete a "true story." As Sam Amago has observed, "the narrator's frequent statements as to the truth of his story may stem from his desire to assuage the reader's doubts to the veracity of his account, but mostly they serve to reveal his own narratorial insecurity." Moreover, as the narrator "continues his project, he becomes more aware of the fact that he will probably never get the story straight. He consequently allows himself more liberty in the construction of his tale."[42] There is a difference between knowledge and information acquisition, and knowing what to *do with* this material, or how honestly to admit one's own role in what story or stories it might tell. Rather than allowing the circumstantial clues to take the narrative in uncertain directions, he selectively winnows them to satisfy a more narrow vision, "trying to give those dispersed notes a coherent meaning and to link them to the facts I knew. [...] But it would actually take me a while yet to reconstruct the story I *wanted to tell* and to get to know, if not each and every one of its hidden aspects, *at least what I judged its essential ones*"[43] (emphasis mine). He applies this imaginative framework not as an effort to challenge the credibility conflicts and doubts that persist, but as way of managing the narrative process to fit the "true story" he wants to tell.

Gretchen Craft has viewed law and literature as bound together by a fundamental fear of the uncertainty of the human condition, and thus focused on providing a "system for making sense of what might happen and for establishing rules to shape or predict possible outcomes."[44] It is, accordingly, this anxiety over what might happen, for what the future holds, that law and literature each seek to allay through their own perceptions. According to Craft, in "law, the unpredictability of actual life is forced into an order that identifies cause and effect, innocence and blameworthiness," allowing "participants to impose a structure on the unsteady progress of the world and to deny the power of blind workings of chance." While literature exposes this fear, she argues that law strives to control it: "The deliberate accumulation of facts creates a convincing fiction" that the combination of circumstances could not have gone otherwise or the consequences been different.[45] Notably, Cercas exposes how the narrator in *Soldiers of Salamis* tries to apply conjecture in ways that seam over the gaps and contradictions of Sánchez Mazas' biography and its connection to a complicated history, allaying anxieties over its, and his own, uncertain direction and choices. The result of this constriction of the imaginative to "control" the text is a false resolution. In a related sense, writer Colm Tóibín has expressed how "straight" biography always contains an argument, but if you ask someone who actually lived it, they'll say "it wasn't like that." And what fascinates biographical novelists, he adds, is "how much information is actually misleading, and how much has information been burned, destroyed. In the end, nonetheless, a partial portrait is offered as a full portrait. And so biography, despite its footnoting and rigorousness, can be actually a kind of falsification of something."[46] Perhaps most importantly, the narrator's actions underscore the limitations of proof approaches to address the kinds of humanistic, ultimately conjectural questions the novel explores.

These issues become most clear in the second part of the novel, which is the narrator's attempt to complete the "sort of" biography, "Soldiers of Salamis," a title that he appropriated from Sánchez Mazas (who purportedly planned to use it for his never-written auto/biography).[47] The narrator has the sense that if he can just pull into coherence the fragments that make up the diary and the facts that he knows of the story more generally, he can achieve the correct placement of the pieces of a puzzle. By combining the three witnesses' stories and the other documentation he has collected, this part of the novel comprises his attempt to reconcile these credibility conflicts and to issue his own convincing verdict of Sánchez Mazas' narrative. Instead, he is left acknowledging that all he can reconstruct is "partial testimonies [...] through the veil of a legend shimmering with errors, contradictions, and ambiguities." As a result, the narrator states that what he relates is not "what actually happened," but rather what "seems probable," not "proven facts, but reasonable conjectures."[48]

Part II: Moral Truths and an Insufficient "Sort of" Biographical Fiction

Although the narrator has managed to fit the evidence into a completed story, he has the sense that a piece is still missing: "The worst of it was I didn't know what part it was. I revised the book thoroughly, I rewrote the order of others. The part, however, did not appear; the book remained hamstrung."[49] The reader, having just finished the relatively dry and unilluminating "Soldiers of Salamis" the narrator has written, knows that what he has said about his version being lacking is true, that we've "learned nothing," as Nathan Richardson has put it, "about what the novel purportedly set out to discover."[50] Despite having filled in many of the details of Sánchez Mazas' story, he has failed to connect this biography to any transcendent questions of human nature, experience, or history. Most significantly, the narrator observes:

> [A]lthough everything I'd found out about Sánchez Mazas over time was going to form the nucleus of my book, *which would allow me to feel secure*, a moment would arrive when I'd have to dispense with those training wheels because—if what he writes is going to have real interest—a writer never writes about what he knows but *precisely about what he does not know*.[51] (emphasis mine)

In completing "Soldiers of Salamis," the narrator has depended upon the facts he learned about Sánchez Mazas as a form of playing it safe. He hasn't had to risk difficult examination of a painful history, his comfortable assumptions of reality, or his own complicity in using the biography of a largely forgettable fascist-turned-bourgeois bureaucrat as a way to prop up his own flagging career as a novelist. And when he's applied fiction, it's been an instrumental means to smooth over these uncertainties.

Referring to the vast epistemological shifts that have taken place over the history of evidence, "from its rise in the Middle Ages in the world of law, its migration to historical writing, and then finally the realm we're most familiar with, journalism," historian Jill Lepore has underscored the transformation of how we manage skepticism with respect to the facts. She emphasizes the decreasing prestige of "humanistic ways of knowing and understanding the world" and the increasing turn to data as a way of managing uncertainty over the truth.[52] Tracing this history with respect to the "large and contentious literature" on the meaning and application of "beyond a reasonable doubt," Barbara Shapiro argues that it was not simply a creation of the courts, but linked to changes in the valuation of different ways of knowing. She notes that early English jurors were to give verdicts according to "the evidence and your conscience," or what was referred to as a "satisfied conscience." Satisfied conscience, Shapiro adds, "is borrowed from casuistry, the theory and practice of making *safe and rational* decisions under conditions of uncertainty."[53] Among growing complexities, she notes that while for earlier generations, moral certainty and belief beyond a reasonable doubt had been synonymous, for contemporary jurors "'moral certainty' began to evoke independent ideas of morality." While some justices expressed concern that jurors might base their decisions on moral standards or emotion rather than the strength alone of the evidence, others expressed the view that "juries *should* act on a 'reflection' of feeling, empathy and experience. Why are we so afraid of the obvious?"[54] Given these challenges, she observes how legal scholars in the twentieth and twenty-first centuries "have returned to probability theory, statistics and mathematical equivalents" in an effort to assert an "objective" and concrete measure to the individual assessment of "reasonable" doubt.[55]

Notably, James Whitman has argued that the reasonable doubt standard as originally conceived was not intended as a standard of proof to protect the accused, but a form of "moral comfort" intended to relieve the moral anxieties of jurors engaged in the disquieting personal responsibility of judgment.[56] While the concept of reasonable doubt assumes that all judgments of human behavior include an element of uncertainty, instructions to jurors have typically tried to equate sufficient certainty "beyond a reasonable doubt" to the expression of "moral certainty," a degree of confidence that courts and their legal advisors continue to struggle to define. In evaluating these ambiguities, Eric Lillquist found that among numerous studies of contemporary jurors' understanding of the certainty required for the reasonable doubt standard, responses varied greatly from 92 percent all the way to 51 percent.[57] By making the determination a probabilistic one, Whitman argues that we have allowed "ease" into the process of judging—forgotten that it is a human decision about the fate of another human being. It is worth considering Whitman's contention in the light of the first two parts of Cercas' novel, and how dependence on selective "facts" can provide a kind of moral comfort that allows us to shift individual responsibility for moral inquiry: "If we can claim that our decision was dictated 'by the truth' we can disclaim personal responsibility for making it."[58] In a similar light, Craft refers to the consoling function of certainty in the law that avoids feeling the pain of the case or the risk that "perhaps the courts filtered the facts the wrong way and reached the wrong conclusion." She argues that this filtering function of both literature and law, "distilling from a sea of meaningful and meaningless details, produces a simplicity that transforms events and subdues their inherent turmoil."[59]

While the narrator relies upon "probable" speculations and "reasonable conjectures" to resolve the uncertainties and contradictions of Sánchez Mazas' biography, he continues to insist that what he is writing is a fully truthful account. Exposing this artificial coherence, Cercas treats ironically the narrator's frequent professions that what he is writing is a "true tale [...] *like* a novel, but instead of all lies it's true"[60] (emphasis mine). The narrator's girlfriend, Conchi, assures him that "imagination is not your strong suit," and "Shit! Didn't I tell you not to write about a fascist? These people fuck up everything they touch. What you have to do is forget all about that book and start another one on García Lorca."[61] Cercas has emphasized that one of the limitations of postmodernism has been confusing irony with sarcasm, seeing literature as a self-referential game. But he contends that responding to postmodernism by avoiding irony is a profound mistake because the function of irony to illuminate contradictions "is the crux of the novel as a genre, and the novel can't ... it mustn't, leave it aside because then it would be reduced to pedagogy. Because then it turns into monolithic knowledge, into propaganda." Unlike factual truth, moral truths, as Cercas defines them, are competing truths, "novelesque," "the most complicated truths, aren't they?"[62] And there is a corresponding distinction between moralism, judgment that closes off questioning, and moral inquiry, which opens to alternative understandings.

In this respect, it is hard not to read the second part of the novel, the narrator's "sort of" biography, as an ironic critique of the unimaginative or the pedagogical and the failure to connect meaningfully to human experience and the lives beyond the text. The conclusion that the narrator comes to is that Sánchez Mazas "probably in his heart, never in his life had he truly believed in anything, and least of all, in what he'd defended or preached. [...] few people remember him today, and perhaps that's what he deserves. There's a street named after him in Bilbao."[63] Instead of "illuminating contradictions," this reductive forgetting glides over anxieties about truth and memory and the unrecognized traces of all the victims and anonymous others without a tale, true or otherwise, written about them or a street with their name. Moreover, it points to other morally comfortable elisions of history that allowed the country to tamp over and silence a conflictive history with a convenient fiction of reconciliation. Cercas refers to the "postmodern" choice of the so-called "Pact of Forgetting" in the Transition, this implicit decision to move swiftly into the present by avoiding the complicated truths and unpleasant realities of the war, the past, the artificial consensus of "no victims and no vanquished."[64] Silence, too, is a kind of storytelling, and often a misleading one.

That even the narrator acknowledges the failure of his version of "Soldiers of Salamis" to open these doubts to examination and to *write about what he does not know*—to ask more self-reflective questions about human nature, history, and biographical truth—is significant. As Cercas observes, "exposing the narrative process is essential." "I love metafiction as a hermeneutic element, as a tool of knowledge." He notes that what changes from postmodernism is that "it's not just a game in which literature looks at itself. *It looks at itself to observe reality. To bring up political, moral, and real problems.* [...] I tell the reader, 'look, this is fiction. This is how it works. I'll show you my doubts, my questions'"[65] (emphasis mine). The questions that Cercas is posing are not only exposing the role of fiction in the construction of biographical truth, but how these fictions connect to other truths about reality and the human condition. Leena Kurvet-Käossar has observed that the effort to write a life "can smooth over archival traces for the sake of narrative coherence; however, these sources are not like pieces of a puzzle that fit neatly into their designated spots. They are fragmentary and nonlinear and expose the fragmentary and nonlinear foundations of auto/biographical impulses themselves."[66] In trying to understand the "missing narrative" that motivates the search for biographical truth, she adds that it is "often via imaginative, fictional means that the narrative is kept afloat through documentary tightropes."[67] Similarly, despite the repeated assertions of the narrator otherwise, Cercas insists that "*Soldiers of Salamis* is a novel, a weird novel, but a novel nonetheless. I was searching for literary truth, not journalistic truth. Literature is a moral, universal truth that manipulates reality."[68] Cercas has argued that while both history and literature involve the search for truth, they are "opposing truths." While historical truth seeks to determine what happened to people in a certain time and place, literary truth, in his view, has the potential to "establish what happens to people under any circumstances."[69]

Indeed, one way of understanding the second section of *Soldiers of Salamis* is to consider how this "sort of" biography functions purposefully, ironically, and metafictively to demonstrate its *insufficiency* as either a flawed biography or a false biofiction. This section thus lays the evidentiary foundation for the emergence of "new tools and interests" such as the need for meaningful biofictional creation that Cercas subsequently explores in the third part. That the narrator employs fiction to avoid the risks of personal responsibility or the moral anxiety of complicated truths both distorts the biographical pact with the reader and misuses the imaginative "to perform the function for which it had been devised," what Cercas describes as the "capacity to make unexpected connections[...]the shaping of paradox."[70] When done well, biofiction acknowledges its function as *fiction* that *uses biography* circumstantially to build the case; the biographical novelist imagines unexpected connections that extend the experience of the biographical subject to our questions in the present, the power, as Michael Lackey puts it, "of human consciousness to evade determinism and thereby to shape an alternative reality into being."[71] Cercas contends,

> [S]o on the one hand, I tell them [my readers] "this is a novel," and on the other, "this is completely true; this happened to me, and it could

> happen to you." It is about shaking the reader's conscience. A novelist must entertain and involve the reader, but his or her ultimate goal should be to make the reader see the world in a different light.[72]

Similarly, rather than a historical verdict or an uncontested biographical truth, writer Colum McCann suggests that what he hopes to achieve through biofiction is "an emotional truth. The human heart in conflict with itself." He adds that he hopes to flare the reader "into the spirit of contradiction [...] not to be didactic, not to tell people how to think or what to think, but *allow* people to feel."[73]

Todd Avery has referred to the salient ethical implications of biofiction "in a very specific context: the present cultural, political, scientific, social and technological moment of 'truthiness', post-truth, alternative facts."[74] He points to the tension implicit to biofiction between the novelist's use of fiction to impart a vision of the world and the deliberate manipulation of historical fact. An important part of this ethical conflict is how it communicates a very lived reality, not only the difficulty of distinguishing truth from fiction, but how we approach responsibility to these distinctions and how honestly we admit our reasonable doubts.[75] Through the second part of the novel, the sort-of biographical "Soldiers of Salamis," the narrator doesn't use fiction to openly imagine new ways of understanding a biographical life or its ability to illuminate other aspects of human experience, but as a mode of simplifying and containing this contradictory reality. And he does so under the guise of representing the truth. In so doing, this section not only fails as biography and as biofiction, but also asks us to think about what truths we seek as readers. Ultimately, post-truth narratives manipulate facts to support convenient fictions, whereas biofictions, when done well, use fictions to better comprehend the real.

Part III: Revising the Search: From Verdict to Biofictional Discovery

One of the essential aspects motivating biofiction is the novelist's freedom to create and renegotiate meaning by using historical and biographical material in imaginative ways. While the first two sections of *Soldiers of Salamis* examine the narrator's biographical search as a means to decide a traumatic history and uncritically reconcile its lingering conflict, the third section of the novel revises the search to reimagine the contradictory and often unknowable motives involved in complex histories. Accepting the persistence of uncertainty does not mean we don't have to come to a decision, to make choices and commitments regarding what to believe, to consider new models for ethically interrogating how and what we believe to be true. The third part of the novel considers how this awareness alters the aims of the biographical search and how it reshapes the kinds of truths the narrator discovers. "There are answers," Cercas contends. "But they are not the answers of journalists, of historians, of judges."[76] For Cercas, manipulating reality is not about factual distortion, but rather about the ability of narrative to have real effects, to transform how we think about the world: "[A] book is like changing life. [...] I want to be changed, but I also want to change the reader's view of life."[77]

For Marc Bloch, the "circumstance becomes a hint, a clue to change the direction of the search, a provocation to ask new questions shedding light on significant phenomena."[78] Within the third part of the novel, a fictional version of Chilean writer Roberto Bolaño provides this clue when he tells the narrator about a chance encounter he had with an enigmatic Republican soldier, Antonio Miralles, who may have been there when Sánchez Mazas escaped. The narrator has a sudden awareness that he may have found exactly the piece to make his story work. He explains to [his girlfriend] Conchi the "error of perspective" that he had committed in writing "Soldiers of Salamis" and that Miralles ("or someone like him") was "exactly the part that was missing in order for the mechanism of the book to function."[79] Bolaño tries to convince him that the real Miralles would only disappoint him, and the only way to finish the novel would be to make up the interview. Bolaño's suggestion—that the "real" Miralles is no longer accessible, and that even if the narrator could find him, he would not seem as convincing as the one that the narrator can imaginatively construct—reflects a familiar postmodern argument of the impossibility of reaching beyond the text. Yet, as Peter Barry has argued, if we agree that the connection to the real has eroded, then "we need to be sure the 'real' is a concept we can do without."[80] The narrator is surprised by his own resistance to simply making up the character, and that finishing the book begins to matter much less to him than being able to speak with Miralles. While the fictional Cercas rejects Bolaño's suggestion and goes on to find Miralles, the real Cercas invents the character.[81] By making this speculative fiction the "missing part" that makes the novel a truthful reflection of human experience, Cercas provides a powerful argument for biofictional creation. The accumulation of biographical evidence can never add up on its own sufficiently to explain (or explain away) the more complex and interesting questions of the novel—not only the graininess of a particular moment, but its relationship to realities of both past and present. Such uses of fiction "narrativize the self not as a game, but in order to enhance the realism of the text and tackle the sociological and phenomenological dimensions of personal life."[82]

The shift in this third part of the novel away from Sánchez Mazas and to the discovery of the missing Republican soldier paradoxically conveys (through this fictional invention) the desire to connect to real histories and identities beyond the text. As Cercas claims, "my aspiration was to lie anecdotally, in the particulars, in order to tell an essential truth."[83] Urged on by his girlfriend, the narrator undertakes an extensive "telephonic pilgrimage" that finally leads him to the discovery of an old man in a nursing home who the narrator believes may have been the soldier. On his way to meet Miralles, the narrator has the expectation that the encounter will uncover the mystery, revealing the fundamental secret that has escaped him: "I thought that soon I would know what he thought when he looked at him [Sánchez Mazas] in the eyes and why he saved him, and then I would at last understand an essential secret [...] It's him."[84]

Yet, Cercas actively disrupts this simple "error of perspective." Rather than affirming identity or providing the answers the narrator had hoped for, Miralles responds ironically to the reasons for his searching: "So what you were looking for was a hero. And I'm that hero, is that it?"[85] Miralles' response reinforces the perception that the effort to order and make sense of these events will always come up against realities that can't be neatly resolved—the unnecessary loss of life in war, lives swept away not by their own convictions but by chance and the decisions of others, the impossibility of knowing why he should have survived when others did not, the apparent meaninglessness of such loss:

> Nobody remembers them, you know? Nobody even remembers why they died, why they don't have a wife and children and a sunny room; nobody remembers, and least of all, those they fought for. There's no lousy street in any lousy town in any fucking country named after any of them, nor will there ever be. Understand? You understand, don't you? Oh, but I remember, I remember them all. Lela and Joan and Gabi and Modena and Pipo and Brigade and Gudayol. I don't know why I do but I do, not a single day goes by that I don't think of them.[86]

The narrator appears to be under the single-minded supposition that by discovering Miralles ("It's him"), and through his direct testimony, he will be able to solve all sorts of questions that had eluded him. This desire for direct answers provides a way of getting around the complexities of a circumstantial reality in which the act of remembering is "by definition, an act of imagination and invention, and the hardest stories to tell have become the stories we need most," those in which there is no ready takeaway—"only the invisible dead, the ghosts who lie in wait."[87] Yet, as the novel outlines the narrator's efforts to find Miralles ("or someone like him") to resolve his story and make it work, it also extends this searching into a broader pattern of what goes missing—the need for someone to play the hero, or, as Annabel Lyon has written elsewhere, the desire for "books and stories that can make sense of our flailing lives."[88] While the third part of the novel appears, on the one hand, to be a simple choice of perspective—a resuscitation of the Republican hero instead of the failed Nationalist one—Cercas doesn't let us off that easily. Contrasting the true character of war with its novelized simulation, Miralles emphasizes the importance of the real lives whose memories are lost or distorted in the effort to force reality into a packaged coherence.

Cercas, for instance, has pointed to the embedded contradictions that were obscured and deferred in fashioning a "morally comfortable" version of post-Franco historical memory that avoided reckoning with a complicated past. "There is this fog of misconception," he argues. "[W]hile historians have done a job, young people don't know the real thing. The collective conscience is not aware of what really happened." He suggests that it creates an artificial ease to say "all Republicans were great, that it was a romantic war. [...] The real truth, the whole truth is what we need to look at."[89] Similarly false is the conception that everyone on the right, or who had benefited from this association, suddenly embraced the same democratic vision and shared history of collective resistance with those they had for so long demonized.

Examining the legitimating process of deciding upon a shared consensus of truth, George Fisher has studied the jury's expanding role in determining witness credibility, or what he refers to as its increasing role as "lie detector." He argues that the authority for truth that was once vested in an external authority—in the power of the oath, for example—has increasingly shifted to the power of the jury. Commenting on the "black box" effect of jury deliberations, by which the process the jury experiences in trying to reach a decision is shielded from view, he contends,

> [B]y permitting the jury to resolve credibility conflicts in the black box of the jury room, the criminal justice system can provide to the public an 'answer'—a single verdict of guilty or not guilty—that resolves all questions of credibility in a way that is largely immune from challenge or review. By making the jury its lie detector, the system protects its own legitimacy.

Moreover, he adds that this expectation has increased over time: "Perhaps the allure of the black box as a means towards apparent certainty in an uncertain world has tempted us to entrust the jury with more and harder questions than it has the power to answer. Today [...] there is almost no kind of credibility conflict we will not ask a jury to solve."[90]

I include Fisher's arguments for a number of reasons. One is how they point to the deepening of responsibility we have to decisions of credibility or trust in a context of constant access to competing information. The other is the attraction of the simple "yes" or "no" answer the narrator Cercas appears to be looking for. Just as we aspired to "strong representations" by which the circumstantial evidence alone would provide assurance of the truth rather than unreliable human transactions, we increasingly try to solve our own experiences of uncertainty and complexity through the hidden processes and immediate answers provided through all sorts of "black box" corollaries. Searching for meaning, we scroll our computers, phones, and other "connected" devices for hours each day in search of circumstantial information that will somehow explain and help us make sense of our lives. In his 2003 article, Thomas Friedman refers to the simultaneous connectedness and emotional distance of a post-9/11 world, marked by more than 200 million searches a day (a number estimated to be closer to 2 trillion in 2020). Reflecting on his visit to Google's Silicon Valley offices, he notes, "You can actually sit in front of a monitor and watch a sample of everything that everyone in the world is searching for. (Hint: sex, God, jobs, and oh my word, professional wrestling usually top the lists.)"[91]

This confusion between what people search for on Google and other search engines and the algorithmic "answers" they receive reinforces an important exploration in Cercas' novel—the difference between the demand for moral certainty and the need for moral truth. James Whitman argues that we experience the world of the trial as a world of "tough, factual questions thrown up by life in a complex society," and the law of criminal procedure as a "set of heuristic rules that help the juror/fact-finders navigate the shoals of uncertainty," a sort-of "puzzle-solving machine."[92] Cercas shows how the narrator initially has the similar expectation that finding Miralles will provide a clear answer to all sorts of puzzles, not only of identity but also of complicated moral choices.

Earlier in this chapter, I referenced Barbara Shapiro's contention that contemporary law has increasingly resorted to statistical, probabilistic calculations to find mathematical equivalents to "beyond reasonable doubt." She notes that a "2006 issue of a new interdisciplinary journal, *Law, Probability and Risk*, contained three articles on the quantification of beyond reasonable doubt and that legal scholars continue to debate whether and how to apply mathematical calculations of probability in legal adjudication."[93] For Jill Lepore, the "larger epistemological shift is how the elemental unit of knowledge has changed." She argues that the transformation from facts to numbers to data as higher-status units of knowledge has altered approaches to truth, and that we have tried to satisfy the devaluation of confidence in factual truth with more and more accumulation of data. Accordingly, in her view, when "people talk about the decline of the humanities, they are really talking about the rise and fall of the fact."[94] By this, I understand her to suggest that we have prioritized the accumulation of information over the investigation, discernment, analysis, and judgment of stories that information might tell us about our lives and selves—the humanistic ways of knowing and understanding each other and our world. We don't have to remember because the computer will do it for us. We don't have to grasp the linkages between concepts that the algorithm has decided for us. Moreover, when we "Google-know," as Michael Lynch, the author of *The Internet of Us: Knowing More and Understanding Less,* contends, "we no longer take responsibility for our own beliefs and we lack the capacity to see how bits of facts fit into a larger whole."[95] Essentially, he argues that we focus only on multitudes of discrete circumstances, and we struggle to see their connection to wider narratives or, I would add, our own connectedness and responsibility to discerning broader truths. By opening biographical facts to speculative, humanistic invention and possibility, biofictions have the potential to contest this contradictory practice that as we've gotten closer to more probabilistic certainty of discrete information, we've actually gotten farther away from the truth.

Cercas writes this novel at a time in Spain when there are active debates about modes of litigating memory that later culminate in the 2007 Law of Historical Memory. While emphasizing the importance of recovering historical evidence and the information they contain, *Soldiers of Salamis* questions whether, even if the differing versions could be agreed upon, all of this material exhumation alone could ever resolve the more complicated truths of memory or provide the kind of completed determination the narrator had first sought. He notes that the price of the convenient fictions of the transition (of reconciliation, of justice, of false "forgetting") is "elusive: it's that fog of mistakes, misunderstandings, half-truths and simple lies [...] that affects everyone like Miralles."[96] Instead of a "crisp and impregnable verdict,"[97] this section of the novel examines how we live and make choices amid the insufficiency of the evidence to solve the questions of moral inquiry that linger. We are trying to reimagine ourselves through data, through information—but in all its overabundance, it doesn't tell us what we really want to know. As Kat McGowan has commented, "the swirl of models and projections, the curves that skyrocket or flatten, offer big-picture predictions that seem to hold all the answers, yet they don't tell anyone anything meaningful about his or her own life. All those charts and spreadsheets cannot answer that most urgent and terrible crisis: *What is going to happen to us?*"[98]

The two key questions the narrator sought to answer—the identity of the mysterious soldier and why he chose to save Sánchez Mazas' life—are never fully answered. While the narrator asks Miralles what the soldier may have been thinking when he looked at Sánchez Mazas after sparing his life, Miralles answers simply "Nothing," suggesting the possibility there was no hidden motivation, no secret to unravel to make sense of the experience and give it firm meaning. Leaving his interview with Miralles and getting into the taxi, the narrator finally asks Miralles if he was, in fact, the soldier. Miralles first answers, "No," and then—as the taxi pulls away—says something the narrator doesn't grasp ("maybe it was a name, but I'm not sure"), and the message remains lost.[99]

For Nathan Richardson, this lack of an answer from Miralles and the popular appeal of the novel among Spanish readers only reinforces the post-silence

Spanish public's disinterest in digging too deeply or problematically into recent history, in effect preferring the "moral comfort" of a non-answer.[100] I read this differently. Ended here, the novel might reinforce the destabilization of meaning that we have come to associate with postmodern thought. Miralles' answer or lack of an answer emphasizes the murkiness of many human decisions, especially in times of chaos and crisis—this wilderness in which it is easy to get lost. It is only afterwards that we create or impose the historical overlay that connects fundamentally lonely, circumstantial moments. Yet, the novel simultaneously suggests that responsibility to the truths of another life and to human connection is, in fact, deepened in this context. Referencing the moral responsibility to private and invisible lives—Colum McCann has argued that "the less known that person happens to be, the more acute the responsibility becomes [...] I have a real responsibility to get [the] story right."[101] Against the view of history or ideology as determining, Cercas emphasizes the importance of individual choices and of private moments such as those between the soldier and Sánchez Mazas or Sánchez Mazas and the narrator. While these moments leave questions unanswered, they appear much more real and defining to their lives than can be explained by the historical record. In order to understand the reality of biographical truths, we need to take into account the resonating effects of these seemingly isolated, contingent moments. "As we know," Nancy Miller has written, "a story about finding always returns to the places where the story got lost. It's also a chance to begin again."[102]

While the novel begins and ends with biographical searching, what transforms are both the questions the narrator wants to answer and how he chooses to manage that uncertainty. The narrator initially wanted to use Sánchez Mazas' biography to solve a conflictive history, to "settle the matter," and to anchor his own indeterminate narrative. Yet, by the end of the novel, Miralles' imagined biography becomes a means to keep alive possibility rather than to close it off, and to arrive at something more ineffable, "when the sayable is everything except what rules us or makes us live or matters or what we are."[103] Despite the insufficiency of factual evidence and the loss of historical traces, it is the creation of the biographical novel that recovers memory and makes vital the speculative intervention of the past into the present. Traveling back home after his visit to Miralles, the narrator reflects in the

> almost empty glass of whisky in front of me, and in the window, beside me, the distant image of a sad man who couldn't be me, but was me, there I suddenly saw my book, the book I'd been after for years, I saw it there in its entirety, finished, from the first line to the last, there I knew that, although nowhere in any city of any fucking country would there ever be a street named after Miralles, if I told his story, Miralles would still be alive in some way, and if I talked about them, his friends would still be alive too.[104]

Cercas has contended that one of the interests that comes newly to light in *Soldiers of Salamis* is to see the "collective as a dimension of the individual."[105] In this way, the seemingly postmodern device of infusing the real with fiction functions not to undermine the real or to suggest that what is conveyed is "just" story, but—as Alison Gibbons has written in a different context—to show "the hermeneutic function of stories in our memories, in our narratives of ourselves and in our relationships with others."[106] In using fiction to revive and give meaning to biographical lives that would otherwise be lost, and simultaneously granting direction to his own evolving history, the novel exhibits what Nicholas Stavris has referred to as "experiments in capturing selfhood or reality."[107] What we see is the powerful interaction of the biographical narrative with our own lives, not as a direct model or allegory but as a form of resistance against mere repetition and a mode of projecting alternatives. Cercas has referred to this connection between past and present as not just intellectual, but an "authentic, essential need" (50). As Ben Lerner has written separately, "I'm probably making this sound too much like some kind of metafictional exercise, when in reality I'm talking about something intensely lived; how each of us is striving to recognize mere chronology into a meaningful pattern, to narrate our pasts in a way that makes the future thinkable."[108]

Cercas argues that at the crossroads of postmodernism is the importance of finding a path forward that produces literature capable of expressing feelings, emotion, morality, without being pedagogical. That biofictions exist alongside more traditional biographies is not because they are failed, lesser than representations that could not fully portray their version of a life. Instead, they explicitly choose to incorporate the fictive in ways that fundamentally change the contract with the reader. A central function of the novel, especially the third part, is the exploration of the reasons for this narrative shift and how it connects to our reality. Noting the increasingly circumstantial nature of contemporary life, the "unmooring of time," in which the "past speaks to us individually and collectively," Megan O'Grady has observed that "a common thread, much less a consensus view of reality, feels increasingly hard to come by." This context has motivated a clarification of the narrative game, its stakes, rules, and positions. Most notably, she argues that "literary authors are looking back not to comfort us with a sense of a known past, or even an easy allegory of the present, but instead—motivated by a kind of clue-gathering—to seek reasons for the way we are and how we got here, and at what point the train started to derail."[109] *Soldiers of Salamis* is a logical place to begin this book in large part because Cercas' biographical novel embodies and embarks on this crisis of the in-between, tipping from postmodern doubt to new tools for truthfully communicating human experience—a kind of mirror for the epistemic challenges we encounter.

Against the loss of connection that results when the "category of the real is eroded," *Soldiers of Salamis* suggests the ever-shifting function of biofiction as a lens, a reflection, and a space for moral imagination (most importantly, perhaps) to perceive our common humanity. The absence of the ability to arrive at a firm historical truth does not mean that we don't have an ethical responsibility to the real lives we imagine. Rather, how we engage with those complexities has profound impact for how we imagine our own possibilities and choices. What matters, as the narrator concludes, is that despite persistent uncertainties "where he's going," "who's accompanying him" or "why," writing Miralles' story still manages to convey a vision for the future, propelling him "onwards, onwards, ever onwards."[110] In this sense, the current growth of biofiction reinforces as much about our effort to manage the uncertainties of the present and future as it does the past. The importance of historical memory, as Miralles demonstrates, is not simply about our moral responsibility to the past, but also how this carries forward into how we understand our lives and human connections, the "openness of extra-subjective imagination that can spur empathy with respect to others."[111]

Writing of the connections between literature and the law, James Boyd White has maintained that findings ("or assertions") and establishing analytical means are "of little value in forming the hopes and expectations that we should bring to imaginative literature."[112] While we tend to think of the role of the juror in the law as simply deciding among competing narratives and corresponding interpretations, each decision, "composed of intermingled interpretations of law and facts, is such an admixture of past and future, of description and hope, of belief about how the world was and aspiration for how the world should be and each decision [...] thereby contributes material from which that world might be created."[113] Seen in this way, biofictions are not only an effort to truthfully reimagine the past but a projection of the kind of social world we yearn for. The shift away from postmodernism involves acknowledging our continued uncertainties without abandoning ourselves deterministically to them. If, as Cercas observes, the "past is never fully past because it is here, acting on the present, forming part of it, inhabiting it," biofiction is not the process of resolving our reasonable doubts regarding biographical lives, but questioning how these narratives imbue the present and open to new conceptions. Coming to a decision about how to narrate the past is not only about determining what happened, but also about how responsibly we envision what is yet to come.

2

Fugitive Biofictions: Antonio Muñoz Molina's *Like a Fading Shadow* and Gabriela Ybarra's *The Dinner Guest*

Antonio Muñoz Molina's *Like a Fading Shadow*[1] (2014) and Gabriela Ybarra's *The Dinner Guest*[2] (2015) seem at first to be unlikely biofictional bedfellows. The first is a dense investigation of a notorious assassin and the second a spare novel involving losses much closer to the author. Yet, together they reveal unexpected connections that deepen the relevance of biofiction to speak to contemporary and universal uncertainties. Both splice auto/biographical documentation and fictional invention in novels were composed as forensic searches. *Like a Fading Shadow* centers on the brief period that James Earl Ray spent on the run after assassinating Martin Luther King Jr. Muñoz Molina hones in on the ten days in 1968 that Ray spent in Lisbon, a city that Muñoz Molina first visits more than a decade after King's death, when he is writing what would become his best-selling novel, *Winter in Lisbon* (1987), itself the story of a chase. *Like a Fading Shadow* reflects both the impressionistic effort to evoke the disorientation of the fugitive and a simultaneous desire to document fragmentary biographical details assiduously, thus solidifying a specific history of disappearance and ultimate capture. The obsessive accumulation of evidence, the profuse inventories of facts Muñoz Molina includes in the novel—once-classified files, interviews, reports, photographs, where Ray eats, what aliases he uses, how his awkward interactions with others unfold—is overwhelming, rather than clarifying. By overlaying the imaginatively documented narrative of Ray's escape to Lisbon with the author's own recollections, descriptions of the emotional state of Ray become conflated and confused with Muñoz Molina's.

In a related fashion, Gabriela Ybarra's *The Dinner Guest* melds her grandfather's abduction and assassination in 1977 by ETA terrorists with her mother's precipitous death to cancer in 2011. While Muñoz Molina highlights an abundance of factual details, Ybarra's sparse novel turns to fragmented reportage in response to the private silences and absences surrounding her grandfather's and mother's deaths. Defending her choice to "freely reconstruct" these events, Ybarra observes, "Often, imagining has been the only way I've had to understand."[3]

Along with the unusual pairing of Muñoz Molina and James Earl Ray, the death of Ybarra's mother from a cancer that appeared to be in remission only to return swiftly and almost invisibly might seem to occur in a different realm, disconnected from the world of politics. Yet, despite the seemingly divided narratives of the terrorist and the writer, the public victim of sectarian violence and the private death of one's mother, these two biofictional novels are aligned in significant ways. Both deal with dramatic political murders. More importantly, both combine the fugitive and the fragment, linking the fugitive unknowability of information and biographical knowledge with the actual, physical escape of the criminal. Despite the vast information surrounding the assassination of Martin Luther King Jr., Muñoz Molina's novel starts with this obscure fragment of Ray's short stint in Lisbon, a bit of information that very few people know, and builds this massive case around it. Alternatively, even though Ybarra's grandfather dies in the very horrifying, public way and his murder by Basque terrorists was widely covered in the Spanish news at the time, she knows very little about it. Muñoz Molina piles up forensic evidence, and Ybarra encounters silence and fragmented details. Through elements of biofiction, the intersection of these two narratives contributes to greater understanding of contemporary epistemological uncertainties and deepens notions of human experience.

The fugitive refers to someone or something that tries to evade detection or capture. In the prior chapter, I described the increasingly circumstantial nature of contemporary life and its relationship to evidentiary and epistemological challenges. I referenced the speed and constant access we have to profuse data, and yet a fundamental rupture in the trust we have in the truthfulness of sources of information. In this chapter, I expand upon the capacity of biofiction to investigate and manage this circumstantial reality. In "Care of Souls," Harvard Divinity School scholars Angie Thurston, Casper ter Kulle, and Sue Phillips characterize the contemporary context as a "crisis of in-between," contending that "as we've unbundled and remixed, we've also isolated and made insecure." By "unbundling"—"the process of separating elements of value from a single collection"—the consolidated authority earlier conferred on a specific canon or confined to a bounded set of sources has multiplied and dispersed, become "unsecured."[4] The effect of this deepening circumstantial reality is, on the one hand, greater individual choice over which discrete, indirect traces to follow, but on the other, less certainty over how they combine to generate a shared conception of reality.

Notably, both authors emphasize the indirect, circumstantial ways they initially became involved with the stories of their biographical subjects. Asked in an interview what motivated him to parallel the lives of Antonio Muñoz Molina and James Earl Ray, Muñoz Molina replied, "It was the result of a series of coincidences. What intrigued me about Ray was not the assassination of Martin Luther King, but the *small, infinitesimal detail* that he spent ten days in Lisbon on the run after committing the crime"[5] (emphasis mine). In describing what drew her to the story of her grandfather's kidnapping and assassination, Ybarra similarly describes how, in grieving her mother, she "*stumbled upon*" the unresolved grief in her family related to her grandfather[6] (emphasis mine). Biofictional creation, then, becomes a way to fill the blanks between isolated points and for Muñoz Molina and Ybarra as narrators to navigate their own losses, "lostness," and uncertainties. The biofictions become circumstantial cases that these authors use to extrapolate and try to make sense of their own lives, and more expansively that we, in reading them, may use to examine our own.

In a relevant sense, Lance Olsen has observed that biographical novels are about how the spaces of the past and selfhood are "constantly elusive, impossible to capture. If we are paying attention, they draw our attention to *something other than what they seem to be drawing our attention to*"[7] (emphasis mine). In this respect, I want to return to the concept of the circumstantial paradigm I referenced in Chapter 1. As characterized by Carlo Ginzburg, the circumstantial paradigm draws together the work of the detective or investigator and that of the historian or biographer. It centers on how pursuing seemingly disconnected signs or "traces" can lead to comprehension of a hidden or otherwise elusive reality. In contrast to direct evidence ("representational, univocal, unconditional"), circumstantial evidence has been defined as "abstract, polyvocal, and probabilistic."[8] Importantly, then, we can consider the biofictional efforts to speculatively fill the gaps among circumstantial details of a life narrative as directed not only to the life under consideration, as a traditional ("straight") biography might, but an effort to point to something else, to a deeper or otherwise unattainable understanding.

We could think of the imaginative linkages in biofiction as a mode of readjusting or modulating the relationship between pure subjectivity and the actuality of lived experience, as Colm Tóibín refers to an "anchored" imagination and Colum McCann argues that we "have to ground the truth somehow."[9] Muñoz Molina fills *Like a Fading Shadow* to the brim with minute details that the narrator (the "I" that parallels many facets of the real Muñoz Molina) contends "anchor [his] speculations."[10] It is, in fact, the minute detail of James Earl Ray's brief time in Lisbon that inspires this novel in the first place. Gabriela Ybarra has referred to how the collection of images, photos, news articles, and Google searches give "more veracity to the text."[11] Both authors reinforce the dichotomous tension within biofiction of concrete reality and creative invention, acknowledging the elusiveness of the truths of any biographical subject and, nonetheless, our simultaneous efforts to pursue access to this missing knowledge. As a form that intentionally navigates the speculative space between the real biographical subject and the fictional construction of another self, biofiction is uniquely positioned to do more than identify the splintering uncertainty of our lives. Rather, by putting into practice the dilemmas we face in confronting both too much information and too little to make sense of the world, biofiction can also model how we navigate this reality, illuminating and transforming literary approaches to the real.

In their biographical novels, Muñoz Molina and Ybarra explore the difference between opening real-life narratives to imaginative possibility and the creation of intentionally misleading fictions. One tries to bring us closer to obscured truths, and the other obscures our confidence in truth. Both writers employ and examine structures of distance and detachment (in time and space, in human relationships, in the organization of the narrative) contraposed against those of intimacy and connection. Through these competing tensions, they suggest the potential of biofiction to pursue connections among isolated, fragmented biographical details and lives as opposed to obfuscating fictions that further reinforce disconnections to the real and each other. In both cases, risks of rupture extend as well to ideological constructions of separatism (sectarian and racially motivated), embedded in violence and negation of dialogue, in contrast to the capacity for ethical engagement with these divisive realities.

Drawing from the concept of the circumstantial paradigm that leads us from the material trace to unexpected connections and meanings, in the ensuing sections I first explore the example of *Like a Fading Shadow* and then of *The Dinner Guest*. I consider how both authors reveal the attraction and limitations of physical evidence to provide clues to the real lives beyond the text, and how intersubjectivity in these works creates points of access bringing past and present into dialogue. Finally, I bring the endings of both works together to consider the ethical implications of the imaginative uses of biofiction to speak to epistemological and hermeneutic uncertainties of contemporary life.

Muñoz Molina's *Like a Fading Shadow*

> *Objects say what we don't; [...] But one still wants to imagine. (Like a Fading Shadow)*

The growth and popularity of biofiction in the past three decades have taken place alongside other marked shifts in cultural and literary perspective, especially with respect to how we approach questions of risk and uncertainty regarding the value of truth and the real effects of our uses of fiction. Along with other literary approaches, biofiction is not static and is open to many adaptations. Its recent expansion has also coincided with the growing perception among many cultural theorists that postmodernism has run its course and is being supplanted by new paradigms less interested in the instability of truth and reality than in how we actually manage those uncertainties to achieve meaningful expression of our lives.

Linda Hutcheon concludes the epilogue to the second edition of *The Politics of Postmodernism* with the declaration that "the postmodern moment has passed" (181). Nicoline Timmer contends that the call for an "alternative vision is heard more loudly. Quite simply put it is not unthinkable that after endless proposals for *de*constructions, a desire to *construct* will break through."[12] "In response to and negotiation" with their postmodern predecessors, Irmtraud Huber explores what new roles speculation and imagination might play in these new realisms, citing the following parenthetical contenders, among others: "Neorealism" (Rebein), "Speculative Realism" (Saldívar), "New Sincerity" (Kelly), "Aesthetics of Authenticity" (Funk), and "Aesthetic of Trust" (Hassan).[13] To that, we might add metamodernism, altermodernism, post-postmodernism, and various others. While the field is still very much in play, there is a common shift away from purely ironic approaches toward the connectedness of language, humans, and reality, and a newly dominant engagement with the connection and consequences of literature and other forms of creative expression for how we live and create our lives. In this vein, Josh Toth contends that "the more corrosive implications of postmodernism have come to buttress a societal trend toward irresponsibility, hyperindividualism, and market-powering uncertainty."[14] Amid the risks of a post-truth culture that discounts facts over what individuals *feel* or choose to be true—that "make-believe becomes real if you believe in it enough"—Toth expresses the call for a "certain thread or form capable of fostering, or renewing, an ethical relationship with the truth."[15]

In a television interview about *Like a Fading Shadow*, Muñoz Molina commented, "I'm not at all interested in postmodern games. To me, it was important to make clear what was true. I wanted to create a novel with the maximum attention to factual details."[16] Just as Cercas noted that perhaps he used to be a postmodern writer, and "maybe now I'm a post-postmodern writer,"[17] Muñoz Molina notes his own shift to fiction more devoted to accessing and understanding reality rather than affirming its uncertainty and artifice. In a 2015 essay, he observes, "I remember a statement a character made in my first novel, of which I was very proud at the time: It doesn't matter that a story be true or false but only that you know how to tell it." He adds that fiction was "my way in the world, but also my out of the world, all the more so. Very often real life seemed confusing and difficult to tackle, whereas the gifts of fiction were always there for the taking."[18] In this sense, he characterizes his earlier use of invention as a means of trying to escape a complicated, muddled, problematic reality. In turn, he describes a subsequent alteration in his perspective, a kind of exhaustion of everything being a fiction:

> I was coming around to thinking that literature would only be worth writing or reading as long as it became almost indistinguishable from life itself. What was the point of making up invented stories since almost anywhere in the world was teeming with real ones, unbound by the narrow rules and worn-out routines of fiction, always unforeseeable, ready to be learned and told?[19]

In the next section, I explore what motivates this change in thinking for Muñoz Molina, and how this shift in approach relates more broadly to the expansion and growth of biofiction as a form.

The structure of this particular biographical novel is significant to prefacing this question. *Like a Fading Shadow* contains three intersecting time frames: James Earl Ray's escape and his time in Lisbon in 1968, Muñoz Molina's researching and creation of *Like a Fading Shadow* in the years just prior to its publication in 2014, and the period of writing his earlier novel, *Winter in Lisbon*, in 1987. As material traces, the spaces of the city of Lisbon point to what Nancy Miller has referred to elsewhere as a "map of meaning and relations" that eludes the auto/biofictional narrator, yet provide "clues, almost an invitation to follow where they lead."[20] Researching the movements of James Earl Ray in Lisbon evokes Muñoz Molina's time there almost three decades prior, "unleashing (in Spanish 'desató', literally un-tying or disconnecting) very powerful feelings that had been buried or hidden away."[21] Sergio Restrepo has argued that Muñoz Molina's intention to be faithful to the use of real elements in this work of fiction becomes a defense of material evidence that calls into question the principles of postmodern literature.[22] Yet, really, what Muñoz Molina calls into question is his own ethical grounding and the limits of his efforts at escape through both fiction and physical distance. That is, in challenging his prior use of literary tools, he is also posing a critical problem for the present: What is the path forward now? Through the dual time frames of Muñoz Molina's novelistic references (mid-1980s and the early part of the decade of 2010), he effectively uses the tools of postmodernism against itself to speak dually to the function of literature and literary truth in the past and the present. He puts into contraposition how *insecurity* (fragmentary, fugitive realities) invokes and ultimately undermines postmodern freedom, and similarly how *isolation* reinforces the problems of the diminishment of reality through self-reinforcing fictions such as conspiracy theories and other embedded issues of post-truth we are experiencing in the present.

From the start of *Like a Fading Shadow*, Muñoz Molina reveals a profusion of heavily researched details he has unearthed about James Earl Ray, and that reinforce both the attraction and deception of the archive as a source of explanation. Muñoz Molina describes staying up late into the night "searching his tracks through the vast sleepless memory of the Internet," his head turning with "dates, names, trivial events—a modicum of reality that it was hard to imagine someone making up."[23] We learn that when Ray was "nine or ten, he would wake to his own screams every night," that "he dreamed that he was blind," that he was scared of falling. He documents everything Ray took in the car with him as he fled the site of the crime in Memphis, the contents of the blue gym bag mistakenly left behind, and what investigators later found in the trunk and floor of the car, down to the bits of facial hair and dried foam on the blades of the disposable razor. "I see," he declares, "his figure take shape before me, his shadow, his entire biography, composed of these minute details, one by one, like broken tiles in the mosaic sidewalks of Lisbon."[24] "Even the most secret lives leave an indelible trace," he writes. Yet, following these disparate traces feels disorienting rather than clarifying, as Muñoz Molina reinforces how "exotic minutiae" and "trivial yet exact details *give a misleading sense of omniscience*"[25] (emphasis mine).

Each networked clue leads to another; there is always another link to click, another circumstantial trace to follow. Muñoz Molina emphasizes the confusion between *access* to information and images, and understanding how those details might be meaningfully connected or what they might reveal. "It only takes a few seconds online to access the archive containing detailed accounts of almost everything he did, places he visited, prisons where he was held, even the names of women who slept with him or shared a drink at a bar."[26] Despite all of the prodigious biographical information that is available about Ray, Muñoz Molina observes that he remains an enigma: still, "nobody has been able to satisfactorily explain his motivations."[27] "It is amazing," the narrator Muñoz Molina declares in *Like a Fading Shadow*, "how much you can learn about a person and still never really know him, because he never said what was most important: a dark hole, a blank space; a mug shot, the rough lines of a facial composite based on disjointed testimonies and vague memories."[28] In one sense, then, this biographical novel seems to be about to what extent we have prioritized, even fetishized, the constant circulation of information over understanding.

It is significant to situate the novel as well within the context of media changes that were reshaping the production and reception of information at the time. The 1968 assassination of Martin Luther King Jr. was clearly a vastly significant criminal act and cultural moment that received expansive global media coverage via television, radio, and print. While the assassination of Ybarra's grandfather not quite a decade later received more localized attention, it was also a political crime against a prominent public figure that generated significant attention in the regional and Spanish media. Moreover, from the perspective of the authors writing in 2014 and 2015, these sources balloon within the current moment of constant connection amid a profusion of fragmented information coming from every direction.

Despite access to so much data, there is a need for imaginative invention to try to fill the gaps and to arrive at those things that would otherwise be inaccessible to us. "Objects say what we don't; they reveal in public what we would prefer to keep secret," the narrator Muñoz Molina claims at one point. "What they say without words makes fiction irrelevant." Yet, he quickly revises this claim. "But one still wants to imagine. Literature is the desire to dwell inside the mind of another person, like an intruder in the house, to see the world through someone else's eyes," however "impossible."[29] Notably, Muñoz Molina underscores a central tension that biofiction both embodies and explores—the desire to access and understand another life as a way to escape one's own, and yet the realization that this refuge is only temporary.

The imagined subjectivity he envisions for Ray often blends confusingly with his own: "I awake inside his mind, frightened, disoriented"; "My dream could have been his and in any case, has everything to do with him, although he did not appear"; "I learned so much about him that sometimes I feel like I am recalling his own memories, places he saw where I've never been."[30] Perhaps most importantly, in tracking Ray's movements in Lisbon, Muñoz Molina reflects back on his younger self while writing his earlier postmodern novel, *Winter in Lisbon*, incorporating a series of repeated images and symbols that reinforce parallel perceptions of distance, disconnection, and lack of attachment. These features relate the risks of mistaking mobility and breadth of options for depth of understanding, and a resultant solipsism or narcissism.

While he describes Ray as constantly on the move ("thirteen months and three weeks, five countries, fifteen cities, two continents, not to mention all the nights in different motels and boardinghouses"), the impression Muñoz Molina creates is claustrophobic rather than one of escape.[31] He characterizes Ray as isolated, paranoid, utterly alone. Underscoring the opacity with which he imagines Ray experienced the world, its "murky consistency," he envisions the fragmented, indirect, and incomplete ways that Ray tries to make sense of reality and his recourse to distorted fictions as an effort at evasion. In Lisbon, "everything must have been strange and confusing" to him, Muñoz Molina imagines. Even basic communication is impenetrable; "people muttered in an incomprehensible language."[32] Muñoz Molina never creates dialogue or has Ray speak. He is effectively "muted"—we know only what others reported Ray to have said and what Muñoz Molina imagines was in his mind. He characterizes Ray as having observed the world for his entire life as an outsider—divided, siloed: "Everything in his life happened behind a wall, visible or invisible; everything was always at a distance."[33]

Retracing his own and Ray's movements in Lisbon, Muñoz Molina uses similar language of distance and fragmentation to reimagine his own state of mind at the time of writing *Winter in Lisbon*. He writes that the first time he went to Lisbon in 1987, "beneath the calm surface of my daily routine was a *juxtaposition of fragmented lives without rhyme or reason* [...] *scattered pieces that did not fit together*" (emphasis mine). Observing that nothing comes easier to him "than the feeling of being suddenly lost," he adds that "much of what I did felt *alien* to me [...] inhabiting *transient worlds that had little to do with one another*, none truly my own"[34] (emphasis mine). He describes his dissatisfaction with his then-job as a municipal employee and his detachment toward his wife and children: "I hid each of my lives in a fragment from the other."[35] He recalls the trip to Lisbon as an effort to escape "all ties, obligations, routines, loyalties."[36] Noting his own "capacity for evasion" (feeling like a "fugitive and a traitor"), he "kept retreating into an intimate paralysis fed almost entirely by fictions."[37]

Yet, in evoking intersubjective parallels among the fugitive experiences and subjectivities of Ray with his own, it seems implausible and unconvincing that Muñoz Molina is attempting to directly conflate or associate his earlier self with a racist assassin with whom he otherwise shared little in common besides the "infinitesimal detail" of their having fled to the same city. Rather, by emphasizing the disassociating escape into invention as a kind of detachment from responsibilities to the real lives and emotional responsibilities beyond the fictional worlds of escape, he provides important clues to how we might read the symbolic function of Ray's biography and to understanding why Muñoz Molina chose to make this novel a biofiction. In fact, it becomes clear that this book isn't as much about grasping or "capturing" the motivations of Ray as it is about examining broader responsibility to the fictions we produce. Instead of emphasizing the fictionality or artificiality of reality, it is about the real implications of works of fiction on how we understand the world and each other. The function of the biofiction, then, examines these layered ways in which the novel reinforces elaborate reminders of, and connections to, the realities beyond the text, posing questions about the "pragmatic consequences and potentials of the fictions we decide to tell."[38]

An important inflection point in *Like a Fading Shadow* occurs when Muñoz Molina clarifies what he *used to* believe versus what he believes "now," at the time of researching and writing this biographical novel about Ray in 2014. He recollects the "simulacra of double lives" he was living at the time of writing *Winter in Lisbon* in 1987, declaring "that is why I was so attracted *then* to stories about spies, traitors, and impostors, novels about fugitives who fake their own death"[39] (emphasis mine). By hiding each of his lives "in a fragment from another," he avoided recognizing the actual consequences of his responsibilities to other lives and to the fictions he created, even the ones he told himself. He recollects how his "girlfriend, or maybe she was my wife by then," complained that the empathy he felt for his fictional characters did not extend to his real relationships: "All that sensibility for characters in books and films, yet you're completely oblivious to those who are actually here for you." Using the example that he couldn't evoke awe or even muster curiosity at the sight of his future child on the sonogram, he describes how "back then," he "thought fiction had to do with the imaginary [...] that real life was elsewhere ... imagination richer and more powerful than reality."[40] Muñoz Molina implicitly associates his earlier narcissism with the creation of narcissistic, self-conscious fiction focused only on itself, on the embedded worlds of fictional discourses rather than imaginative linkages that strive to "see the world through someone else's eyes," and thus to deepen understanding of reality and humanity.

By emphasizing the postmodern un-securing of fiction's ties to the real, Muñoz Molina also re-examines the effects of this fracturing on our ethical connections to one another and the role of literature in communicating this consciousness. As I wrote in an earlier essay, "in the postmodern context so well-delineated" in *Winter in Lisbon*, "not only are individuals capable of traveling in a matter of hours over vast distances, but as the relationships between the characters demonstrate, there are no overriding social bonds or other responsibilities which tie them to one place."[41] If Muñoz Molina's earlier novel, then, was about conveying these insecure ties to our situatedness and to human relationships, his perspective "now" as he writes the biofiction shifts to how to try to overcome this distance, to come closer to imagining and understanding the interwoven realities of our own and others' lives. As opposed to either simply cataloguing or documenting, or alternatively, fully escaping into the fictional, the question becomes what we *do* with these fragments to meaningfully make sense of them. In a related sense, Irmtraud Huber has commented on the shift to what she calls reconstructive fictions: such works "ask how fictions contribute responsibly to the world we live in, assessing the danger of solipsistic isolation inherent in a postmodern refusal of meaning, raising ethical questions of representation in the face of *real death and pain,* considering *the pitfalls of escapism*, and re-evaluating the ways our lives continuously shape and are shaped by dreams"[42] (emphasis mine).

Much of the second part of the novel, for example, explores what distinguishes the deceptive fictions of James Earl Ray that want to "supplant reality" from fictions that deepen understanding of reality and human experience.[43] Ray is of course himself a powerful symbol of the absence of human connection or connectedness. Muñoz Molina demonstrates how this solipsism and isolation extend to Ray's use of fictions as sources of destructive disengagement that invoke very real consequences of terror and violence. Virtually all of Ray's relationships are formed by fictions of falsity and distrust, or interactions that are purely transactional. Muñoz Molina writes of Ray, "He had never slept with a woman who was not a prostitute. With a knowing grimace, *based mostly on fictional experience,* he would say to one of the other inmates in the prison that women were only for using and throwing away, that a man on the run should never trust them"[44] (emphasis mine). Isolation feeds his disconnection: "He perceived the world in an indirect manner, with a degree of distortion that was consistent, but he did not know how to calculate":

> He could not trust anything. There was no way to know what was true. [...] He imagined there had to be a method, a code to understand these things, to distinguish truth from lies, like those machines that could decipher enemy messages, a sure way to get reliable information, and perhaps intercept messages between the powerful, the people who own the world, the Jews, the ones who control everything from a distance, the communists.[45]

Most influentially, Muñoz Molina underscores how Ray's access to information about the world is always decontextualized, always in incomplete fragments that never challenge but merely confirm his prejudices, disinformation, and conspiracy theories. Critically, these distortionary narratives conflate in Ray's mind with the very real consequences of King's murder, "live reports about black people rioting [...] the cries, the explosions, the breaking glass, the police sirens."[46] Muñoz Molina is not concerned here with showing the postmodern dilemma of how the simulacra has supplanted the real or the fundamental fictionality of discourses of reality. Instead, what he underscores are the concrete ways in which Ray's isolation and human disconnection fuel his entrenchment in destructive fictions that have profound effects on real lives and histories.[47] As Ray is about to shoot King, Muñoz Molina writes, "the image that was constructed so meticulously in the *laboratory of his mind is now real*"[48] (emphasis mine).

In describing his initial trip to Lisbon as an effort to escape the responsibilities and emotional ties of real life, Muñoz Molina refers to his memories from that time as already "contaminated" by fiction.[49] Writer Edurne Portela has referred to a "contaminated" imagination as one that is damaged or diminished by the effort to cover with silence and evasion complicated or uncomfortable truths, avoiding critical inquiry and engagement.[50] Why does Muñoz Molina relate this earlier "contamination" of his life by fiction to the much deeper and more destructive isolation of Ray? Once again, Muñoz Molina does not convincingly suggest a direct comparison. More allusively, he dislocates the narrowness of Ray's biography from its own temporal confines, illustrating the wider potential to misuse fiction as a means of escaping complex truths through emotional detachment and knowledge polarization.

Arrogant ideologies make themselves immune to revision by evidence, encouraging what Jose Medina has called "active ignorance." This arrogance has its roots in insecurity, a fear or threat that is real or imagined.[51] Arrogant ideologies are associated with conspiracy theories because their insularity from challenge allows them to confirm repeatedly and add to a litany of what one believes to be true. Notably, then, Ray becomes an extreme symbol not only of failures of prolonged insecurity of meaning and truth, but also with the epistemic threats we face in the present, of so-called "post-truth." The conspiracy theories and echo chambers that have degraded contemporary epistemological truths are amplified by algorithms that feed and amplify what we already think we know, reinforced through siloed networks. As Stephen Marche has contended, "The reduction of experience to identity, speech to performance, and thought to language games has resulted, not in more sophisticated and nuanced appreciation of ourselves and others, or in more compassion, but in near-total myopia and self-absorption. Post-fact is, first and foremost, a turning away from the mess of the world. We have *closed* rather than opened"[52] (emphasis mine).

One of the central epistemic challenges we face in the present is the confusion between the use of an "ethical imagination" to open complex truths of reality to challenge and reconsideration and "contaminated" fictions that close off inquiry and reinforce intellectual and ideological solipsism. How do we move from hermetic answers to more hermeneutic possibilities that examine the meaning of fictions in our lives? Muñoz Molina does not suggest that the antidote to post-truth contagion is a return to simple or absolute truths. In his defense of the biographical novel, Jay Parini argues that any effort to understand another life is always a matter of subjective selectivity; he quotes Stephen J. Gould's assertion that we view what we "are trained to view—and observation of different sorts of objects often requires a conscious shift of focus, not a total and indiscriminate expansion in the hopes of seeing everything." That is, this shift of focus and "fruitful selectivities" among the facts of a life allow us to connect to unexpected discoveries that can never be more than partial and open to new examination.[53] Here, I want to consider an important shift in Muñoz Molina's use of biofiction within the novel as a way of expressing this reality. In *Like a Fading Shadow*, Muñoz Molina asserts that *before* "I believed the task of literature was to create perfect forms, symmetries and resonances that imbued the world with an order and significance it otherwise lacked" (i.e., to *impose* this artificial order and meaning on reality). But gradually, he insists, "I began to realize [...] the highest aspiration of literature is not to improve an amorphous matter of real events through fiction, but to imitate the unpremeditated, yet rigorous order of reality, to create a scale model of its processes."[54] I understand this to mean the use of fiction as a kind of simulative model, a subjective experiment that does not dodge the complexities of our realities, but instead actively encourages our effort to consciously shift focus in order to discern alternative ways of perceiving and understanding human experience.

Muñoz Molina's discussion toward the end of *Like a Fading Shadow* of the different possible endings to his biographical novel provides a potent example. As a novelist, he notes that he has all sorts of choices that one cannot always control so neatly in real life. He suggests that one possible ending if we "look at the story under the clear austerity of the facts" is to conclude it with Ray's departure at the Lisbon airport for Heathrow. He can show Ray having passed the limits of airport security, unaware that he would soon be captured at his destination. He could leave the story "as a game that remains within the strict limits of the board [...] [u]nlike real people, they [the characters] have the power to vanish without a trace."[55] Real people leave traces on the earth, make mistakes they can't correct, impact the lives of others, face real consequences for their choices. Ultimately, the biographical "ending" he chooses is to fictionalize a version of what Ray actually does in real life once he is captured and in prison. Despite having confessed, Ray creates his own fictionalized story of another perpetrator who killed King, a shadowy figure named Raúl. (How different is this from his other aliases, one wonders?) While Muñoz Molina fills in the fictional details, the facts of this ending align closely with the conspiracy narrative that the real biographical Ray created of another killer and which some, including members of the King family, later believed.

By selecting this imaginative ending to Ray's biography, a fictional version that to some degree becomes "true," or believed to be true by some people, Muñoz Molina's biofictional creation simulatively suggests the risks to truth are also about the responsibilities to the ways we use invention—not to *supplant* reality, but to expand our perceptions of other subjectivities. While, within the confines of the novel, Muñoz Molina can choose whatever ending to the fiction, in the actual reality, we have to continue to discern between the fictional and factual, between imaginative linkages that deepen connections among diffuse realities and each other, and competing versions that falsify and degrade that trust. Rather than resolve this complexity, biofiction compels us to straddle the worlds of the invented and the real. The choice of how we employ fiction to inform our realities is up to us. By straying from fact to comment on the elusive process of capturing biographical truth, biofiction reveals the tension between reimagining another life and the autobiographical freedom or compulsion to escape and rewrite one's own.

The Dinner Guest

> "Circumstantial evidence is a very tricky thing," answered Holmes thoughtfully. "It may seem to point very straight to one thing, but if you shift your own point of view a little, you may find it pointing in an equally uncompromising manner to something entirely different."
>
> (Arthur Conan Doyle, *Adventure 4—The Boscombe Valley Mystery*)

In *Like a Fading Shadow*, Muñoz Molina exposed how access to profuse and constantly circulating information has not made our biographical lives easier to understand. It has in many ways become harder to know who or what to believe amid so many circumstantial clues and claims to truth. Against this profligacy, Gabriela Ybarra's *The Dinner Guest* explores how silence and absence, what we avoid or fail to see, are also fugitive parts of this unbundled world. In classifying her work as a novel, Ybarra emphasizes the imaginative linkages she creates in order to articulate the fragmentary details surrounding her family's biography and to try to fill these gaps and erasures to make sense of her own. She examines the capacity of fiction to build a circumstantial case for how these biographical fragments might meaningfully connect and the broader story they can reveal.

The Dinner Guest is a split narrative, divided into two parts that increasingly intersect. As with *Like a Fading Shadow*, the novel centers around three main points in time—the more remote past surrounding her grandfather's assassination, the recent past of her mother's illness and death in 2011, and the time of writing the biographical novel, starting in 2012. The first part of the novel involves her investigation and imaginative reconstruction of the story of her grandfather's kidnapping and murder. In the second half, her efforts to revisit the details of her mother's illness and recent death predominate, although intersected by fragmented stories involving terrorist threats earlier faced by her father and grandfather, and by her evolving mindset as she composes the novel. While she largely employs emotional distance and the cool tone of a journalistic report in the first half, as she relates her mother's illness she inserts herself more, noting the linkages to her own self-discoveries in the process: "I always feel that I'm a detective of my own life."[56]

The title itself points to how some of the most powerful things are those that are not physically present or accessible, but that continue to act on our realities—however covertly. As Ybarra writes, "The story goes that in my family there's an extra dinner guest at every meal. He's invisible, but always there. He has a plate, glass, knife and fork. Every so often he appears, casts his shadow over the table and erases one of those present. The first to vanish was my grandfather."[57] In this allusive way, Ybarra alludes both to the actual kidnapping and disappearance of her grandfather in 1977, six years before she was born, and to the persistence of this violent loss to affect her family profoundly, even as its details are withheld and the story vanishes from discussion. In her novel, Ybarra observes how real things that seemed distanced, such as her grandfather's assassination and the actuality of ETA terrorism, were perceived as fictions that "she didn't know how to assimilate as real," whereas the intensely lived experience of her mother's death needed fiction to make it graspable. In an interview she says, "Until I wrote this book, I never realized I had related to the reality of terrorism as if it were a fiction. So, the book is an exercise in reality. I had to abandon the fiction to enter that history. But I also had to invent to fill its gaps."[58]

> Ybarra argues that the novel is an "imaginative reconstruction" because "memory is always fiction and, in the case of my grandfather, I had to make up big parts of his kidnapping because nobody in my family would tell me anything about it. For many years, my family lived as though these traumatic events had never happened. I could infer their pain through their silences, but lacked a story; the only information I had came from the newspapers. In the case of my mother, I did know the story quite well, but reality is often too complicated to make believable, so I had to twist it."[59]

Reconstructing the story of her grandfather's abduction and murder becomes a circumstantial case not only because of the absence of witnesses at the time of his death, but because the silence surrounding the story requires her to reconstruct it indirectly from scattered clues. The two deaths also interconnect circumstantially to inform how she interprets and tries to mutually compose their meanings. As Ybarra comments,

> My mother's death brought back my grandfather's death. Before it, the killing was just a pair of handcuffs in a glass case next to the bronze llamas that my parents brought back from Peru. The tedium of the illness recalled the tedium of the wait during the kidnapping. My father began to talk about blood-stained rosaries. It would be months yet before I understood his pain.[60]

In the "Author's Note" prefacing the novel, she informs the reader that she first heard the story of her grandfather's disappearance when she was eight. A school friend, who happened to be a grandson of the prosecutor on the case, told her that they "fished her grandfather's body out of the Nervión estuary with a trawl net, the kind that Galicians use to catch anchovies." Years later, she adds, the granddaughter of the medical examiner told her that her grandfather had "dissected [Ybarra'] grandfather's body after it was discovered bound hand and foot and run over by a train." Ybarra says that for many years she took these stories to be true "and mixed them with conversations overheard at home to make up a versions of [her] own."[61] That she remixes these false narratives with disjointed snippets of conversations reinforces the multiplicity and insecurity of the evidence on its own to reveal the truth of what happened. "I googled my grandfather's name and visited archives. I took many notes on what I read, faithfully transcribing news stories and opinion pieces. But the scenes that I imagined ended up filtering into my account."[62] As Lily Meyer of NPR has suggested, Ybarra is anxious to enter a past reality but unable to do so. This "anxiety gives [the] fiction a purpose," filling the gaps and creating the imaginary linkages that the fragmentary, nonlinear traces alone fail to offer.[63]

Ybarra demonstrates the repeated search for convincing material evidence—images or artifacts that will secure the story—and their insufficiency. Referencing "epistemological blind alleys," Anne Rüggemeier has characterized such objects as "epistemology's other: they turn the focus on the things that cannot be known, the stuff that resists (narrative) sense making."[64] The spare prose of the first section (forty pages) regarding her grandfather's kidnapping is composed of fragmented, circumstantial details. Whereas *Like a Fading Shadow* was overflowing in its verbosity (at more than 500 pages in the original Spanish), *The Dinner Guest*'s slim frame highlights the importance of documentary evidence to reveal what is omitted. Ybarra seems to be trying to anchor the story to these tangible evidentiary clues. Among others, these include segments of various newspaper articles, images of her father in the "French-made" aluminum handcuffs used by the kidnappers, published letters from her grandfather to his children during his time in captivity and their replies; an altered crossword puzzle with coded messages the family hoped the grandfather would see; notification on balled-up sheets of notebook paper from the terrorists that they had killed Javier Ybarra; directions and a map to where to find the body; and explicit descriptions from the autopsy reports. The accumulation of these fractured details—the expanding *body of evidence* she compiles—is viscerally connected with real bodies, with the story of identifying and recovering the actual *body* of her grandfather and his material remains.

Whereas Muñoz Molina delved imaginatively into the mental subjectivity of James Earl Ray, Ybarra avoids imagining the interiority of her family members/biographical subjects. Instead, with precise, surgical detail she reports the actual physical interior of her grandfather's body. For example, "upon performing the autopsy, Dr. Toledo, medical examiner at Basurto Hospital, determined that his intestinal walls were atrophied, evidence that […] he had been given almost nothing to eat during his confinement." A few pages later, she adds, "during the autopsy, it was discovered that my grandfather had traces of grass in his stomach and that it had been at least three days since he'd defecated, even though excrement was discovered in the hideout that the police found sometime later."[65] While Ybarra provides a great deal of information about her grandfather's violent death, it is notable that she includes so much opacity within all these notes, information, and factual specificity.

We are reminded that the spaces marked by violence and loss—the Basque region, her grandfather's body, her mother's body—are not just imagined, but real existences and sites of trauma. On the one hand, the evidentiary details she uncovers seem to provide her a certain reassurance of the truth of the story she is uncovering. Ybarra says in an interview,

> Although this is not explicit in the text, it was very shocking for me to see my father's grieving face in the newspapers; it also impressed me to realize that my father lost his father when he was about the same age as

> me when I lost my mother. When I saw all the photographs and the news, *I couldn't deny the murder of my grandfather was true.*[66]

Writer Carolyn Kraus has referred to the reassurance of documentary evidence "that might have lent my story credibility and anchored it in the physical world ... [a] yearning to establish material connections to [my] past, 'true' connections that could not be repudiated, dreamed up, or eradicated."[67] Yet, Ybarra also provides repeated examples of the narrative cross-examining itself and challenging the certainty of what she had just reported. At one point, she provides a disconnected list of a number of things that "weren't true." Did the kidnappers who burst in one May morning bind all the children to the brass bed, or did her father's youngest sister hide in a wardrobe? Did her grandfather ask the kidnappers to kill him on the spot, or did he say, "The worst you can do is shoot me?"[68] These uncertainties highlight the powerful role of the circumstantial, the speculative, and of absence in sharing her judgments and efforts at discovery.

Referring in a different context to the recent expansion of "documentary poetry," Mary Pinard has captured insightfully some of this complexity. She observes, "Twenty-first documentary culture goes beyond simply recording the history of something or the fact that something happened. And it represents the *fracture* that probably led to that thing happening. So you can bring a lot of different materials to bear, everything from calculations to newspaper articles to footnotes. This documenting is an acknowledgment of the fracture." Silence, in contrast, is a kind of rejection or suppression of that rupture and of its pain, "the fracture of the environment, of the family." And we could add to that the kind of repeated "fracture" that we see with terrorist violence, with repeated trauma, "a compound fracture about a hundred times over—bones sticking through the surface." Pinard adds, these works "about breakage are on the surface distancing—they're about exploding pieces away. But there has to be some work to bring the pieces toward each other [...] ideally, toward some sort of healing, but not always."[69]

Ybarra shows how the search and documentation of facts can provide an illusion of a kind of control over the chaos of existence. Her father assuages his anxiety over her mother's devastating diagnosis by taking copious, meticulous notes: "Start of Ernestina's illness" in which the potentiality of creating an artificial anus is described with exacting detail.[70] After her mother's death, Ybarra spends the hours before her flight to Madrid averting the sight of the city her mother had occupied but instead calculating the weight of the buildings, the number of windows and floors of a skyscraper, "but neither my phone's calculator or I can handle the load."[71] As with *Like a Fading Shadow,* excessive documentation or *data* does not resolve the unanswerable, deeply human questions that the narrator wants to discover.

Even the information Ybarra does have plentiful access to, such as internet searches, generates a sense of absence and distance. For example, Ybarra has to google the story of her grandfather's kidnapping and assassination in order to learn about it, no differently from anyone else with no connection to the family. Throughout the book, Ybarra makes repeated references to these Google searches. Her mother repeatedly searches for information regarding her cancer. Ybarra searches for information on her grandfather and later in the novel about the ETA terrorist who tries to kill her father. These searches for answers to deeply complicated and complex questions occur alongside myriad, mundane others. Such examples reinforce the ease of searching and apparent solutions against the essential emptiness of the profuse but insufficient, unsatisfying answers they provide. Ybarra immediately follows this disappointing search with another for the poet Robert Walser, who died alone in the snow by suicide, and who is now "buried" with 300,000 other images of himself on Google Images. A few pages later, transitioning to the time of writing the book in 2012, after the death of her mother, she describes finding herself unable to reconstruct her image. Searching on the internet, she finds only one picture of her as a young woman. The rest are of gravestones. All of these searches reinforce the perception of continued distance and absence, despite so much apparent access. As author Ali Smith writes,

> The web's metaphor, its *numinous promise of answers to undreamt questions*, belies its limitations as a tool of connection [...] for the Internet's charm is also a kind of *deception* about a whole new way of feeling lonely, a *semblance of plenitude* but really a new level of Dante's inferno, a zombie-filled cemetery of spurious clues, beauty, pathos, pain, [...] a great sea of hidden shallows.[72]

Moreover, there are not only evidentiary gaps, but also emotional space she has to fill as well. She describes how when her mother got sick, she realized that "my father, my sisters and I had gotten used to being apart because she [her mother] *bridged the gap*"[73] (emphasis mine). Her mother is the connective thread that assimilates these fragmented, circumstantial parts into a common thread. Surely, most of us have had friends or family members like this, and we struggle to know what to do in their absence or how to fill the space of what had previously given that common group and shared story a feeling of coherence. Reflecting on her choice to make this novel a biofiction, rather than a memoir or a biography, she says,

> I imagined as I researched. There were many things that I didn't know, so I couldn't have imagined them before beginning my research. [...] During the writing of the first part of the book—the part about my grandfather—I was always trying to come closer to my father ... I always

> think of *The Dinner Guest* as a *ritual of grief and an exercise of truth* in which *I use fiction to help me assimilate* the deaths of my mother and grandfather.[74] (emphasis mine)

Important to understanding Ybarra's novel and the relevance of biofiction in this process of "assimilating" these two disconnected losses is her effort to use factual details to bridge this absence. Various critics have observed how Ybarra actively invents while simultaneously employing a narrative voice that feels distant—precise and analytical. Yet, it is actually when the fiction breaks through to show how the author and the biographical lives she examines have used silence and distance as a way to avoid engaging with complicated truths that the novel becomes most affecting.

At the end of the first section of the novel, Ybarra describes how despite the proximity of ETA violence in her life, she had "*lived at a remove* from the conflict"[75] (emphasis mine). By this she means she had been able to avoid acknowledging its realness or its continued implications in her family's life and that of her country more broadly. She notes how she and others had been able to isolate and insulate themselves from the violence.

> During the roughest years at the beginning of the eighties—the so-called *años de plomo*, or Years of Lead—the neighbors pretended nothing was happening; they played tennis, had cocktails, went out sailing and visited the open-air restaurants of Berango. The tension was under wraps. A car in flames, a dead body, and a few hours later everything returned to normal.[76]

With her family's move to Madrid when she is twelve (a decision she describes as an effort to shield the family), she is further insulated from this reality: As Bryony White has written in another context, such violence "is often portrayed at a remove; it is mundane, glanced at, yet *painfully and overwhelming present*, as most systemic violence is"[77] (emphasis mine). Most significantly, the suppressed violence of terrorism, her mother's cancer, and her father's silence all become interconnected, as Ybarra examines both the use of imagination that silences what we don't want to see, keeping it safely a fiction, alongside the redemptive power of fiction to transform the way we understand a complex reality.

One of the most significant ways in which Ybarra links the narratives of her grandfather and her mother is to consider the relationship among differing approaches to eluding difficult truths. Ybarra observes that her mother's first instinct was to "hide her illness. [...] Her reaction to illness was resistance. 'Nothing's wrong here. This isn't killing me. Look how well I am.'" She adds, "Sometimes I even believed it myself."[78] When her mother starts experiencing concerning symptoms of pain throughout her body, she "pretended it was her muscles that hurt, not her bones." Her father also avoided considering more serious possibilities. "Don't worry," he said as he stroked her face, "this must be side effects of the chemo."[79] Yet, while Ybarra depicts her family as first turning to self-protective fictions that deny the silent metastases occurring within her, an important transformation in the book is her mother's swift acknowledgment when she learns the truth. This breaking of the silence contrasts with the withholding of the story of Ybarra's grandfather, and how denying it happened even though it had changed her father's life dramatically, made it a story that imposed itself so much more forcefully.

Ybarra's sparse, evocative style also makes this work feel like the architecture of a poem, and it is evident that she pays a lot of attention to how things physically connect to *proximity* in the narrative. There is a profound spatial component to *The Dinner Guest*. Ybarra explains how in addition to cyber-surfing, in the effort to process her mother's death, she decided to physically revisit all the places she had been with her when she was sick. Much of the second half of the novel situates us in that landscape, which is similarly inconclusive. As we revisit with the narrator the hospital's radiation department where her mother was treated, she notes, "I feel the same lethargy I felt a year ago. The same fog in the head. [...] I've only been in this room for five minutes and I want to leave."[80]

The shifts in the narrative back and forth between the illness of her mother and the research into the terrorist threats that affected her grandfather and father, a kind of toggling between frames and landscapes, become important signals as to how to read the "circumstantial clues" to the novel. In this way, it seems illuminating that her perception of terrorism as a kind of distant fiction is the immediate prelude to the second half of the novel, and her recalling: The afternoon of April 4, 2011, my mother called me and said: "Gabriela, 'I have cancer, *but it's really nothing*'" (emphasis mine). She adds, "A few hours later she boarded a plane and sat on her tumour all the way to New York."[81] Ybarra thus connects the self-protective fictions of her mother (and herself) with other ways of "*living at a remove*," of avoiding difficult truths.

Ybarra carefully documents the details of her mother's decline in ways that are less narrative than evocative—describing what it was like to undress her mother and hold her fragile, childlike body, naked, in the hospital shower, and detailing the restrictive diet she has to eat to protect her ravaged colon: "Now she only liked soft, cold food and was eating gelatin from a bowl."[82] When her mother is told that her cancer's "silent metastasis" had explosively spread and she has little time left, "her first reaction was to fall apart. But then she reflected and let it be known she was glad no one had hidden anything from her. She found acceptance in the time it took her to eat the yoghurt on her meal tray."[83] Ybarra has commented in an interview that one of the things she was interested in exploring was about getting closer to the intimate truths of our humanity and our actual physical (and not only emotional) vulnerability. She observes that there were moments of great beauty in integrating death as something more natural, perhaps as opposed to more insidious silence, a shadow.[84] This openness has something to do with coming closer to the more transcendent truths of our lives. As Rebecca Guevara has said of Colum McCann's *Letting the Great World Spin*, it also points to a larger realization, amid the world's complexities, of "mingled sadness and appreciation for the world's beauty that slips by unnoticed under the thoughtless or cruel acts that obscure it."[85]

Colum McCann has talked about how biofictions ask readers to go in and question ideas for themselves to "open up the moment for a little while so that others can peek inside and see what we don't want or refuse to see."[86] Examining not only her father's silence related to her grandfather's death but her own avoidance or "not seeing" of the implications of terrorism on her family becomes intricately entwined with coming to terms with her mother's death. Significantly, political separatism is itself a kind of "fragment" or effort at breaking away.

Again, Ybarra uses the structure of the narrative to show these interconnections. She marks temporal parallels: "a month and half after my mother died, on October 20, 2011, ETA announced a final halt to armed conflict."[87] In addition to the attack on her grandfather, Ybarra interrupts the narrative of her mother's decline and death with short side investigations that try to reconstruct the suppressed stories of attempts on her father's life when she was a teenager by an ETA member who went by the name of Miguel. At the same time, the details of what happened are destabilized by the fictions needed to reconstruct these uncertain histories: "A policeman came into the lobby and shouted: "There's a package bomb!" My cousin threw up her arms and dropped the package. The postman tossed the mail in the air; the letters hit the box with the bomb in it while my cousin's arms were still raised. *Or at least that's how I imagine it*."[88] She describes "spending the morning googling" Miguel, finding information about his family, a YouTube account created by someone by the same name as him. ("I don't know whether it's real or fake.") She writes that none of this scares her, but then she imagines Miguel in front of the computer and doesn't know what to feel. "Looking at pictures of him, I feel the same way I do when I look at images of cancer cells. I don't think about the threat, but about the story conjured up."[89] Bodies of evidence, physical bodies, the body politic ... all become entwined here. She says of the violence related to ETA, "We never talked about it."[90]

David Jiménez Torres has related *The Dinner Guest* to another recent novel, Fernando Aramburu's *Patria* (translated as *Homeland*) that also explores the effects of the Basque conflict and ETA terrorism on its victims.[91] Jiménez Torres argues that while *Homeland* situates the violence and the pain in the heart of Basque society, Ybarra dislocates it from this context, connecting it to more universal contexts and experiences of loss. He contends that Ybarra exemplifies the perspective of the new generations for whom the relationship with the violent past of ETA is secondary, told by others.[92] The narrator's references to Pompeii or the Empire State Building highlight this loss of historical and geographic specificity to ETA and its victims. Further, he suggests that the abrupt jumps between the grandfather's story and her mother's confuse the ability of the reader to differentiate the two deaths. In part, he presents the critique that connecting these two deaths diffuses the power of the political, or the suggestion that "everything" is political. Yet, he also observes that dislocating the violence of ETA from its most habitual markers reduces the capacity to exercise a narrowly pedagogical or Manichean function to those decades of violence, opening them to wider understandings, an affective process he connects to Edurne Portela's call for an "ethical imagination." In fact, as he indicates, the narrator of *The Dinner Guest* herself begins her novel by observing that imagining may sometimes be the only option for how to understand a fragmented, complicated narrative and its silences.

In her exploration of the "silence" and "complicity" surrounding the effects of ETA violence, writer Edurne Portela states, "I am part of this history, and my perspective in telling it is that of a witness; a witness, however, who for many years, if not indifferent to the problem of the violence in the Basque region, nonetheless ignored it, elected *not to try to understand*, because it was too complicated and too emotionally difficult"[93] (emphasis mine). She asks herself how she can now tell the story of this "wounded, fragmented and still polarized society"[94] of which she is a part. In particular, she notes the complexity of a past in which the majority of the young people felt antipathy and had more fear of the national police and the civil guard, even though the great majority of these youth rejected the violence of the ETA organization and its nationalist aims. In so doing, she points to other layered fractures in Spain's recent history.

While Ybarra is part of a younger generation than Portela, she alludes similarly to this complex mixture of proximity, distance, and denial. She looks up one of her old school friends on Facebook, googles his contacts, several of whom have been in prison, and finds pictures of him with ETA members. She recalls that "one day he told me that at home they'd said he couldn't be my friend. He told me that he had two cousins in jail. I managed to convince him that not talking was stupid, and we continued to hang out until I moved to Madrid. Sometimes I wonder if he ever thinks of me." Against this familiarity, she looks up videos on YouTube of an ETA member showing caches of weapons and at pictures of ETA commandoes. She notes, "I have a hard time coming to terms with them, because accepting their humanity means recognizing that I'm capable of the same things they are. My conscience felt easier when I imagined that they were crazy or that they weren't people. Martians. Fiction."[95]

Differentiating what she refers to as a contaminated imagination (silenced, indifferent), Portela emphasizes the possibilities of an ethical imagination to arrive at greater understanding of complex, difficult realities. This doesn't mean, from her perspective, agreement with the perspective of another, but one that tries to imagine what motivates the other outside of narrow prescriptions of identity, political associations, and the constriction of ideology. She calls for "imagining, thinking, and feeling our own emotional, perspectival responses to these events not from the narrow perspective of moral denunciation or ideology, but from affective spaces of discomfort and uncertainty."[96] Similarly, Colum McCann refers to the idea that "we need to hold contradictory notions in the palms of our hands at the same time. [...] There is an overwhelming feeling that we cannot embrace nuance as agilely as we used to. There is the refusal to accept opposing ideas, an inability to recognize that our own ideas can stand in perfect opposition to one another."[97]

Portela has argued that she needed to situate her attentions specifically on the Basque region and not to escape or avoid engaging with the complexity of the violence there by conflating its experience with that of other places, to imagine how we might reconstruct those broken social ties. However, one of the strengths of *The Dinner Guest* as a biofiction is exactly that Ybarra *detaches* and *dislocates* the experience of terrorist violence from the isolated Basque context, inserting it into a much broader context of human suffering, silence, and the relationship we have with death and dying. How much easier it would be to suggest that these experiences have nothing to do with us, and that they are unfamiliar.

"Every culture is built upon defense mechanisms," argues biographical novelist Olga Tokarzcuk. "This is quite normal, the way we try to suppress everything that is not comfortable for us."[98] Her role as she sees it is to force her readers to examine aspects of their own history—their own, or their nation's—that they would rather avoid. *The Dinner Guest* suggests that biofiction can have a redemptive function not only by showing us the points of fracture, but also by examining processes of healing, human connection—how we try to draw the fragments together in ways that make the future imaginable. The more substantive truth is not limited to a specific time or place, but to the effort to pursue human understanding and to transcend the domination of silence and avoidance of difficult, complicated realities. At the end of *The Dinner Guest*, Ybarra returns to the spot in the woods where her grandfather was killed. And while the distance remains, it is not the space of loss or what is missing that comes into focus. Rather it is the sense of coming closer to the interconnected threads of their lives and evolving stories: "As I take notes I think about my grandfather, my mother, and my father. About my mother telling us: 'Live lightly.' About my grandfather saying 'The worst they can do is shoot me.'"

Conclusion

In the final chapters of *Like a Fading Shadow*, the narrator Muñoz Molina travels to Memphis, to the Lorraine Motel where Martin Luther King Jr. was killed, now a civil rights museum. In the carefully replicated room that Ray once occupied, Muñoz Molina discovers a vertical showcase "where all the objects I had read about and seen in photographs are on display": the bullet, the binoculars, the flimsy bed, green blanket and dirty sofa, dusty Christmas ornaments on the mantelpiece. "Everything is organized and tagged, like the fragmentary objects of those remote everyday lives preserved in the display cases of museums; material traces of a lost world."[99] Objects may "say what we don't," but Muñoz Molina affirms that some things elude understanding: "the intensity of that injury, the vehemence of its hate and its mix of vulgarity and ignorance cannot be translated."[100]

The past, he argues, is "a theme park." All of these objects seem distanced and disconnected from the realities they harbor, from their real effects. You can

> pose next to the life-size figures that cover the wall as if you had been in one of those marches, walking right next to Martin Luther King. You can enter the cell where King was held in Birmingham, Alabama, sit on a bed identical to his, read, projected on the wall, the letter he wrote on loose sheets, in the margins of the newspaper [...] But who could know how that darkness felt, the sound of the bolts and the cries of the prisoners, who could know the insidious doubt in the middle of the night, the suspicion that all this sacrifice is in vain and that he has brought even more suffering to others, the thirst of the soul, the secret cowardice.[101]

Literature, he has contended, "is the desire to dwell inside the mind of another person [...] to see the world from someone else's eyes." Leaving behind the mind of James Earl Ray, he imagines what Martin Luther King Jr. might have been thinking in the moments leading up to his assassination. In doing so from the perspective of invention, of fiction, he is not trying to actualize some secret truth of what King may have been thinking or to deepen his biography. Instead, he is exploring a more conflicted, contentious interiority that interrogates the narrow version of King as a martyr, the reductive simplicity of the symbolism projected onto him. He imagines King thinking,

> He had never wanted to be put on a pedestal, but they did it anyway; they elevated him to this earthly sainthood and then disowned him for not living up their impossible expectations. They turned him into a heroic statue only to throw stones at. Shame was one of the his most assiduous secret afflictions, throbbing deeper than the weight of his obligations [...] the gap between what others chose to see in him and who he really was. There is no public figure who is not an impostor.[102]

Why does Muñoz Molina use biofiction to imagine King's subjectivity in this way? Emma Donoghue has argued that if biofiction is done smartly, it "shouldn't be cozy and desirable and an escape to another era, but it should actually make us uncomfortable. It should provoke us."[103] The imaginative view that Muñoz Molina constructs of King's inner dialogue underscores how the biographical images we create can so readily be smoothed into deceptive fictions, resolved symbols that avoid our having to examine other uncomfortable truths regarding the persistence of division and fracture—of racism, of separatist violence, of trauma. We can create symbols that challenge and interrogate, but we can also universalize "at a remove," in ways that dilute nuance and close off complexity. Yet, as Ybarra's work explores, the effort to isolate and to insulate ourselves from difficult, conflictive realities is a fragile refuge. That silence is imposed does not resolve the unsettled realities underneath, or prevent them from resurfacing. One of the central possibilities of biofiction in response is to expose what we "do not want or refuse to see," to acknowledge and contend with these layered contradictions.

Returning to the quote with which we began this chapter, that "as we have unbundled and remixed, we have also isolated and made insecure," I want to close by suggesting how biofiction might reorient us amid this circumstantial reality, reinforcing its particular contemporary relevance. As Muñoz Molina and Ybarra have explored, fictions can provide a fugitive attempt at escape—decontextualizing and distancing us from engaging with difficult or complicated realities. However, fiction can also be used to remix and to *recontextualize* seemingly disconnected lives and perspectives, bringing together contradictory ideas and images that might otherwise remain isolated from one another and from examination of their real effects. In so doing, biofiction has the potential to embolden the ethical imagination, opening to the complicated, transformative pursuit of embodying and reimagining the human condition.

PART TWO

Speculative Truths and Derivative Fictions

3

Entertaining the What-Ifs in Rosa Montero's *The Madwoman of the House* and *The Ridiculous Idea of Never Seeing You Again*

Writer Rosa Montero has referred to biographies as "existential maps" to navigate a confusing world. In this way, she describes using the biographical lives in her fictions as "enormous screen[s] onto which to project these possibilities."[1] As she puts it, "Perhaps each one of the events of our lives could have gone ten different ways. [...] By playing out the what-ifs, the novelist experiments with these potential lives."[2] Rather than documenting a specific life as a biographer might, many biographical novelists immerse themselves in the life of a historical figure to speculate not only on alternate pasts but as a mode of projecting options for navigating the present. Such authors of biofiction emphasize the benefits of variance, playing out multiple options that run contrary to dominant, totalizing narratives. Drawing from financial approaches to risk and uncertainty, the following two chapters consider this *speculative* potential of biofiction.

Relating shifts in cultural logic to developments in literary strategy, the three differing models I have put forth in this book are not exclusive, but intersecting. The prior chapters considered how writers of biofiction approach evidence, uncertainty, and decision-making within an increasingly circumstantial context. In what I termed the *circumstantial model*, these writers respond to contingent, competing, and often fragmented claims to biographical truth and meaning. Amid a profusion of indirect claims, we have to decide who and what sources to trust—which version(s) to invest in as credible. Economic theorists have also considered how "the decision to trust resembles a 'leap' not justified by calculation," but anchored in *as-if* assessments requiring faith and judgment.[3] The language of financial approaches to speculation, leveraging indeterminacy as a source of potential gain, provides a useful paradigm to examine the expanding pull of biofiction. Financial speculation both refers to qualities of risk—the gamble or guess about likely changes in market value—and retains traces "of the older definition of speculation as a *conjectural contemplation of a subject, the imagination of possibilities*"[4] (emphasis mine). That biographies can be used as a means to try to anchor reality (hedging against the risks of uncertainty) and a means to speculate on its possible versions (through acceptance of greater volatility) makes biofiction a particularly apt instrument to negotiate the complexities of contemporary life.

By framing important features of the development of contemporary biofictions around the concept of the speculative, I focus on three particular aspects. One, how perceptions of uncertainty and risk shape investment in the biographical subject as a source of fictional experimentation and creative potential. Two, is what I refer to as the tendency toward the specular. While part of the biographical novelist's freedom comes from projecting the imagined subjectivity of another life, these works also expose the embedded interactivity of the life under consideration with that of the author, engaging across temporalities to act on how we read both past and present. Three, the effects of the dispersion of authority and meaning to the growth of derivative instruments, including derivative biographical lives. By derivative lives, I mean biographical narratives derived from another life but liberated from valuations based solely in factual data or historical specificity. Such imagined versions, no longer anchored to the original source, can become independent sources of investment and exchange.

Observing that the fictionality of derivatives and other speculative instruments has intensified since the 1980s, Sherryl Vint argues that the reliance on subjunctive modes (if … then) and "their orientation toward the future makes this fictionality like speculative fiction."[5] Writers of biofiction have similarly seized upon the tools of speculation to engage with endemic risks and uncertainties of life and biographical knowledge that have deepened in the contemporary context. As referenced in the introduction to this book, Alison Gibbons has referred to a "shifting dominant cultural logic" that has made the world feel more uncertain, volatile, and precarious.[6] In his analysis of risk, Peter Bernstein maintains that the proliferation of derivative instruments such as futures and options, or what he calls "side bets," is symptomatic of the perception of enhanced uncertainty. While derivative instruments are intended to control the risks of uncertainty by determining "who takes on the speculation and who avoids it," they can also add complexity and indeterminacy by distancing from the underlying source as the market shifts from trading "real assets" to trading risks.[7] The market of derivatives over the past decades is as astronomical as one quadrillion dollars by some estimates and ten times the world's GDP. In *Capitalism with Derivatives,* Dick Bryan and Michael Rafferty claim that the growth in derivatives (starting in the 1970s, but exponentially since the 1990s) has made the world "more dynamic and more fragile, more complex and more integrated."[8] This description echoes the theologians' claims referenced in the last chapter, that as "we've unbundled and remixed, we've also isolated and made insecure." According to Ulrich Beck, a key feature of contemporary life is wrestling with the new set of manufactured risks and opportunities we have brought into existence. Both Beck and Anthony Giddens see these at least partly in biographical terms. Beck refers to "precarious biographies and inscrutable threats that affect everybody and against which nobody can adequately insure."[9] Giddens contends that "a puzzling diversity of options" means we have to "create, maintain, and revise" a set of constantly changing biographical narratives.[10]

Rosa Montero has argued that while the world has always been uncertain, "we are more conscious of that uncertainty." In turn, she asserts, "making evident that reality and fiction are connected makes the world a little bit more unpredictable, allows this chaos to make its way a little bit into our books. [...] The aim is still to make sense of a life. If not, we wouldn't have a reason to make art at all."[11] Her prolific works of fiction and nonfiction have engendered widespread critical and popular success spanning the period from the end of the Franco dictatorship (1975) to the present.[12] A journalist, novelist, essayist, and cultural commentator, Montero's strategic blending of the factual and imaginative intersects with her insights on the speculative nature of contemporary life. This chapter draws on my 2017 interview with her and two of her works of and about biofiction: *The Madwoman of the House* (*La loca de la casa,* 2003) and her more recent *The Ridiculous Idea of Never Seeing You Again* (*La ridícula idea de no volver a verte*, 2013).[13] *The Madwoman of the House* sits at the intersection of autofiction, literary essay, and biofiction. She integrates fictionalized versions of episodes in her own life with various biographical vignettes of writers and artists whose lives serve as templates or "paradigms" for the coexistence of the real and the imaginative with which biofiction engages. In so doing, she creates a fictive game with the reader that experiments with multiple possibilities. Her biofictional novel, *The Ridiculous Idea of Never Seeing You Again*, derives from a brief diary of Marie Curie to reveal a very different view of the scientist than that of her published biographies.[14] Describing it as a "supremely mixed product, a hybrid," she calls it "an autobiography of me that is not an autobiography; it is a biography of Marie Curie that is not a biography; it is an essay that is not an essay."[15] In so doing, she opens these suggestive details of Curie's life as a "paradigm, a referential archetype from which to explore the questions swirling through my head."[16] Suggesting, as Paul Dimaggio has with respect to the future, that the past is also "an ambiguous canvas capable of multiple interpretations," Montero examines how these differing versions also shape our current realities and choices.[17]

Biofiction as Strategic Choice

Montero's claim that she is using Curie's life as a way to question a dominant view of reality and to open it to alternative visions is an important distinction differentiating the speculative intentions of biofiction from the representational aims of biography. As I observed in Chapter 1, the choice of creating a biofictional work is not the default when one struggles to compose a convincing biography and decides fictionalizing will simply have to do. Biofiction has differing aims and a different contract with the reader. Montero goes to great lengths, for example, to distinguish the separate expectations she has as writer and reader for both of these forms. She asserts, for example, that if she wants to know about the life of a particular historical figure or biographical subject, she wants to "read a well-written biography" so that she knows that what she is reading "is true, or at least documented." Rather, she argues that while there are great novels that incorporate real people as characters, when done well, these don't only illustrate the life of the person but intervene as a "means to this broader search for the meaning of existence [...] to create an impressive fresco of the human condition."[18] What's more, she contends that this biofictional approach "provides the uncertainty that [...] reveals the incredibly murky frontier between fiction and reality, or rather, *it makes us conscious of reassessing our reality*. And this is a really good thing"[19] (emphasis mine). In so doing, Montero conveys the liberties of the biographical novel to unsettle established views of reality in ways that traditional biographies and purely fictional novels cannot achieve. Montero points to the literary freedom of "greater space," of "doing something riskier."[20] I see this process as incorporating uncertainty into the model of using biography to try to better understand the world. Instead of discounting outliers or the unpredictability of outcomes, for Montero these "what-if" options create opportunities to avoid determinism and to envision unexpected potential.

Commenting on the ways that changes in genre respond to and revise our understandings of the "historical present (any present, including this one)," Lauren Berlant has claimed, "requires rethinking how to convert incidents into exempla that can hold up the sense of the world." By this, she suggests how discrete, circumstantial events become symbols or models that make "worlds available as process-in-formation and in potentiality," or what she refers to as envisioning "new realisms."[21] It is significant that Montero links the use of biofiction not with its capacity to shape purely imaginary worlds, but with its effects on how we experience and *reassess* reality. This clarification also points to important ways in which biofiction differs from imaginative fiction that does not incorporate biographical lives as characters. By immersively venturing into the realm of possibilities, the writer of biofiction brings the past into dialogue in ways that can generate rethinking our options and potential pathways in the present. As Laura

Cernat has thoughtfully summarized: "Unveiling the dynamics at stake in the contemporary sociopolitical landscape through the use of past figures is a means of projecting new realities in the future and promoting social change."[22]

Hedging and Speculating

Mainstream economics has dedicated substantial effort to creating theories that attempt to do away with uncertainty by reducing it to calculable risks that can be "readily" assessed and managed. Yet, despite the fact that new derivative instruments to manage the risks and complexity of the market turn up at a bewildering pace, more information has not led to more certainty. Instead, as Peter Bernstein observes, "[d]iscontinuities, irregularities, and volatilities seem to be proliferating rather than diminishing."[23] Furthering this claim, Mark Taylor observes that "greater complexity brings more volatility and instability, which in turn create unavoidable uncertainty and insecurity." Drawing on the philosophical connections between differing contexts, Taylor suggests that the "resurgence of market fundamentalism" is not isolated from other aspects of culture that strive to "restore" simplicity and clarity: "While claiming to be realists, these true believers imagine an ideal world at odds with the new realities emerging in network culture. The dream of a rationally ordered world where every risk can be hedged is as old as time itself. All such schemes are designed to escape time and history and thereby overcome the inescapable insecurity of life."[24]

An important factor compelling the growth in biofiction is the extent to which writers and readers incorporate uncertainty and speculation into the model of how we experience and shape our expectations of reality. A "hedge" is a means of protection. In the financial markets, hedging is a form of defense against unexpected volatility. One hedges in an effort to eliminate known risks and speculates, conversely, in order to capitalize on the potential opportunities of uncertainty. We can communicate these strategies in literary terms as hedging against unexpected shifts in meaning and value, or speculatively opening oneself to the greater risk of variance associated with conjecture. Such trades are often offsetting pairs, so that one investor absorbs greater risk and the other pays for the corresponding "security" of more certainty. As the interplay of imperfect information, the process of assessing and appropriating risk—speculating on the inaccessible details or possibilities—enriches an understanding of the contradictory impulses within biofiction. Using biography becomes a vehicle to manage this uncertainty *and* a means to speculate on possible options projected through the lives of others. Montero puts both of these aspects in contraposition. She emphasizes how from the point of view of the novelist, speculating on the biographical possibilities "you are free to live your life in other lives." At the same time, she views transferring this speculative risk onto another life story as a form of "safely" gaining order or control over the perception of a chaotic reality. "[I]t allows you to live your life in a more controlled fashion because you enter into these other lives and these help you to imagine other ways of seeing and understanding the world."[25]

From the perspective of the writer of biofiction, fictionalizing biography might be considered a risk of being considered unserious (for example) or that people won't take the narrative seriously as "just story," "just fiction." Montero observes, for example, "for decades she hid her most imaginative self and fomented the logical side of her writing because the intellectual and rational were the domain of men," and the way to gain respect within that normative world, whereas imagination and fantasy would be considered "frivolous diversions of women."[26] For this reason, she adds, her first novels were all more traditionally realist in tone. However, Montero's novel *The Madwoman of the House* is a playful reference to freeing imagination from its gendered repression and isolation from reality, in turn liberating both realism and life—"much freer."[27] There is also the narrative payoff of deferring or projecting one's own risk of uncertainty onto another life story, playing out possibilities that way. Another upside potential is better reflecting reality beyond the constraints of straight biography or facts alone. As we have seen, biography—while it often claims to completeness—is also a simplified, artificialized model. There are profits from being able to imagine beyond and to stretch the limits of this model, more accurately reflecting the blend of fiction with the real in our lives.

In her earlier *Stories of Women* (1995), which reappraises the biographical narratives of women who official histories largely excluded or otherwise undervalued, it is notable that she starts with Agatha Christie. Montero suggests that Christie's public persona was a deliberate elusion: "She spent her life hiding things, concealing flaws, misrepresenting virtues, constructing for herself an impressive imaginary figure. In fact, she was a great fraud, a keen impostor. She feigned, for example, an image of complete and calm control over existence, to the point of coldness and detachment, when in reality she was a woman full of passion and fears."[28] Montero draws attention not only to this carefully constructed image, but also to the role of biographical recognition itself as a powerful institutionalizing element that can artificially "lock in" distortions. These derivative versions, originally intended to hedge against uncertainty and authoritatively control the direction of the biographical narrative, became sources of their own unpredictable exchange. She describes, for example, Christie's disappearance one December evening, abandoning her car in the middle of the highway, doors left open, her coat and suitcase left in the car. The mystery of her disappearance was never resolved, even when she was found having dinner in the hotel where she had spent the last ten days. She had lost her memory and registered under the name of her husband's mistress, even putting an ad in the paper requesting that anyone who might know a woman by that name seek her at that address. Montero notes that Christie makes no mention of this in her thick autobiography: "It must have frightened her too much."[29] Her fear of uncertainty is so great that she uses hedging as a way of avoiding risk to the point that she becomes at odds with her own reality and lost even to herself.

Significantly, Montero's biofictional works are very much explorations into how individuals approach these "inescapable insecurities," or wide-ranging life risks, suggesting that perhaps the emphasis on limited or narrowly bounded expressions of biographical possibility has to do with hedging our own fears over the unpredictable nature of reality. She comments that many biographies artificially manipulate the story of a life to conform to an ordered vision that does not convey the real or underlying complexities of a life, observing the "fondness we humans have for retouching our biographies," to give "the appearance of order to the absolute chaos of existence."[30]

Managing Loss

According to rational expectations theory, individuals make use of all available past and present information when making decisions, and these expectations include their forecasts for the future. Under this model, any misaligned valuations are quickly incorporated, so that the aggregate valuation of the market is considered to accurately reflect the "real" or underlying value (in effect to be "right" or "justified" in its assessment). This hypothesis of "efficient markets" thus discounts the effects of incomplete knowledge or information that might otherwise be unknown or withheld, as well as the possibility that individuals might act "irrationally" against their best interests. Contrastingly, Montero engages with what we can gain from delving into stories of instability, absence, and what has gone missing from the official histories. Instead of the price of "security," which one might incorporate through hedging, Montero emphasizes strategies that explore how we manage the "inescapable insecurities" of potential loss or risk of finding ourselves lost. As she expressed in conversation with me, "The perception I have of the world [is that it is] unstable, confusing, a reality that could fall to pieces any moment and leave everything in shards. [...] I have the sensation that life is very tenuous, in essence that you can become lost at any moment. The truth is you can always wander astray, become lost to yourself." In turn, she adds, the biographical novel is interested in the effect of this instability on our lives, "the price of insecurity."[31]

One of the key features of speculation is the willingness to take on greater exposure to the risk of loss in exchange for the upside potential of gains. Both *The Madwoman of the House* and *The Ridiculous Idea* incorporate narratives of loss, both real and imagined. In *The Ridiculous Idea*, Montero uses Curie's biography and the grief she suffered at the sudden death of her husband Pierre as points of intersection with Montero's loss of her husband, Pablo Lizcano, in 2009. Yet, in noting her "desire to use her [Curie's] life as a measuring stick for understanding her own,"[32] she points to more universal questions of loss and disorientation—the effort to create "an emergency map that can indicate the path through so much emptiness."[33] In this converging of the autobiographical and the biographical, Montero emphasizes the *specular* or reflective nature of any biographical creation, refracted through the author's own experiences and subjectivity. Her narratives suggest that our identities are not continuous, but are marked inevitably by loss—to memory, to time, to the differing versions of ourselves we can no longer grasp. What is irrational is to pretend these gaps and absences don't exist or to negate the powerful influence on how we experience identity and reality. As she observed in conversation with me, "If you ask the first person on the street, he or she would tell you in their own words, the world is confusing, you can't be sure of anything or anybody. So, novels, as the imaginative expression of the self, reflect this collective unconscious, and this collective unconscious happens for a reason—because nothing is certain, not even the self."[34]

Montero highlights the narrative of a disappearance as a structuring moment in *The Madwoman of the House*, relating the story of her (wholly invented) twin sister's frightening disappearance from the park where the two were playing as children. Her sister is gone for three frantic days; yet, when she returned Montero never learned what happened. "Within a few months, the story of the disappearance of my sister had become one of those taboos that are so common in families, one of those cloistered and secret places where nobody goes."[35] Yet, toward the end of the novel, Montero suggests that we *suppose* for a moment that she does not actually have a sister, and that as a result, this strange incident in which her sister disappeared never actually occurred. "Even so," she adds,

> this chapter on the absence of my sister and the silence of my family would be the most important for me of the whole book, the one that would have taught me the most, informing me of other deep silences in my childhood, silent gaps that I know are there, but that I would never have been able to access through my real memories, which are equally untrustworthy.[36]

While Agatha Christie's story was true, Montero positions her own fictionalized biography as equally vulnerable to the risks of loss and instability. There are many ways for people to disappear—often without knowing so. Maybe they are following a hunch, or chasing a rabbit down a hole, or asking for forgiveness. All we know is that the disappearer leaves in search of something. The disappearance of Montero's imagined sister perhaps serves this purpose as well as the imaginative search for something by the author that can't be accessed in real life or through factual discovery alone.

In *A Field Guide to Getting Lost*, Rebecca Solnit notes how children "seldom roam now, even in the safest places," and how roaming can be about "developing self-reliance, a sense of direction and adventure, imagination, a will to explore, to be able to get a little lost and then figure a way back." In this way, as Solnit contends, "lost" has "two disparate meanings. Losing things is about the familiar falling away, getting lost is about the unfamiliar appearing." In this way, she suggests, becoming temporarily lost is a process "in which the world has become larger than your knowledge of it."[37] The risk of loss, in this way, is a source of demonstrable gains that wouldn't be possible by simply retaining what we already know or find familiar.

Notably, the speculative invention becomes an instrument to both incorporate loss *and* access gains in understanding that would not have been possible from "straight" biography that adhered only to known facts. Montero refers to this as the "real-imaginary"—"the truth of the lies in the novel—something that can often convey a more profound truth than the real-real."[38] As Jens Beckert has suggested in an economic context, this speculative imaginary permits individuals to "move beyond inherited thought-patterns and categories by bringing them in an as-if world in which given reality is surpassed and a different one considered."[39]

While in Montero's works the volatility and viability of multiple biographical alternatives in the contemporary context are indeed destabilizing, this variance is also a source of invention and creativity. Interestingly, referencing the "binding and unrealistic" hypothesis of "complete and perfect information" on which so much of traditional economic theory depends, economic theorist Roberta Patalano has explored the role of imagination and projected narratives in creating a fuller picture of human decision-making and individual agency. Drawing on research related to uncertainty in economics by George Shackle, she contends that realistic choice does not imply a selection among a bounded set of exogenously determined options, but "consists in first creating, by conjecture and reasoned imagination on the basis of mere suggestion offered by visible recorded circumstances, *the things on which hope can be fixed*"[40] (emphasis mine). Speculative imagination in Montero's work often acts similarly, not only as a mode of addressing what has gone missing, but also as a form of hopeful searching for what is possible.

Accordingly, in "What if You Could Do It All Over? the Uncanny Allure of Our Unlived Lives," Joshua Rothman examines the power of our speculative lives to act on our real choices and experiences. As he observes, "swept up in our real lives, we quickly forget about the unreal ones," those "unrealized possibilities" that "through their persistence, shape us." What, he asks, "do our unreal lives say about our real ones?"[41] Montero considers these possibilities in *The Madwoman of the House*. For example, she explores the dispersive possibilities of a single memory at three different points in the narrative, slightly altered each time and with different outcomes. The core of the story is this: She (the biofictional Rosa Montero) is in her early twenties and out for a night of festivities with her friend, Pilar Miró, who introduces her to a famous American actor whom she refers to only as "M." There is a mutual attraction; the two drink a lot, and she drives him back to his temporary apartment in the Tower of Madrid, "the tallest building in the city at that time"; it had been the "pride of Francoism, a rather ridiculous, phallic fantasy of modernity."[42] The story deviates in its directions from here, contrasting with its simple resolution in one case to two others in which the inability to find her keys or identification or alternatively to remember what room, or on which floor M lives, creates problems. In one instance, M suddenly collapses and the fictional Montero, unable to identify the apartment, can neither send help nor return to let him know where she's gone. In the other two versions, either because she is mad at herself for sleeping with the famous M, or determines he must be a cad to whom she is just another hanger-on; she flees the apartment in either humiliation or ire.

When coupled with the multiplicity of stories, for instance, the location of M's temporary apartment suggests an ironic view toward the image of the tower as a symbol of authoritarian, paternalistic control. In differing versions of the story, Montero arrives to find her car, left parked outside the Tower, surrounded by the "frightening grey-coated police of Francoism."[43] In part, we can consider both the use of these images and the dispersion of biographical options she provides the narrative, as challenges to this deterministic view of social reality. In contrast to conformity with the rigid rules and gendered constraints of life under the Franco dictatorship, even its waning years, she associates the speculative uncertainties of the contemporary context with the vitality of change and with biofictional opportunities to reveal the validity of other interpretations and possibilities.

Similarly, Montero demonstrates how her own images of M are constantly shifting: "If before I had invented a despicable M, after that night, I dedicated myself to exploring an incredible one."[44] In contrast to the story about her imagined sister, these versions of a single memory are not traumatic, nor even significant in terms of having a marked impact on the life of the Rosa Montero in the novel. In fact, in one of the versions, she runs into M years later and he fails to recognize her, or perhaps even recognize his own self in the story, "because none of these identities formed part of our current narratives any longer."[45] So, why does she include them? By creating alternative fictional worlds that experiment with the limits (and limitations) of historical reality, these narratives point to an important freedom of biofiction to rewrite stories from the past to create different outcomes or possible futures. These options revise the expectation that there is only one clear answer or defined path. The flip side of paralyzing uncertainty amid a multitude of options is the opportunity to reimagine one's life and the world.

Montero has said, "We start from the assumption that within us are multiple selves; we don't believe in the self as a cohesive identity any more. Before, we understood identity as something holistic and largely unchanging across a trajectory [...] everything was scheduled along a certain path. But now, everything is chaos."[46] The concept of speculation is that it is just a moment in time; amid the velocity and profusion of the present, it constitutes a strategy to take advantage of differences in information, or the perceived variability of expectations. If there is little risk of variability, there would be no need to protect or hedge against these potential changes, or alternatively to open oneself to risk in the hopes of being right about a specific valuation. In this sense, the speculative does not constitute a full portrait, but a temporary stopover within a vaster and mutating trajectory. Commenting in an interview, she contended that she uses biography in this way as a form of experimenting with imagined realities, adding, "I'm delighted that there is no obligation to determine these stories."[47]

Fictional Expectations and Real Experiments in *The Ridiculous Idea of Never Seeing You Again*

We can examine Montero's speculative biofictions through the lens of what economist Jens Beckert has referred to as "fictional expectations." In contrast to rational expectations theory, Beckert argues in *Imagined Futures: Fictional Expectations in Capitalist Dynamics* that "under conditions of uncertainty, assessments of how the future will look share important characteristics with literary fiction; most importantly, they create a reality of their own by making assertions that go beyond the reporting of empirical facts. Fiction *pretends a reality where the author and the readers act as if the described reality were true*"[48] (emphasis mine). Noting that fictional expectations are not limited to the economy, but relevant in all spheres of human action, Beckert defines these as "imaginaries of future states of the world" that orient decision-making even though this reality is unknown. "As is the case with fiction in literature, the defining feature of fictional expectations in the economy is that they create a world of their own into which actors [individuals] can project themselves."[49] Referencing the work of Wolfgang Iser, Beckert contends that "this fiction-ability of humans is a source of innovation and novelty," as individuals "can imagine a world different from the existing one and 'inhabit' this world" through creative imaginings that "transcend the known and thereby motivate decisions that create newness."[50] By focusing on how literary notions of fictionality offer a useful framework to examine the powerful influence of the imaginative in the behavior of economic decisions, this paradigm offers a corollary lens to examine the speculative appeal of biofiction as part of a wider cultural logic.

We tend to associate speculation with projections regarding future events. Yet, this speculation also works in reverse. If using the past cannot necessarily predict future disruptions correctly, Montero suggests that limiting oneself to dominant narratives can equally occlude the contingent possibilities of the past and their residual, resurfacing effects. Montero has said that what the novelist does

> is to develop these multiple alterations, these refracted versions [derivatives] of reality, the same way that the musician composes diverse variations of an original melody. The writer takes an authentic nugget of existence, a name, a face, a small anecdote, and begins to modify it one thousand and one times, substituting ingredients or giving them another form, as if one were applying a kaleidoscope over a life and spinning indefinitely the same fragments to produce a thousand different figures.[51]

Rather than being contained by existing models, we can consider how biofictions speculatively play out the what-ifs of unrealized options "as if they were true" to uncover new ways of seeing and experiencing reality. As well, Montero suggests how biofictions, as instruments of imagination, like theories, models, and forecasts, can take on the risks of unexpected or overlooked details that traditional models have overlooked. Incorporating these factors can be the impetus to realize an inadequacy or to spark revision and change in what we believe or how we aspire to understand the world.

Montero's *The Ridiculous Idea* takes a biofictional approach to the life of scientist Marie Curie, who built her career through discoveries and experimentation with radioactive elements. It is also productive to consider how the process of scientific inquiry to test the boundaries of the known as well as Curie's non-normative status as a woman in the sciences at a time when that made her a complete outlier speak to the narrative experimentation in Montero's work. Pointing to the relative lack of "genuine realist-experimentalists," Lauren Berlant has wondered, for instance, "why we have so few principles of experiment in the humanities [...] as though we can't afford to admit that we are trying things out and only partially, slowly clarifying problems." She contrasts this reticence with approaches in the sciences, where "they have no problem admitting the proximity of profound incrementality to great leaps." In the sciences, everything tends to be a "hypothesis," a "theory"; there are very few *laws*. Even gravity is explained through the *theory* of relativity. There is no reason literary narratives that explore the real can't take on a similar form of experimentation, open to frequent challenge and review. In turn, she contends that among the limiting features are the "reproductive demands of disciplines, with their beautiful staircases," suggesting that reductive or proprietary views of genre and their norms inhibit more speculative questioning of established orthodoxies.[52] Similarly, writer Jose Ovejero has referred to the "realism of indeterminacy," observing that we often over-emphasize the interpretation of fictional representations and give too little attention to how we understand reality. He adds, "We ask ourselves how why a writer says something, but we don't ask ourselves why these things happen in real life."[53] In this sense, we can consider how the expectations of biofiction liberate fiction from interacting only with purely invented worlds; they simultaneously incorporate the role of speculation and uncertainty in shaping options for how we incrementally and contingently understand and perceive possible actions within actual, lived reality. In this next section, I explore how "fictional expectations" and the speculative potential of biofiction that we see in Montero's work are reflective of this experimentalist paradigm with the real.

Martin Fridson has described common features of speculation as "bets against the consensus view."[54] One of the key features of speculation involves judging when a specific asset may be misvalued or inaccurately discounted, along with the desire to exploit this disparity to profit from the validity of other interpretations. Drawing on the brief diary of Curie's following her husband's sudden death (having been run over by a horse-drawn carriage), Montero actively challenges the consensus view of Curie's life, opening it to alternative conceptions. She explores how Curie's biography deviates from dominant interpretations, examining how contradictory, obscured, or more subjectively experienced information invests biographical uncertainty with unexpected returns. As she puts it, "once you enter into a life" more subjectively, more speculatively, you "grasp things that more orthodox, more externally focused biographers would likely not have captured," things a traditional biographer would miss.[55] She emphasizes how Curie's life, this serious scientist whose work centered on rational, empirical observation and analysis, deviated from normative expectations into more imaginative, emotive realisms, and how consensus biographical models have overlooked many revealing, revisionary variables. Montero demonstrates how Curie struggled to liberate herself from all sorts of conventional expectations of gender and other limiting factors in order to invent not only scientifically but to project an alternative future. According to Montero, she was an "other," what Montero refers to as a #Mutant. She says this admiringly, "*be*," she advises a "woman without a place, or in search of another #place."[56] Montero thus implicitly links

Curie's experimental path with the idea of experimentation as resisting determinism and the effort to bring a new world into being.

Just as Montero lauds the itinerant, mutable, instability of Curie's positionality, or her drive to exceed the limited spaces of opportunity offered ambitious women in her era, Montero's frequent use of hashtags throughout the text demonstrates how her perceptions of Curie's biography are developing rather than static, and interconnected to other ideas in-progress that surface throughout. As she reflects, these hashtags provide symbolic clues indicating that "these are themes and ideas in construction throughout the book."[57] Moreover, as Maryanne Leone has argued, "embedding the contemporary phenomenon of hashtags" shows other interconnections between past and present contingencies and parameters, suggesting the pertinence and transferability "of Marie Curie's gender-based exclusions, restrictions, and expectations for women of the twenty-first century."[58]

Alluding to the spatial sense of mapping, Montero contrasts what she calls a "horizontal" or journalistic perspective with a "vertical, disordered" approach, "characteristic of the special vision with which at times (at night before falling asleep, one afternoon while driving home), we think we glance, for an instant, the substance of life, the heart of chaos."[59] A horizontal approach implies a linear, causal progression. The vertical, in contrast, leaps from line to line, simultaneously eliding discontinuities and gaps and incorporating these disruptions into the unfolding biographical narrative. Hashtags open to other spaces of participation and discourse beyond the singular, authoritative space. They gain strength, fade, or adapt through the risk of being open to the investment and involvement of others. In his consideration of fictional expectations within a context of uncertainty, Jens Beckert refers to how imaginaries freed from the constraints of rational, expected value can create new opportunities. Perhaps, as Beckert has suggested, by not being bound to the limits of past models of expectations, speculative imaginings of the future—untethered from prior patterns—have much higher degrees of freedom. Similarly, Montero uses Curie's biography to divert from the expected biographical formula, opening it to a more episodic and creative vision.

Curie earned not one but two Nobel prizes: one, together with her husband, Pierre, in 1903 in physics and another individually in 1911 in chemistry. Including Curie, there have only been four female laureates ever in chemistry and two in physics. Montero emphasizes not only how unorthodox Curie's path was at the time, but also how likely to be discredited or ignored altogether. She refers to the biographies of four other female scientists in differing eras whose contributions male mentors or colleagues sought to make invisible. For example, Montero provides the example of Rosalind Franklin, who discovered the foundations of the molecular structure of DNA. Franklin, who died young of ovarian cancer, probably from exposure to X-rays, may not have known that Watson, Crick, and

Wilkins appropriated her work on DNA and used it as their own. Worse yet, Montero suggests, is that neither Watson nor Crick ever mentioned Franklin, nor recognized her contributions. "Although, at least," Montero adds, this story is known. "I wonder how many other cases of espionage, unacknowledged appropriation, and parasitism there must be" that have never been made public.[60] In underscoring these obscured or depreciated histories of women who contributed to science, Montero is particularly interested in how, amid spaces of loss and uncertainty, speculative challenges to normative expectations can revise expected, explanatory models and suggest alternative trajectories. "The concept of biography as an emergency map, as an existential map," she contends, "reflects this question: 'How do we learn from the world?'"[61] As Jens Beckert has stated with respect to fictional expectations, such "imaginaries can transcend the known and thereby motivate decisions that create newness."[62]

Montero, for example, explores what she sees as suppressed or devalued facets of Curie's biography that reassess its potential and capacity to illuminate more universal questioning. In the words of Roberta Patalano, "creative rethinking of the parameters of a decision situation based on imaginaries makes it possible to recognize links in a 'new narrative texture.'" In this sense, according to Kendall Patton Bronk, the imagined can be "subversive of an established order."[63] Instead of stabilizing around commonly held external valuations, Montero shows how a more specular, biofictional view can inhabit and express internalized factors that destabilize popular conceptions. For example, Montero observes that "what came through" in reading Curie's diary was "how passionate she was, how different from the cold, scientific image with which she has been portrayed."[64] Exploring this complexity, she revises the predominant biographical narrative explaining the shift in Curie's career after Pierre's death. People claimed, Montero asserts, that Marie Curie was a lesser scientist in the second half of her life and "that these changes happened with the death of Pierre, that he was the brains." In refuting this sexist view, Montero argues that in addition to her journals and the work she did, we also have how her father influenced her. "Well, that's what Marie Curie 'herself' communicated to me once I began to immerse myself in the facts of her life."[65] Montero thus projects herself beyond what a traditional biographer would, adopting a speculative vision that allows her more freedom to imagine Curie's choices and portray them against the limiting "law of the father," which—we might add—Curie surpassed. Rooted in the facts of Curie, she feels free to use imagination to see how it shapes the life of this serious scientist as much as reason and intellect did.

Montero observes that Curie formed part of an elite vanguard that predicted the instability of the atom—paving the way for all sorts of later discoveries about its structure. Yet, in July 1902, when Curie wrote to her father elated at her discovery, her father patronizingly replied, "Now, you possess quantities of radium at your disposal. But if we think about all you've done to achieve this, it may turn out to be costliest chemical element of all. What a shame that all of this work will only be of theoretical value!" Applying the hashtag, #Honorthyfather, Montero notes that Curie's father died six days later and thus never got to see his daughter receive the Nobel Prize only a year later. "Although now that I think about it," she adds, "he would probably have found something disagreeable to say about it."[66]

Why does Montero give so much importance to this story? To explain why, I connect its relevance to two different aspects of speculative imagination and show why these are important to the speculative aims of biofiction. In so doing, I elaborate on the concept of fictional expectations, and also consider how imagined expectations can shape real outcomes and act on the contingency of possibility. Let me start with the concept of how explanations themselves can either narrow or expand opportunities for understanding. Max Haiven has observed that so much of the "seemingly scientific and technocratic calculation and manipulation of risk" comes down essentially to the explanatory narratives we create—"an intimate human world, animated by belief, communication, and indeed culture."[67] Similarly, in a *Hidden Brain* podcast episode ("Story of Stories"), host Shankar Vedantam notes that when his guest, psychologist Tania Lombrozo, elaborates on "extracting the structure of the world in a way that's generalizable," what he understands her to mean is "that explanations, and to some extent stories, too, are about constructing models for the world. They allow us to cut through confusion to distill complexity into simplicity." Lombrozo responds that "part of what explanations do is that they relate our observations, which are highly variable, changing from moment to moment, to something more like a simple underlying structure that allows us to predict how things might go in the future. It's a way to try to extract order and regularity from what might otherwise seem disorganized and unsettling" (or what Montero describes as the "absolute chaos of reality"). Yet, as Lombrozo suggests, explanations can also make us less curious, because perhaps "we tend to over-rely on our own story that we construct and under-rely on those other sources of evidence that may or may not fit into our story so nicely."[68]

In this way, to the extent we build our assumptions of reality around these bounded, binding explanations and models, as we saw with the case of Agatha Christie, they can actually lock in distortions or a mis-valued but predictable, prescriptive view of the world. Of course, we are well aware of how power and authority shape the meaning of stories into dominant orthodoxies that crowd out options. Beckert observes, for example, how market-influencing stories stem from powerful investors, bank analysts, economists, central banks, and other high-ranking actors who "shape expectations" and "anchor" valuations turning their fictional expectations into "self-fulfilling prophecies."[69] In this way, too, we can see how powerful expectations such as those of Curie's father may have altered her choices and unlived lives.

At the same time, Montero suggests the limits of our efforts to exert authority over derivative lives and their meanings. For example, she poses the question, "Was Marie Curie's father as demanding as I've indicated? I think so, but the reader has the same facts as me and will need to decide what to believe."[70] Beckert has emphasized that the term "fictional" should not be taken to mean that these "expectations are false or mere fantasies, only that expectations of the foreseeable future inhabit the mind not as foreknowledge, but as contingent imaginaries. [...] Contingency negates the idea that expectations are correct in the aggregate," and that anyone is able to predict which one of them will be accurate.[71] That is, in a context of uncertainty, we are not all going to settle on a consensus of what to believe (nor from Montero's perspective would we ever want to). Such expectations can never be actual forecasts but "merely projections." If, for Beckert, "fictional expectations" emphasize how future imaginaries shape present action, for Montero, speculating on divergent visions of the past also implicates the pliable possibilities of how these speculative visions might act on our understandings of the present. Such experimental visions with the real have the potential to revise and open all sorts of previously unimagined possibilities.

While Beckert argues that a key difference between fictional texts and speculative expectations under conditions of uncertainty is that "readers of novels are not interested in putting fictional descriptions into practice, while actors in the economy based their real world decisions on the expectations they hold," Montero's speculative biofiction suggests otherwise.[72] In fact, as Montero demonstrates, our imaginative projections and "unrealized" lives (the what-ifs) have powerful effects on the actual choices we perceive. The biofictional world takes on added relevance because it speaks to how we understand the possibilities of lived reality. Montero has said that Curie's biography provided her "with a certain connection, to *play out through her life* in a way, these questions that were nagging at me, like a conversation with her *that are in many questions for all of us*"[73] (emphasis mine) As Montero expresses it, projecting her vision of Curie's biography encouraged her to examine important questions on her own:

> How to live better, to achieve more plenitude in life, to better capture the moment, how to live with less anxiety, how to free oneself from the mother/father stranglehold that can destroy your life as it threatened to do to poor Marie Curie, who spent half of her life trying to prove to her dead father that radium had an important purpose.[74]

By considering versions that might otherwise have been closed off, this speculative view of biofiction creates models that chart divergent options to navigate the ambiguity and flux of contemporary life.

Montero considers the complicated relationship between writing and living a life throughout both *The Madwoman of the House* and *The*

Ridiculous Idea. However, toward the end of *The Ridiculous Idea* she makes an important connection between literary and scientific experimentation, and the uncertainties that each engages with and provokes. As Montero discusses with respect to Curie's research, "Marie discovered and measured radioactivity [...] superhuman, luminescent rays that cure and kill, that burn cancerous tumors with radiation or scorch the body with atomic destruction."[75] She thus refers to both the benefits and the risks of human creation and the responsibility to the realities in which we intervene. It is not coincidental that Montero links this tension to the uncertain borders of fiction and reality, and our responsibility to the speculative visions we imagine and create. She notes that the connection between biographical reality and fiction is an ambiguous and complicated territory in which many authors have foundered. Montero observes that it is never easy to know where to stop, up to what point it is licit to tell another person's story or not, and how to manage the "always radioactive substance of the real."[76]

In this respect, it is useful here to consider a point that Beckert makes. He asserts that the fictional character of expectations in the economy is something that those speculating in the markets go to great lengths to conceal. In this way, even if the models and projections are "as-ifs" or "what-ifs," it is necessary to believe that they will come to fruition to be effective. In contrast, while biofictions imaginatively project onto a biographical life, the contract with the reader is not one of concealing this speculative use of fiction. Montero argues that she has used Curie's life as a "paradigm, a referential archetype." She doesn't pretend to the completeness or finality of this projected model. Where she suggests individuals become lost is when they use fiction not as a means of challenging reality to better understand the uncertain, incomplete, and evolving nature of the human condition or the "world in its greater complexity" but as a means to conceal this honest inquiry or to deepen deceptive fictions. In both *The Madwoman of the House* and *The Ridiculous Idea*, she refers to the example of Truman Capote as someone who used fiction to leverage a false view of the real, buying into the artificially inflated and unstable creations of fame, coming undone in the process. By intervening instrumentally and self-interestedly in the real-life fates of others to do nothing more than benefit his projected image, Montero suggests Capote undermined the meaningful aims of both fiction and journalistic truth. María Fernández describes, in this way, how this biographical novel incorporates as its "real protagonist" the "human condition and its ability for creation and destruction of oneself and the 'other'; or what is the same, its own capacity for both rebirth and death at its deepest level of meaning."[77]

Montero's biofictions and her interview comments related to this form reinforce an experimental, experiential approach to how we experience and narrate the real, in which lives that are "safely" and completely explained come across as artificially so. In both literature and life, she speculates on a world in which it is easy to get lost, a world in which things, people, and meanings frequently slip away. Montero describes these moments as grasping an idea only to feel it slip away again, like glimpsing the immensity of a whale and then watching it submerge again below the water: "better said, only fragments of this back, flickers of this whale, pinches that let you sense the unbearable beauty of the whole animal, but before you had time to do anything, before even being able to speculate on its volume and size, before having understood the meaning of its piercing stare, the incredible creature submerges and the world remains quiet and deaf and so empty."[78]

Just because things are complicated and unresolved does not mean we just throw up our hands and say the truth doesn't matter, or that an uneven, transitional, and potentially changeable truth is no different from a false view of the world—that we shouldn't strive to imagine powerful and elusive meanings we can't fully grasp.

Through the uncertain contours of biofiction, Montero pits anxiety over becoming lost amid the chaos of reality against the simultaneous literary experiment of opening these narratives and lives to unexpected value and possibility. By entertaining the what-ifs, Montero suggests we can distance ourselves from simply affirming the anecdotal details of a reality we expect to find and instead reveal a dispersion of options. Incorporating risk and uncertainty into the model of how we imagine a life, such speculative biofictions suggest we are free to experiment anew.

4

Fraudulent Pasts and Fictional Futures in Javier Cercas' *The Impostor* and Adolfo García Ortega's *The Birthday Buyer*

Biofictions often challenge master narratives that consecrate one dominant perspective and disregard many others. A number of recent Spanish biographical novels center on recovering or reimagining these alternative histories, in particular those shaped and suppressed by authoritarianism and the inheritance of violence. This chapter focuses on two novels that approach the construction of derivative lives from the conflicting narrative outlooks of victim and false victim of historical trauma. In what he refers to as a work of non-fiction "saturated with fiction,"[1] Javier Cercas' novel *The Impostor* (2014) exposes the counterfeit biography of Enric Marco, the once-leader of Spain's most prominent organization for Holocaust survivors.[2] By counterfeit, I mean that Marco knowingly presented his forged biography as true. In actuality, Marco was never a deportee or in the Nazi concentration camp as he claimed—and, far from fighting fascism—had volunteered as a guest worker for the Third Reich. Conversely, Adolfo García Ortega's *The Birthday Buyer* (2008) draws on history and invention to speculate on the conceivable experiences of Hurbinek, a three-year-old victim of the Holocaust encountered by Primo Levi in Auschwitz, and his possible futures had he lived.[3] In so doing, he draws on the potential of these derivative creations to liberate Hurbinek's brief biography to imaginative reinventions, suggesting that one of the functions of biofiction is to give life to voices that would otherwise remain silenced.

These two works inform each other in compelling ways. Each alludes to how the Holocaust in real and symbolic forms relates to the history of

Spanish fascism under Franco and the process of reinvention (individually and collectively) that followed the end of the dictatorship. Both examine moral quandaries elicited by Primo Levi regarding the Holocaust as the ultimate symbol of that which escapes explanation or human understanding. Beyond these historical features, each self-consciously explores the ethical risks and possibilities of biofiction to create lives both invented and informed by real people. While *The Impostor* uses biofiction to expose derivative versions that falsify connection to the actual biographical and historical realities from which they originated, *The Birthday Buyer* explores the vitalizing capacity of the fiction writer to create and proliferate prospective lives.

In financial markets, derivatives refer to contracts (types of "options") between two parties whose value is *derived from* an underlying asset. Rather than owning a tangible asset, the derivative involves speculative expectations regarding the value of its future direction. As I have suggested earlier, we can also understand these instruments in a literary sense as narratives derived from real-life sources and as agreements between writer and reader that reflect expectations. Readers, for example, expect to know whether to evaluate the derived life as fictional or factual, or how closely it hews to its source. Both writers and readers will be interested in whether, and to what extent, the writer's fictional use of the biographical life adds value by expanding our understanding of reality and the world.

Lucia Boldrini has noted how ethical questions are at the core of biofiction, especially with regard to the appropriation of other subjects' stories without their consent, or, alternatively, giving voice to someone "whose voice or story may have been forgotten, even erased from history."[4] As Boldrini adds, "Each choice involves the opposite ethical risk: either refuse the appropriation of another's voice, but leave them without any voice; or give them the possibility of having their history represented, but at the cost of substituting one's voice for theirs, appropriating it, and with that, their identity."[5] While, on the surface, the narrator of *The Birthday Buyer* and Cercas' Enric Marco employ similar arguments for using the fictional life of another, putting these two works in comparison exposes critical differences, shedding important light on what might constitute an ethical use of biofiction. To what extent is it justifiable for writers of biofiction to assume and invent an unlived life of another individual, when—as in the case of Marco—that was a kind of identity theft in real life?

The narrator of *The Birthday Buyer* professes that even though he was not "Jewish, Russian, or any of the victims of persecution, humiliation, and elimination [...] crushed and erased simply because they existed, he *felt* like a victim, any one of those victims." In imagining possible futures for Hurbinek, "perhaps the most victim of them all," he knew he was "*legitimized by a sense of justice*"[6] (emphasis mine). By assuming the narratives of real Spaniards who experienced the Nazi concentration camps, Marco similarly claimed, "I've lived through everything I tell, but only in another place;

I only changed the setting to make known the suffering of the victims."[7] In *The Impostor,* Cercas uses the tools of biofiction to create an invented dialogue between himself and Marco, in which he explores and defends the *novelist's* right to imaginative creation of real-life figures in contrast to Marco's fraudulent appropriations. *The Impostor* thus emphasizes a key distinction separating the openly fictional from deceptive fictions presented as factual. Yet, Cercas has also received criticism from some scholars for giving further attention to Marco's story, thus further depriving the real victims of their voices and the validity of their histories.[8]

As these examples suggest, *The Birthday Buyer* and *The Impostor* adopt and examine diverging approaches regarding the creation and use of derivative lives. This chapter thus explores the risks and responsibilities of using fiction to reinvent the narratives of real, historical lives—tensions that biofiction embodies and that speak directly to contemporary ethical challenges of epistemology, trust, and belief. Just as Colum McCann has argued that the "manipulation of what is true and not true" is what the contemporary biographical novelist is "flaring up against,"[9] Cercas has argued that "the problems of the [nineteen] thirties are the problems of the present in a clearer way than it has ever been." Noting the failure to distinguish between factual deception and literary invention, Cercas adds, "We have returned to epic, emotional politics, haven't we? [...] Tons of lies being said without penalty."[10] The problem of post-truth, or "truthiness" as Stephen Colbert famously popularized it, prioritizes what "feels" true, whether or not it is supported by factual evidence. By actively interrogating the intervention of fiction in the narratives we invest in as true, I will argue that many biofictions actually guard the effort to pursue truth and the capacity to distinguish it from imposture. In making this argument, I consider three main aspects. First are determinations of trust and the consensual fictional compact with the reader. Second is the use of metaphor and symbol as tools of inquiry and human connection, rather than self-interested imposition. Third is the aim of the fiction to grant imaginative access to not only represent a life, but to transform a vision of reality.

I start by considering how Cercas uses biofiction in *The Impostor* to examine broader questions regarding the responsibility to reinvent a life or the past, especially with regard to what he refers to as the "industry" of historical memory during and following Spain's transition from dictatorship. In contrast to the abundance of historical and fictionalized information about the Holocaust that infuses Marco's fraudulent biography, the facts surrounding Hurbinek's brief life are almost non-existent. Turning to García Ortega's efforts in *The Birthday Buyer* to draw and deviate from the lives of Hurbinek and other real individuals connected to his sparse biography, I explore the possibility to create not only divergent pasts but redeem possible futures. In so doing, I relate this process to the concept of futures in the financial sense of speculative options. Finally, I put the two novels in dialogue. What makes some derivative lives more worthy of our investment than others? By examining the choices of how unled lives imbue the present, these works explore the humanizing potential of biofictions to lay bare the uses and misuses of fiction in the dominant narratives we create, and the risks and responsibilities as moral agents who must live with the consequences.

Risk and Return: Fictionalized Truths vs Truthful Fictions

In an interview I conducted with Cercas, he observed, "Biofiction, as you've denoted it, is very dangerous. You take a lot of risks. But a writer that doesn't take risks is not a writer, he's a scribe. [...] Risks are normal because you are working with real people."[11] Michael Lackey has argued that biofictional writers are more interested in their own vision, so they are using rather than representing the biographical subject.[12] We can think of this approach as employing the literary invention of the biographical subject as a means of achieving a fuller, more creative version or reality. Yet, in the case of a living subject like Marco who had already perpetrated such great lies, we can also think in terms of manipulation or exploitation for one's own advantage, of being "used" by another subject. In using Marco's biography to consider the "ease with which people can be misled," Cercas also explores the risk of being similarly co-opted—"the fear that I would be accused of playing into Marco's hand, of trying to understand him, and in doing so, to forgive him, of being complicit with this man who had mocked the victims of the worst crime in human history."[13]

Contemporary social theorist Anthony Giddens has argued that the self is reflexively made. By this, he means not that the self is a set of fixed traits, but an individual's own reflexive beliefs and changeable understanding of their biography. Yet, that we continuously create and revise our biographical narratives does not mean that the self can be wholly fictive or deny the importance of external reality to the ongoing story of the self and remain credible. Much of Cercas' novel, for example, includes his meticulously researched documentation into the construction of Marco's false biography and how he so convincingly falsified the archive and co-opted the stories of others to forge this derivative identity. Referring to Marco as truly a "mobile fiction," Cercas comments, "As I was working, I felt Marco had invented not only his time in the Nazi concentration camp of Flossenbürg, but had also invented his whole life."[14] Cercas is particularly concerned with how Marco disengages the materials and narratives of other people's lives and embeds those into his shifting biography.

By the time Marco was exposed by historian Benito Bermejo in 2005, he had been riding the big lie of being a Holocaust survivor for almost three decades. He had published his false testimony in one of the first books about Spaniards deported to the concentration camps and given hundreds of talks and speeches, many educating young people about the crimes and abuses committed by the Nazis. He professed to having been a valiant member of the Republican cause in the Spanish Civil War, of being arrested as a resister in France and handed over to the Gestapo, of his torture and suffering in the concentration camp. In reality, Marco had volunteered to go to Germany as a member of the group of workers Franco sent to help Hitler's cause (in Marco's case servicing German torpedo boats). He was imprisoned briefly abroad for reportedly spreading communist propaganda on the job site, but was quickly released and never experienced any time in the concentration camps.

In fact, Marco assimilated just enough material from the archive and other's biographies to make his story credible. For example, as Cercas reveals in his research, Marco appropriated the name of Enric Moné, an actual Spanish prisoner of the Flossenbürg camp, declaring that it was just a misspelling. Drawing from common tropes of Holocaust depictions and what he had appropriated from others' testimonies, Marco took a "thread of reality and laced, crocheted, or otherwise spun it into a fanciful decorative piece."[15] Cercas in turn laces Marco's manipulations with the Spanish nation's and his own capacity to use fiction as a mode of reinvention, and then to believe or "buy into" these fictions. The novel thus becomes one of investigating broader questions of how fiction intervenes in the real—its relationship to history and human nature. Marco's fictionalized versions were evidently emotionally riveting enough to bring members of the Spanish parliament to tears when he spoke before them as President of the Friends (Amical) of Mauthausen, the Spanish concentration camp survivor's group he led beginning in 2003 (having been a member since 1999). Cercas argues that Marco's derived biography was especially convincing because it incorporated just enough truthful particulars to conceal its deception, commenting that "plausible lies [...] [e]ffective lies, are a mixture; they contain some element of truth."[16]

We can consider derivative lives as drawing initially from actual biographical sources; however, just as derivatives in the financial market can be traded in their own right, these derivative lives can become detached from their underlying ("real") assets and become sources of independent exchange. This paradigm provides a helpful model to consider Marco's efforts to trade on his falsified biography, its circulation, and Cercas' literary investment in trying to understand the implications of its wider contagion. This is especially so, given that for Marco the derivative life proved so much more valuable than the real one.

Marco, for example, does not have ownership over the biographical narratives he claims, but uses these derived versions as instruments for enhancing his own underperforming biography. As Marco described to Cercas in an interview he conducted with him as research *The Impostor*, he felt almost "obligated" to create a heroic past for himself as a means to redeem his "terrible life," his "suffering" childhood, his lack of luck.[17] In effect, Marco sought to increase the present value of his biography through the fictionalized derivations of others' real traumas, exchanging his experiences of loss and failure for those of recovery and resurgence. Arbitrage refers to the effort to exploit the differential in values across different markets or derivative forms. By hedging his bets that these derived fictions would not be discovered, he simultaneously sought to enhance his derivative value through arbitrage and to claim a stake in the memorialized histories of Spanish victims of Nazi persecution.[18] Moreover, Marco's fictionalized biography serves as a powerful metaphor for the risk of acceding to dominant fictions rather than opening them to investigation and challenge. The ready acceptance of Marco's derivative fictions suggests how images that are emotionally charged and that match an expected, desired narrative can gain credibility and dissuade challenge, distorting or ignoring the separation of truthful facts of a life from their imaginative constructions. As Cercas emphasized in an interview,

> It's clear we need fiction, because reality is always insufficient—when it's not terrible or overwhelming. [...] But it's also true we need reality; we can't survive with fiction alone. This what the protagonist of *The Impostor* cannot understand: he invents another life—a heroic, epic, sentimental life—to free himself from the cowardly, mediocre, and dreadful greyness of his own life.[19]

Part of the risk that Cercas explores with respect to derivative fictions is not only that these versions begin to circulate on their own and overtake connection to actual, lived realities, but that they diminish the value we place on truth. For example, Cercas emphasizes repeatedly how Marco not only co-opted others' experiences and narratives of the Holocaust into his unfolding biography, but began to convince himself that the emotional truth of this falsified version was just as valid as the real, even more so. He suggests that Marco's identification with his derived identity is so utter that "after a certain point he was no longer pretending." In a photograph of survivors of Flossenbürg in which Marco is among the group, Cercas observes, "[i]f you didn't know he was one of them, nothing would give it away. In effect he *is* one of them."[20] "I'm an impostor, but not a liar or a fraud," Marco declares in an interview for *El País* in 2011, six years after his biography had been exposed as a fake. "All I did was distort my own story. I became the voice and right-hand man of the deportees because I also suffered imprisonment in Germany. Tell me, what is the difference between jail and a concentration camp?"[21] Employing this specious, surrogacy argument, Marco declares that although a particular event may not have happened to *him*, it is part of a broader collective history in which he may "rightfully" claim a share.

Importantly, the kind of false equivalency that Marco makes between these two very different experiences demonstrates the dangerous slippage—the risks of the derivative. That derivatives are not tethered to the underlying asset or originating source does not mean that the real sources (the lives that have unknowingly collateralized his fiction) do not exist, and that there aren't actual survivors and victims who would have given anything to have gone to jail rather than the concentration camps. This slippage represents a loss of connection to the real lives that suffered. Marco is so (self-interestedly) invested in the profit of the derivative reality that he avoids entirely, or loses any concern for, at the very least, the important truth there is something real there underneath to start with. In one sense, this evokes the source of criticism that some scholars have lodged at Cercas, as well, for drawing renewed attention to Marco's story, and thus conceivably letting his story overtake the real histories he usurped.

When asked how we might judge the moral dimensions or limits of when an author has "betrayed a historical figure," Laurent Binet has argued that "the limit is when fiction becomes falsification, when one is slipping into a kind of revisionism."[22] While Cercas argues that Marco took this to an extreme level, part of the risk of telling the story of Enric Marco is that we fail to consider our own vulnerabilities to convenient, revisionist fictions, that Marco's story is merely moralistic or pedagogical. That is, *The Impostor* also explores the false security of convincing ourselves that Marco's narrative has nothing to do with our own. Beyond probing the motivations of Marco, Cercas explores the shared risk of depending upon derivative fictions that conform to the image we want to construct for ourselves rather than risk exposure of more ambivalent motives.

In this regard, one element at the heart of *The Impostor* is the biofictional interview Cercas creates with Marco. Within the novel, Cercas invents a conversation between a literary version of himself and an imagined Marco. He interviews the real Marco at various points and includes the transcript of one interview at the end of the book. So, why include this fictionalized interview? Is Cercas just making the fictional Cercas reveal what he wanted him to say, rather than what he actually revealed when he spoke with him? In fact, Cercas has stated that he wrote this section of the book first, when Marco's case first broke, and later returned when he decided to write the novel. In this sense, biofiction enters the world of truthiness and speaks its language in order to point out the fraudulent, or truest yet unspoken, stories. This section becomes a structuring part of the book that reframes the conversation away from being about the deceptive fictions of Marco to the ethical risks and responsibilities of fiction more broadly.

As Cercas expressed in an interview, "To me, this dialogue is the most important in the book. [...] I don't think the book could exist without that chapter." He added,

> [W]hat meant something, or could mean something, was to create a struggle to the death between fiction and reality in this book. I mean between the lies that Marco had told, his fictions, and the truth hidden behind those fictions. [...] This book is a struggle between fiction and reality, but it's also a struggle between Marco and me, I mean between two impostors.[23]

By referring to himself as an "impostor," Cercas ironically suggests the surface parallels between the novelist who fictionalizes reality in order to achieve a poetic or moral truth about the nature of reality and the human experience and someone like Marco who misappropriates fact to impose a convenient, self-interested fiction. Through the biofiction, Cercas creates a dialogic "struggle" between these competing approaches and the damaging risks of falsely confusing them. This chapter ("The Flight of Icarus," Chapter 8) is the focus of my subsequent analysis.

"The limit is when fiction becomes falsification." (Laurent Binet)

Rather than biographical truth, Cercas flags that he is exposing the reality of the fiction in this biofictional section of *The Impostor* by emphasizing that he is "*fantasizing* an *imaginary conversation* with Marco."[24] He's making a point by telling us that he's fictionalizing, while Marco doesn't acknowledge this. A central issue that emerges immediately in this ironic, imagined dialogue is the association Cercas establishes between Marco's derivative lives and the reinvention of individual and collective histories as part of the historical memory movement in Spain. By exposing the "reality of the fiction" in this way, Cercas illustrates this is not just metafictive play drawing attention to the textual construction of the fiction, but implicates how these fictions intervene in our realities.

In the immediate wake of Franco's dictatorship (post-1975), both political left and right avoided dredging up the past for fear of unsettling the nascent democracy. While this is often referred to as the "Pact of Forgetting," it is quite clear no one actually forgot, but instead redefined individual and collective narratives. Cercas has emphasized how Marco was reinventing himself at the same time as many Spaniards were reinventing their pasts. In this sense, Cercas draws on the concept of something derivative as of questionable authenticity as well as dependent on another source. He relates this fraudulent realness to the marketing of historical memory following Spain's transition from dictatorship, in which he argues many people revised or repackaged their biographies to conform to the politically convenient fiction of a shared history of collective resistance and democratic aims. He contends that while few succeeded in inventing a whole new identity, the majority were content to "titivate or embellish their past."[25] Cercas argues that almost no one challenges Marco's story despite its inconsistencies because it fits a wider, popular narrative: the victim of fascism who becomes the heroic image of a resurgent democracy, divesting a problematic history of "its ambiguity, the complexities, the gaps and fears and dizziness and contradictions and asperities and moral chiaroscuro of genuine memory and genuine history."[26]

In Cercas' imagined exchange with the fictional Marco, he has Marco compare the invention of his derivative biography with Cercas' biofictional invention of the neglected republican hero, Miralles, in his popular novel *Soldiers of Salamis*. Suggesting they both used the same tools, the fictional Marco contends that Cercas similarly profited from the "so-called industry of memory" his novel helped foster, providing readers with the emotional narrative they wanted to hear rather than examining more nuanced realities. Cercas replies, "You're not trying to tell me that my novel is to blame for the apotheosis of historical memory? I'm vain, but I'm not stupid." To which Marco retorts that Cercas' novel is at least partly to blame, arguing that "people needed to weep for the elderly, forgotten Republican in that asylum in Dijon, for the friends he lost in the Civil War, just as they needed to weep over the things I said in my talk about Flossenbürg, about the Civil War and my friends during the Civil War."[27] While the narrative Cercas argues that his invention of Miralles was legitimate because, as a novelist, he "lied with the truth [...] legitimately in the way that novels lie," the imagined Marco further counters,

> I did exactly the same thing as you—no, I did it much better than you. I invented a guy like Miralles, except that this Miralles was alive and visited schools and talked to children about the horrors of the Nazi camps and about the Spanish inmates there, and about justice and freedom and solidarity; This man was leader of the Amical de Mauthausen, and thanks to him people began to talk about the Holocaust in Spanish schools, thanks to him people discovered that Flossenbürg camp existed and that fourteen Spaniards died there.[28]

This imagined exchange is important for a number of reasons. Through the biofiction, Cercas ironically plays out the post-truth arguments that Marco and some of his real defenders used to justify his actions, in which the invented real *feels* more true and is thus more compelling than the actual truth. Marco not only claimed his false biography and its "alternative truths" were not emotional lies, but that its derivative fictions more effectively conveyed the experience of what it was "really like" than those who actually experienced it, thus publicizing "truths" that needed to be known.[29] That is, the derivative begins to define and revalue the real, rather than the other way around.

Cercas carries this literary play further to acknowledge some of the criticisms of self-interest leveled against his own use, and later critique of the historical movement in Spain. Most importantly, in having Marco conflate or diminish the truth of facts of historical memory of actual survivors as "distinct from Marco's imaginary passage through Flossenbürg [...] as opposed to purely fictional constructs,"[30] Cercas sets the stage for his exploration of the distinction between the novelist's legitimate use of reinvention to invent derivative lives and Marco's post-truth deceptions.

Any quick Google search will produce all sorts of results suggesting how "reinventing yourself" is often perceived as a positive self-improvement goal rather than a deception: *How to Reinvent Yourself and Change Your Life for the Better*, *Ten Companies That Successfully Reinvented Themselves, The Power of Reinvention*, just to name a quick few. Moreover, we can think of countries that have successfully reinvented themselves, including many post-communist or post-dictatorship countries such as Germany following the fall of the Berlin Wall. These have been heralded as success stories. So, when does reinvention become a dangerous fiction rather than a smart overhaul? When, as Laurent Binet suggested, does fiction become a falsification?

Cercas observes that when the Marco scandal broke in 2005, many people wondered how Marco "could have duped so many people for so long with such a monstrous lie."[31] In part, Cercas suggests that Marco both revealed and was a consequence of the general lack of education in Spain surrounding the Holocaust. While Spain was technically neutral in the Second World War, Franco nonetheless sided with the same fascist powers that had provided him military aid in the Spanish Civil War. Further, Franco had forged a Nationalist mythology around a united Castilian culture that denied pluralities of faith, ideology, and regional identification. Even after the end of the dictatorship, Spain was slow to incorporate Holocaust literature and education. Primo Levi's work, which García Ortega uses as a starting point for *The Birthday Buyer* and which Cercas references in *The Impostor*, was not published in Spain until 1987. And it was not until 1997 that the first novel by a Spanish author that dealt with the Holocaust was published (Maria Àngels Anflada's *The Violin of Auschwitz*), and that was in Catalan, not Spanish. Given these absences, as with those around Spain's unresolved legacies of the Civil War and dictatorship, for Cercas, as Christopher Taylor contends, "it's a deeply unamusing irony that when people did start concerning themselves with the past, one of the voices that spoke to them obsessively of silences and lies and heroic truth-telling was engaged in Trump-style projection."[32]

Cercas uses the biofiction to inventively illustrate how Marco's discourse filled these absences with the sentimental discourse people wanted to hear rather than engaging with more complex realities. Cercas has the fictive Marco justify how his derivative narrative took hold, challenging Cercas with the claim that he employed the same [fictional] instruments that Cercas used to insert his own invention:

> Do you really believe that [...] if they'd truly cared about it, my lie would have passed for the truth, my deception would have been believed? Look, with your novel you proved that many people had forgotten the Civil War and in particular those who lost the war, or at least you made them believe they had forgotten, but with my imposture, I proved that in our country the Holocaust didn't exist, or no-one cared about it. [...] The difference is that you were acclaimed for doing it, and I was made a pariah.[33]

In the absence of nuanced, fact-anchored consideration of individual and national histories and their myths, Cercas exposes the risk of derivative fictions that fail to interrogate a complicated history or uncomfortable truth but simply confirm an "alternative truth," which is really a euphemism for a lie. But this leads to the most important argument Cercas explores in this biofictional exchange, in which he seeks to distinguish the legitimate creation of derivative lives as a novelist from post-truth distortions such as Marco's. A central aspect that Cercas emphasizes is the different contract that the fiction writer has with the reader. In "Literary Hoaxes and the Ethics of Authorship," Louis Menard associates false Holocaust narratives with other literary hoaxes that are flat out violations of the "autobiographical pact," the implicit guarantee that the narrative voice or subject is truthfully telling his or her own life story.[34] In analogy, the biographical pact gives similar reassurance from the perspective of the biographer to tell the story of a person's life with as much accuracy as possible, and not to strategically or consciously alter the facts. The novelist's contract with the reader is different. As Michael Lackey has suggested, writers of biofiction can "unapologetically change facts about an actual historical figure, and they usually convert their biographical subject into a symbol with which readers can connect."[35] As I have argued with respect to derivative contracts, writers of biofiction can do this because they build these expectations into their model.

The biofictional Cercas similarly argues that the novelist can do this because unlike Marco, who is claiming to factual accuracy and the truth of his biography, the fiction of the novelist with the reader is consensual. A key difference, he emphasizes, is that the novelist acknowledges the use of fiction, whereas Marco denied it. As the biofictional Cercas tries to explain to a defensive "Marco" in their imagined interview:

> The problem is that you weren't a novelist [...] Because everyone knows that the novelist deceives, but nobody knew that you were doing it. Because the novelist's deception is consensual and yours was not. Because the novelist has a duty to deceive and you had a duty to tell the truth. Those are the rules of the game and you broke them.[36]

In *Impostors: Literary Hoaxes and Cultural Authenticity*, Christopher Miller suggests that the postmodern concept that the fact/fiction distinction was unstable and always contestable was appealing as an intellectual game that played with readers' expectations, but less so when "the world turned," and "he realized that fakery was no longer just a classroom sport." Miller contends, "It is harder to see the fun in deception when the fate of the world seems to depend on resisting lies, 'alternative facts,' and 'fake news.'"[37] These comments of Miller bring us closer, I believe, to the structuring role of Cercas' use of biofiction in *The Impostor*. Cercas explores the critical importance of distinguishing legitimate, ethical uses of fiction to which we "consent" from imposed, unauthorized fictions. He also highlights the shift from the flexibility of truth as purely a textual game of experimentation to one that acknowledges very real consequences of manipulating the differences between fictional play and reality—the very real risks and responsibilities we have to the fictions we invest in as true.

In a review of *The Impostor*, Mario Vargas Llosa accurately portrays the slipperiness between a truthful fiction and fictionalized truths, and then seemingly falls victim to it himself. Calling Cercas' book a "subtle essay on the nature of fiction and the ways in which it can invade our lives and transform them," he contends,

> We live in an age when confidence tricksters are everywhere around us and the vast majority of them—bankers, government officials, political and union leaders, judges, academics—lie and commit crimes to become rich [...] and their stories amount to nothing more than the predictably crooked dealings of petty thieves. At least Enric Marco did what he did with broader horizons—and yes, why not, for less egotistical reasons [...] Fiction has replaced reality in today's world and, for that reason, the everyday characters of the world no longer interest or entertain us. Fantasists do.

He adds that it is "not surprising that in such times" figures like "the giant Enric Marco have been able to perpetrate their misdeeds—forgive me, I mean their heroic deeds. But don't blame novelists; they just tell the stories their readers would like to live."[38] Notwithstanding his ironic characterization of Marco's heroism, Vargas Llosa's proposition that just because something moves us or has some positive consequences, its truth value becomes secondary or the sympathetic attraction of the derivative fiction even justified is exactly the risk that Cercas plays out in his biofictional dialogue with Marco. The danger of suggestive metaphors that claim to the authenticity of true memory is in part that they become believed, or more believable than real, historical truth. The greater risk is that when stories (such as Marco's) are proven false, no one cares. The risk of post-truth is that not just that the derivative overtakes the truth, but that the distinction between factual truth and invention loses significance. This is especially so, given that Marco's reinvention is a type of forced erasure of other's real suffering, as much as a derived fiction.

Certainly, an important distinction Cercas is also making is that the ethics of aesthetics, the ethics of biofiction, are absolutely different and critically so, from the ethics of factual representation. "Leaving aside these contradictions," as he has stated in an interview, reduces "it to pedagogy [...] into monolithic knowledge, into propaganda."[39] In this context, Cercas (or at least his biofictional avatar) suggests that it is even more essential to discern the differences between the rules of fiction and those of reality for rewriting the past for deriving alternative lives.

Notably, Cercas reinforces his own susceptibility to the desire for reinvention and the uncertain role of fiction in that process. In the concluding section to the imagined exchange between Cercas and Marco, Marco asks Cercas why he titled his article about him in the newspaper, "I am Enric Marco." Cercas says that it's because of a German biopic by that name. To which the imagined Marco apocryphally replies, "Bullshit: you called it that because you knew from the beginning [...] that I'm your [imagined] reflection," that "in defending me you defend yourself. [...] The truth is that you are me."[40] While Cercas suggests that Marco took it to a destructive extreme, he also considers how fictions imbue all of our realities and narratives, and that it is up to us to acknowledge them. When writing the opening paragraph of *The Impostor*, something Cercas said he did only when finished with the book, Cercas acknowledges his own potential complicity in reinventing his own and other's derivative fictions, the ongoing struggle over how truthful knowledge is formed and our responsibilities for its use that the biofictional section of the novel prominently plays out.[41] Was it ethical of him to use Marco's story? I think so, but that is of course open to debate. When done well, biofictions don't reinforce what is resolved about a life, solidifying the historical or real-life individual, but instead employ that narrative to ask more paradoxical questions of us. They speak to conflicts within ourselves; they ask us to consider our own specular and conflicted roles in what we invest in as true.

Investing in Speculative "Futures" in Adolfo García Ortega's *The Birthday Buyer*

A novel examines not only reality but existence. And existence is not what has occurred, existence is the realm of human possibilities, everything that man can become, everything he's capable of. Novelists draw up the map of human existence by discovering this or that human possibility. But again, to exist means "being-in-the-world." Thus, both the character and his world must be understood as possibilities—Milan Kundera, *The Art of the Novel*[42]

While Cercas' novel uses biofiction to examine the misuses of derivative invention and to contrast them with the truths of honest fiction, Adolfo García Ortega's *The Birthday Buyer* explores the redemptive potential of biofiction to imagine speculative possibilities for lives otherwise disempowered and silenced by history. At the start of this chapter, I posed the question of what justifies deriving a fiction from another person's biography. Returning to that question, I consider what the differing approaches of these two authors can tell us about the uses of biofiction to respond to and inform the present in meaningful ways. As the title suggests, the narrator of *The Birthday Buyer* "buys" *aniversarios* (or anniversaries, translated into English as birthdays) what we can understand in either case as unled lives, speculative *futures*. As the narrator says, "I want Hurbinek to exist. To exist once more. To exist for longer. To be an existence that endures. To lead an *invented, possible life*. Manufactured by me"[43] (emphasis mine). The argument that we come to biofiction, as Chika Unigwe has suggested, for possibilities rather than historical truth, is perhaps nowhere clearer.[44] In contrast to a manufactured truth, García Ortega suggests that he imagines openly in the function of the novelist, manufacturing these fictional alternatives as a way of giving life to lost potential. While these are futures in a subjective and subjunctive temporal sense, we can also conceive of them in a financial sense as derivative options. Like a speculative investor, the narrator "buys" (in the form of invented options) these futures for Hurbinek and other real-life individuals associated with his brief life.

What exactly does the author mean by "buying"? Unlike the transactional nature of assuming other lives in *The Impostor*, García Ortega offers a different intent here, but what is the "cost" or what is being exchanged in the process? García Ortega seems to suggest the moral, human cost of reimagining lost possibility. Each "purchased" biography forms the basis of an imagined, speculative past and future. Yet, this approach also raises ethical questions. Is it right for García Ortega, from the space of fiction, of imagination, to speak for those who actually suffered the Holocaust? García Ortega was asked in an interview how he could write with such intimacy about life and death in Krakow and Auschwitz without having been there—"an astounding achievement, but some may call it charlatanism." García Ortega has argued that his imaginative linkages were what drew him most closely to try to "understand what the victim feels. The fact that I did not experience it myself does not deny me the right to write about it."[45] This defense suggests the ethical conundrum of many works of biofiction. While, on the one hand, there is the act of creating imagined lives for those otherwise forsaken by history, there is seemingly the ethical risk or tradeoff of some form of appropriation.

As with the metafictional Javier Cercas within *The Impostor*, the narrator in *The Birthday Buyer*, while never directly named, seems a loosely autofictional proxy for the author. As the biographical source for his novel, García Ortega draws from the sparse description in Primo Levi's 1963 memoir, *The Truce* (also known as *The Reawakening* in the United States): "Hurbinek was a nobody, a child of death, a child of Auschwitz."[46] Levi describes a mute child who "looked about three years old," perhaps born in Auschwitz and knowing nothing else, evidently subjected to medical experiments and other horrors that left his legs paralyzed. Presumably left to die, he is cared for meticulously by another camp prisoner, fifteen-year-old Henek, who has been tasked with selecting which children are sent to the gas chambers. While Hurbinek "fought like a man, to the last breath, to gain his entry into the world of men," Levi writes that he "died in the first days of March 1945, free but not redeemed. Nothing remains of him. He bears witness through these words of mine."[47]

García Ortega continues Hurbinek's story, picking up where Levi left off forty-five years earlier, to imagine alternative pasts for Hurbinek and the derivative possibilities of what might have been had he lived. As García Ortega has expressed in an interview,

> Hurbinek stands for all the dead Jewish children, all the Jews who died in the death camps. It was important to me to write a novel [...] because I believe that literature has a very important role in the documentation of reality, at times even more important than that of institutional history. I wanted to use imagination to tell the truth. I did not want to write *only about what was, but also what might have been.*[48] (emphasis mine)

In my analysis of the novel, I link these various threads to consider the imaginative creation of speculative futures, the role of symbol and metaphor as sources of empathy and connection, and finally the effort of biofiction to not simply reveal alternative possibilities but to transform the perception of the world of the reader.

Structure of the Novel

The narrator of the novel is a Spaniard who describes feeling overcome for years by the story of the Holocaust and his sense of identification with the victims ("feeling" Jewish, "feeling" a victim).[49] Consumed with understanding the unfathomable, he is initially traveling to Auschwitz "to probe the reasons behind that massacre, that annihilation, to find out who the guilty parties were, to ascertain the historical truth. I wanted to know the *details*."[50] Yet, the narrator never arrives at the concentration camp. Along the way, he has a terrible car accident and finds himself in a hospital in Frankfurt. The frequent refrain throughout the novel that "I was going to Auschwitz, but not anymore" underscores that the journey he is taking is no longer a physical one but a projected, imaginative space.

As Antonio Muñoz Molina has commented, "the novel is not speaking of the historic Auschwitz, but of our consciousness and imagination of Auschwitz sixty years later."[51] Auschwitz is a symbol, a metaphor for all sorts of unanswerable losses that continue to imbue the present. While the narrator says he wants to know the details of the Holocaust, the importance of the novel is not, as he claims, reconstituting or discovering its historical details. Like arriving at Auschwitz, knowing more facts would not solve the more perplexing, existential questions he wants answered:

> I repeat: what do we we know about Hurbinek? Nothing really. [...] What do we know about one another? [...] And if we don't know how people react in extreme conditions, how millions perished at the hands of the Nazis, at least we know enough to understand the pain, anguish, loneliness and fear felt by others. We feel compassion; we are human. But are we?[52]

The narrator has argued that he "feels a *responsibility* to give Hurbinek a future," that he is "legitimized by justice."[53] Yet, he also acknowledges that telling Hurbinek's story won't help Hurbinek. "What use is an invented life to him?" Instead, he says, "It *is* of use to me, in no small way to invent his life," contending that it is the "only path to redemption both he and I can take"[54] (emphasis mine).

It is clear that the supposition that "going to Auschwitz" would ever have clarified or explained anything is itself a fiction. The accident frees the narrator to take the journey in a purely imaginative direction, liberates him that way, but there was never any way to get there besides imaginatively. García Ortega has said in an interview that he "devoted a year and a half or so to reading history books and memoirs about the Holocaust, Auschwitz, and Krakow. Only then did I go back to writing about Hurbinek."[55] Yet, no matter how many survivor accounts you read, you are not going to get any closer to really understanding or fathoming what it was like, or how such inhumanity could transpire—to some sort of explanation, which is impossible. No matter what, it would always have to be an imaginative process that tries to understand what to *do* with this reality, rather than to truly understand what happened.

In trying to "give life to Hurbinek" and the ever-broadening "range of possibilities," the first thing the narrator imagines is what he refers to as Hurbinek's "pre-life" in the concentration camp.[56] "I think Hurbinek lived just that length of time not to have memories," he contends.

> Except for rare exceptions, all our memories begin *after* we are three, not before. That's why I'm horrified to think that Hurbinek, with all his strength and desire to live, only experienced a pre-life, only lived a strange extension of his mother's uterus. And yet all he lived in that time without memories was the permanent suffering, pain and fear that were his food, his playthings, the air he breathed.[57]

García Ortega thus gives critical importance not only to Hurbinek's implied silence (through his lack of understandable language) but also as a symbol of someone without memory—a pre-memory that he then imaginatively expands.

Importantly, García Ortega's first-person narrator does not only speculate on the lives of Hurbinek, but his parents, Primo Levi, and Henek. In conjuring Hurbinek's brief life and death in the camp, the narrator counters his suffering with the heroic vision of the gentleness and compassion with which he imagines Henek cares for him. The narrator observes,

> I find what binds me to Henek is his love for Hurbinek. [...] I love Henek because I want to be Henek. I don't know what portion of Humanity Henek is, but I do know that without him, without Henek, what Adorno said would be absolutely right, that after Auschwitz it would have been impossible to write poetry. Or anything else.[58]

The narrator declares that "we know that Henek was really Belo König—Primo Levi says that, when he relates how the Polish nurses who couldn't face looking after Hurbinek changed König to Henek."[59] He imagines Henek's life after the end of the war, including envisioning his burying Hurbinek along with Primo Levi, at the foot of a small tree. While he says that "we know" (do we?) that his wife never heard him speak about the real Hurbinek, his wife recalls him telling their sons the story of a tree that contained the spirit of a small, legless boy and that called Henek's name. "But she didn't know the source of that story, just as she didn't know that a tree that held Hurbinek's spirit grew in a place in Poland that the Germans once called Auschwitz."[60]

In *The Rewakening*, Primo Levi describes that Henek had been deported to Auschwitz with his whole family, all of whom besides him had been killed. In order to survive, Levi writes that Henek had "organized" himself as a Kapo, and it was his job to choose when there were selections at the children's Block. "Did he feel no remorse?" Levi poses. "No. Why should he? Was there any other way to survive?" With this question, Levi alludes to the impossible ethical complications of life in the camps, what he referred to in a later essay as the "gray zone."[61]

On a surface level, it might seem here that Enric Marco and García Ortega (via his narrator) use the same tools of sentimental fiction and the creation of a heroic vision to reinvent the past. However, whereas Marco professed to the historical truth of his heroic fiction, García Ortega openly projects a redemptive possibility for the world through his *biofictional* Henek, making him a metaphor or literary symbol representing the redemptive capacity of humanity. As the rescuer of Hurbinek, he has to fulfill the choice of how to redeem the awful choices and situation imposed on him, demonstrating care in the face of incredible cruelty and horror. Rather than acceding to a view of human possibility as determined by dominating social, historical, and political forces, this image of Henek suggests the power of individual moral responsibility. Thus, just as Auschwitz takes on the metonymic symbolism for evil and the degradation of the human spirit, García Ortega's biofictional Henek suggests the power of human connection and the ethical obligation we have to one another even alongside the worst threats to our common humanity.

In the novel's Chapter Three (III), García Ortega invents the possible motivations of Primo Levi's contested suicide in 1987, subjectively associating his survivor's guilt with the tortured thought "that he had forgotten the number tattooed on Hurbinek's arm"—again imagining the resounding echoes of Hurbinek's life despite its brevity and silence.[62] This significance is further deepened in Chapters IV and V, in which García Ortega invents the lives of a possible family of origin for Hurbinek, drawn from the lives of real victims to whom he dedicates the novel. As he expresses, "I also dedicated the book to all of the characters appearing in it who really did exist, even if under different names."[63] Notably, each of the vignettes, many focused on the prewar courtship and love story of his imagined young parents in Poland, is introduced in relation to its position as pre- or post-Hurbinek's death, which becomes a kind of historical anniversary (the opposite of the birthdays the narrator buys back). For example: "1936: Nine years before Hurbinek's death"; "1945. Seven months after Hurbinek's death"; "1965. Twenty years after Hurbinek's death," etc. The last vignette of the section, "1960. Fifteen years after Hurbinek's death," ends with a list of the uncertain fates of the children—including three who died in Auschwitz—born to Hurbinek's imagined grandmother, Raca Cèrmik. While official history and biography are typically documented by the dates of the births and deaths of famous individuals, it is significant that García Ortega structures the "before" and "after" of his characters' lives based upon Hurbinek's death, a life that his "grandmother" Raca will never "wonder after the soul of Hurbinek," because "she doesn't even know he existed. Life kept that hidden from her."[64] Even in its absence of real historical recognition or individual memory, Hurbinek's death thus becomes the point of inflection around which the other lives and histories circuit. As Joshua Rothman has expressed, such unled, unreal lives "make us feel the precariousness and the specificity of the way things are."[65] The novel, in turn, centers on the tension between a destructive reality and the competing implication of all of these unrealized, unled lives that might have been.

It is almost impossible to get through the realist dystopia of Chapter VI ("That Gap There in the Collarbone.") and retain any hope for humanity. The narrator reports in relentless detail the torturous and murderous actions against children in Auschwitz. This is the chapter in the book that contains the least imagination. As he has contended in response to criticism regarding the cataloguing of these horrors, "I'm only imagining what reality has carried out," suggesting that it is important not to escape into the fantastical or to divest these events from the real, because these unfathomable events actually happened and should be acknowledged.[66] It is especially notable that García Ortega strategically centers the novel with the subsequent chapter (VII, "Actors in a Miniature Theatre") in which, having already derived invented pasts related to Hurbinek, he imagines possible futures had Hurbinek survived. In so doing, he projects these speculative lives for Hurbinek onto a series of other individuals the narrator encounters in the present: among them, a railway worker in Budapest, a Spanish writer, a Russian set designer, a Polish filmmaker—a series of eight potential lives. In the ensuing section, I consider the structuring importance of these *futures* to refocusing the aims of the biofictional narrative, and I position this argument in relation to theories of speculation and speculative investment.

Hurbinek's Speculative Futures

The narrator claims he

> felt under a responsibility to give Hurbinek a future, a future that occasionally led me to look for him concealed within the personality of a man called Pavel Farin. [...] Perhaps Hurbinek really lives on as that individual, Farin the Russian. A life that was *inserted,* decided by me, the creator of his future. Why not? Why couldn't he have more lives? Other possible lives? (emphasis mine)[67]

In *Speculative Everything*, Anthony Dunne and Fiona Raby state that "for us, futures are not a *destination* or something to be strived for, but a medium to aid imaginative thought—to speculate with." They are, then, "not just about the future, but about today as well, and that's when they become a critique."[68] In this vein, "the purpose of speculation is to *unsettle the present*, rather than *produce the future*"[69] (emphasis mine). This view of the speculative is instructive when considering the function of the biofictional speculation that García Ortega employs in imagining alternative futures for Hurbinek. These projected lives provide a series of scenarios that not only imagine how Hurbinek's existence might have evolved alternatively (the what-ifs), but in so doing comment on our own present and the possibility to create a different, more just future. As Sherryl Vint has argued, "the practice of speculative fiction at its best, then, can work to compel belief in different kinds of possible futures, ones that begin from the experiences and points of view of those whose lives are made invisible [...]."[70]

In the financial context, *futures* are a type of derivative option that try to settle in the present the uncertain exchange value of something that will take place at a future date. In this way, such derivative instruments turn to an uncertain future and strive to protect against risks by *securing* the present value of the future. As I have suggested, however, García Ortega flips this version of futures on its head, *unsettling* the present rather than settling, engaging with uncertainty rather than resisting it, and in turn using imagined *futures* to refigure the value of the present instead of the other way around. In so doing, García Ortega embraces narrative experimentation that can never undo the real, horrific experimentation that was done to Hurbinek but can only project forward counterfactual parallel worlds of the human possibilities that were lost.

Through this specular, subjective experimentation, the biofiction functions in García Ortega's novel, then, as a source of creative potential and freedom against the delimiting forces of an oppressive history. The ethics of the biographical novel in this way become an antidote to despair and paralysis, a mode of acting on the present. Vint refers, in this spirit, to "speculative fiction's power to imagine the world otherwise—to register what is missing from this world and compel belief in the possibility of a different one."[71] She further references what she calls "promissory futures," which reveal a kind of indebtedness to those who have been disempowered from the privilege and profit of speculative investment while undergirding it with their labor. However, we could also think of this promissory vision as the obligation García Ortega (via his narrator) implies those who did not suffer the trauma of the Holocaust owe those who did, that is, the responsibility to invest in alternative futures and carry forward the memory of those otherwise excluded from realizing these options.

Notably, the authors of *Speculate This!* contrast exploitative speculation that seeks to quantify and contain risk to generate individual profit at the expense of others—as we could categorize Marco's hedging his bets against exposure of his false pasts—against affirmative speculation that embraces uncertainty, contingency, and difference to multiply rather than reduce possible futures. Speculation, they argue, "is always essentially about potentiality: a reach toward those futures that are already latent in the present, those possibilities that already exist in the here and now [...] which is, in effect, the ability to become different from what is present."[72]

It is useful to examine closely some of the imagined futures that García Ortega creates for Hurbinek and how he narrates these. Rather than any conceivability that Hurbinek survived, these options all remain firmly planted in the realm of hopeful fictions. In *The Principle of Hope*, Ernst Bloch has referred to speculations of another world, fueled by "affective apprehension of the inadequacy of the present, that offer traces of a better world that he characterizes as Not-Yet-Consciousness."[73] This transformative impulse is what distinguishes speculative fiction from mere futurism, according to Philip Wegner, who argues that we should understand such speculative narration as a *method* for imagining, rather than a set of genre conventions, "a form of engaging with the world rather than a content."[74]

García Ortega develops eight different lives for Hurbinek, had he survived, each derived from brief encounters with real people that evoke for him an image of who Hurbinek might have become. The narrator reminds us repeatedly of the provisional nature of these derivative versions. If he wasn't Pavel Farin, a famous theater set designer, a "prestigious, even mythical figure [...] *or else*, Hurbinek metamorphosed into an employee of the Budapest train system, one Jozsef Kolunga."[75] He prefaces the subsequent possibilities with similar conditionals: "Or else," "Or perhaps," "Or else this possibility." As the narrator has suggested, he "inserts" or projects onto the lives of these real individuals a series of alternative, speculative futures for Hurbinek. This narrative process is thus reminiscent of the approach to speculative biofiction by Rosa Montero, who contended that she used the biographical subject as an enormous screen onto which to project possibilities, thus investing these imagined lives with her own creative vision.

In addition to a Russian set designer, a Hungarian tram conductor, and a Spanish writer, the narrator also considers the options that Hurbinek might have become a Polish/French actor, a Bulgarian conductor, an English botanist whose "real profession" is a collector of antiquities, an Israeli photographer, a radio journalist. The diverse geographies of these individuals reinforce the function of Hurbinek as a more universal symbol, as García Ortega expressed in an interview, "transforming him to the sphere of metaphor."[76] Moreover, each of these individuals elicits a form of recognition on the part of the narrator that he associates with his invented image of Hurbinek. Given how little information is known about Hurbinek, these glimpses are subjective, visceral impressions that inspire the speculative fictions. For example, imagining Hurbinek as Jozsef Kulunga, the Budapest tram operator, the narrator observes passing

> a man in a tram driver's uniform who walked with the help of sticks in Zsigmont Móricz Square tram station. I don't remember his face, because I only saw him from the back, and for a few seconds at that, as he was disappearing through a door into an area that was off limits to non-authorized personnel. *It was then that I began to imagine Hurbinek had survived* (emphasis mine).[77]

It is significant that in varied instances of these experimental narratives the paralysis, silence, and traumatic memories of Hurbinek are prominently revised. While his legs remain physically handicapped in these scenarios, he often gains possibilities of freedom and mobility. For example, "the legs of little Jozsef (since he was baptized with that name as a Catholic in the Central Parish Church) strengthened and when he could walk, his father started to take him to the Tram System's canteen."[78] Or, as the Spanish writer, Pablo Orgambide, for whom traveling" was never a problem, since that limp of his ... only weighed on him when he forgot to conceal it, never stopped him from leading the life he wanted to lead."[79] Similarly, the narrator envisions speculative futures for Hurbinek in which rather than silence and the inability to have his efforts at language understood, he is recognized for his creative expression, writing the biography of Adolph Hitler, as the only world-famous seated orchestra leader on the planet, or as Pavel Farin, the creator of set designs that were "new worlds, full of playfulness and whimsy, that he could create as he wished, and even create as works unique on the face of the world."[80]

Moreover, in the majority of these speculative reinventions, the Hurbinek that has "metamorphosed" into these other's biographies has no recollection of his prior existence. So, as Pavel, while "his face held traces of Hurbinek, he would never recognize [...] that strange child he once was"; as Pablo Orgambide, "his father got a number tattoo as well, so he could tell his son it was an ancient family rite, a numbering that affected various members of the family over generations, an absurd explanation that Pablo accepted." As Paul Roux, "he has a few problems with his legs, where he lost a great deal of sensitivity, though he doesn't know when or how."[81] Jacob Paul has observed that "memory (and its implicit subjectivity) has always been at the center of postwar responses to the Holocaust. Holocaust museums are devoted to the memory of the event, but what they mean by memory is not the physiological act of recalling former experience, but *installation of a memory* in those who have not experienced the thing itself."[82] Notably, in "uninstalling" Hurbinek's traumatic memories from his past and these imagined futures, he also acts to *install* the recognition of these absences in the reader, who—unlike Hurbinek's speculative selves—presumably has no direct experience with this traumatic history. At the same time, he frees these speculative versions of Hurbinek (via his imagined futures) from his oppressive history as a victim of fascistic violence to offer the possibility of different symbolic meanings.

Hurbinek is an interesting symbolic choice since, as the narrator argues, he was on the cusp of memory—did not have the language to codify his experiences. The loss of these traumatic memories he suffered seems a kind of gift, but then so much of Holocaust memory culture is about making sure that these realities aren't forgotten, that we never forget so as not to repeat them. Hurbinek can't actually participate in memory culture, but in becoming a symbol of what invokes it—of the underlying real—his derivative versions are actually what help to explore the possibilities of all that was lost, not only his individual suffering.

We could think of both the absences that García Ortega illustrates and the possible lives onto which he imaginatively projects lives that Hurbinek never actually lived as kinds of *negative spaces*. Yet, as Joshua Rothman poses, "isn't the negative space in a portrait a part of that portrait?" He adds, "in the sense that our unled lives have been imagined by us and are part of us, they are real; to *know what someone isn't*—what [they] might have been, what [they] dreamed of being—this is to know someone intimately." [...] When we first encounter people, "we know them as they are, but with time, we perceive the auras of [unlived] possibility that surround them."[83] He references the work of Andrew Miller in describing the emotion this experience evokes as "beauty and heartbreak together." Miller's expression offers a pertinent reflection for the implications of the last three vignettes García Ortega includes, in which the speculative reinventions of Hurbinek come closer to acknowledging their connection to Hurbinek's real origins in Auschwitz.

As Augustus Hubbard, prospector for the Antiquities Department of Sotheby's, he receives a letter from one of his stepbrothers who has been investigating "their true identity for several years, at Gus's expense." According to the narrator, the letter "tells him about Auschwitz, a place that he, Gus, could never have imagined was linked to his life (or in fact, to his death, I would suggest.) [...] Look at your arm, and draw your own conclusions," the letter concludes. "What Gus had always thought of as the incomprehensible features of a whimsical tattoo, turned out to be numbers that were hardly legible even if you stretched the skin. Night is falling in Bangkok and suddenly he has ceased to be Augustus Hubbard, art valuer."[84] With the life of Israeli photographer, Icek Bienenfeld, he heads off on a European tour whose itinerary includes visits to the concentration camps, including Auschwitz. "He chose the last one, because it was where he had been born twice," although he remembers nothing of either. "His brothers, sisters, uncles, aunts and cousins? Did they ever exist? [...] Hurbinek was returning to Auschwitz and was returning by himself."[85]

Yet, immediately following, García Ortega begins the next speculative biographical vignette ("The life of Walter Hanna") with the statement, "Hurbinek was going to Auschwitz, but not anymore."[86] The parallel of this line with the narrator's own ("I was going to Auschwitz, but not anymore") reinforces in this last of the eight alternative lives that García Ortega creates for Hurbinek a strong intersubjective connection with the narrator. Hanna, "an ironic, seductive radio journalist specializing in sports," suffering from AIDS and with little time left, is in a hospital in Germany because, like the narrator, he was in a car accident while driving to Auschwitz. The narrator observes that "Hurbinek will never make it to Auschwitz. At least for a second time." And yet, he adds,

> something that is still possible, an absurd hope: that Walter Hanna, the journalist whose voice in Greece is as famous as Melina Mercouri's, is

> *really* inhabiting the same present as myself, the very same day, the very same hour as I imagine him [...] And it could be absolutely for real, it could be true that at the very moment when I am rescuing Hurbinek from the dead and giving him a life, the real Walter Hanna, or whatever his name is, is there in that hospital, because he was *really* born in Auschwitz and had *really* made the journey, his life's last, that far. Then Hurbinek had certainly lived *über alles*, above all else, as the hymn goes.[87]

How might we explain the implications of this intersubjective parallel that neither the narrator nor "Hurbinek" (in any of his derivative manifestations) will reach Auschwitz? To understand, I return to the claim referenced earlier in this section that speculative "futures are not a *destination,*" but "a medium to aid imaginative thought" and "*unsettle* the present." By having neither return to Auschwitz, to the past site of historical trauma, García Ortega revises the physical journey with the speculative potential of the biofiction to experiment with alternative, more life sustaining, worldviews. By not returning to a concrete past or arriving at a specific future, we keep the redemptive possibilities of the future in play. Rather than the historical Auschwitz acting on the present, it is what we *do* with the past going forward that matters. As Sherryl Vint has suggested, such speculation does not focus on risks and probabilities, but on "change, ideally change that moves the world" toward greater awareness of, and commitment to, the human responsibilities we bear to one another.[88]

Spectral Pasts and Tangible Traces

> And all the lives we ever lived and all the lives to be
> Are full of trees and changing leaves. (Virginia Woolf,
> *To the Lighthouse*)

Rather than real biographies, the speculative pasts and futures that García Ortega creates, then, become symbolic spaces (realities he "buys up"). By asking us to consider "what might have been," they open up to what *could* be. Yet, as much as this novel conditionally, contrary-to-fact, imagines, it is populated by specters, the ghostly presence, of the many absent individuals who in reality were deprived of these potential lives. As García Ortega's narrator suggests, very young children who perish leave barely a trace, especially if the adults who would tend to the recollections of their fleeting lives disappear alongside them. How do these lives, which become haunting, symbolic ghosts, relate to the speculative paradigm I have suggested? In Spanish cultural studies and post-dictatorship studies more broadly, spectrality has often referred to the ghosts of past traumas that have not been recognized. As Jo Labanyi has argued, "ghosts are the traces of those who were not allowed to leave a trace."[89] Under this paradigm, lives that have been silenced and erased, "leaving only their ghostly traces," are "bound to return and haunt the present." Jose Colmeiro contends that the "reappearance of ghosts in Spanish post-Franco culture has almost everything to do with the repression of the past. [...] The return of the past in spectral form would be thus a symptom of the collective inability to deal with it properly, but it can also offer the possibility of rectification, acknowledgment and reparation."[90] This is what Labanyi refers to as addressing the ghosts, rather than denying them or becoming possessed by them. We can understand this metaphor of the presence and present of ghosts not only in terms of the Holocaust or of Spain's history under fascist dictatorship, but in relation to the legacy of any such violent repression.

This metaphor is usefully applied to the final chapters of *The Birthday Buyer*, in which the narrator first speculates on the experiences of the imagined parents of Hurbinek, Sofia, and Yakov, after their arrivals to the concentration camps (including the birth of Hurbinek), and Sofia's desperate efforts to shield him from suffering and death. These are followed by two chapters titled "The Plural Life of Objects" and "The Tree of Photos from this World," which explore the few objects of Hurbinek that accompanied him through his brief life, and the story of Hurbinek's tree that Henek (Belo König) invented for his son. As opposed to "pre-memory," as the narrator characterizes Hurbinek's absent memories, Marianne Hirsch has put forth the concept of postmemory. Under this paradigm, those who did not directly experience a traumatic past, nonetheless, may feel its effects through "imaginative investment, projection, and creation."[91] The physical record of memory through photographs and other objects is a prominent instrument of postmemory. Such memory objects tell us, she suggests, as much about the present-day desires of those who hold onto them as they do about the past.

Documenting the few objects that existed "*with* Hurbinek" that "passed through his life" (and thus hold a *trace* of him), the narrator asks, "Where did they come from, who touched them, who owned them, who loved and used them before and after him?"[92] These few items include the handful of items he touched and that touched him: a metal mug, buttons, a little wooden doll used in Dr. Mengele's clinics to calm terrified children prior to the monstrous experiments conducted on them, the scarf that Primo Levi hid under the sleeve of his uniform after Henek had buried Hurbinek under a large tree. The scarf, the narrator argues, became the impetus for Levi to write about Hurbinek. "He knew nothing about the child's past and refused to hazard any possible future for him. However, the dirty scarf and its dragon stuck in his memory forever."[93]

These ghostly objects, like Hurbinek's lost biography, bear no witness on their own. It is our responsibility to listen to what they tell us, and thus imaginatively carry forward their signification. García Ortega writes that Henek, for example, told the story to his son of a "tree whose trunk housed a very pale being with the face and body of a little boy, a legless little boy. He named this astonishing being Hurbinek, and entitled the story, 'Hurbinek's tree.'"[94] At the end of the novel, the narrator declares that "in the tree of photos from Hurbinek's dreams there are two photos" on which his gaze lingers. One, a "photo Hurbinek would never see," is of the imagined mother of Hurbinek, Sofia, which captures her in a happy moment before war and loss, but which is in turn "lost among the debris from the building when the Nazis demolished it." The other is a photo of the narrator's accident. "There is no hope," the narrator suggests, "might be a caption for the photo," given that the accident appears so horrific as to be unsurvivable. However, he adds, maybe "I was born anew that day, perhaps Hurbinek was born within me as well."[95] He imagines that photo hanging on the tree as part of a strange dream. Preparing to leave the hospital and Germany behind, the narrator remembers reading how Primo Levi's family could recognize him when he returned after the war, and he speculates on how his own family will react when he arrives home.

> I haven't changed over these three weeks, and my daughters will easily recognize me, I am sure, but deep down, I *have* really changed. [...] I have revisited the last century, I have entered into its horrors and imagined its grey epicenter in the short life of little Hurbinek, the three-year-old Jewish boy. Thinking, researching and telling all that has changed me. Of course it has. I now know I was going to Auschwitz, but not anymore.[96]

Cercas has argued that the most important obligation of the novel "consists of expanding our understanding of the human condition"—the form of the novel needs to keep changing and entering unexpected territory in order to "leave us changed, different than before."[97] In a similar vein, Christopher Schaberg has suggested the capacity of the best literature to *unmoor* us, to shake us from the security of complacency and into the uncertain, creative spaces "into and through the world all around."[98] García Ortega demonstrates this transformative vision by focusing on what changes about the narrator through the process of reimagining and inventing these real lives, creating the speculative biofiction. The narrator does not arrive at a new physical place on this journey, but inhabits a different view of reality and his own ability to act. The reality that is transformed is not that of the Holocaust—those brutal facts are firmly cemented—but the potential to be changed by creative invention in place of the destructive absences wrought by power, to demonstrate the living possibility of that history in the present and of our ability to make of it something regenerative.

Rather than acceding to the idea of human possibility as determined by dominating social, historical, and political forces that disempower our authority or control, the image the novel creates of Henek and his tree suggests the power of individual moral responsibility. For every Enric Marco, there is the counter-possibility of the choice of care for those who cannot speak on their own behalf, which is also the author's project. In this context, Ernst Bloch has referred to the power of imagination oriented to what he calls "positive astonishment" cultivating more than one's own circumstance, of imagining what might improve the world as opposed to "negative astonishment," which manifests itself merely in one's own better position within an unchanged world. While Cercas' novel points to the misuses of fiction to appropriate the traumatic pasts of others, *The Birthday Buyer* highlights our shared responsibility to move beyond affirming the truth of a painful history to speculate on what that means for the present moment. Just as Henek reimagined Hurbinek's tree to give hope to his son, Emma Donoghue has commented, "So I suppose I see every biographical novel I write as having tree roots. These roots are reaching toward that past historical moment but of course they are reaching from right here. And it affects both ends."[99]

As I cited in Chapter 1 of this book, Javier Cercas has observed that "the past is never fully past because it is always here, acting on the present, forming part of it, inhabiting it." Through the imagined spaces of biofiction, the derivative lives of Hurbinek, of Enric Marco, and of other real and false victims continue to exist, and it is our choice what directions we take their narratives—to what degree they transform our perceptions of the world and the possibilities to inhabit a more livable present. The problems of the present include the responsibility of how we fictionalize real lives and speculate on their derivative possibilities in order to realize more just futures.

PART THREE

Critical Play in Biofictional Games

5

Playing for Real: Simulated Games of Identity in Lucía Etxebarria's *Courtney and I* and *Truth Is Nothing but a Moment of Falsehood*

In the preceding chapters, we considered how writers have used differing forms of biofiction to respond to a circumstantial, speculative reality. The following two chapters explore how the world of the early twenty-first century of constant immersion in networked, virtual worlds has prompted writers to experiment with new forms of biographical fiction as narrative games that reveal and reconfigure the interactive relationships involved in narrating a life story. The process of writing a life is often framed as a struggle for authorship or control of the biographical representation among multiple stakeholders. Rather than documenting a life as a biographer might, these biographical novelists immerse themselves in the life of a biographical figure not only to speculate on alternative possibilities, but also to actively intervene and play out these options as one would a simulation. Patrick Jagoda, for example, has argued that games serve as a form for "staging, encountering, processing, and testing experience and reality in the twenty-first century."[1] All biofictions might be perceived as simulations in the sense that they are attempts to create an invented model of something real. However, simulations also suggest a design characterized by specific features: simultaneity, the intervention of multiple participants, and the necessity for adaptive response. We can thus see the creation of these biographical narratives as constantly adapting multiplayer games in which varied, often competing "players," including the biographical subject, try to control the outcome—each with his or her own stake regarding whose version wins out.

Within this context, Lucía Etxebarria is emblematic of a writer who has been particularly zealous in drawing attention to herself and her biographical image across multiple media, thus linking self-creation and promotion with consumption of her literary work. Etxebarria burst onto the Spanish writing scene in 1997 with her best-selling first novel, *Love, Curiosity, Prozac and Doubts*, and subsequent works earned prominent and lucrative literary awards, including the Nadal and Planeta prizes. Yet, critics have often depreciated her success as the result of provocative marketing rather than true literary talent. As Christine Henseler has observed, she is an "author whose outrageous promotional tactics have enchanted and bemused some, angered and alienated others, while gaining the attention of most of the Spanish reading public."[2] While once a popular and critically successful author, by 2013, her riches to rags, crash and burn story would ultimately invoke more doubt than love, much of this due to the damaging intersection of her public selves and her published works. How does she model and then lose control of the biofictional game? This chapter examines how Etxebarria's carefully constructed public persona intersects with her creation of herself as a fictionalized character embedded in the biographical narrative and vying for control of its direction. Game theory and game studies provide alternative modes to examine the network of relationships perceived as shaping biographical identity within contemporary reality. Accordingly, I apply strategies from other games of simulation where individuals play an intervening role in the construction of fictionalized narrative identities.

Among Etxebarria's works, for example, are a number of biofictional narratives that stretch and play off the borders between the real and the fictional, the biographical other and her own self-creation. Drawing on the work of Patrick Jagoda, Henry Jenkins, Marie-Laure Ryan, and Jan Simons, among other theorists intersecting the areas of game studies, narratology, sociology, and cultural studies, I argue that Etxebarria creates biofictional games in which she operates not only as an extradiegetic author. She also prominently breaks the fourth wall to blur the lines between her identities outside the text and her biographical avatars within the narrative, all of which ultimately escape her authorial control. As I asserted earlier in the introduction to this book, she thus alters the biographical novelist's role from external creator or operator of the simulation to one knowingly immersed in the game of its unfolding direction, competing for control with other players. These narratives include *Courtney and I* (2004),[3] a reinvention of her 1996 quasi-biography of the American grunge-rock couple, Kurt Cobain and Courtney Love, and *Truth Is Nothing but a Moment of Falsehood* (2010).[4] While *Courtney and I* models games as experiments for enacting and resisting the social construction of biographical identities, *Truth Is Nothing but a Moment of Falsehood* puts the game into action as a playable simulation.

For example in *Truth Is Nothing but a Moment of Falsehood*, Etxebarria creates and brings to virtual life via "his" own Facebook page and media strategies a fictional musician, Pumuky, who went on to draw vast numbers of real-world followers. I consider Etxebarria's use of technology and various media to stretch the limits of narrative representation through the lens of what Henry Jenkins and others have referred to as transmedia storytelling, in which integral elements of a fiction are not vertically integrated but dispersed horizontally and systematically across multiple media and modes of delivery. Users speculate and play on the gaps and uncertainties in these unfolding stories through their own narratives. Finally, I consider how Etxebarria has both promoted this permeability and fallen victim to lowered barriers to cultural participation in the construction of public, "published" identities. In the past decade, having sworn off publishing more books that she declared too heavily pirated and therefore no longer profitable, Etxebarria has increasingly been reduced to scandal-ridden celebrity status, most notably in a short-lived reality TV appearance. Forced to exit this televised game, she described in *El País*, "I got involved in something I couldn't control."[5] By applying concepts of game theory and game studies, I consider how Etxebarria's example shows the risk of participatory formats to both create and desecrate meaning and literary value.

What's Changed? Interactive Biofictional Games and Spain's Gen X

Game theory focuses on strategies to manage the uncertainty of dynamic interactions and to negotiate revised rules of play. Jan Simons observes that the "matrixes, diagrams, and other graphics of game theory do not represent actual game play by 'real' game players, but model the choices available to the players and simulate the reasoning behind the players' strategic choices."[6] Yet, in referring to a "game theory" approach to biofiction, I am not only suggesting a theoretic angle. Patrick Jagoda has argued that game theory has contributed fundamentally to the broader culture through the "extension of games from the status of hobbies and pastimes to a form capable of modeling every aspect of economic, political, and social life."[7] Reinforcing the "broader imbrication of games with lived experience," he contends, "games are not merely alternative realities that become, by the early twenty-first century, coextensive with the world; importantly, they are at once models of the world and *in* it."[8] This doubling of the game, both as simulative design of the real and mode of immersive experimentation within that world, has accelerated in contemporary life, especially since the turn of the millennium. How do these interactive games intersect with biofiction's narrative adaptations of real lives?

One obvious way to see this is through the expansion of social media and other forms of intervening in networked identities. "Friending," "following," and otherwise projecting versions of oneself across multiple platforms further destabilize the line between self-creation and the reception or involvement of others in that process. The uses of social media stretch the limits of traditional autobiography and biography to reflect a fundamental shift in the construction of narrative identities and the multiple ways we mediate relationships through these derivative selves. Perhaps most importantly, these auto/biographical placeholders are not merely unidirectional, but demand interaction—replies, "likes," comments, memes, retweets, etc. These sites become entry points through which readers also project themselves as characters into purportedly dialogic relationships among the participants of the virtual world. Instead of passive observation, these forms draw us into the existence of another's story, requiring constant response and engagement. Writer Jose Ovejero has referred to the "compulsion to multiply oneself through followers that at the same time diffuse" our presence, this "necessity to intervene with frequency" in order to affirm one's existence and value.[9]

As auto/biographical creation and response have become more immediate, immersive, and interactive—more game-like—biofictional forms have understandably adapted. Thematically and stylistically, Spain's Generation X (born 1965–80) reflects a changed worldview from earlier trends of post-dictatorship narrative. Lucía Etxebarria (b. 1966) is one of the most visible and polemic members of Spain's Gen X, and one of its few women writers. As we have seen with writers such as Javier Cercas and Antonio Muñoz Molina, various popular writers in the last decade of the twentieth century and first decade of the twenty-first wrote biographical novels re-examining Spain's recent past and unearthing alternative histories long suppressed under authoritarian rule. While these authors also had little to no memory of life under dictatorship (1939–75), they are well aware of its effects. Spain's Gen X authors, in turn, demonstrate scant interest in exploring its resonances. If the characters in these writers' works perceive themselves as liberated from the constraints of their parents' generation, they are simultaneously stymied by the acceleration and abundance of only short-term options in the present. The aimless bartending and other Spanish versions of McJobs and the gig economy that appear in many Gen X novels are emblematic of apparent freedoms marked by uncertain realities. The real jobs did not materialize, nor did the rejections of old values mean there were new ideals ready to shift into place. This economic situation exacerbated profoundly during the economic crisis from about 2008–13, in which Spain's young people (especially those under thirty) had over 50 percent unemployment and the Spanish government imposed austerity measures. While Etxebarria herself was a highly published adult author by this point, a number of her protagonists come of age with economic precarity and malaise as their backdrop.

As a demographic, Generation X came of age during the consumer boom of a newly democratic Spain. Mass media and accelerated technologies offered new spaces of biographical production and consumption, most notably through the expanding reach of the internet and social media. The narrative interests of this generation and after thus reflect the expansion of networks, along with shifting models of subjectivity and identity. Rather than contesting models of authority centered on dictatorship, power and influence are projected and played out through fluid entities of media images and commodity culture, along with the new expectations and desires these representations evoke. In Etxebarria's narratives, these images and networks are not distinct from "real" life, but expanded platforms for communicating how biographical identities are perceived, negotiated, and potentially fictionalized. How these dispersions of the self are reflected through interactive biofictional games sheds critical light on shifting experiences of subjectivity and the experience of identity that continue to form dominant aspects of contemporary life.

Games of Fame, Spectacle, and Kitsch in *Courtney and I*

With *Courtney and I,* Etxebarria revises the subject of her 1996 pseudo-biography of the rock couple Kurt Cobain and Courtney Love, *The Story of Kurt and Courtney: Put Up with This!* (*La historia de Kurt y Courtney: ¡Aguanta esto!*), substituting herself prominently in the title spot formerly occupied by Kurt in relation to Courtney.[10] While Courtney's relationship to Kurt had earlier predominated much of her public image, Etxebarria now claims this managing role. This alteration provides us with a clue to the mutability of Etxebarria's position as both authorial "biographer" and sharing the spotlight as co-biographical subject. Kurt Cobain was the lead vocalist for the American grunge band, Nirvana. His status as a rock legend in the 1990s amplified to a type of cult status with news of his death by apparent suicide in 1994. The volatile relationship between Courtney Love, lead vocalist for the band *Hole*, and Cobain (whom she married in 1992) and with whom she had a child had also long been fodder for public controversy. Etxebarria claims with intentional vagueness that she began *Put Up with This!* "when she was twenty-seven, twenty-eight, or twenty-nine," choosing to revisit this biography approximately a decade later because she had constructed her earlier version of Courtney based mostly on Courtney's own declarations of her life and "it was clear that Courtney would be the first to have an interest in idealizing her life." However, "now that the Internet exists and a number of biographies and articles have come to light," Etxebarria says she "sees things very differently."[11] Contesting her own earlier representation, Etxebarria says she now feels a more visceral, almost *eidectic* identification with Courtney.[12] Rather than idealize or defame her, she wants to immerse herself using "imagination and the great capacity to open oneself to new stories and spaces," in order to reveal a different biographical image of Courtney that should "convert itself, should *exist* as a live experience, in constant even conflictive evolution."[13] In enacting this evolving biofictional version, it is notable that Etxebarria relies upon her own immersive, imagined vision of Courtney— ("It doesn't interest me so much who Courtney is as who we think she is")—as well as the derivative constructions of others, while rejecting what Courtney herself may have thought.[14]

As the title *Courtney and I* self-consciously advertises, the biographical narrative is not only about Courtney, but also about Etxebarria. Just as Courtney's public image was before largely shaped in relation to Kurt, Etxebarria's projection of herself in this framing position as the substitute partner indicates her intention to supplant this defining role. This is complicated by Etxebarria's own ambiguous positioning, identifying imaginatively ("eidetically") with Courtney as though she were herself embodying her emotions and experiences, and as the seemingly distinct, subjective "I" of herself as author. In this respect, we can consider her adaptive narrative as biofictional reimagining and contingent game with Etxebarria as both designer and player. She substitutes herself in the position previously occupied by Kurt, and as parallel interlocutor of Courtney's constructed images—both mirror and game controller. On the one hand, this seems to be an effort at a type of feminist rewriting of Courtney's narrative; yet, Etxebarria's exclusion of Courtney herself from the process also undermines this supposedly shared female liberation.

Because Etxebarria intervenes so profoundly in evaluating and reshaping versions of Courtney, it is tempting to read her narrative autofictionally. And, indeed it is in part a self-referential commentary on the construction of Etxebarria's own public personas. However, what makes her narrative a biofictional and a critical game is how Etxebarria plays *through* the biographical figure of Courtney, while forgetting that her own [Etxebarria's] biographical selves are equally open to the appropriation and adaptation of interested players in other narrative games.

Etxebarria maintains toward the end of *Courtney and I*, for example, that what she has created is an elaborate game in which the image of herself within the narration may be just another fictional character—a game no different perhaps from the way she has led us to a specific image of Courtney. She claims, "But I have not been talking about actual people. What I have been talking about are icons, representations, myths. And it is for this reason that intentionally I have put forth a game, and I have made you arrive here at the hands of a character that in her day dressed in Zara pants and a t-shirt that said 'Psychobitch.'"[15] Yet, at the same time that she inserts herself as a potentially fictive character within the narrative, she also tries to exert external authority over this representation because she is the one designing and operating the game.

However, what exactly is the game that Etxebarria thinks she has created for the reader? Patrick Jagoda suggests how interactive games as modes of experimentation and investigation rather than presenting players with problems to be solved instead "*make problems*" that call into question the underlying structure of our social and economic order, or make us reflect critically on the constructed nature of our subjectivity[16] (emphasis mine). We could also think in terms of what Greig de Peuter and Nick Dyer-Witherfeld have called "counter-play," which is unruly innovation that exploits the rules and structure of traditional game play and uses it to disrupt those norms. If this is the case with Etxebarria's game, what are the problems she makes, and to what degree is hers a subversive game of counter-play?

In game theory, the source of uncertainty is based in the interactive network of relationships among the characters. Each player's move is constrained by what he or she thinks other players will do, or what options others choose. Etxebarria presents the biofictional game as an interactive process that disrupts the biographical subject as the center of the narrative or the stability of authorial control over its direction. One of the problems that Etxebarria's game explores (and creates) is the confusion and conflation between persona (or fictional character) and person, or how mythologized, distortionary, and highly suspect versions become codified as "real," become real in that sense. This is not only a problem for Courtney, but also for Etxebarria, as I will discuss.

Etxebarria demonstrates how these problems of persona proliferate in the derivative worlds of social media and diverse online identities. On the one hand, social media makes everyone feel like a celebrity, feel like they are being seen or able to become public selves, mirroring famous people's celebrity. Etxebarria actively mines this performative reality, both performing that celebrity and inviting her readership to interact with her directly via her social media. She sees herself as in charge of that process, but also falls into a series of mirrors that undermine that authority; she forgets that other people are part of that dynamic as well, and can reduce her to cheap celebrity.

We can think of persona in this regard as the game-playing self, the image that one wants to perform or publicly play out. However, we can also think of the images that other players project *onto* these virtual, performative characters, thus considering how the intentions and desires of other players (their shifting desires and decisions) change the game. And we may ask who is designing the rules of the game, and how (or whether) players operating within its system may successfully adapt or challenge these constraints. Moreover, in so demonstrably breaking the fourth wall and addressing the reader directly, she implies that we, the real-world readers, are also implicated in the narrative game she is playing. We are also now involved in the dissolution of barriers between the fictional and the real worlds that she has created and not certain how to assess the realness or declarations of the various players.

As Etxebarria repeatedly emphasizes, in re-booting the narrative game to expose and challenge the fictions surrounding Courtney, she has no interest in exploring the veracity or reality of Courtney's biography but what her shifting image *represents*. Courtney, she says, "interests us only as myth."[17] Referring to Baudrillard's theory of simulacra, she suggests that especially when someone becomes famous (and here she includes herself) their image transcends the real and enters into the *hyperreal*, becoming a "screen onto which a society and its public project their illusions, desires, and deficiencies."[18] Etxebarria refers in various instances to her own fame and celebrity in the decade since she initially wrote about Courtney: "I have become famous—'famous' in quotes,"[19] and contending that one becomes a celebrity only when "their biography becomes part of a wider 'mythical metanarrative,' in which their admirers and detractors invest themselves self-interestedly."[20]

In addition, while Etxebarria references Debord's theory of the spectacle—the false realities produced by the endless regeneration of commodified images that draw us in through their clickbait—her narrative is more reflective of game world than spectacle alone. As Patrick Jagoda observes, while the "society of the spectacle was founded on separation and hierarchy," the game world is "interactive, participatory, and increasingly networked," so that individuals don't passively consume the commodified fragments of others' biographical images, but play into and solicit these myths for their own ends in response to shifting desires and efforts to gain advantage.[21]

For example, Etxebarria reproduces an array of uncertain claims made by diverse players, including Courtney herself, who have competing stakes in the representation of her biographical narrative. Among others, these include passages from the biography ("hagiography," in Etxebarria's framing) of "the close friend of the diva," Poppy Z. Brite[22]; references to the heavily edited diaries of Kurt, letters that circulate on internet sites, polls that allow users to vote which Courtney doll they would prefer from "Kinderwhore" to "Rock-Glamour"[23]; descriptions of the efforts of the British filmmaker, Nick Broomfield, whose biopic not only accused Courtney of being manipulative and a climber, but also of being the actual killer of her "mythified husband."[24] Suggesting the box office benefits of Courtney's purported manipulations in trying to block the film, Broomfield has asserted in an interview for *Rolling Stone*, "So it sort of became a different film. It became a film about why someone was trying to stop the film from happening. In a way, it became a more interesting film. Courtney started defining the film, then, which was like, 'What part did she have in his endgame' kinda thing."[25] Etxebarria argues that these derivative interpretations of Courtney were disconnected from the "real Courtney," but were what others *projected onto her*, playing out these conflicts through their representations of her. Notably, Etxebarria uses an example from her own life to make this case, suggesting that an interview in which she came off looking poorly was because the interviewer, a journalist going through a messy separation, had projected her own drama onto Etxebarria: "Although she transcribed my words, she didn't transcribe my message, but her own."[26]

Another problem that Etxebarria both presents and creates, then, is *her* ambivalent positioning in relation to Courtney and the biographical games she is representing. Is she external to the game redesigning the trajectory and rules by which we should read Courtney's narrative? Or is she an internal player projecting onto and role-playing the tensions surrounding her own image? In exposing the crowd-sourced fictions of Courtney's biography, hasn't she similarly used Courtney-as-avatar? Consider, for example, the relationship among narrative strategies and digital games of identity in which players shift from purely external, exploratory observers to what Marie Laure-Ryan has referred to as internal, ontological modes of play. Rather than remaining outside the game, the user in the internal mode projects herself as a member of the fictional world, through either an avatar or other interactive first-person placeholder within the unfolding narrative. Additionally, the exploratory versus ontological dichotomy reflects the ability of the player to influence events in the virtual world. In contrast to an approach where the player can explore all aspects of this world but has no power to change it, the ontological approach assumes the decisions of the user affect the evolving narrative and have the capacity to alter events.[27]

In Etxebarria's biofictional texts, the "biographer" frequently becomes a player rather than only an outside observer or commentator regarding the life of the biographical subject. Against the external, exploratory view of the traditional biographer who sublimates her presence in the narrative, Etxebarria flaunts the ability to project her subjectivity into the story, both publicly and as a hidden player. She actively underscores the shift of the biographer's role from external creator or operator of the simulation to one knowingly embedded in the game, so that subject(s), player(s), and biographer(s) share and compete for control of the narrative game.

Throughout *Courtney and I*, Etxebarria explores how much of what has been represented about Courtney constitutes false models. Notably these "false" versions share prominent similarities with publicized criticism of Etxebarria. She suggests that we tend to read Courtney's life through the filter of the dangerous or destructive female. She asserts that because Courtney has been converted into the modern embodiment of an ancient myth associated with the emergence of patriarchal cultures—"the *femme fatale*, the devourer of men"—the facts surrounding Courtney's life have been selectively managed to present the corresponding image of her.[28] When applied to the music scene, this myth crystallizes in the legend in which the girlfriend/wife, through her self-interested manipulations, destroys and brings down the fall of the band.[29]

In Etxebarria's view, this myth evokes the path of Kurt and Courtney from counterculture heroes to the allegorical death of the iconic Gen X *grunge* movement (with Kurt's death) and the concomitant transformation of Courtney from authentic "kinderwhore" to plastic "Made-Up" (in the sense of both cosmetic and fake) Courtney or "Barbie Versace."[30] In Etxebarria's telling, Courtney's physical transformation and increasing social conformity suggest not only her simulative "avatar," but also real, physical self has become completely controlled by the normative design of a traditional gendered game, and is no longer transgressive. She resists this for Courtney and for herself, stating that she strongly preferred Courtney-Kinderwhore, whose appropriation of this look (according to Etxebarria) recognized that one could be "feminist at the same time as coquettish, and even a little tacky."[31] This insistent defense of sexual and gendered agency resounds against a number of public criticisms of Etxebarria herself; in turn, she vicariously refutes these critiques lobbied against her through her defense of the earlier transgressive Courtney. The images she puts forth of Courtney thus actively overlap and become confused with the reality of Etxebarria.

Not only Etxebarria blurs the distinctions between herself as author, biographical subject, and fictional construction. For example, there is a tendency for readers to interpret Etxebarria's works through the lens of her persona, and to read her novels in the context of this biographical self as *either* expressions of refreshing resistance or publicity-stunt conformity with market forces. Etxebarria's combative and highly sexualized public image has invited frequent controversy. It is noteworthy, in turn, that Etxebarria defends the "aggressive," provocative, "self-aware" appropriation of the image of Courtney-Kinderwhore against the collapse of this image into the commercial(ized) "Made-Up Courtney."[32]

Amid these strategic shifts in image, Etxebarria suggests that the *real representation* of Courtney was lost along the way. As she underscores, what interests her is not what Courtney actually is, but how we play her—what her image represents, or what we think that is. If this is the case, we may wonder what difference it makes if we concentrate on Courtney as a character within a game, rather than uncovering the real. Yet, Etxebarria simultaneously laments one form of representation for another she finds less authentic. According to Etxebarria, the fictions of Courtney do not only infuse her biographies, but also begin to reshape how Courtney defines herself in response, including revising her body through plastic surgery. These simulated versions of a life, then, do not just mask the real but begin to distort and replace it. That is, the fictions escape the textual or imagistic world of persona and begin to reshape and redefine the real, physical *person*. Through this process, Etxebarria presents the construction of biographical identity as a mutable, interactive game in which she and others can intervene. Yet she still wants it both ways—claiming that as author/designer of the game (who "made us arrive" at the interpretation of Courtney's biography she wanted us to see), she can convey what really matters, those "essential" details that remain.

When Etxebarria observes, "I can't help but ask myself to what extent Courtney is not a victim of her own persona," the reader also can't help but ask to what extent Etxebarria is not speaking of herself.[33] She is hyper-aware of the different ways of inserting herself into the text as a character, but it is not just about authorial identity bleeding into auto/biographical selves in her books, but how these creations of herself extend into her real life. By confusing these boundaries, not only her fictional avatars, but Etxebarria's authorial identity risks becoming under attack. This blurring of person and persona means that potential criticisms become not only about not liking her book, but personal—extending the game to her identity.

Playing out versions of Courtney's biographical images is thus also a way for Etxebarria to try to reclaim and take control over not only Courtney's but also *her* own public image or avatar. As an article from *El País* reflects,

> Even Etxebarria recognizes that she has her own avatar and that she lives in permanent opposition to it: it is that public image that exists of her as a strong, controversial woman prone to making tone deaf statements. According to Etxebarria, this is not the real Lucía, although she has inadvertently contributed to creating the image. "The avatar's power is so strong in the popular imagination that it takes a lot of mettle to endure it," she admits. [...] My public persona creates problems independently of what I myself do."[34]

While Etxebarria's desire to manipulate this avatar, to have agency (and play, rather than be played) is reinforced through her self-insertion into the narrative world, this role remains blurred. From the point of view of the author/designer, she wants simultaneously to set the rules and revise the game. Yet, while she has claimed (or pretended?) that the game was all *hers,* she neglects that she is also a networked biographical character in others' narrative games—with their own strategic intentions.

Significantly, what Etxebarria underscores is awareness of and interaction with the myths associated with one's biographical image. "It was *kitsch* (the difference between kitsch and tacky is that kitsch has an awareness of itself. Tacky doesn't know what it is an, and instead tries to be elegant, while kitsch consciously transgresses the rules of good taste with a clear ironic and self-referential intention."[35] Kitsch, then, suggests one is in on the game. As Etxebarria suggests, kitsch reflects playful awareness of something as artificial. Kitsch only works if the audience is complicit in the intentionality of the fake. That is, they have to get the joke. The garden gnomes or plastic flamingos placed in the garden are only successfully kitsch when they are understood as ironic imitations. Moreover, we have to consent to the fact that the kitschified derivative is now purely commodified and no longer connected to the object or identity it was originally intended to evoke. But, Etxebarria's ambivalent position—blending the simulative into the experience of contemporary reality while exhorting the loss of one more "real" to the artificial—makes this assurance harder to evaluate and infuses this playfulness with a certain anxiety. If this is all just a "game," then who or what determines the rules, the participants, and who is "in on" the humor?

If enjoyment of kitsch depends upon playful awareness of the game, Etxebarria's ambivalent status—both inside and outside the game—highlights the confusing separation of biographical reality from the proliferation of its myths, leaving only the spectacle. Concluding *Courtney and I*, Etxebarria reminds the reader that she has not been talking about real lives, but about icons, representations, myths. Yet, how does she distinguish this if she does not have an underlying, even fuzzy, understanding of who the "real" Courtney is? Indeed, by self-identifying with Courtney and then affirming that the images of her cannot be trusted, she makes her own biographical identity and authorial voice similarly untrustworthy. Just as we cannot be sure that the Lucía Etxebarria-as-avatar who negotiates the text is the same as the real Lucía Etxebarria, we have no guarantee that her portrait of Courtney is any more real. By drawing attention to how mythologized, distortionary, and highly suspect versions take hold, Etxebarria demonstrates susceptibility to her own subjective, specular alternatives.

Enacting the Game in *Truth Is Nothing but a Moment of Falsehood*

In *Courtney and I*, Etxebarria creates a biofictional game with herself as designer and player creating and contesting the social constructions of Courtney's (and by projection, Lucía's) publicly shaped identities. In *Truth Is Nothing but a Moment of Falsehood*, she goes beyond describing the interactive story world and enacts the game as a playable simulation that extends across varied media. In this section, I consider Etxebarria's use of technology and various media to stretch the limits of biofictional representation through what Henry Jenkins has referred to as transmedia storytelling. Transmedia storytelling is a process where "integral elements of a fiction" and its characters are "dispersed systematically" across multiple media or delivery channels. As a result, Jenkins argues, media consumers become "hunters and gatherers moving back and forth across different narratives trying to stitch together a coherent picture from the dispersed information."[36] These revisions in the way that complex stories are transmitted and adapted through interactions with readers reflect broader transformations in participatory culture, "profoundly altered by a succession of new media technologies which enable average citizens to participate in the archiving, annotation, appropriation, transformation, and recirculation of media content."[37] In turn, I see expanded participation through new media as central to the strategies of Etxebarria to draw the reader into her own auto/biographical spaces and to engage with narratives and characters across various platforms. Through the construction of her own "transmedia story," Etxebarria's construction and promotion of *Truth Is Nothing but a Moment of Falsehood* is an example of a multiplayer game carried out through varied media with Etxebarria as a hidden player.

The novel itself narrates the mysteries surrounding the death of Pumuky—the leader of a band called *Sex and Love Addicts*—and efforts to unravel the truth of what happened. Did he take his own life? Did someone else shoot him? Various people with a connection to Pumuky (girlfriends, lovers, friends, his manager, neighbors, mothers of friends) all claim knowledge of the real backstory. The reader has access to these differing clues and interview-style testimonies, but it is not clear how or whether these can ever be pieced into one credible narrative. Through this dispersive game, the biographical narrative remains open to the uncertain invention and intervention of networked sources, each with their own self-interested claims on how the narrative plays out (See Appendix A, Figure 5.1). As I will describe, the story world is complicated further by the fact that Etxebarria creates a real-world and social media presence for the fictional character of Pumuky and other members of the band that predates and prefigures their presence in the novel, and infuses her own biography in these identities. [See Appendix B]

Significantly, *Truth Is Nothing but a Moment of Falsehood* is a simulated, biofictional game because Etxebarria becomes a hidden player, assuming the "biographical avatar" of her created character, "Pumuky Guy Debord," among others, and playing out these selves through her social media presence, YouTube video, and other user-based formats. However, unlike a transparent or honest biofiction that affirms its fictional intentions and creative play, Etxebarria built interest in the novel through a series of orchestrated deceptions (what might be called "spectacles") intended to attract the reading public to interact with the simulated lives both outside and inside the novelistic space. For example, Etxebarria created a readership and fan base for Pumuky through Facebook, YouTube, and other media as a "real" biographical identity *before* she introduced him as a fictional character in the novel. For months prior to the release of the novel, Pumuky had "his" page on Facebook (one populated by Etxebarria as hidden player) with some 3,000 "friends" and a music video by Sex, Love and Addicts on YouTube—in which Etxebarria herself prominently appears—believable enough to invite a record offer from Sony. (Sony managers resurface as players in the novel.) Other features include a faked news report declaring the death of Pumuky, and showing a visibly distraught Etxebarria.

Given this unusual framing, I will concentrate on the structure of the novel through its external-facing design and promotion rather than on the contents of the storyline in order to explore the interplay that Etxebarria creates with the characters in the novel and her own biographical identity. Etxebarria uses social media to toy with how the simulated images and identities may not only mimic but also construct what we accept as real; however, this strategy also serves to create or multiply the difficulties readers face in distinguishing Etxebarria's creative production from the auto/biographical representations she shares on her public-facing profiles. For example, Etxebarria "plays" through multiple characters from the novel on social media. Prominently, through Etxebarria's adoption of the persona of Pumuky by her creation and "insertion" via "his" Facebook page, Pumuky becomes an alter ego "without anyone knowing" of her involvement, as she declares.[38] Further, when Etxebarria decides to "kill off" Pumuky, she uses Facebook to reveal the news through another biographical self-avatar and character in *Truth Is a Moment of Falsehood.* Through the character of "Romano," self-declared best friend of Pumuky, Etxebarria copies a post onto *her own* Facebook page that Romano has purportedly written on Pumuky's Facebook "wall": Romano writes on February 2, 2010:

> I am truly surprised about everything that's happened, that people question the existence of Pumuky. Pumuky has been more than real; he has been hyperreal. He has lived a life much more sincere than the majority of users of Facebook, who can't reveal anything about their lives because they are afraid that their girlfriend or their boss will read their profile ... Not real? What is real and what is not real? We live in a world in which the frontiers of reality and fiction don't exist anymore. The vast majority of the profiles on Facebook don't correspond to real, physical people with names in the Civil Registry and this does not keep them from interacting, relating to one another, EXISTING, in essence.[39]

The appearance of Romano—whose last name "Debord" clues us to the parallels with Pumuky's Facebook identity (Pumuky Guy Debord) and with the title of Etxebarria's novel itself, *Truth Is Nothing but a Moment of Falsehood* (citing from Guy Debord's *Society of the Spectacle*)—proliferates the play of identity while linking it to the essence of Etxebarria's novel. On the one hand, the use of Facebook to profile Pumuky and to build audience interest across social media appears to function simply as an elaborate spectacle or publicity stunt. At the same time, Etxebarria plays off these online narrative strategies to register the difficulty of distinguishing between the simulated and what we accept as real. For example, "Romano" writes in another reposted note on Etxebarria's wall (February 2, 2010) referring to

Etxebarria as both Lucía and "Olga," another character in *Truth Is Nothing but a Moment of Falsehood:*

> I remember that Lucía told me some time ago the story of when she was little and the clown from the TV show Fofó died, and she got to school and saw all of the little girls crying and she didn't understand why, since they didn't know the damn clown from Adam, and it wasn't like it was their uncle or their grandfather. Olga was old enough to know the clown was on the TV and not actually in her life ... In the same way, lots of people who did not know Pumuky cried for him because to them he was real, as he continues to be for us.[40]

By assuming these multiple online identities (Olga, Romano, Pumuky, Etxebarria "herself"), Etxebarria reveals how these supposedly individual auto/biographical selves become multiple, biofictional selves and sites of interaction whose realness among her readership may not be that different from that felt by the fans/followers of Fofó. However, while exposing this uncertainty, she also reinforces problems of trust that she herself manipulates. As Amanda Haas suggests, "if an avatar was once a projection of the human body and human values, as the Internet grew in popularity it was flattened into a mask. [...] [I]n the mixed-use spaces of the Internet—where some people were playing themselves and others were hoping to play tricks—avatars became ambiguous." She suggests that while on Facebook, you are supposed to just be "you," this "tech fantasy" means "proliferating online platforms have prompted us to create more and more conceptions of ourselves to send off into the world," and when the world becomes too much, to "let your avatar—a being who is endlessly malleable"—take over.[41]

Indeed, following Pumuky's "death," Etxebarria—inserting herself through Romano—decries the intervention of others in shaping and mythologizing *her* image. Thus, the identity confusion that the transmedia expansions of the novel both create and explore does not deal only with Pumuky, but self-consciously affects the author herself, mediated through Facebook and other platforms. Similarly, as we examined with respect to *Courtney and I*, Etxebarria acknowledges that her public personas take on their own lives. For example, comparing the false "avatars" in the press with the real Lucía to the game that Etxebarria plays in assuming her own fictional avatars, "Romano" writes on Etxebarria's Facebook page:

> In the same way, Lucía lives facing an avatar that does and says things that she doesn't do or say: she has never beaten up a renter, nor has she neglected to bathe her daughter, nor has she ever said that if she were a man, she would be in the academy ... But there exists someone with her name created by the media that carries out a life parallel to her own. In fact, things have gotten to the point where on Facebook Lucía has had

> to give up my original name so that they would not confuse her with this woman, who is called Lucía Etxebarria, and in her private profile has another name and another identity. And nobody has considered it until now a macabre game.[42]

McKenzie Wark refers to critical play through the "trifler," a player who subverts the aims of the simulation game and explores the limits of its rules and mechanics. Notably, we observe Etxebarria's use of trifler identities within the simulated game *both* as novelistic play and as fictional avatars that try to control *her* image and revise her "real" profile. However, as much as these stand-ins serve to contest versions of her public image she refutes, they also detach and slip away from Etxebarria as their creator. As she herself argues in reference to Pumuky, "I created him … such that the character took on his own life and there came a moment when I was completely outside of myself. You would have to call a psychoanalyst to explain what happened."[43] Just as we have seen with other derivatives, the speculative instruments we use to anchor or diversify potential valuations have a way of escaping determination and our control, especially when they no longer demonstrate connection to any underlying foundation.

Speculative Identities and Fanfiction

Elaborating on the construction of Etxebarria's novel as an interactive game, we can consider these strategies through what game designer Neil Young refers to as "additive comprehension," referring to the ways in which each additional text contributes a "new piece of information which forces us to revise our understanding of the fiction as a whole."[44] Rather than produce greater comprehension, however, in *Truth Is Nothing but a Moment of Falsehood*, these additions expose missing elements and fragmentation. Similarly, Jenkins argues that transmedia texts often "result in what might be seen as gaps or excesses in the unfolding of the story; that is, they introduce potential plots which cannot be fully told or extra details which hint at more than can be revealed. Readers, thus, have a strong incentive to continue to elaborate on these story elements, working them over through their speculations, until they take on a life of their own."[45]

Accordingly, fanfiction describes a process in which individual readers (so-called "fans") take aspects of the story and/or its characters and create their own narratives from it. This creative reworking opens up the creative work to "what if" scenarios not fully explored or explained in the original version. While "fan appropriation and transformation of media content" has often been derided for this derivative aspect, these strategies reflect transformations that allow readers to become "active participants in new patterns of media production and consumption."[46] As Jenkins describes, fanfiction becomes a means of rejecting the "definitive version produced, authorized, and regulated by some media conglomerate [or other authorizing power]. Instead, fans envision a world where all of us can participate in the creation and construction of central cultural myths."[47] In this sense, fanfiction becomes a challenge to the effort to singularize or rein in control over the fictionalization of biographical identities. Rather, anyone can speculate on the nature of these identities and imagine their future directions.

We can explore this concept of fanfiction both in terms of Etxebarria's pseudo-biographical novel, *Truth Is Nothing but a Moment of Falsehood*, and in terms of her own fans' (and anti-fans' or critics') participation in her image and narrative identities—the biofictions they create of *her*. Etxebarria's novel investigates the differing versions of aspects of Pumuky's life, what may have happened, and what may have led to his death, through the perspective of multiple individuals connected to (and "followers of") the "band." While not fans in a traditional sense, these characters are both "readers of" and "players in" his life, as each interacts with and sends his narrative in a differing direction. Additionally, each of the characters has his/her own incentives for wanting the story to unfold a specific way, either to absolve guilt regarding potential complicity in the outcome of Pumuky's unhappiness or simply to present themselves in the most positive light. Similarly, there is the acknowledgment that this speculation is a form of a game. At the beginning of the novel, Romano describes his desire not to try too hard to figure out Pumuky as a way to keep the game going: "I don't want to take apart the toy to figure out exactly how it works, only to end up understanding how it functions but not being able to play [with it] anymore."[48] In this sense, Romano takes on aspects of the role of the "trifler" as Wark has described it: "If a cheat is someone who ignores the space of the game to cut straight to its objective, then a trifler is someone who ignores the objective to linger within the space."[49]

Etxebarria's use of social media conforms to the creation of transmedia identities that seduce spectators/readers to intervene and become players in the narrative games of the text. Jenkins has argued that while transmedia fictions "create a unified and coordinated entertainment experience," viewers/readers are quick to perceive the gaps and to speculate on these through their own fictions. In this sense, the creators lose control over the singular or "coordinated" direction of the biographical narrative to the imaginations and stories of other participants.[50] Similarly, in *Truth Is Nothing More Than a Moment of Falsehood*, Etxebarria suggests how a firm image of Pumuky splinters into multiple literary recreations. Yet, despite Etxebarria's claims that what she wanted to show with this novel is that "no one is in possession of the truth," and that the same story, seen from thirteen different pairs of eyes, "is for each one a different story," she simultaneously laments this loss of control or authority over her own biographical image and story.[51] In almost identical terms to those she places in the "voice" of her (other) alter-ego

Romano on her Facebook page, Etxebarria decries the falsity of many of these published identities—what she alludes to as simulated—which in her view have overtaken the truth or the "real" Etxebarria in the public imagination. She declares, "I have had the experience of having an avatar, another person who lives in the hyperreality and that has done things that I have never done or said. When you live with an avatar, it consumes you. I have had a bad experience with all of this."[52]

Through her self-created avatar, Romano, Etxebarria contends on her Facebook page that what we decide to believe about an individual is not based upon uncovering some concertedly hidden truth, but more about creating a comfortable myth of a definitive explanation. As "Romano" asserts, "And in that way we create a fantasy and we pass it off as the substance of reality."[53] In turn, each of the characters takes the story, or their piece of it, in their own chosen direction, applying their own myths onto the essential framework and details. Similarly, the novel leaves open to interpretation the question of who has seduced whom into a myriad of myths. As one of the characters describes: "Pumuky wasn't more than ... something like a screen onto which so many people projected" their aspirations.[54]

We can contend that a similar process takes place through the interactions on Etxebarria's Facebook pages and through her participation across social media. Readers use these spaces to speculate on her (and their) identities and relationships, projecting their own myths and imagining her as they choose. In thinking about the blogs and social media sites that many of us zealously read and contribute to, and which authors (including ourselves) use as potent tools of self-construction and promotion, I am curious. To what extent, in constantly revising and re-casting ourselves to forge connections with readers, to "seduce" people into reading about us and our lives, do we find ourselves still lost, no closer or more certain of what we were seeking to know in the first place? To what extent do these attempts at autobiographical creation and biographical consumption mislead us into having discovered something real—the "real" Lucía Etxebarria, for example, or perhaps simply having established some elusively "real" connection with a present but absent individual in the first place. Alternatively, if it is all "just a game," what are we getting out of it? This blurred distinction or knowledge can extend not only to what we consume of what writers say is true about themselves or others, but to our own awareness of the uncertain boundaries between the real and the fictional, the biographical other and our own self-creations.

In this sense, the novel captures the unique cyber-characteristics of the contemporary context, in which the increasingly networked nature of our reality of constant access to images and information is coupled with a sense of absence and perpetual searching. In statistics, the coefficient of determination refers to how accurately a model explains and predicts an outcome based upon the correlation to independent variables. In Etxebarria's novel, as the last chapter title "Coefficient of Flight from the Desired Object" suggests, the myriad correlations among lives and stories and information lead us no closer to a sense of certainty or clarity regarding the "desired object." Rather, the novel reinforces the continued distance of the characters and the lack of resolution. Upon comparing the multiple versions of Pumuky's story, how the lies, misinterpretations, and deceits cloud the perception of those who surround him, the reader is left to decide the end of the novel. The object of the search—the figure of Pumuky—remains absent, and the mystery unsolved. The reader is left with only a multiplicity of options regarding who Pumuky may have been and what might have motivated him. He (like Etxebarria?) might be any of these, or none of them at all.

"Coefficient of the Flight from the Desired Object"

"Look for us" on Facebook, YouTube, and MySpace, Etxebarria invites the reader at the end of *Truth Is Nothing but a Moment of Falsehood* (see Appendix B). In this sense, she suggests that the narrative is not just contained within the pages of the novel but extends into other biographical purportedly "real" expressions of Etxebarria's and her readers' lives and selves. As I have described, she specifically created this reality a priori the characters' appearance in the novel, building the narratives of the characters across multiple media and inviting their "friends" to follow them across various platforms. At the same time, once having let the reader in on her game she maintains the ruse and co-opts the reader into continuing to play along. On Etxebarria's Facebook page, Romano describes how easy it was to open the profile of Pumuky on "his" page. The password was the name of his mother, Charlotte. Of course, at this point the reader knows that Etxebarria, Pumuky, and Romano are all the same person—so of course it is easy for "Romano" to know the password. However, in this way Etxebarria also plays with the illusion of a key or hidden password that will unlock the secrets and let us in on the real biographical identity of another person.

Amid the shifting narrative identities, there is the sense that if we could only figure out the design—get outside the game—we could determine who or what to believe. But there is the simultaneous consciousness that we are embedded *in* the game, and there is no outside or objective observer to declare a firm answer, a concrete winner or loser, a decisive end to the search. Etxebarria seems to want it both ways: to suggest she is in control of the game as designer and at the same time that there is no distinction between game and reality, or at least no way to distinguish between the real and the simulation. Yet, if this is the case, Etxebarria neglects that she is also part of other's biographical games, with their own hidden players.

One of the stories from Etxebarria's pseudo-biographical collection, *A Love Story Like Any Other*, perhaps best explores what happens when readers become hidden players.[55] The vignette "A Heart on the Ceiling"[56] tells the story of a Spanish writer invited to a conference in Montreal. At the conference, she befriends one of its organizers (Adrian) who introduces her to one of his friends (Gabriel). On the last night of the conference, amid a mutual attraction, the protagonist and Gabriel fall into what appears to be a one-night stand, as the Etxebarria-figure is leaving the next day. Yet, once apart, the two undertake a virtual relationship through email and phone sex, which begins to seem more real and satisfying to the protagonist than her own tangible reality.

The story then investigates what happens when she actually tries to enter the simulated world and to make it real. A few days before a planned visit to finally go and visit Gabriel in person, he tells her that he has met someone else. Since it is so close to the date of the trip, Gabriel's roommate, Adrian, convinces her to go anyway as his guest. The visit is initially very awkward, as the protagonist and Gabriel carefully avoid each other. However, toward the end of her trip, the sexual attraction crystallizes amid a torrid scene of lovemaking on the top of an apartment building roof, as various onlookers in other buildings voyeuristically look on. While the protagonist has built her image of the relationship with Gabriel on the character she created for him in her secret game, Etxebarria's narrative reinforces the extent to which they are both objects of play in the simulation games of other spectators. While Gabriel insists that the reason his roommate encouraged her to make the trip was out of courtesy, the protagonist doubts otherwise, noting that Adrian himself later told her that he had been in on their "game," listening to their telephone conversations. These hidden listening sessions gave him the opportunity to play out his fantasy, to substitute himself in the role of the protagonist and imagine *himself* with Gabriel.

Notably, the protagonist thought the game was all *hers*, and that she had control over its direction and evolving narrative. Yet, through Adrian's involvement, she has become in essence an unknowing character in *his* game, one that in turn manipulates hers to conform to his desired reality. The traditional view of the voyeur is purely exploratory, to use Ryan's term, in that the spectator's involvement does not affect the narrative events themselves. Instead, in this case, the role of the voyeur alters the history of what takes place. Adrian gives the appearance of being fully outside the game that Gabriel and the protagonist have constructed, when in reality he is another hidden player, altering the conditions by which the narrative develops.

The progressive loss of the real to the simulated, and the further dispersion of that authority through the intervention of other players, has added significance when considered in terms of Etxebarria's insistence that she has based these characters on real lives. The permeability in Etxebarria's work between authorial persona and her characters' lives has often shaped critical reception of her work. Through her personal blog, Facebook, Twitter, interviews, and most recently participation in a reality TV show, Etxebarria's approach reflects low barriers to participation with her readership. Just as with other transmedia story spaces, users are quick to perceive the gaps and excesses in *her* biography and to speculate on these through their own narratives. In turn, Etxebarria has both promoted this permeability and fallen victim to it, showing how the interactive construction of biographical identity (especially the pursuit of celebrity) can overshadow the value of literary production.

At the end of 2010, Lucía Etxebarria's Facebook site was removed or "deactivated" by Facebook. An article in the newspaper *El Mundo* (November 24, 2010) indicates that Facebook closed two of her profiles in late 2010.[57] One of these closed accounts was attributed to Pumuky Guy Debord, including references to the invented character's exploits "involving drugs and sex." The other was a personal profile, which, while belonging to the author, used a pseudonym ("a false name"). In turn, Etxebarria denounced the "censorship" of the social network and the erasure of her correspondence of over a year and a half, "along with thousands of photos, poems, reviews, and commentaries of immense sentimental value from friends and fans." While her public-facing Facebook page has since reappeared, these developments are a clear example of how (perhaps at the hands of a biographical other) identities, images, and narratives can similarly slip away.

Endgame

What should we make, if anything, of Lucía Etxebarria's precipitous fall from media darling to literary pariah, of her exiting the world of publishing, even appearing in a televised reality show ("Summer Camp"), in which she very literally becomes a participant in a shallow game world of others' design? Is this version of her narrative arc just an easy way of resolving a complicated biography? Reconstituting the rules of Etxebarria's own game, that "it doesn't interest [her] as much who Courtney is as who we *think she is*," it would be very easy to substitute Etxebarria here in Courtney's place. We could resign Etxebarria and ourselves to her contention that the myth is inseparable from the real. Yet, I have argued throughout this book that a limitation of postmodernism or an element of its exhaustion is to forego the effort of narrative to creatively transform reality and to see it only as a self-referential game, as fiction that only reflects on itself rather than trying to reveal something real, in the sense of more transcendent. In so doing, Etxebarria demonstrates the limitations of her approach to exceed beyond the reflexivity and permeability of the simulated with her biographical reality.

Etxebarria has wanted to project herself as an internal, ontological player; yet, she has often remained external and exploratory to the lives she imagines. She has been innovative in imagining the interactive design of biofictional creation by dispersing representations of herself and her narratives across multiple platforms and inviting her readers to play into those constructions. However, she has missed a critical aspect of biofictional play, which is to deepen understanding of interiority as a means of engaging with the gaps and uncertainties of our biographical lives. In this context, transforming biofictional play aspires to what Gibbons, Vermeulen, and van den Akker refer to as "a renewed need or wish to experience the world as possessing depth, as *real*, even amidst a lingering postmodern skepticism."[58] One of the key features of biofiction is the effort to enter into the speculative subjectivity of another individual and for the writer to immerse him/herself in simulated fashion as a way of reaching beyond the limitations of the textual world. Yet, while Etxebarria enters into others' lives, she has remained largely a surface player, perceiving biographical identity as shaped only by manipulation, invention, and construction.

As Thomas Malaby has suggested, "as it is played, [a game] always contains the potential for generating new practices and new meanings, possibly refiguring the game itself."[59] Etxebarria's approach demonstrates the risks of the contemporary, "gamified" reality of constant immersion in which we can so readily play into the construction and revision of others' biographical narratives for self-interested aims. Yet, the relevance of biofiction is the capacity to continue to adapt and refigure the networked versions of our biographical lives to generate new meanings. Etxebarria is right that we should revisit the constructions of our myths, but not with the aim of simply simulating them in different form. As writer Lauren Groff suggests, to create new narrative paradigms within our networked reality, we would have to break with the idea of the "Disney-given hero, or maybe the Greek-given idea, of a single hero who is able to save us all. Because that's not how history really works. It's a collective action when good things happen."[60] Beyond endlessly constructing and deconstructing icons, representations, and myths, or being determined by the interventions of other players, we can interpret the gaps in biographical narratives as opportunities for adaptive design and collective experimentation with these evolving modes of interactivity. In so doing, rather than seeing biofictional co-creation as the loss of authority and autonomy, we can employ it to keep real human possibility in play.

Appendix A

Maze of Interconnections: Networked Map Etxebarria includes in *Truth Is Nothing but a Moment of Falsehood*

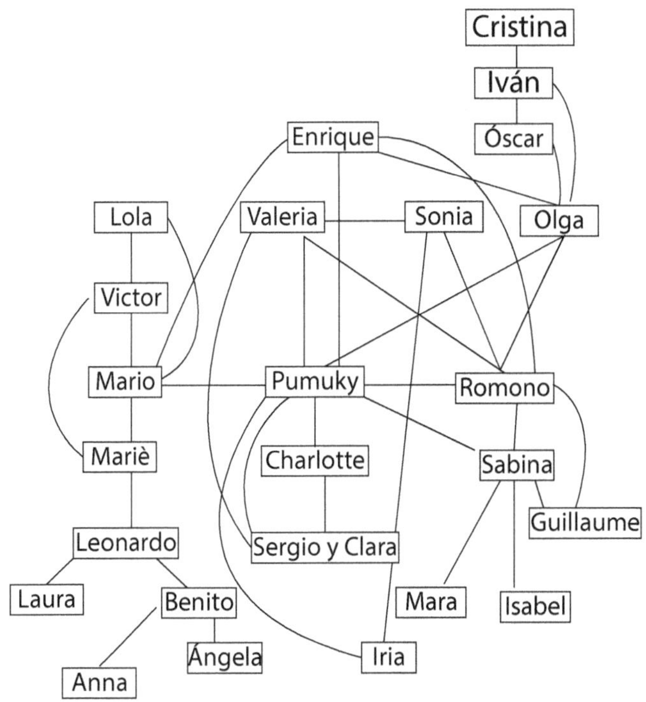

FIGURE 5.1 *Addendum at end of* Truth Is Nothing but a Moment of Falsehood.

Appendix B

"Look for us on Facebook with these identities:"
Búscanos en Facebook con estas identidades:
Romano Debord
Pumuky Guy Debord
Lucia Etxebarria
SLA en MySpace:
www.myspace.com/ sexandloveaddicts
Coge palomitas de SLA en YouTube:
www.youtube.com/watch?v=fqRe5V2QbdA

Appendix

6

Literary Afterlives and Paratextual Play: Elvira Navarro's *The Last Days of Adelaida García Morales* and Antonio Orejudo's *The Famous Five and Me*

This chapter considers novels by Elvira Navarro and Antonio Orejudo that use diverging strategies of paratextual play to reimagine the interconnections among two biographical writers' creations and their literary afterlives. In *The Last Days of Adelaida García Morales* (2016), Navarro explores the ethical complexities and competing motivations of the process of biofictional creation through the backstory and decisions surrounding the making of a fictional documentary of the late author, Adelaida García Morales.[1] *The Famous Five and Me* (2017) also creates an immersive biofictional game that documents the making of a type of sequel or "spinoff."[2] Spinoffs appropriate and adapt originating works, often in ways that critically reimagine the present by de-emphasizing fidelity to the predecessor version.[3] Orejudo appropriates and imaginatively interacts with the literary afterlives of characters from a favorite childhood series, relocating them to a Spanish context and interweaving their afterlives with his past and present in ways that challenge the ethical choices of his own generation.

In his original definition, Gérard Genette defines paratext as a "threshold," an "undefined zone" between the textual and outside world. These include "those liminal devices and conventions" that mediate its reception, including titles, prefaces, forewords, epilogues, notes, and afterwords (peritexts), but also external elements such as interviews, reviews, and correspondences (epitexts).[4] These elements can both frame and subvert the authority and intention of the originating text, opening it to alternative understandings. Game scholars have more recently broadened Genette's concept to incorporate "any element that forms a figurative threshold of a text and that grounds it in a socio-historical context," without limitations on authorship, including criticism and journalism, fanfiction, alternate reality games, tie-in novels or spinoffs, and transmedia storytelling. Moreover, as Jan Švelch observes, the concept of paratextuality was originally introduced as part of larger typology of *transtextuality*, intended to tackle relationships among "texts, cultural practices, and socio-historical circumstances."[5] Along these lines, Navarro and Orejudo play across and between the indefinite worlds of biographical invention and the surrounding sociohistorical reality, evoking political, moral, and other real problems beyond the text. Most importantly, these works demonstrate how participatory formats challenge the autonomy of "authorized" narratives and biographical identities, revising and expanding their interpretative and real effects within alternative contexts.

I use the term paratextual play to emphasize the dynamic interaction among multiple stakeholders both within and outside the text competing for control over the production and reception of biofictional meaning. Steven Jones has argued that "what Genette saw as a limited device supplementing the main text can now be taken to describe an everyday and essential character" that often subverts the primacy of the main text.[6] In his view, popular games "[are] predominantly paratextual. That is, the formerly limited role of the paratext, to serve as a threshold or transactional space between the text and the world, has now moved to the foreground, has become the essence of the text."[7] This shift underscores the relevance of player/audience perspective to influence and intercede in the side of production, which has been a more dominant focus of Genette's model. As a form that actively intervenes in the liminal space between responsibility to the recorded life of the nominatively real biographical subject and the freedom of imaginative creation, biofiction embodies the negotiated crossover between these discursive claims. Each derivative version or "spinoff" creates a new opportunity to reboot: to reposition and imagine anew the possible extensions and permutations of a biographical life. Furthermore, I consider how the uncertainty of these strategic interactions can be examined through the concept of game theory and the structure of game play.

Elvira Navarro's *The Last Days* creates a fictional account of recent events preceding the author's death and the subsequent efforts on the part of characters with only peripheral knowledge of García Morales to affirm their versions of her uncertain biography. Despite widespread recognition and acclaim for her novels *The South* (*El sur seguido por Bene,* 1985), made into a famous film by her then-husband Víctor Erice, and *The Silence of the Sirens* (*El silencio de las sirenas,* 1993), García Morales died in relative obscurity. Inspired by what she says was a real anecdote in which García Morales went to a Cultural Ministry office seeking 50 euros so that she could visit her son in Madrid, Navarro's fictional narrative is less a biographical profile than an exploration of the risks and responsibilities we have in evoking the myths, silences, absences, and enigmas of another life. What unfolds is the intersection of two fictional narratives—one involving the Cultural Office employee who denied García Morales the financial assistance, and another by a film director seeking to make a documentary about the late author, drawing from far-flung witnesses with sparse insights into her life. Intervening in these competing narratives is the critical voice of Navarro, who exposes the hypocrisy of self-interested players who manipulate memory and biographical narrative to their own advantage. In so doing, Navarro calls into question the ability to convey honestly who García Morales may have been or what kinds of biographical truth are possible. Notably, in using García Morales' life as a paradigm to explore these issues, Navarro has in turn been the subject of criticism, most notably by García Morales' ex-husband, film director Víctor Erice, who has accused Navarro of self-interested appropriation. Through interviews and other media in which Navarro has contested these claims, the paratextual framing that Genette described as conditioning the intentionality and interests of the author (and other authorizing partners, such as the publisher) becomes a contested space regarding the ethics of Navarro's text and of biofiction more broadly.

While in *The Last Days*, Navarro creates a "false documentary" in the mode of fiction, Antonio Orejudo's *The Famous Five and Me* creates a different form of secondary co-creation. The childhood characters of the "Famous Five," a popular series by British author Enid Blyton that Orejudo grew up reading, are reimagined in their adult versions through narratives that intersect and blend with the biographies of the author's own childhood friends and himself. The author invents a biofictional version of his friend and fellow writer, Rafael Reig, who within the fiction writes a prominent sequel (*After Five*) imagining the characters' lives forty years later. The strategy of having Orejudo play as a simulated character "in" the embedded spinoff created by "Reig" and simultaneously as creator of the narrative game involving real and fully invented players embodies the fluid threshold between playing into others' fictional lives and revising one's own. Within the novel, the spinoff functions to reexamine the author's earlier reception of the series to comment satirically and critically on his own generation then and now.

Game Theory and Narrative Strategy

The term "model" (circumstantial, speculative, game theory) within this book communicates how forms of biofiction reveal, respond to, and revise approaches to uncertainty and risk across diverse fields and ways of knowing, suggesting how the world informs literary experimentation and vice versa. A model simplifies something more complicated in an effort to produce understanding. Markedly, in *Radical Uncertainty*, John Kay and Mervyn King describe game theory as an "effort to turn a mystery into a puzzle."[8] Kay and King underscore how such models are not effective as direct representations of reality because they cannot express the actual uncertainty and contingency of life; instead, they must be understood narratively, suggestively. They use the Prisoner's Dilemma as an example. In this prototypical game theory scenario, two prisoners have to make decisions about whether to confess or not without knowledge of what the other chooses. They can either betray the other for personal gain or assume the uncertain risks of cooperation. As the authors observe, the Prisoner's Dilemma is not actually talking about the criminal justice system. "A small-world model is a fictional narrative, and its truth is found in its *broad insights rather than its specific detail*" (emphasis mine). The protagonist in these models is "not an actual person or business, but an artificial construct, every bit as much a conceit of the author as is Sherlock Holmes"[9]. Rather than fidelity to mimetically representing a biographical life, the use of biographical figures in a fictional work can similarly model and provide insights into complex dynamics within an interconnected reality.

As a framework for conceiving social situations among competing players whose decisions affect and are impacted by the possible decisions of others, game theory serves as a useful backdrop for examining the biofictional interplay in these two works. A key facet is how multiple players—readers, critics, biographical subject(s), and others with vested interests in how a life story is told—can increasingly intercede in the process of paratextual framing, subverting the primacy or authority of a precursor or predominant version. For example, the choices that Navarro explores through the competing strategies of the characters within the novel ultimately prefigure and play out in real-life polemics regarding the novel's publication, mediated largely through competing paratexts. Varied players claim a stake in the dispute over the freedom of the biographical novelist to her fictional vision. The textual game and the debate over its after-effects on real lives thus generate their own strategic interaction that engages with the risks, responsibilities, narrative payoffs, and ethical limits of biofictional creation. This is not an ancillary or sidebar discussion, but one that feeds back into, and challenges the interpretation and reception of, Navarro's novel.

Orejudo's *The Famous Five and Me* adopts a different form of paratextual game play. Orejudo creates a biofictional spinoff within the novel in which the earlier choices of the characters in their fictional, serialized storyworld are reimagined through future interactions that cross back and forth across the fictional threshold to reappraise the author's perceptions of his own generation in the present. The characters' childhood representations as successful, daring explorers working collaboratively in pursuit of a shared mission give way in their adult versions to passivity and tacit participation in the dominant, materialist games of others, emphasizing consumption, self-interest, and zero-sum competition at the expense of ideals. Through the "small world narrative" of the spinoff, Orejudo revises precursor forms of the characters while questioning existing social and political paradigms in which his generation has tacitly or with more complicity benefited from and played into, positing the powerful ways that games intervene in realities. As Patrick Jagoda suggests in a different context, these writers are interested in the more challenging questions of "how immersive and interactive game worlds can enable players to experiment with the reality of both the neoliberal subject and a world that is perpetually in flux."[10] Thus, while, on the one hand, a game-like world of paratextual play suggests the dispersion of authorial control, it also opens to the possibility of critically examining alternative modes for understanding and imagining more ethical and participatory realities.

Paratexts and the Ethics of Biofictional Prerogative in *The Last Days of Adelaida García Morales*

Elvira Navarro has emphasized repeatedly that her novel is a work of fiction and not intended as a biographical portrait of Adelaida García Morales. As she has asserted, García Morales is the "catalyst but not the protagonist of [her] book." Instead, she argues that she uses her biographical character as a "paradigm" that, by reflecting on precariousness and the uncertain construction of memory and identity, sets in motion the ethical conflicts involving two fictional protagonists: the Cultural Affairs assistant and the documentary filmmaker.[11] Navarro has said that one of her principal motivations for writing the novel was to examine the silences and absences surrounding the figure of García Morales, despite her earlier literary prominence and inclusion among canonical Spanish writers of the late twentieth century. When García Morales died in 2014, Navarro notes in an interview, it seemed she had been gone for a long time.[12] There was little publicity recognizing her death or acknowledgment of her literary impact, and the limited press regarding her achievements often highlighted the influence of her earlier marriage to filmmaker Víctor Erice. So, when Navarro received two emails from writer friend and sociologist, Rosario Izquierdo Chaparro, the story of the disappearance of the author from public life and abandonment by the cultural institutions and network within which she had once been a leading voice seemed to Navarro to contain broader insights. Defending her choice to fictionalize the life of the author and its difference with biography, Navarro has asserted, "I didn't research the author. This wasn't the objective I sought, but to be faithful to the impression of strangeness and fear that her disappearance invoked in me, as well as the sensation of injustice that invades me when I see the indifference toward cultural heritage and memory that there is in this country."[13]

As referenced previously, Lucia Boldrini has examined the tension implicit within biofiction between historicity and the freedom to liberate the biographical subject to new imaginings. This involves both the opportunity to give voice to someone whose story might otherwise be silenced or misapprehended, and the potential implications of appropriating another person's biography while substituting one's own perspective and narrative reconstruction for theirs, without their consent.[14] As I have argued in this book, and García Morales' example highlights, there are also real costs involved in remaining silent—avoiding the moral risks of speaking through another but remaining complicit with dominant interpretations that deny the expression of alternative possibilities. Navarro's novel illuminates and puts these ethical conflicts in contraposition through the internal conflicts of the characters within the novel and across the threshold of the text through the critical reception of readers and critics who weigh in on these questions. Navarro's use of García Morales' real name and details of her life prompted substantial controversy regarding what right she had to "appropriate" the author's life, and challenging whether her creative intentions contributed new insights or were more self-interested. Professor and literary critic Ana Caballé affirms that "this debate is more pertinent than ever" because of the recent profusion of works blending the real and the fictive. For her, the question is what this inspiration in real life offers—"a new way of seeing things, a new creation," or simply the expression of "more or less anecdotic details" that result in exploiting another's story.[15] Thus, the very questions that the novel itself explores with respect to the implications of representing another life also play out in the real, extratextual world through the ethical debates surrounding Navarro's freedom to use the figure of the late author in her biofiction.

Through alternating chapters, the novel examines the ethical and creative dilemmas of the two fictional protagonists. The Cultural Affairs assistant who (within the novel at least) denied García Morales the 50 euros she requested tries to justify her decision in an effort to ameliorate her guilt and fear of blame over her unwillingness to extend help to the author. Her principal preoccupation is whether to put together some type of tribute that might offer cover for their bureaucratic inaction and place the Cultural Affairs office in a better light. Ultimately, this also fails to transpire, undermining her "noble" intentions: "The idea of hosting a tribute, given the scant reverberations over the death of the author, went from being an obligation and a solution" for the problem in which she'd become embroiled to a "noble, romantic project in which she felt deeply invested, but in which she would not expend any more energy. [...] What's more, there was no sense spending an already meager budget on an event that nobody would attend. Hardly anybody in the town knew she was living there. Very few, in fact, even knew of her."[16]

The ethical conflicts of the documentary filmmaker involve the difficulty of getting past the mythology of biographical narratives surrounding the figure of Adelaida García Morales, as the fictional director engages with a series of characters, all of whom feel authorized to put forward their own theories regarding her silence, her withdrawal from the world, and her mental health. The filmmaker chooses to interview three people who claim knowledge of the author at different times in her life: a childhood friend, the mother of a school friend of García Morales' son, and a psychiatrist who treated the author. They offer conflicting and contentious testimony, each trying to dominate the conversation and demonstrate how the other is wrong in their representation of the author. The director increasingly questions not only what is real or imagined regarding their versions of the author, but also debates the appropriateness and sufficiency of her original documentary aims and strategies to reveal the enigmatic figure of García Morales. When she edits the film she has collected, she is not happy with the result. "*Hadn't she always considered her documentary a type of free recreation or atmospheric sequel to the novels of García Morales and of the fictional character, not actual person, that she was? Wouldn't it make sense, then, to shift to fiction*? She would reaffirm this idea, reminding herself that people often confuse verisimilitude with what is verifiably true, and that it would be better for the film to discount this false perception from the start, to make clear that her production did not seek to represent the actual life or work of anybody"[17] (emphasis mine).

In Genette's original definition, the paratext, especially in the "epitext," which is outside the boundaries of the book but part of its reception, establishes a "transactional space of exchange" with the sociohistorical reality.[18] Much of the epitextual discussion surrounding *The Last Days* has to do with the intentions and authority of Navarro to appropriate and fictionalize details of García Morales' life. Significantly, the narrative game within the novel of competing motives and strategic interactions with respect to the life and fictional afterlife of Adelaida García Morales ultimately models the tensions and ethical debates that take place in the immediate wake of the publication of Navarro's novel, interacting with *its* textual afterlife. While for Genette a key feature of paratext was that "the author or one of his associates accepts responsibility for it," under the more expanded definition of games theorists, this threshold extends to the interplay among multiple stakeholders.[19] Jonathan Gray has contended that "it is not only the triangle of producers, texts, and audiences that requires scholarly attention but also the links and spaces between these elements, which are to a large degree enabled by paratextual phenomena," conditioning all three.[20] In the subsequent section, I explore how the textual afterlife of

Navarro's novel intersects with the dynamics within *The Last Days* and its paratextual framing to open the novel to wider questions regarding the ethical boundaries of biofiction.

The Critical Afterlives of *The Last Days of Adelaida García Morales*

Soon after Navarro published *The Last Days*, García Morales' ex-husband Víctor Erice published an outraged essay in Spain's most circulated newspaper, *El País*, with the following headline: "A Stolen Life."[21] In this essay, Erice denounces the appropriation or "theft" of his ex-wife's biographical identity, accusing Navarro of "banalizing her memory as a writer" and trivializing "her identity as a human being." Erice pointed to the book's cover description as a "kind of false documentary in the form of fiction." "Curiously enough," he asserts, "Navarro had no problem affirming that she didn't really know anything about the last days of Adelaida García Morales beyond the allusive anecdote, and that she hadn't tried to research further. Given these circumstances, I can't help but ask on what *moral* and *intellectual authority* Elvira Navarro appropriated the name [of the author] for herself."[22] Elaborating further, he points to Navarro's declaration at the end of the narrative in the paratextual "Clarifications" that her book "is a work of fiction. Everything that it narrates is false and in no way should be read as a chronicle of the last days of Adelaida García Morales." He contends, "This reference to the 'false' character of her own narration betrays a basic confusion of Navarro with respect to literary creation. Because narrative fictions truthfully achieved [...] are not defined by inspiration *necessarily* in the real, but achieve on their own—without having to refer externally to their sources—a greater sense of truth." Lastly, he concludes that Navarro used García Morales' name out of self-interest, without concern for the damage it might cause third parties. "More than one person might ask themselves," he writes, whether her use of the author's real name "did not possess an obvious marketing aspect. Because it seems clear that if Elvira Navarro had titled her book *The Last Days of Paquita Martínez* it would not have produced the oversized media and commercial attention from which the novel is benefiting."[23]

It is worth noting that Erice refers to various paratexts within Navarro's novel, while making very little reference to the content of the novel itself, noting that his attention was drawn, along with the title and cover description, to addendums titled Epilogue, Clarifications, and Credits. He comments that this last section includes a "hodgepodge of references—many of them from the internet, inexact, and in part bibliographic—more appropriate of essays and biographies that seem destined to tell us something, rather than a made-up story with a substratum amply documented." Notably, Erice references the two emails from Izquierdo Chaparro, which Navarro includes in full within the "Clarifications" section, and which she has indicated were the inspiration for her novel. However, he ignores his own mention in one of them, in which Izquierdo writes, "And according to the doctor, Víctor Erice had broken off all contact with her [García Morales]."[24]

The criticisms that Erice raises regarding questions of ownership and intention related to biofiction's creative use of biographical lives are not new. "I hope each one of us owns the facts of his or her own life," Bethany Layne has quoted Ted Hughes' letter to *The Guardian* contesting "the repeated removal of his family's name from Sylvia Plath's grave."[25] As Layne reflects, "Hughes would no doubt have been horrified by their subsequent appropriation in biographical fiction, in texts such as Kate Moses' *Wintering* (2003), and *The Ballad of Sylvia and Ted* (2001), the latter doubly outrageous for being penned by his sometime mistress."[26] She adds, "There remain, however, many unanswered questions about the custody battle of the facts of a life that biographical fiction effects. Did the subject, contra Hughes, ever own such facts to begin with? Is it a forcible takeover or a negotiated sharing? And why has the post(postmodern) post-truth world proven so hospitable for these facts to be contested?"[27] Michael Lackey has argued that "biofiction appropriates a subject's life and works by way of revealing a personal vision, regardless of the factual accuracy of the portrayal." But he has gone on to ask, "Should writers have total freedom with regard to altering facts about their biographical subject?"[28]

Notably, Erice's essay similarly "appropriated" and framed much of the ensuing dialogue regarding Navarro's novel, often overtaking critical discussion of the novel itself. An *El País* article notes that while the book launch in Barcelona had been planned for soon after its publication on September 22, "nobody foresaw that it would coincide with the article that the filmmaker Víctor Erice" had published the day before. "I knew that I was entering into a risky zone," Navarro is quoted as saying, and yet "I explain throughout that it is a fiction [...] I put it on the cover and in two other explicit mentions; I couldn't put it on each page."[29] A profusion of other articles appeared with such titles as "Erice-Navarro: Novels Retouched with Photoshop"[30]; "Toxic Fictions"[31]; and "Fiction Also Hurts," subtitled, "The article by Víctor Erice sparks a debate about the limits of fiction in literature." Within this essay, Maribel Marín Yarza inquires, "Should a writer impose limits when playing with reality and fiction so as not to hurt people that have been made into characters? Is everything game in literary creation? To what point is it fair to use the name of a person and invent a life that is not researched?"[32] In a separate piece, Javier Rodríguez Marcos writes, "It's possible that, as the author states, the protagonist of *The Last Days of Adelaida García Morales* is not the *historical* Adelaida García Morales, but everything revolves around her: from the title to the bibliography. It is strange that the family would remain on the margin of so much documentation."[33]

While critical reviews of a novel have always affected their reception, what seems significant here is that so little of this debate has to do with the *actual novel* of Navarro and how much emerges and circulates from the paratexts (the "buzz" or "anti-buzz") around it. We could think of this as the legends or *mythology* surrounding Navarro's text. In turn, while Navarro expresses an intimate knowledge of a number of García Morales' works, she makes a point of not doing additional research by consulting with her relatives or others close to the author. Is she right to do this? An important feature of the post-postmodern context is the speed and ease with which we can access all sorts of secondary information without knowledge of how accurate or carefully vetted it may be. For example, the two emails from Rosario Izquierdo Chaparro that Navarro includes in the "Clarifications" contain a number of contradictions that are never resolved. These emails themselves are based on "hearsay" reports of what Izquierdo Chaparro had heard from others about the details of García Morales' request.

In fact, Navarro's biofiction of García Morales and the paratextual play that it has inspired both incorporate these questions and exhibit the risks and responsibilities involved in the ongoing fictional construction of literary afterlives. As I have suggested, *The Last Days* plays out many of these ethical questions within the text, conflicts then further replayed through the media (as "trending topic") in the critical reception to her novel. What would it constitute to betray a biographical figure in a biofiction? Does García Morales' ex-husband have any more claim to the facts of her biography than Navarro does? What *does* Navarro gain by using García Morales' real name that wouldn't have been possible if she had, as Erice suggests, given her a fictional name such as Paquita Martinez? The following section examines these questions further, referring both to how they emerge within the text and in the paratext in its broadest sense—the threshold or mediation between the text and the real identities in the world.

Defending Navarro's biofictional use of García Morales' real name, writer and *El País* literary critic Carlos Pardo observes, "Navarro's book belongs to a tradition of works that question why a successful author is erased from the map." He contends that using García Morales real name is essential because it is exactly that silence and erasure of the real biographical figure of García Morales and her literary production that Navarro's book seeks to redress. "Nobody asked Mörike for *Mozart's Journey to Prague* nor Büchner for *Lenz* to provide documentation or to consult with the family. I think this book is being judged as if it were an official biography or journalism." Pardo argues further that "the most generative literature is that which plays with the uncertainty between reality and fiction. [...] The limit of literature is the obligation to narrate what is possible, to exceed the boundaries of where history can go, and to transform possibility into the creation of questions."[34]

Further refuting Erice's perspective on Navarro's novel, Cristina Morales, in an essay titled "Elvira Navarro: A Question of Authority" has claimed that with the publication of his article, "the floodgates opened. Others piled on, calling Navarro indecent and a perpetrator of an immoral act." Countering these claims, Morales argues that these attacks are not only directed at Navarro. What Erice and his supporters "under the pretext of pain and emotions (justifying that, moreover, by means of the media infrastructure granted [him] by virtue of the authority he holds [...]")—are attacking, in her view, is "a way of understanding literature, a form of writing, and an appreciation of the creative process."[35]

Navarro plays out through the director her own metaliterary reflections regarding her choice of biofiction. Toward the end of the novel, amid the crisis that the director experiences when she reviews the preliminary version of her documentary and decides to abandon her earlier approach, she announces three decisions regarding her creative process that will guide the revision of the film. The first two of these are that in depicting the re-encounter with the writer García Morales, the film will take as its point of departure the part of the novel by the author that Erice did not finish filming, and that it should take place in a small town in Seville. Despite its title, the earlier film never completed the portion of the novel in the south. In contrast to the excess of realism she claims Erice erroneously relied upon, the director determines her imaginative vision of García Morales "could not be of this world," because she contends, [for her] "she was not real."[36] In this sense, the director opts for her own creative spinoff, "a *type of free recreation or atmospheric sequel to the novels of García Morales and of the fictional character, not actual person,* that she was" (emphasis mine). These facets are important because they reclaim the direction of Adelaida García Morales' biofictional afterlife with the imaginative continuation of the author's novelistic creation, rather than leaving it with the version of her ex-husband.

Yet, the third choice is the most significant. For example, explaining her choice to shift gears and to construct her film as a fiction, the director observes:

> For a while longer, she would vacillate about the benefits of introducing, as a secondary thread, the views of a number of experts about the narrative of the writer, but ultimately not even this small digression seemed tolerable. The idea of pursuing such an established path would end up paralyzing this radical form in which being wrong, even a complete failure, is better than abdication. What is the obligation to offer the perspectives of experts when the power of her relationship with García Morales doesn't have to do with the [external] validation of her work, but with intuitions, with such amorphous material that only the creative process could give shape to?[37]

I'm thinking deeply here about how for many years García Morales had chosen to live in relative anonymity and remain "unknown" rather than be perceived, appraised, or judged—by other mothers, husbands, children, psychiatrists—which feels like at least part of why the earlier documentary form starts to feel wrong or immoral to the director. The filmmaker, via Navarro, chooses instead a more imaginative direction that draws from her own private relationship to the writer's work—not to create a biographical, but a subjective, intuitive vision. It seems significant, moreover, that the Cultural Affairs assistant, while ultimately avoiding a public tribute, still finds her own way to discovering the late writer's work and to leave a note in her mailbox that communicates that privately held acknowledgment.

Rather than trying to capture the biographical image of García Morales, to *represent* the real, which—as Navarro has contended in an interview, would be just another fiction—she separates the aims of biofiction from aims of *resemblance* to those of *creative adaptation*. That is, rather than seeing the difficulty of fully reproducing the "real" as a failure, it offers the possibility of discovering new modes of access and understanding that would not have been possible through facts or testimony. Gary Botolotti and Linda Hutcheon have observed the critical tendency in contemporary culture to denigrate adaptations, as "secondary and derivative in relation to what is usually and (tellingly) referred to as the 'original.'" Yet, they argue that the "fidelity to the 'original' could, in fact, be seen as irrelevant to the actual evaluation of the 'success' of the adaptation for two reasons." One, the adaptation or biofictional version stands on its own merits. More importantly, the risks of shifting away fidelity concerns open up new ways of "thinking about the human desire to tell and retell certain stories, resetting them in wildly different times and places, and using a wide variety of media to do so."[38] The character of the psychiatrist in the novel is an example of those who, using their authority, seek to impose the dominance of their perspective and to limit the freedom to imagine alternatives. In the epitextual space, Erice's criticism could be understood similarly. It is significant, in turn, that it is the female director who ultimately decides that the film must be a fiction.

In the "Epilogue," Navarro lists a series of biographical details that the director found on the internet. She notes that "as the documentary, titled *The Last Days of Adelaida García Morales*, avoided the biographical perspective, the facts are not checked. There is contradictory information, and surely more than one false or imprecise detail."[39] While this seems emblematic of navigating the uncertain post-postmodern context we live in, the effect is to emphasize both the profusion of biographical data and its limitations or relevance to convey the "broad insights" or imaginative vision and "fictional world narrative" the director puts forth. Navarro has claimed that she sought to honor García Morales by continuing to grapple with the incompleteness of her memory and the many possible permutations of her literary creations. By using the real name of García Morales, Navarro engages with the ethical questions regarding the intervention in another life and that permeate the world outside the text in a way that would not have been possible without occupying the thresholds of both bio and fiction. As Andrew Fleshman has written elsewhere, games in critique "may challenge the player by making her question what it means to succeed or fail." Instead of "winning" and imposing a singular, authorizing view or "losing" and "quitting" the game, Navarro's narrative suggests a process of ongoing reappraisal and redefinition. The games of paratext in *The Last Days* leave biographical intention and authority actively in play.

Biographical Games of Spinoff and Social Critique in Antonio Orejudo's *The Famous Five and Me*

In *The Famous Five and Me*, Antonio Orejudo interweaves fictionalized elements of his biography and that of fellow writer, Rafael Reig, with the imagined adult lives of the characters of the "Famous Five," a popular children's book series by Enid Blyton written between 1942 and 1963, the year that Orejudo and Reig were born.[40] Orejudo's book draws part of its ludic inspiration from Blyton's first "Famous Five" book, *Five on a Treasure Island*, and plays out the invented futures forty years later of Julian, Dick, Anne, and their cousin Georgina/George. (The dog, Tim, is no longer present for obvious reasons.) Within the novel, this future history becomes the best-selling spinoff, *After Five*, apocryphally written by Orejudo's real-life friend, Reig. As part of the speculative game, Orejudo ("Toni") becomes a character in Reig's novel, accompanying The Five through their time in Almeria, Spain, where Orejudo lives in reality. By reterritorializing The Five from England to Spain and interacting with their adult versions in his own contemporary reality, the former characters of Blyton's series become players and biographical subjects of experimental play in Orejudo's world just as he interacts in theirs. This breakage of the "magic circle" that cultural historian Johan Huizinga described "as the boundary that demarcates a space of play, separating the activities of games from everyday life" suggests not only how Orejudo becomes immersed as a player in the fictional world, but also how the actions of the fictional players interface with real social, political, and economic concerns.[41] Orejudo's novel is the most "hybrid" of the biofictional works I explore in this text. Orejudo creates the biofictional figure of his real-life friend and fellow author, Reig, himself the creator within the text of the fictional character, Orejudo. Yet, the novel also actively imagines how the fictions we create actively intervene in and revise our real lives, enacted through these biofictional selves.

In this regard, I pursue two modes of analysis. One is to consider the spinoff, *After Five*, within the novel as a type of appropriation and transformation of the "biographical lives" of Orejudo and The Five that we might characterize as an immersive game of fanfiction. In the expanded definition that some games theorists have espoused, fanfiction and other transmedia constitute further examples of paratextual play, mediating the threshold between the fictional and biographical worlds. In turn, the second is to examine how Orejudo, participating as overall author/designer, adaptively experiments with the lives of the characters in ways that critically play out dominant challenges and failures confronting the actual biographical lives of his generation outside the text.

Games can "become critical and experimental when they short circuit dominant norms and conceptions of mastery and power," for example, exposing and challenging contingencies of choice, control, difficulty, and success or failure.[42] In his novel, Orejudo depicts the collaborative ideals of a generation just hitting adolescence at the start of the post-Franco democracy as giving way to passive accommodation with neoliberal political and economic systems that perpetuated self-interested inequalities structured as competitive play among imbalanced winners and losers. As Andrew Fleshman has characterized it, "successfully playing the game precipitates a larger and more significant social failure."[43] Orejudo has described that he read the "Famous Five" series when he was a young adolescent (ages ten to twelve), about the same age of the characters in the books, at a time when he observes that Spain was at a similar cusp of transition from the authority of the patriarch, Franco, to post-dictatorship freedoms. It is this in-between generation that, according to the narrator, Toni, has moved through history without actively participating in creating or challenging the operating systems of the society. Orejudo has suggested in an interview that they arrived too early to be active participants in the democratic transition and too late for the anti-austerity (so-called "Indignados" or 15-M) protest movements during the deep financial crisis of 2008–13, when unemployment spiked over 50 percent for young people. By playing out the adult lives of The Five within a recent Spanish context, with himself as a fellow character, Orejudo adapts the trajectories of The Five to examine critically the choices, outcomes, and possibilities of real lives beyond the text.

Fanfiction and Participatory Culture

The first parts of *The Famous Five and Me* center on the childhood friendships of Toni, the influence of the stories of The Five on his generation, his university years, and the discussions of Reig's *After Five* at various academic and fanfiction conferences. In fact, the novel begins with the fictional Orejudo's presentation of Reig's *After Five* at a conference of the Blyton Foundation. I have argued throughout this book that a critical facet of the expansion and experimentation of biofiction is the interactive ease with which we can constantly play into and revise our own and others' biographical narratives across multiple platforms. Referring to the growth and immediacy of "participatory culture," Henry Jenkins has argued that "patterns of media consumption have been profoundly altered by a succession of new media technologies which enable average citizens to participate in the archiving, annotation, appropriation, transformation, and recirculation of media content." Jenkins has observed the intersection of two significant and competing cultural trends. One is the trend toward media convergence, in which media ownership is "concentrated in the hands of a smaller and smaller number of transmedia and transnational conglomerates" that seek to horizontally control content across diverse media. Through a vast "series of intertextual references and promotions," a successful product will thus "flow across media until it becomes pervasive within the culture at large—comics into computer games, television shows into films, and so forth." He argues that fans "reject this idea of a definitive version produced, authorized, and regulated by some media conglomerate. Instead, fans envision a world where all of us can participate in the creation and circulation of cultural myths." In turn, they contest this increasingly privatized culture by treating mass culture "as if it offered them raw materials for telling their own stories and resources for forging their own communities. [...] Fan culture, thus, represents a participatory culture through which fans explore and question the ideologies of mass culture, speaking from a position sometimes inside and sometimes outside the cultural logic of commercial entertainment."[44] In this sense, fanfiction becomes a refutation of efforts to singularize or rein in control over biographical identities. Rather, anyone can speculate on the nature of these identities or narratives and imagine their future directions.

Significantly, the "multiple, dynamic, and often contradictory relationships" between convergence and participatory culture play out within the many strands and strategic interactions within Orejudo's text, through the creation of dispersive fictional universes and at the same time the characters' lack of awareness or intentional disregard of their co-optation in networked systems of commercial influence. As Caroline Levine has characterized, "At any given moment we know that we cannot grasp crucial pathways between nodes, and this points to our more generalized ignorance regarding networks. We cannot ever apprehend the totality of the networks that organize us."[45] For example, the fictional Orejudo and Reig create expansive transmedia points of entry for fans to participate in the creation and circulation of content related to The Five, beginning with their founding of the literary magazine *The Five*, during their university years. The narrator, Toni, observes that the Enid Blyton society had originally just been a simple club of readers and fans of the writer's work. However, it was the funding through the pharmaceutical conglomerate, LABS™, which provided the support for the expansion into a wide variety of platforms. Among these are the annual role-playing Fiveday celebration, The Five-Fetish Fair, talks, colloquia, and excursions to locations mentioned in the books, not to mention the acquisition of an expansive archive and even the purchase of the "Villa Kirrin" mentioned in the books as a center of reference. LABS™ also provides the experimental drug that treats Reig's sudden illness, allowing him to write the best-selling spinoff, *After Five*, in which the biofictional Reig does not simply adapt the Famous Five series but plays into their imagined adult lives as an immersive game with Orejudo as a character.

Fanfiction is defined as "the creative appropriation and transformation of existing popular media texts by fans who take stories, worlds, and/or characters as starting points and create their own stories based on it."[46] Such works do not necessarily reinforce the existing structures of the earlier model, but through their derivative versions interactively offer the possibility for contested understandings that transform meaning. In the earlier discussion of *The Last Days of Adelaida García Morales*, I referred to competing ethical claims regarding biofiction's appropriation of another life story or alternatively of its capacity to give voice to understandings of a life that might otherwise remain silenced. The use of fanfiction within Orejudo's novel, developing the afterlives of "The Five" and incorporating a biofictional version of himself in their narrative world, incorporates both of these elements. Appropriating these characters provides a vehicle for Orejudo to play *through* these imagined afterlives both to expose damaging aspects of the original series that he overlooked as a child, and to rewrite these lives in the present in a way that critically examines his own cultural present. Peter Lunenfield has argued that "the backstory – the information about how a narrative object comes into being – is fast becoming almost as important as the object itself."[47] The novel suggests how as a child he had "projected onto" the characters his own desires, unquestioning of the ethical flaws he later notices as an adult, such as the overwhelming emphasis on money and privilege.[48] In the fictional *Fiveday* conference, for example, the participants "settled accounts" with the legacy of the "sexist, racist, and fascist Enid Blyton." Orejudo describes how the first year that [the biofictional] Reig presented *After Five* at the conference, "the Blyton Foundation filled with fans who came up to him to congratulate him and to tell him that he had helped them to see things through his eyes, through those of Reig; that his voice had merged with that of Enid Blyton"—transforming her vision through the use of her characters.[49]

Narrative Immersion and Video Games

By making the lives of the fictional characters of The Five simulatively "real" through their blending and involvement in his world, while making the biographical figures of himself and Reig fictional characters in their stories, Orejudo relates narrative immersion with the interactive experience of video game play. In playing a video game, we enter as avatar into the fictional world of the game, and, as part of that simulative world, the other characters become real to us. As the narrator Orejudo writes,

> [E]ach time I that I opened one of those covers illustrated by the great José Correas—whose drawings did not seem to me ancillary additions that could be overlooked, but natural extensions of the text—I didn't feel like a reader of a fiction, this would come later; I felt like one of the characters. And I would close the covers of the book just as exhausted as Julian, Dick, Ana, Jorge, and *Tim;* as if I had also rowed, as if I had also dived deep into the sea to inspect the sunken ship [...] in an experience as intense and real as that of videogames today.

He adds, "My son also leaves his room exhausted after spending the afternoon hiding from enemy soldiers, devising ambushes, developing plans and managing sophisticated weaponry."[50] This is thus far an unsurprising claim—that narrative immersion in other's lives is replicated in interactive formats such as video games that emerged in the later part of the twentieth century. However, where Orejudo further twists this claim is in the immediately subsequent lines. He incorporates one of the fictional characters of The Five, "Dick" (who he writes "Now goes by Richard"), in producing and authorizing the game being played by his son, in charge of ensuring its "verisimilitude" and "technical sufficiency" ("if we pay attention to the credits") in his role as president of Activision, a developer of exceptionally lucrative, first-person virtual war games.

A few elements here merit consideration. First, we note how Orejudo—by playing within and along with the game he has designed—creates an ambiguous threshold among fictional and biographical identities, leaving the reader uncertain at this point as to the "realness" of Dick/Richard. In an interview, Orejudo has said, "Many days we don't know if what we are living is imagined or not. It is this sense of perplexity we have because we are immersed in realities that are really hard to believe. And this is the novel: a type of adaptive play of a book [...] a settling of accounts with those who are part of my generation of acquiescence."[51]

Moreover, Orejudo (as empirical author) creates an implicit linkage between the virtual game world and the "gamified" reality of neoliberal competition revealed through the career trajectory, financial interests, and ownership of the game conveyed through Dick's fictional biography. "Gamification," as Patrick Jagoda defines it, "marks a condition of seepage or doubling through which game mechanics and activities influence work, leisure, thought, and social relations—key ways people interface with reality today."[52] Orejudo describes how Richard had earlier abandoned his studies to enlist in the army, a decision that "cost him dearly." The difference between the traumatic experiences Dick suffered in the war contrasts with the enjoyment of the virtual game:

> I have watched my son play out a role in the campaign of a limited edition for collectors of UK Wars 3, where there is a recreation of the Battle of Mount Longdon, which resulted in the final victory for the British troops in the War of the Malvinas. The virtual battle is supervised personally by Richard, who participated in the real episode when he had just turned nineteen.[53]

The narrator Orejudo adds, "Reig tells us in *After Five* that Richard was surprised by the naturalness 'with which the rash decision to enter combat became an irremediable reality.'"[54]

It is only at this point in the novel that it becomes clear that we have crossed an artificial threshold and entered into the spinoff, *After Five*, written by Reig. *After Five* goes on to communicate how, following his wartime experiences, Richard dedicated himself to private industry related to security, founding the lucrative company You & Me™, which earns its wealth protecting mining production in Africa. When he turned fifty, he sold that to start the equally profitable company selling video wargames. Thus, in Reig's version, Dick's earlier idealism and acknowledgment of the real costs of war are converted into the production of virtual games, and whose measures of success are conditioned purely by monetary goals and market forces based on the "protected" exploitation of natural resources.

Patrick Jagoda argues that games have become an "exemplary cultural form that serves as a prominent metaphor of everyday competition and success." He further describes this *gamified* reality, a term that derives from behavioral economics, as the "use of game mechanics in traditionally nongame activities"—a form that economic, social, and cultural life increasingly takes in the present. In the early-twenty-first century, he asserts, "business, consumerism, crowdsourcing, dating, education, exercise, healthcare, labor, marketing, research, social media applications and warfare—just to name a few areas—have all increasingly adopted the logic and structure of games."[55] Moreover, he links the effort to "level up," as we might conflate socioeconomic status and achievement in a video game, with the extension of similar rewards ("likes," "badging," "achievement points," etc.) that shape subjectivity and interpretations of success around the values of the neoliberal market. He argues that games that inundate the present are "action-oriented meditations that shape a wide range of encounters with the contemporary situation, especially in the way that they interweave economic principles with the experiences of contemporary life."

Summarizing Jagoda's argument, Andrew Fleshman observes that games have the "striking and dangerous power to reinforce neoliberal norms of unlimited consumption, individualistic self-absorption, and zero-sum competition." However, by building off game theoretic concepts of modeling our strategic interactions with one another as a way of better understanding the world, "they also have the potential to lay bare the contradictions and distortions of neoliberal subjectivity" and to reinforce the potential of adapting the game.[56] In the subsequent section, I explore how Orejudo uses the spinoff, *After Five*, as a role-playing game and a game with the reader that foregrounds and undercuts the gamified realities of the adult characters. In so doing, he plays out the implications of this model for his generation as a biofictional player *within* the fictional spinoff, *After Five*, and in interaction with the layered functions of challenge and social critique from *outside* the diagetic space of narrative play as author/designer.

After Five: Gamification and Contingent Games

Thomas Malaby has described games as *processes* of adaptation. "As it is played, it always contains the potential for generating new practices and new meanings, possibly refiguring the game itself. [...] Games are, like many social processes, dynamic and recursive, largely reproducing their form through time but always containing the possibility of emergent change."[57] This description is especially relevant to our consideration of the experimentation associated with biofiction as a form of recursive play. The real lives being imaginatively reinvented may function as models that help us better understand the operations of existing realities, or they may be revised in ways that allow us to speculate on unrealized possibilities and divergent outcomes. Similarly, we might consider how the interaction of The Five with Orejudo as biofictional character in *After Five* refigures Blyton's earlier narrative, *Five on a Treasure Island*, and replays many of the challenges faced by Orejudo's generation to comment on then and now. As Malaby has further elaborated,

> The potential sources of contingency that are arranged and calibrated in games are the same sources we encounter throughout our lives. They are just semi-bounded in the designed game. It is therefore the fact that games have this fundamental quality of multilayered contingency that allows them to both mimic and constitute everyday experience, and this is what makes well-designed games compelling.[58]

In imagining the fictional biographical afterlives of the series' childhood characters, the narrative game of *After Five* models various conflicts and contingent realities that members of Orejudo's and Reig's generation experienced in post-1980 Spain to the present. These contingencies include the lack of clear thresholds between the parameters of fiction and those of the real, as *After Five* metafictively demonstrates. Additionally, as Malaby expresses, these games are shown to have real connections to the social world: "Everyday experience and game arenas, each filled with uncertainties, can inform each other through metaphor [...] but they can also be the site for real stakes and real consequences."[59] For example, problems with drug addiction (particularly heroin) deeply affected Orejudo's generation. The cover of his book shows an image of six childhood friends, including him. Only three of those friends survived; the other three died of drug overdoses.

Within Orejudo's text, The Five and their imagined "afterselves" become experimental subjects that "compress particular experiences and model small subsets of the present world," modeling and satirizing its gamified logic. For example, in *After Five*, Ana, along with her former husband, Chad Elson, a member of the punk band, The Shots, become addicted to heroin (she's able to finance their habit, ironically, through the money she inherited from her father's sale of his needle-manufacturing business) and she becomes HIV-positive. While Ana survives, she also experiences an ideological reversal, embracing a rigid conservatism and becoming part of the extreme right that defends Brexit, while opening a bar whose name is a tribute to Margaret Thatcher. Later, she remarries a friend of the fictional Orejudo, an entrepreneur with whom she and her siblings found a new company, MULTIPLE CHOICE™, which makes them lots of money providing businesses with any resources they request, including human subjects for pharmaceutical experimentation.[60] The ironic play on pharmaceutical companies is especially telling as it reduces physical health as a basic public good to its utility as a source of corporate profit.

In Reig's spinoff, all of the characters make self-interested decisions that demonstrate a lack of awareness or willful ignorance regarding the human consequences of the wider networks in which they are embedded. Ana marries a friend of the narrator, Román Soler, whose business provides human subjects for experimentation. Julian works as an ethics auditor for the ironically named "GOOD THINGS," another pharmaceutical company, but has no idea what is actually taking place. When Georgina, as an investigative reporter, wants to expose the company's fraud and corruption, Julian is fired for stealing company information. Yet, even after he is let go, his siblings and he continue to invest in the company that fired him for whistleblowing. As Román tells Julian: "It's one thing to lose faith in human beings and another altogether to lose a business opportunity."[61] Similarly, Orejudo's Reig pokes fun at the hypocrisy and celebrity adulation of corporate CEOs, noting that "in the same chapter dedicated to Julian, Reig transcribes a video that he says he found on the internet." The video shows the CEO of GOOD THINGS, "moving from one side of the stage to the other like a rock star. A little before he died, his friend Freddie Mercury—says Reig—had taught him how to fill the stage with electricity and synergy." In the video, he says, "I tell you: there is an effort underway to recover innocence, an effort to make public service compatible with entrepreneurial profit. [...] GOOD THINGS is not an NGO, but a business [...] decency and justice are profitable. We are not creating social welfare; we are creating the capitalism of the twenty-first century."[62]

Within the gamified reality, "neoliberal rationality disseminates," according to Wendy Brown, "the model of the market to all domains and activities—even where money is not an issue—and configures human beings exhaustively as market actors, always, only, and everywhere, as *homo economicus*."[63] This statement demonstrates a clear expansion of the "game theoretic" model of the Prisoner's Dilemma in which competitive self-interest trumps collaboration to broader expressions of cultural logic, until "gamification functions to colonize greater and greater swathes of our psychological, interpersonal, professional, and social lives."[64]

Nowhere is this paradigm clearer than in the ending to *After Five*. As I have described, *After Five* is a spinoff of the original Blyton story, *Five on a Treasure Island*. The general format of the "Famous Five" series is the collaboration of the children to discover and defeat a dangerous source of disorder, often a criminal. In *Five on a Treasure Island*, the children's explorations lead them deep into the dungeons of Kirrin castle, where they discover a map to hidden treasure. Two of the children are locked in the dungeons by the criminals who want the gold for themselves, but the other children help them escape and they are able to capture the crooks and recover the gold, which the authorities determine legally belongs to Georgina's family, making them rich. As is clear from this example, the story structure emphasizes collaboration (over competition), trust in authorities, and shared reward for their work ("leveling up"). In the original stories, the children confront a specific threat: "thieves, criminals," as Orejudo observes in an interview. "And they help to restore order by capturing the bad people." However, in his version, The Five as they get older realize that the threat is not external—that they themselves are the source of the disorder. This change in the paradigm dramatically changes the meaning of the game to revise not only the past series, but through the biofictional presence of Orejudo and Reig, to comment on the contemporary context. It should not be lost on us that Orejudo uses imaginative experimentation with fictional and biofictional subjects in ways that subvert and critique real modes of using and exploiting real lives, especially those with the least social and economic capital.

Toward the end of *After Five*, Georgina takes the fictional Reig and Orejudo to a sixteenth-century castle that had been originally built to protect the mines of alum common to Almeria. The castle, now owned by an Englishman named Jim, has been converted into a type of hostel for refugees who use its hidden tunnels and passageways to escape the immigration authorities. There, they were being trained to adapt themselves to the "economy of scarcity" as the "economy of the future." As they discover, not only are the refugees working and living there part of a human factory of adolescents providing "raw material" for GOOD THINGS, but MULTIPLE CHOICE™ is a co-contributor in this process, teaming with GOOD THINGS for years to provide raw material and human subjects in all parts of the world; in fact, they share ownership. As Orejudo has described in an interview, it seemed "very provocative to construct this version of himself that gives up writing to be super happy as an investor."[65] *After Five* concludes with a picnic, which Orejudo attends, along with Reig's adopted son named Mazen, who had lived for some time in the factory of Jim the Englishman. When Julian mentions that Georgina had thought about writing an exposé about the horrors of the human factories where young people were essentially indentured, "Mazen seemed relieved that she had decided not to," given that if she had written that report, it might have threatened dismantlement of the multitudes of similar locations throughout the world, "with catastrophic consequences for many people." And so, the novel ends, "They didn't talk again about the matter." Instead, they went back to their picnic filled with "*organic, fresh* and above all *fair trade* delicacies."[66]

Orejudo thus revises the original paradigm of The Five through an immersive biofictional narrative that satirically exposes the gamified nature of contemporary life and implicates his generation, who are both players and passive beneficiaries, complicit in its unfair rules through their self-interested failure to do anything in response or even to acknowledge their own involvement. In a sense, Orejudo has created a type of "Alternate Reality Game" (ARG). ARGs are at the crossroads of fan-based creation, collective game play, and media convergence. ARGs are role-playing games that allow fans to cross back and forth between the fiction and the material world. That is, fans *play along*, but the media company ultimately authorizes and controls the structure of the game. Similarly, through the experimental game of the biofictional narrative, Orejudo critically exposes individual participation in a neoliberal reality that models a competitive, self-interested game and that has pervaded economic, social, and cultural life during his adulthood; he plays out these outcomes for the original series of The Five, as if he were narrating a game theoretic model. As with biofictions, which take an individual life and "replay" it under different conditions, the process of immersive interaction with these lives as characters allows us to critically examine the limitations of these models and to imagine how we might generate new and more just modes and rules of play.

Concluding Thoughts

Biofictions constitute thresholds between the situated reality of a real biographical subject and the experimental play of fictional creation. Similarly, games theorists have contended that social texts and popular interactive games have increasingly become paratextual, crossing between the invented world and lived reality and involving the wider participation of players to intervene in and adapt the game. In this way, paratextual play constitutes an opportunity not simply to support the existing rules of engagement, but to challenge and revise the authority of the original version. Patrick Jagoda has described experiments as "inherently artificial constructions that nudge and modulate reality's constellation of potentials in ways that allow for observation that would have otherwise been impossible. Games, too, are artificial constructions that can compress particular experiences and model small subsets of the present world."[67] Extending this model, I have argued in this chapter that Navarro's *The Last Days of Adelaida Garciá Morales* and Orejudo's *The Famous Five and Me* demonstrate salient examples of paratextual play, narrative games, and biofiction. In this way, these works compel attention to the interaction among multiple players to not only shape and generate new biographical meanings, but to challenge and imagine otherwise how we live and understand the world as an ongoing process of refiguring the game itself.

Coda: Biofiction's Antidotes to Post-Truth

Biofictions, as I have demonstrated throughout *Derivative Lives*, constitute thresholds between the situated realities of actual, biographical subjects and the imaginative potential of fictional creation. Thus, while deriving from real sources, biofiction also liberates fiction from interacting only with invented worlds. Instead, these works invite us to experiment with our biographical lives and to use fiction to evaluate and shape real-world concerns. Throughout this book, we have considered how writers use biofiction to respond to, revise, and reimagine the intervening effects of circumstantiality, speculation, and immersive interactivity on how we experience and represent our own and others' lives. A central thesis has been that these biofictional strategies are not limited to literary outlook but reflect broader rearrangements in cultural logic that involve other disciplines and modes of inquiry that similarly contend with uncertainty and the speculative risk of conjecture. Accelerating in the past few decades, the speed, profusion, and anonymity of networks of information and images have vastly multiplied the capacity to produce derivative identities across multiple platforms, while making it harder to authenticate the originating sources of these abundant circumstantial details or to affirm their truthfulness. The expansion and popularity of biofictions are both an outgrowth of this dispersive reality, and a mode for navigating this context, modeling alternatives for how we manage and rethink its possibilities and pitfalls.

Writing this book during a global pandemic has been a powerful reminder of how quickly uncertainties and risks can proliferate. The uncertainties we face are not only the risks of physical dangers to ourselves and our planet, although those are very real, but also to the confidence and trust we have in sources and claims to veracity. As *Oxford Dictionary* expressed in making it their 2016 word of the year, the risks of post-truth are not only that people confuse fact and fiction, but more significantly that the value of truth no longer matters. I have argued that the risks and responsibilities of how we use fiction to understand our world and each other are greater in the context of the circumstantial, speculative, game theoretic world under threat from post-truth. In this concluding section, I want to think about how—by pushing us to examine critically the connection to factual realities and the distinct, but equally significant responsibility to the truths of fiction—biofictions offer potential antidotes against post-truth contagions. At their best, biofictions engage directly with the contemporary epistemological crisis to ask us what kinds of truths we hope to achieve.

The Limits of Facts

Oscar Wilde claimed, "The English are always degrading truth into facts."[1] I began this book with Javier Cercas' *Soldiers of Salamis*, which marked a turning point in the expansion of the biographical novel in Spain. While the narrator accumulates all sorts of factual details, he is initially unable to connect this information to any transcendent questions of human nature, experience, or history. As the circumstantial model explores, we have prioritized the accumulation of data at the expense of the discernment, analysis, and judgment of what those clues might tell us about our lives. Meaningful truths, these writers suggest, cannot be simply about what we know but exactly about what we fail to understand, what Cercas calls "moral truths,"[2] the "shaping of paradox."[3] Moreover, both Cercas and Antonio Muñoz Molina reflect upon the shift from postmodernism's fractured relationship between fiction and the real, and biofictional truths that strive to reconnect fiction to the realities of our lives.

Hidden and Uncomfortable Truths

The biofictional writers included in this book have explored both how we navigate a world of too much information and too little real knowledge. We can build mountains of distance as both Gabriela Ybarra and Muñoz Molina suggest, with factual accumulation alone. Just as Ybarra argues that imagination has sometimes been the only means of understanding, imaginative linkages can become the necessary threads to weave together isolated strands. Some biographical novelists explore truths that would otherwise remain hidden, either because of an absence of information or because they are shrouded in silence. Or they may engage with uncomfortable truths that might otherwise be reduced to facile fictions, opening up the moment, as Colum McCann has observed, to "see what we don't want or refuse to see."[4] In *The Dinner Guest,* Ybarra suggests that biofiction can have a redemptive function not only by exposing the points of fracture, but also through the healing process of trying to seam the fragments together. In a different way, Muñoz Molina reinforces Emma Donoghue's claim that biofiction done well should "actually make us uncomfortable. It should provoke us."[5] In using biofiction to invent Martin Luther King Jr.'s thoughts in the moments just prior to his assassination by James Earl Ray, the imaginative view that Muñoz Molina constructs of King's inner dialogue challenges popular simplifications of King as a symbol. In so doing, he explores how biographical images we consume can so readily be smoothed into palliative fictions that avoid our having to confront uncomfortable truths regarding the persistence of division and fracture—complicated issues of race, of separatist violence, of trauma. One of the central tasks of biofiction is to expose and contend with these unsettled and contradictory realities.

Speculative Truths

Exploring what might happen or could have happened differently is at the heart of the next provisional truth biofiction explores. These speculative truths consciously revise biographical lives and open them to the risk of conjecture in order to imagine unexpected possibilities. Beyond the capacity to shape purely imaginary worlds, it is significant that Rosa Montero links the use of biofiction with its effects on how we experience and reassess reality. This clarification also points to important ways in which biofiction differs from imaginative fiction that does not incorporate biographical lives as characters. By entertaining the "what-ifs," Montero's uses of biofiction challenge dominant, totalizing narratives. Through multiple alterations, we can revise expected models, realizing an inadequacy or suggesting alternative trajectories that spark revision and changed perceptions in how we understand the world. Both Montero's and García Ortega's biofictions use literary experimentation with biographical lives as a way of opening these life narratives to unexpected value and possibility that might otherwise have been overlooked, while considering the ethical risks and responsibilities of speculative investment in another's life story as a kind of existential map for managing our own uncertainties. Similarly, García Ortega uses imagined biographical futures and derivative lives to both critique and unsettle the present.

Alongside the upside potential of taking on the speculative risk of conjecture, in *The Impostor*, Javier Cercas takes the most direct examination of the risks of derivative lives that deny or distort the use of fiction by presenting it as fact, thus actively violating the biographical pact with the reader. That Marco's monstrous lies were so convincing is emblematic of the damaging effects of derivatives that bear no connection to the real lives and historical truths from which they were supposedly sourced. Such works suggest that individuals become lost when they use fiction not as a means of challenging reality to better understand the uncertain, always incomplete, and evolving nature of the human condition, but as a means to conceal or evade this inquiry and thus to deepen deceptive fictions.

Playful Truths

Alongside their more official versions, we are performing biofictions all the time, as we create and intervene in derivative selves and avatars through social media and other online identities. As Mary Holland has observed, "most recently, technological developments alter our sense of what is real and our ability to represent it in altogether new ways with ever-increasing computational power, the internet, virtual reality, technology, and digitization simultaneously destabilizing and exploding our sense of what reality is, while offering more sophisticated ways of representing it."[6] I have argued that biofictional experimentation and adaptation have been shaped profoundly by the immersive and interactive ease with which we can play into and revise our own and others' biographical narratives. By "playful truths," I am not implying that such biofictions are playful in the sense of ironic distance from reality. Instead, through very different modalities, the game-like biofictions of Lucía Etxebarria, Elvira Navarro, and Antonio Orejudo suggest that biofictional games can be critical, experiential, and experimental. These works thus function to question dominant norms and conceptions of rules of neoliberal competition, challenge gendered norms and conceptions of mastery and power, and expose difficult decisions of choice and control regarding the fictions we create.

Concluding Thoughts

As I hope to have shown throughout this book, there are ethical implications not only for how we assess the value of biographical truth, but also how we approach the uses of fiction to reinvent real lives. I have argued that the contract with the reader matters, and that there is a profound difference between using literary fiction openly to speculatively imagine reality as opposed to deriving convenient fictions and presenting them as fact. I have contended that the aims of fiction matter. There is a difference between post-truth that tries to manipulate biographical fact with the aim of imposing a particular view of reality and fiction that opens biographical lives to imaginative inquiry in the hopes of discovering new truths. And there is a profound distinction between the transactional use of another's story for self-interested gain and the effort to envision another's subjectivity and worldview in order to expand the possibilities for empathy and human connection beyond our own individual experiences.

With biofiction, life becomes literature and literature reveals the fragility, flexibility, and flux of our biographical lives. Without providing firm solutions to the circumstantial, speculative, gamified nature of contemporary life, biofiction will continue to resonate and seek ways of mapping us through this uncertain landscape. "How will you go about finding that thing the nature of which is totally unknown to you?" the philosopher Meno asks Plato.[7] The stakes of contending with biographical uncertainty offer the potential reward of seeing the world anew, of discoveries we didn't even know we were looking for. If we stay safely with only the "facts" we know about our lives, biofictions suggest also how much we might lose. Biofiction, in this way, is about extending the boundaries of the self and of biographical knowledge of another; alongside the risks of imaginatively going beyond the contained certainties of what we think we know, we venture into the territory of unexpected possibility.

NOTES

Introduction

1 Alain Buisine, "Biofictions," *Revue des Sciences Humaines* 4, No. 224 (1991): 7–13.
2 Rosa Montero, "Speculative Subjectivities and the Biofictional Surge," Interview by Virginia N. Rademacher, in *Conversations with Biographical Novelists: Truthful Fictions across the Globe*, ed. Michael Lackey (New York and London: Bloomsbury), 160.
3 Montero, "Speculative Subjectivities," 167, 158.
4 Peter Bernstein, *Against the Gods: The Remarkable Story of Risk* (New York: John Wiley & Sons, 1996), 8.
5 Anthony Giddens, *Modernity and Identity: Self and Society in the Late Modern Age* (Stanford: Stanford University Press, 1991), 3.
6 Alison Gibbons, "Postmodernism is Dead. What Comes Next?" *Times Literary Supplement Online* (June 22, 2017), https://www.the-tls.co.uk/articles/public/postmodernism-dead-comes-next/.
7 Javier Cercas, "Resisting the 'Dictatorship of the Present' in the Biographical Novel," Interview by Virginia N. Rademacher, in *Conversations with Biographical Novelists: Truthful Fictions across the Globe*, ed. Michael Lackey (New York and London: Bloomsbury, 2019), 50–1.
8 Jonathan Sturgeon, "The Death of the Postmodern Novel and the Rise of Autofiction," *Flavorwire* (December 31, 2014), https://www.flavorwire.com/496570/2014-the-death-of-the-postmodern-novel-and-the-rise-of-autofiction.
9 Ben Lerner, "An Interview with *The Believer*," Interview by Tao Lin, *The Believer,* No. 101, https://believermag.com/an-interview-with-ben-lerner/.
10 Brooks Landon, "Extrapolation and Speculation," in *Oxford Handbook of Science Fiction*, ed. Rob Latham (New York: Oxford University Press, 2104), 25.
11 Judith Merril, "What Do You Mean: Science? Fiction?", in *The Other Side of Realism*, ed. T. Clareson (Madison: University of Wisconsin Press, 1971), 60.
12 Colm Tóibín, "The Anchored Imagination of the Biographical Novel," Interview by Bethany Layne, in *Conversations with Biographical Novelists: Truthful Fictions across the Globe*, ed. Michael Lackey (London and New York: Bloomsbury, 201), 231. Layne combines this phrasing in the title for her interview, in which Tóibín describes his biographical novel *The Master* as "a work of pure imagination," but one in which "you're anchored, you're getting an anchor from certain facts and that anchor is not merely factual but emotional."

13 Robert Tally, "Meta-Capital: Culture and Financial Derivatives," *Cultural Logic* 17 (2010), Special Issue on Culture and Crisis. Ed. Joseph G. Ramsey, https://ojs.library.ubc.ca/index.php/clogic/article/view/191529.

14 Colum McCann, "Contested Realities in the Biographical Novel," Interview by Michael Lackey, in *Conversations with Biographical Novelists: Truthful Fictions across the Globe*, ed. Michael Lackey (New York and London: Bloomsbury, 2019), 138.

15 In reference to related hybrid life-writing forms, Alison Gibbons has referred to autofiction as "an explicitly hybrid form of life writing that merges autobiographical fact with fiction." She adds, "Autofiction is, to my mind, a broad genre, containing novels that conform to this strict definition, but also other forms in which the central character does not take the author's name (e.g. at all, they take a variation of the author's name, or they remain nameless), such as the related modes of fictional autobiography and fictional memoir as well as autobiographical fiction." Robin van den Akker, Alison Gibbons, and Timothy Vermeuluen, *Metamodernism: Historicity, Affect, Depth after Postmodernism* [London and New York: Rowman and Littlefield, 2017], 120–2). Notably, Gibbons' view of the expansion of autofiction, as I have also suggested with respect to biofiction, responds in part to an exhaustion with postmodernism's distance from real-world concerns, and a desire to connect fictional experimentation to situated lives and realities beyond the text. See, especially p. 130 of her chapter, "Contemporary Autofiction and Metamodern Affect," in *Metamodernism*, cited above.

16 Montero, "Speculative Subjectivities,"164–5.

17 Ibid., 167.

Chapter 1

1 For readability, I have referenced the English translation. The original version in Spanish, *Soldados de Salamina* (Barcelona: Tusquets), was first published in 2001. The English translation by Anne McLean, *Soldiers of Salamis* (New York and London: Bloomsbury) was published in 2004. All in-text citations are from the English version with the original Spanish cited in parentheses in the endnotes, followed by the page number from the 2001 edition.

2 Javier Cercas, "Resisting the 'Dictatorship of the Present' in the Biographical Novel," Interview by Virginia N. Rademacher, in *Conversations with Biographical Novelists: Truthful Fictions across the Globe*, ed. Michael Lackey (New York and London: Bloomsbury, 2019), 50, 52.

3 I interviewed Javier Cercas in October 2017 in Barcelona. This interview is published in *Conversations with Biographical Novelists: Truthful Fictions across the Globe,* cited immediately above. This chapter references my interview as well as those others have conducted with Cercas.

4 Christopher Schaberg, *The Work of Literature in an Age of Post-Truth* (London and New York: Bloomsbury, 2018), 12.

5 Cercas, "Resisting the 'Dictatorship of the Present'," 52.

6 Mary Holland, *The Moral Worlds of Contemporary Realism* (New York and London: Bloomsbury, 2020), 216.
7 Cercas, "Resisting the 'Dictatorship of the Present'," 49.
8 Michael Lackey, "The Rise of the Biographical Novel and the Fall of the Historical Novel," *a/b: Auto/Biography Studies* 31, No. 1 (2016): 33–58.
9 Michael Lackey, *Truthful Fictions: Conversations with American Biographical Novelists* (New York and London: Bloomsbury, 2014), 48.
10 Cercas, "Resisting the 'Dictatorship of the Present'," 50.
11 Barbara Shapiro, "Circumstantial Evidence: Of Law, Literature, and Culture," *Yale Journal of Law & the Humanities* 5, No. 1 (1993): 240.
12 In James Whitman, "The Origins of Reasonable Doubt," *Yale Law School Faculty Scholarship Series* (2005), digitalcommons.law.yale.edu/fss_papers/1. See also James Franklin, *The Science of Conjecture: Evidence and Probability before Pascal* (Baltimore: Johns Hopkins University Press, 2005), 63.
13 Barbara Shapiro, "Beyond Reasonable Doubt: The Evolution of a Concept," in *Fictions of Knowledge: Fact, Evidence, Doubt*, eds. Yota Batsaki et al. (New York: Palgrave MacMillan, 2012), 26.
14 Michael Wood, "Afterward," in *Fictions of Knowledge: Fact, Evidence, Doubt*, eds. Yota Batsaki et al. (New York: Palgrave MacMillan, 2012), 215.
15 Nicholas Stavris, "The Anxieties of the Present," in *Supplanting the Postmodern: An Anthology of Writings on the Arts and Culture of the Early 21st Century*, eds. David Rudrum and Nicholas Stavris (New York and London: Bloomsbury, 2015), 353.
16 Alison Gibbons, "Contemporary Autofiction and Metamodern Affect," in *Metamodernism: Historicity, Affect and Depth after Postmodernism*, eds. Robin van den Akker et al. (New York: Rowman and Littlefield, 2017), 130.
17 José Ovejero, "Toda la verdad sobre mi adicción al sexo," *Esto no es un blog* (April 26, 2017), https://joseovejero.com/2017/04/26/toda-la-verdad-sobre-mi-adiccion-al-sexo. ("Pero no se debe ridiculizar la nostalgia, que siempre es el testimonio de una carencia; como el dolor fantasma, nos recuerda que hemos perdido un elemento necesario en nuestras vidas, y lo echamos de menos, y nos duele su ausencia"), https://joseovejero.com/2017/04/26/toda-la-verdad-sobre-mi-adiccion-al-sexo.
18 Mary K. Holland, *Succeeding Postmodernism: Language and Humanism in Contemporary American Literature* (New York and London: Bloomsbury, 2013), 201.
19 Hans Hansen, "Modes of Remembering in the Contemporary Spanish Novel,"*Orbis Litterarum* 71, No. 4 (2016): 277.
20 Linda Hutcheon, *A Poetics of Postmodernism: History, Fiction, Theory* (New York and London: Routledge, 1988), x.
21 Shane Hegerty, "Losing the War but Winning the Literature," Interview with Javier Cercas, *Irish Times* 71, No. 4 (June 2003), https://www.irishtimes.com/news/losing-the-war-but-winning-the-literature-1.361789.
22 Richard K. Greenstein, "Determining Facts: The Myth of Direct Evidence," *Houston Law Review* 45, No. 5 (2009): 1827, 1805.
23 Cercas, "Resisting the 'Dictatorship of the Present'," 64.

24 Nathan Richardson, "'No Pensar', or Does the Contemporary Novel of Memory Really Want To Know?": *Tiempo de silencio, Corazón tan blanco, Soldados de Salamina* and beyond," *Letras Hispanas* 7 (2010): 6–7.
25 Javier Cercas, *Soldiers of Salamis*, trans. Anne Mclean (New York and London: Bloomsbury, 2004), 80. Translation of *Soldados de Salamina* (Barcelona: Tusquets, 2001) ("fugitivas alusiones en memorias y documentos de la época, relatos orales de quienes compartieron con él retazos de sus aventuras, recuerdos de familiares y amigos a quienes refirió sus recuerdos—y también a través del velo de una leyenda constelada de equívocos, contradicciones y ambigüedades [...] Así pues, lo que a continuación consigno no es lo que realmente sucedió, sino lo que parece verosímil que sucediera; no ofrezco hechos probados, sino conjeturas razonables"), 89.
26 Ibid., 137, 138 ("una suerte de biografía"; "A la segunda relectura la euphoria se trocó en decepción: el libro no era malo, sino insuficiente, como un mecanismo completo pero incapaz de desempeñar la función para la que ha sido ideado porque le falta una pieza"), 143, 144.
27 Among others, Samuel Amago, "Narrative Truth and Historical Truth in Javier Cercas *Soldados de Salamina*," in *True Lies: Narrative Self-Consciousness in the Contemporary Spanish Novel*, ed. Amago (Lewisburg: Bucknell University Press, 2006), 144–65; Nathan Richardson, "'No Pensar', or Does the Contemporary Spanish Novel of Memory Really Want to Know?: *Tiempo de silencio, Corazón tan blanco, Soldados de Salamina* and Beyond," *Letras hispanas* 7 (2010): 2–16; Robert Spires, "Depolarization and the New Spanish Fiction at the Milennium,"*Anales de la Literatura Española Contemporánea* 30, Nos. 1–2 (2005): 485–512.
28 Cercas, *Soldiers*, 8 ("excusas para la nostalgia de los viejos y carburante para la imaginación de los novelistas sin imaginación"), 21.
29 Cercas, "Resisting the 'Dictatorship of the Present'," 50.
30 Ibid., 55.
31 Julian Baggini, "Truth? It's Not Just about the Facts," *Times Literary Supplement* (September 21, 2017), https://www.the-tls.co.uk/articles/post-truth-philosophers.
32 Cercas, *Soldiers*, 40 ("un relato real, un relato cosido a la realidad, amasado con hechos y personajes reales, un relato que estaría centrado en el fusilamiento de Sánchez Mazas y en las circunstancias que lo precedieron y lo siguieron"), 52.
33 Ibid., 137 ("una suerte de biografía de Sánchez Mazas que, centrándose en un episodio en apariencia anedótico pero acaso esencial de su vida- su frustrado fusiliamiento en el Collell- propusiera una interpretación del personaje y, por extension, de la naturaleza del falangismo o, más exactamente, de los motivos que indujeron al puñado de hombres cultos y refinados que fundaron Falange a lanzar el país a una furiosa orgía de sangre"), 143.
34 Richardson, "'No Pensar'," 7.
35 Cercas, *Soldiers,* 30 (2001, 42).
36 Miller, *What They Saved: Pieces of a Jewish Past* (Lincoln: University of Nebraska Press, 2011), 5. I am grateful to Leena Kurvet-Kaössar for her observations on this point. See "The Archive," *a/b: Auto/Biography Studies* 32, No. 2 (2017): 355–8.

37 Cercas, "Resisting the 'Dictatorship of the Present'," 62–3.
38 Alexander Welsh, *Strong Representations: Narrative and Circumstantial Evidence in England* (Baltimore: Johns Hopkins University Press, 1992), ix, x.
39 John Loftis, "Review of *Strong Representations: Narrative in Circumstantial Evidence in* England," *Rocky Mountain Review of Language and Literature* 47, No. 1.2 (1993): 116. Welsh argues that from late eighteenth century to end of nineteenth century in England, "narrative consisting of carefully managed circumstantial evidence, highly conclusive in itself and often scornful of direct testimony, flourished nearly everywhere—not only in literature, but in criminal jurisprudence, natural science, natural religion, and history writing itself" (Welsh, *Strong Representations, ix*).
40 Shapiro, "Circumstantial Evidence," 229; Shapiro, "Beyond Reasonable Doubt," 29.
41 See also Pfeiffer, *From Chaos to Catastrophe? Texts and the Transnationality of the Mind* (Berlin/Boston: DeGruyter, 2019). Pfeiffer frames the development of the biographical novel as a means for managing unpredictable patterns when replacements for "failing total conceptions of the world and life must be found." He also claims that intimate linkages between biography, history, and novel begin to appear in the eighteenth century, around the same time as Welsh asserts that circumstantial evidence becomes prominent in law and English narrative.
42 Samuel Amago, *True Lies: Narrative Self-Consciousness in the Contemporary Spanish Novel* (Lewisburg, PA: Bucknell University Press, 2006), 152, 153.
43 Cercas, *Soldiers,* 49, 58 ("Lo releí varias veces, tratando de dotar de un sentido coherente a aquellas anotaciones dispersas, y de ensamblarlas con los hechos que yo conocía"; "Pero lo cierto es que tardé todavía algún tiempo en terminar de reconstruir la historia que quería contar y en llegar a conocer, si no todos y cada uno de sus entresijos, si por lo menos los que juzgaba esencial"), 60, 69.
44 Craft, "The Persistence of Dread in Law and Literature," *Yale Law Journal* 102, No. 521 (1992): 522.
45 Ibid., 536–7, 526. See also James Whitman's ("The Origins of Reasonable Doubt") analysis of the development of the "reasonable doubt" standard in response to the moral "dread" of jurors.
46 Colm Toíbin, "The Anchored Imagination of the Biographical Novel," Interview by Bethany Layne, in *Conversations with Biographical Novelists: Truthful Fictions across the Globe*, ed. Michael Lackey (New York and London: Bloomsbury, 2019), 224.
47 Cercas, *Soldiers*, 137, 63 ("una suerte de biografía de Sánchez Mazas"); "Before he left, Sánchez Mazas told us he was going to write a book about all that, a book with us in it. He was going to call it *Soldiers of Salamis*; strange title, don't you think?" ("Antes de marcharse, Sánchez Mazas nos dijo que iba a escribir un libro sobre todo aquello, un libro en el que apareciéramos nosotros. Iba a llamarse *Soldados de Salamina;* un título raro, ¿no?"), 143, 73.
48 Ibid., 80 ("Así pues, lo que a continuación consigno no es lo que realmente sucedió, sino lo que parece verosímil que sucediera; no ofrezco hechos probados, sino conjeturas razonables"), 89.

49 Ibid., 138 ("Lo malo es que yo no sabía cuál era esa pieza. Corregí a fondo el libro, reescribí el principio y el final, reescribí varios episodios, otros los cambié de lugar. La pieza, sin embargo, no aparecía; el libro seguía estando cojo"), 144.
50 Richardson, "'No Pensar'," 10.
51 Cercas, *Soldiers,* 137–8 ("aunque todo lo que con el tiempo había averiguado sobre Sánchez Mazas iba a constituir el núcleo de mi libro, lo que *me permitía sentirme seguro*, llegaría un momento en que tendría que prescindir de esas andaderas, porque—si es que lo que escribe va a tener verdadero interés—un escritor no escribe nunca acerca de lo que conoce, sino precisamente de lo que ignora"), 143–4.
52 Jill Lepore, "The Academy Is Largely Itself Responsible for Its Own Peril," *Chronicle of Higher Education* (November 13, 2018), https://www.bunkhistory.org/resources/3505. Jens Beckert, *Imagined Futures: Fictional Expectations and Capitalist Dynamics* (Cambridge, MA: Harvard University Press, 2016), also observes in a note (8) how the parallel development of fictional worlds and approaches to probabilistic certainty contributed to a general awareness of the contingency of social reality and rules for dealing with these uncertainties.
53 Shapiro, "Beyond Reasonable Doubt," 20–1.
54 Ibid., 29, 31.
55 Ibid., 33–4.
56 Whitman, "The Origins of Reasonable Doubt," np.
57 Eric Lillquist, "Recasting Reasonable Doubt: Decision Theory and the Virtues of Variability," 36 *UC Davis Law Review* 85 (2002): 112. Barbara Shapiro has similarly referenced these vast disparities of interpretation, noting recent experiments seeking numerical equivalents for "beyond reasonable doubt" for jurors and judges ranging from a low of 0.6 to a high of 0.9, with judges at the high end and jurors at the low end ("Beyond Reasonable Doubt," 2011, 33).
58 Whitman, "The Origins of Reasonable Doubt," np.
59 Craft, "The Persistence of Dread," 530–1, 522. See also Julian Baggini, "Consolations for a Post-Truth World": "But that process of stripping away is removing, from actual phenomenon being discussed, complexity, ambiguity, nuance … and a lot of things that are really important to understanding the phenomenon. When you try to translate any kind of real-life problem into a neat, logical form, you're almost always simplifying it. We need a kind of blend—we need not just tools of logic (which are important and valuable—I'm not denying that) but also tools of judgement, and of inductive and abductive reasoning which can also inform."
60 Cercas, *Soldiers,* 57 ("Es un relato real. […] Será como una novela—resumí—. Sólo que, en vez de ser todo mentira, todo es verdad"), 68.
61 Ibid., 57, 138 ("Es solo que, en fin, querido, me parece que la imaginación no es tu fuerte"), 68; ("¡Mierda!—dijo Conchi—. Ya te dije que no escribieras sobre un facha. Esa gente jode todo lo que toca. Lo que tienes que hacer es olvidarte de ese libro y empezar otro. ¿Qué tal uno sobre García Lorca?"), 144.
62 Cercas, "Resisting the 'Dictatorship of the Present'," 53, 56.
63 Cercas, *Soldiers*, 132, 134 ("Es probable que para entonces ya no creyera en nada. También lo es que, en su fuero interno, nunca en su vida haya creído

en nada; y, menos que nada, en aquello que se defendía o predicaba. [...] Hoy poca gente se acuerda de él, y quizá lo merece. Hay en Bilbao una calle que lleva su nombre"), 138, 140.

64 Javier Cercas, "From Conversations about *Soldiers of Salamis*." Extract from *Diálogos de Salamina: un paseo por el cine y la literatura* (Tusquets, 2003), *Words Without Borders Magazine*, https://www.wordswithoutborders.org/article/from-conversations-about-soldiers-of-salamis. Cercas has recently been more critical of the historical memory movement, in particular the 2007 "Law of Historical Memory." For further reading, see Giles Harvey, "Why a Champion of Reparative Justice Turned on the Cause," *The New Yorker*, January 6, 2020.

65 Cercas, "Resisting the 'Dictatorship of the Present'," 64.

66 Kurvet-Kaössar, "The Archive," *a/b:Auto/Biography Studies* 32, No. 2 (2017): 355.

67 Kurvet-Kaössar, paper presentation at the American Comparative Literature Association (ACLA) Annual Conference, Utrecht, Netherlands (July 2017).

68 Rafael Méndez, "Cercas pide que se desconfíe del narrador de "*Soldados de Salamina*," *El País* (July 2, 2002), https://elpais.com/diario/2002/07/03/cultura/1025647206_850215.html. ("Es una novela, rara, pero una novela. Yo buscaba la verdad literaria, no la del periodismo. La literaria es una verdad moral, universal, que manipula la realidad").

69 Javier Cercas, "The Third Truth," *El País* (English edition), (July 6, 2011), https://english.elpais.com/elpais/2011/07/06/inenglish/1309929650_850210.html.

70 Cercas, *Soldiers,* 138 ("como un mecanismo completo pero incapaz de desempeñar la función para la que ha sido ideado porque le falta una pieza"), 144; Cercas, "Resisting the 'Dictatorship of the Present'," 57, 53.

71 Michael Lackey, *Conversations with Biographical Novelists: Truthful Fictions across the Globe*, ed. Michael Lackey (New York and London: Bloomsbury, 2019), 10.

72 Javier Cercas, "Javier Cercas: The Perils of War and Fame," Interview with Carlos Rodríguez Martorell, *Criticas,* August 1, 2005.

73 Colum McCann, "Contested Realities in the Biographical Novel." Interview by Michael Lackey, in *Conversations with Biographical Novelists: Truthful Fictions across the Globe*, ed. Michael Lackey (New York and London: Bloomsbury, 2019), 139.

74 Todd Avery, "Pseudo-Quotations and Alternative Facts: Lytton Strachey and the Ethics of Biofiction in the Post-Truth Moment," in *Biofiction and Writers' Afterlives*, ed. Bethany Layne (Newcastle upon Tyne: Cambridge Scholars Publishing, 2020), 28.

75 Julian Baggini makes a useful distinction between "creating truths" and "being creative with the truth," or lying. To him, creating truth acknowledges the power of what we do to "create different realities," not just describe the ones that are already there. See Julian Baggini, "Consolations for a Post-Truth World," *3 AM Magazine*, https://www.3ammagazine.com/3am/bagginis-consolations-post-truth-world.

76 Boyd Tonkin, "Javier Cercas Interview: Picking over the Wounds of Spain's Recent Past," *The Independent* (June 8, 2014), https://www.independent.co.uk/arts-entertainment/books/features/javier-cercas-interview-picking-over-the-wounds-of-spain-s-recent-past-9500996.html.

77 Hegerty, "Losing the War."

78 Karolina Polasik, "Historian an Investigating Magistrate. Carlo Ginzburg's 'Circumstantial Paradigm.' Marginalia," *Sensus Historiae* II (2011): 47–8.
79 Cercas, *Soldiers*, 163 ("le conté a Conchi, mientra comíamos en self-service, la historia de Miralles, le expliqué el error de perspectiva que había cometido al escribir *Soldados de Salamina* y le aseguré que Miralles (o alguien como Miralles) era justamente la pieza que faltaba para que el mecanismo del libro funcionara"), 167.
80 Peter Barry, *Beginning Theory: An Introduction to Literary and Cultural Theory* (Manchester: Manchester University Press, 2002), 90.
81 Cercas has said that all of the characters in the novel are real, with the exception of Conchi. Yet, while Miralles is based upon a historical individual, he is essentially anonymous, and the character that Cercas develops is predominantly a fictional construction.
82 Alison Gibbons, "Postmodernism Is Dead. What Comes Next?" *Times Literary Supplement Online* (June 22, 2017), https://www.the-tls.co.uk/articles/public/postmodernism-dead-comes-next/.
83 Cercas, "Resisting the 'Dictatorship of the Present'," 53.
84 Cercas, *Soldiers,* 160, 177 ("'Es él'" [...] "pensaba que pronto sabría si Miralles era el soldado de Líster que salvó a Sánchez Mazas, y que sabría también qué pensó al mirarle los ojos y por qué lo salvó, y que entonces tal vez comprendería por fin un secreto esencial"), 165, 180.
85 Ibid., 197 ("Así que lo que andaba buscando era un héroe. Y ese héroe soy yo, ¿no?"), 199.
86 Ibid., 199 ("Nadie se acuerda de ellos, ¿sabe? Nadie se acuerda siquiera de por qué murieron, de por qué no tuvieron mujer e hijos y una habitación con sol; nadie, y menos que nadie, la gente por la que pelearan. No hay ni va a haber nunca ninguna calle miserable de ningún pueblo miserable de ninguna mierda de país que vaya a llevar nunca el nombre de ninguno de ellos. ¿Lo entiende? Lo entiende, ¿verdad? Ah, pero yo me acuerdo, vaya si me acuerdo, me acuerdo de todos, de Lela y de Joan y de Gabi y de Odena y de Pipo Y de Brugada y de Gudayol, no sé por qué lo hago pero lo hago, no pasa un solo día sin que piense en ellos"), 200–1.
87 Megan O'Grady, "Why Are We Living in a Golden Age of Historical Fiction?" *New York Times* (May 7, 2019), https://www.nytimes.com/2019/05/07/t-magazine/historical-fiction-books.html.
88 Annabel Lyon, "Irony-Free Reality TV," *Geist* 53 (Summer 2004), https://www.geist.com/fact/columns/irony-free-reality-tv/.
89 Hegerty, "Losing the War."
90 George Fisher, "The Jury's Rise as Lie Detector," *Yale Law Journal* 107, No. 3 (1997): 575.
91 Thomas Friedman, "Is Google God?" *CNN.com* (June 29, 2003), https://www.nytimes.com/2003/06/29/opinion/is-google-god.html.
92 Whitman, "The Origins of Reasonable Doubt," np.
93 Shapiro,"Beyond Reasonable Doubt," 33.
94 Jill Lepore, "The Academy Is Largely Itself Response for Its Own Peril", *Chronicle of Higher Education* (November 13, 2018), https://www.chronicle.com/article/the-academy-is-largely-itself-responsible-for-its-own-peril/?cid2=gen_login_refresh&cid=gen_sign_in.

95 Cited in Lepore, "After the Fact: In the History of Truth, a New Chapter Begins," *The New Yorker* (March 14, 2016), https://www.newyorker.com/magazine/2016/03/21/the-internet-of-us-and-the-end-of-facts.
96 Cercas, "From Conversations about *Soldiers of Salamis*."
97 As characterized by George Fisher in "The Jury's Rise as Lie Detector" (1997): "And the jury, in loyal support of the system's legitimacy, has issued crisp and impregnable verdicts," 581.
98 Kat McGowan, "Numbers Are Failing Us," *Boston Sunday Globe*, April 26, 2020 K1.
99 Cercas, *Soldiers,* 203 ("tal vez fue un nombre, pero no estoy seguro"), 205.
100 Richardson, "'No Panser'," 11.
101 McCann, "Contested Realities," 136.
102 Miller, *Pieces*, 229.
103 Cercas, *Soldiers,* 207 ("todo excepto lo que nos gobierna o hace vivir o concierne o somos o son"), 208.
104 Ibid., 207 ("lo vi entero, acabado, desde el principio hasta el final, desde la primera hasta la última línea, allí supe que, aunque en ningún lugar de ninguna ciudad de ninguna mierda de país fuera a haber nunca una calle que llevara el nombre de Miralles, mientras yo contase su historia Miralles seguiría de algún modo viviendo y seguirían [sus amigos] viviendo también siempre que yo hablase de ellos"), 208.
105 Cercas, "Resisting the 'Dictatorship of the Present'," 52.
106 Gibbons, "Postmodernism Is Dead."
107 Stavris, *Supplanting the Postmodern*, 356.
108 Ben Lerner, "This Week in Fiction," *The New Yorker* (June 10, 2012), https://www.newyorker.com/books/page-turner/this-week-in-fiction-ben-lerner.
109 O'Grady, "Why Are We Living."
110 Cercas, *Soldiers,* 208 ("sin saber muy bien hacia dónde va ni con quién va ni por qué va, sin importarle mucho siempre que sea hacia delante, hacia delante, hacia delante, siempre hacia delante"), 209. Notably, this is the last line of the novel.
111 Schaberg, *The Work of Literature*, 11.
112 James Boyd White, *From Expectation to Experience: Essays on Law and Legal Education* (Ann Arbor: University of Michigan Press, 1999), 54.
113 Greenstein, "Determining the Facts," 1830.

Chapter 2

1 Antonio Muñoz Molina, *Como la sombra que se va* (Barcelona: Planeta, 2014), trans. Camilo A. Ramírez, *Like a Fading Shadow* (New York: Farrar, Straus and Giroux, 2017). All original Spanish citations and English translations are from these editions. For readability, I have referenced the English edition in all in-text citations, with the original Spanish cited in parentheses in the endnotes followed by the page number from the 2014 edition.

2 Gabriela Ybarra, *El comensal* (Barcelona: Caballo de Troya, 2015), trans. Natasha Wimmer, *The Dinner Guest* (London: Penguin, 2018). All original Spanish citations and English translations are from these editions. For readability, I have referenced the English edition in all in-text citations, with the original Spanish in parentheses in the endnotes, followed by the page number from the 2018 edition.

3 Gabriela Ybarra, *The Dinner Guest*, 1–2 ("Esta novela es una reconstrucción libre […] A menudo, imaginar ha sido la única opción que he tenido para intentar comprender," *El comensal,* 11–12).

4 Angie Thurston, C. ter Kulle, Sue Philips, *Care of Souls*, https://sacred.design/wp-content/uploads/2019/10/CareofSouls.pdf. Notably, as a description of this crisis of in between, Thomas Lea has referred to how the "twenty-first century reader can comfortably regard a work of fiction with cynicism *and* credulity, outrage *and* ennui, optimism *and* despair, without needing either a cohering sentimental narrative, or any balance between these states." [Thomas] Lea, *Twenty-first Century Fiction: Contemporary British Voices* (Manchester: Manchester University Press, 2017), 15.

5 Antonio Muñoz Molina, "Antonio Muñoz Molina: 'La literatura tiene la obligación de comprender,'" *El Periódico*, https://www.elperiodico.com/es/ocio-y-cultura/20141213/antonio-munoz-molina-literatura-tiene-obligacion-comprender-3769649.

6 Gabriela Ybarra, "Imagining Truths: In Conversation with Gabriela Ybarra," Sarah Timmer Harvey, https://www.asymptotejournal.com/blog/2019/06/20/imagining-truths-in-conversation-with-gabriela-ybarra/.

7 Lance Olsen, "The Biographical Practice of Not-Knowing, Interview with Michael Lackey," in *Truthful Fictions: Conversations with American Biographical Novelists*, ed. Michael Lackey (New York and London: Bloomsbury, 2014), 194.

8 Kevin Jon Heller, "The Cognitive Psychology of Circumstantial Evidence," *Michigan Law Review* 105, No. 2 (2006): 25.

9 See interviews with Colum McCann by Michael Lackey and Colm Tóibín by Bethany Layne in *Conversations with Biographical Novelists: Truthful Fictions across the Globe* (New York and London: Bloomsbury, 2019).

10 Antonio Muñoz Molina, *Like a Fading Shadow,* 9 ("El hecho de entrar en el hotel daría un anclaje físico a todas mis especulaciones, volvería tangible lo que hasta ese momento pertenecía a las ensoñaciones y a los duermevalas de los libros"), 19.

11 Ybarra, "Imagining Truths."

12 Nicoline Timmer, *Do You Feel It Too: The Post-Postmodern Syndrome in American Fiction* (Amsterdam and New York: Rodopi, 2010), 21. https://brill.com/view/title/30394.

13 Irmtraud Huber, *Literature after Postmodernism: Reconstructive Fantasies* (London and New York: Palgrave MacMillan, 2014), 6.

14 Josh Toth, *Truth and Metafiction: Plasticity and Renewal in American Narrative* (New York: Bloomsbury Academic, 2021), 24.

15 Toth, *Truth and Metafiction: Plasticity and Renewal in American Narrative*, 8, 29.

16 Antonio Muñoz Molina, interview by Óscar López, *Página 2* (December 1, 2014), https://www.youtube.com/watch?v=8ySR6pM_uRA ("Yo, los juegos

posmodernos, decir que la realidad y la ficción son lo mismo, a mí eso no me interesa nada. Para mí en la novela era importante dejar claro aquello que es cierto, es decir, construir una novela con lo máximo de materiales no inventados").

17 Javier Cercas, "Resisting the 'Dictatorship of the Present' in the Biographical Novel," Interview by Virginia Newhall Rademacher, in *Conversations with Biographical Novelists: Truthful Fictions across the Globe*, ed. Michael Lackey (New York and London: Bloomsbury, 2019), 50.

18 Antonio Muñoz Molina, "On the Experience of Fiction," *Hudson Review* LXVIII, No.1 (Spring 2015), https://hudsonreview.com/issue/spring-2015/.

19 Molina, "On the Experience of Fiction."

20 Nancy Miller, *What They Saved: Pieces of a Jewish Past* (Lincoln: University of Nebraska Press, 2011), 4.

21 Antonio Muñoz Molina, "La literatura tiene la obligación de comprender" (Literature Has the Obligation to Understand), Interview with Elena Hevía, *El Periódico* (December 13, 2014), https://www.elperiodico.com/es/ocio-y-cultura/20141213/antonio-munoz-molina-literatura-tiene-obligacion-comprender-3769649 ("desató cosas que estaban muy escondidas").

22 See Sergio Restrepo, "Pos-simulacro e hipermodernidad en Como la sombra que se va," *Nomenclatura: Aproximaciones a los Estudios Hispánicos* 5 (2017).

23 Muñoz Molina, *Like a Fading Shadow,* 5 ("Me quedé hasta muy tarde buscando sus rastros por la memoria insomne de internet [...] me volvían a la imaginación fechas, nombres, hechos mínimos dotados de la consistencia quitinosa de lo real, lo que nadie puede inventarse"), 12.

24 Ibid., 5, 8 ("cuando tenia nueve o diéz años se despertaba todos las noches con sueños pavorosos, más asustado todavía por sus propios gritos [...] Se esforzaba por despertar y abría los ojos y no podia ver, porque había desembocado en otro sueño sucesivo de ceguera. [...] y las que se encontraron luego en el maletero y en el suelo del coche, hasta los pelos y los restos de espuma seca adheridos a las hojas de una maquinilla de afeitar desechable. [...] Voy viendo su figura formarse delante de mí, su sombra, su biografía entera, hecha de esos detalles minimos"),13, 17.

25 Ibid., 45, 44 ("los datos triviales y exactos permiten una sensación engañosa de omnisciencia";"El pasado está lleno de pormenores exóticos"), 70, 73.

26 Ibid., 4 ("Basta teclear unos segundos en el portatíl para internarse en los archivos donde se conserva el testimonio de casi todas las cosas que hizo, los lugares donde estuvo, los delitos que cometió, las cárceles en las que cumplió condenas, hasta los nombres de mujeres con las que pasó una noche, o con las que tomó algo en la barra de un bar"), 10.

27 Muñoz Molina, Página 2.

28 Muñoz Molina, *Like a Fading Shadow,* 5 ("Es asombroso todo lo que se puede llegar a saber de una persona de la que en el fondo no se sabe nada, porque nunca dijo lo que más habría importado que dijera; un hueco oscuro, un espacio en blanco; una fotografía en una ficha policial; las líneas toscas de un retrato robot hecho a base de testimonios fragmentarios y recuerdos imprecisos"),11.

29 Ibid., 272 ("Las cosas dicen lo que uno calla; revelan obscenamente en público lo que uno habría preferido que quedara en secreto [...] Lo que ellas cuentan sin palabras vuelve irrelevante la ficción. Uno sigue queriendo imaginar. La literatura es querer habitar en la mente de otro, como un intruso en una casa cerrada, ver el mundo con sus ojos, desde el interior de esas ventanas en las que no se parece que se asome nunca nadie. Es imposible [...]," 453.

30 Ibid., 3, 4, 6 ("El miedo me ha despertado en el interior de la conciencia de otro; el miedo y la intoxicación de las lecturas y la búsqueda; [...] El sueño del que he despertado podía ser suyo, aunque él no apareciera; [...] He llegado a saber tanto de él que me parece recordar cosas de su vida, lugares que él vio y yo nunca he visto"), 9, 10, 13.

31 Ibid., 3–4.

32 Ibid., 70 ("La gente hablaba murmurando en su idioma incomprensible"), 113.

33 Ibid., 176.

34 Ibid., 27, 7 ("Debajo de una superficie tranquila mi vida era una yuxtaposición sin orden de vidas fragmentarias, un sinvivir de deseos frustrados, de piezas dispersas que no cuadraban." [...] "Nada es más fácil que sentirse de repente perdido; más fácil para mí, al menos." [...] "Una gran parte de lo que hacía me era ajeno"), 45, 15, 45.

35 Ibid., 30 ("Me escondía de cada vida en la otra"), 50.

36 Ibid., 96 ("Me había desprendido de todas las ataduras, las obligaciones, los horarios, las lealtades de mi vida"), 154.

37 Ibid., 80, 58 ("como un fugitivo que también fuera un traidor"; "me iba recluyendo en una especie de parálisis íntima alimentada casi en exclusiva de ficciones"), 130, 93–4.

38 Huber, *Literature after Postmodernism*, 219.

39 Muñoz Molina, *Like a Fading Shadow*, 204 ("por conatos o simulacros de dobles vidas"; "Por eso me atraían tanto entonces las historias de espías, de traidores y de impostores, las novelas de fugitivos que se hacen pasar por muertos y se esconden bajo una nueva identidad"), 336.

40 Ibid., 31, 33 ("mi novia, o quizás ya mi mujer, me dijo: 'Tienes tanta sensibilidad para los personajes de las novelas y de las películas, y no ves a quien está cerca de tí.'"; "Tenía esa convicción tan enfermiza [...] de que la vida verdadera estaba en alguna otra parte, de que la imaginación es más rica y poderosa que la realidad [...] y las historias de ficción mucho más perfectas que el desvenir desorganizado y repetitive sin lustre de los hechos reales"), 51–2.

41 Virginia Newhall Rademacher, "Postmodern Quest and the Role of Distance in Antonio Muñoz Molina's *El invierno en Lisboa*," *Ciberletras: Revista de Crítica Literaria y de Cultura* 18 (2007), https://www.lehman.edu/faculty/guinazu/ciberletras/v18/newhall.html.

42 Huber, *Literature after Postmodernism,* 218.

43 Muñoz Molina, *Like a Fading Shadow*, 131. The narrator states, "Sometimes fiction wants to supplant reality, sometimes it settles for adding certain secondary details" ("La ficción unas veces quiere suplantar la realidad y otras se conforma con añadirle pormenores secundarios"), 208–9.

44 Ibid., 109 ("Nunca se había acostado con mujeres que no fueran prostitutas de bajo precio, de las que se ofrecían en la calle. A un compañero de la prisión

le decía siempre, con una mueca de experiencia en gran parte ficticia, que las mujeres eran para usar y tirar, que un hombre en peligro no podía fiarse de ellas"), 173.

45 Ibid., 170, 171–2 ("El mundo exterior le llegaba de una manera indirecta, con un grado de distorsión del que era consciente pero que no sabía calcular"; "No podia fiarse de las informaciones que le llegaban. No había manera de estar seguro"; Él imaginaba [...] que tendría que existir un método, un código que le permitiera compender todo aquello, distinguir la verdad de la mentira, lo todavía actual de lo anacrónico o lo desacreditado, como las máquinas de descrifar mensajes enemigos que tenían los servicios de espionaje durante la guerra, un procedimiento seguro para distinguir lo que era cierto y fiable [...] y quizás hasta para interceptar los mensajes que se intercambiaban entre sí los dueños del mundo, los poderosos, los judíos, los que mangoneaban todo sin dejar huella, los comunistas"), 275, 276, 277.

46 Ibid., 173 ("Oía a predicadores que anunciaban la inminencia del Apocalipsis o la llegada de Jesucristo en una nave extraterrestre. Oía la transmission en directo de los disturbios que provocaban los negros en las ciudades durante las noches de verano, explosiones de bombas y fragores de incendios y de cristales rotos de comercios asaltados, sirenas de policía y temblores de edificios quemados que se derrumbaban"), 280.

47 As an example of the disassociative processes of dangerous false narratives that foment credence in extremist ideologies and conspiracy theories, Muñoz Molina provides a provocative model via his imagined representation of Ray's subjectivity and interior monologues.

48 Muñoz Molina, *Like a Fading Shadow,* 274 ("La imagen construída tan meticulosamente en el laboratorio de su conciencia se ha vuelto real"), 457.

49 Ibid., 129 ("ya contaminados de ficción"), 205.

50 See Edurne Portela, "Puntos de partida: Cuestión de imaginación," in *El eco de los disparos. Cultura y memoria de la violencia* (Barcelona: Galaxia Gutenberg, 2016), 18–30. In a related interview, Portela contrasts the capacity of an "ethical imagination" to transform a reductive, Manichean contaminated imagination by opening to nuance and complexity; the ethical imagination, in contrast, "is that which provokes us and pushes us to reconsider our own convictions." Interview with Xandru Fernández, *El Cuaderno* (June 2017), https://elcuadernodigital.com/2017/06/05/edurne-portela/.

51 Referenced in Michael Patrick Lynch. "The Value of Truth," *Boston Review* (March 1, 2021), https://bostonreview.net/philosophy-religion/michael-patrick-lynch-value-truth.

52 Stephen Marche, "David Shields 'Reality Hunger' in the Age of Trump," *Los Angeles Times Review of Books* (August 5, 2017), https://www.lareviewofbooks.org/article/david-shieldss-reality-hunger-age-trump-write-now/.

53 Jay Parini, "Fact or Fiction: Writing Biographies versus Writing Novels' from *Some Necessary Angels: Essays on Writing and Politics*," in *Biographical Fiction: A Reader*, ed. Michael Lackey (New York and London: Bloomsbury, 2017), 300.

54 Muñoz Molina, *Like a Fading Shadow,* 181 ("Yo creía entonces, en esos años en los que aún no te conocía [su esposa Elvira Lindo], que la tarea de

literatura era inventar formas perfectas, hechas de simetrías y de resonancias que dieran a la experiencia del mundo un orden y un significado del que otro modo carecía. [...] Muy poco a poco, en otra vida futura, me fui dando cuenta de que [...] [a] lo más que se puede aspirer lo inventado no es a mejorar mediante la ficción la materia amorfa de los hechos reales sino a imitar lo que mirado con atención en su orden impremeditado y sin embargo riguroso, a convertirse en una maqueta de sus formas, en un modelo a escala de sus procesos"), 293–5.

55 Ibid., 217 ("A diferencia de personas reales disponen de la potestad de desvanecerse sin rastro"), 357.

56 Ybarra, "Imagining Truths: In Conversation with Gabriela Ybarra."

57 Ybarra, *The Dinner Guest*, 3 ("Cuentan que mi familia siempre se sienta un comensal de más en cada comida. Es invisible, pero está ahí. Tiene plato, vaso, y cubiertos. De vez en cuando aparece, proyecta su sombra sobre la mesa y borra a alguno de los presentes. El primero en desparecer fue mi abuelo paterno"), 15.

58 Gabriela Ybarra, Podcast interview, *Vostok Seis* (July 30, 2018), https://www.vostokseis.com/episodios/gabriela-ybarra.

59 Ybarra, "Imagining Truths: In Conversation with Gabriela Ybarra."

60 Ybarra, *The Dinner Guest*, 44 ("La muerte de mi madre resucitó la de mi abuelo paterno. Hasta entonces, para mí el asesinato eran solo unas esposas metidas en una vitrina al lado de las llamas de bronce que mis padres trajeron de Perú. El tedio de la enfermedad llamó al tedio de la espera del secuestro. Mi padre empezó a hablar de rosarios manchados con sangre. Yo aún tardaría varios meses en comprender su dolor"), 60.

61 Ibid., 1 ("Escuché por primera vez la historia a los ocho años. Un compañero de clase en el colegio, nieto del fiscal que había llevado el caso, me explicó cómo su abuelo pescó el cadaver del mío en la ría del Nervión con una red traiña, del tipo que usan los gallegos para capturer boquerones. Años más tarde, la nieta de un médico forense, compañera de clase en otro colegio, me confesó que su abuelo había diseccionado el cuerpo del mío después de que lo encontraron atado de pies y manos arrollado por un tren cerca de la estación de Larrabasterra. Durante muchos años tomé las dos historias por ciertas y las mezclé con conversaciones escuchadas en casa hasta elaborar una versión propia"), 11.

62 Ibid., 1–2 ("Metí el nombre de mi abuelo en Google y visité hemerotecas. Tomé muchas notas sobre lo que leí: transcripciones literales de noticias y reacciones. Pero las escenas que imaginaba terminaron filtrándose en mi crónica"), 12.

63 Lily Meyer, "Breaking Down the Doors to the Past in the *Dinner Guest*," *NPR* (May 29, 2019), https://www.npr.org/2019/05/29/726346251/breaking-down-the-doors-to-the-past-in-the-dinner-guest.

64 Anne Rüggemeier, "Beyond the Subject—Towards the Object? Nancy K. Miller's *What They Saved: Pieces of a Jewish Past* (2011) and the Materiality of Life Writing," *European Journal of Life Writing* 5 (2016): 38.

65 Gabriela Ybarra, *The Dinner Guest*, 31, 34 ("Al hacerle la autopsia el doctor Toledo, forense del hospital de Basurto, determinó que tenía las paredes intestinales pegadas, síntoma evidente de que [...] casi no le habían dado de comer durante su confinamiento; En la autopsia se descubrió que mi abuelo

tenía restos de hierba en el estómago y que llevaba por lo menos tres días sin defecar, a pesar de que en el zulo que la policía halló algún tiempo después habían aparecido excrementos"), 45, 48.

66 Gabriela Ybarra, "Imagining Truths: In Conversation with Gabriela Ybarra."

67 Carolyn Kraus, "Proof of Life: Memoir, Truth, and Documentary Evidence," *Biography* 31, No. 2 (Spring 2008): 245.

68 Ybarra, *The Dinner Guest*, 16 ("No es cierto que …"), 28.

69 Mary Pinard. Personal interview with Virginia Newhall Rademacher, August 2020.

70 Ybarra, *The Dinner Guest,* 47 ("Principio enfermedad Ernestina. Notas de su marido"), 64.

71 Ibid., 125 ("He intentado calcular el peso de los edificios. He contado las ventanas y los pisos de un rascacielos y he estimado lo que podían pesar, pero ni la calculadora del teléfono ni yo hemos sido capaces de soportar tanto cargo"), 151.

72 Ali Smith, *There But For The* (London: Penguin Press, 2006), 159. https://www.amazon.com/There-But-Novel-Ali-Smith/dp/0375424091.

73 Ibid., 119 ("mi padre, mis hermanas y yo nos habíamos acostumbrado a nuestra ausencia porque ella la amortiguaba"), 144–5.

74 Ybarra, "Imagining Truths: In Conversation with Gabriela Ybarra."

75 Ybarra, *The Dinner Guest*, 40 ("Por lo demás vivía ajena del conflicto"), 55.

76 Ibid., 39 ("Durante los años más duros de los ochenta, los llamados años de plomo, los vecinos simulan que no pasa nada: juegan al tenis, toman el aperitivo, salen a navegar y visitor los merenderos de Berango"), 54.

77 Bryony White, "The Gaze of Others," *Times Literary Supplement* (April 30, 2021), https://www.the-tls.co.uk/articles/open-water-caleb-azumah-nelson-review-bryony-white/.

78 Ibid., 79 ("Su reacción frente la enfermedad fue la resistencia. Aqui no pasa nada. Esto no me mata. Mirad cómo me encuentro de bien. Y me lo creía a ratos"), 99.

79 Ibid., 91 ("'No te preocupes,' le dijo mi padre mientras le acariciaba la cara, 'estos deben ser los efectos secundarios de la quimoterapia'"), 113.

80 Ibid., 64 ("Siento el mismo letargo de hace un año. La misma densidad en la cabeza. […] Llevo solo cinco minutos en este cuarto y me quiero ir"), 82.

81 Ibid., 45 ("La tarde de 4 de abril de 2011 mi madre me llamó por teléfono y me dijo: 'Gabriela, tengo cáncer, pero no es nada.' Unas horas después se subió a un avión y se acomodó sobre su tumor hasta que llegó a Nueva York"), 61.

82 Ibid., 83 ("Ahora solo le gustaba la comida fría y blanda y cenaba gelatina de un bol"), 129.

83 Ibid., 98 ("Su primera reacción fue desmoronarse. Pero luego reflexionó y dió a entender que estaba contenta de que nadie le hubiera ocultado lo que pasaba. Alcanzó la aceptación en lo que tardó en comerse el yogur de la bandeja de la comida"), 121.

84 Gabriela Ybarra, Interview on *Vostok Seis*, https://www.vostokseis.com/episodios/gabriela-ybarra.

85 Rebecca Guevara, "Review: *Let the Great World Spin*," *Writing Waters Blog* (April 27, 2012), https://thewritingwaters.wordpress.com/2012/04/27/let-the-great-world-spin/.

86 Colum McCann, "Contested Realities in the Biographical Novel," Interviewed by Michael Lackey, in *Conversations with Biographical Novelists: Truthful Fictions across the Globe*, ed. Michael Lackey (New York and London: Bloomsbury, 2019), 139.
87 Ybarra, *The Dinner Guest*, 116 ("Un mes y medio después de que muriera mi madre, el 20 de octubre de 2011, ETA anunció el cese definitivo de su actividad armada"), 141.
88 Ibid., 67 ("Un policía entró en el portal y gritó: '¡Hay una bomba!' Mi prima levantó los brazos y tiró el paquete al suelo. El cartero lanzó la correspondencia por los aires; las cartas golpearon la caja del explosivo mientras mi prima seguía con los brazos levantados. O así me la imagino yo"), 86.
89 Ibid., 69, 70 ("He encontrado una cuenta de YouTube con un usuario que tiene el mismo nombre y los mismos apellidos que él. No sé si es falsa o verdadera." [...] "Ninguno de los vídeos que he visto me ha dado miedo, pero luego he imaginado a Miguel frente al ordenador y no sabría describir lo que he sentido. Sus retratos me provocan sensaciones similares a las imágenes de las células del cancer. No pienso en la amenaza, sino en la ficción que me sugieren"), 88, 89.
90 Gabriela Ybarra, Interview on *Vostok Seis,* https://www.vostokseis.com/episodios/gabriela-ybarra.
91 Fernando Aramburu, *Patria* (Barcelona: Tusquets, 2016). Translated as *Homeland*, trans. Albert MacAdam (New York: Pantheon, 2019).
92 David Jiménez Torres, "El espacio de las heridas: violencia, afectos, y context en *Patria* y *El Comensal*," *Bulletin of Spanish Studies* 96, No. 7 (2019): 1077–94.
93 Portela, *El eco de los disparos*, 21 ("Yo soy parte de esa historia y mi punto de vista para contarla es el del testigo que por muchos años, si no indiferente al problema de violence en el País Vasco, sí le dio la espalda, eligió no querer entender porque hacerlo resultaba demasiada complicado y emocionalmente agotador").
94 Ibid., 21.
95 Ybarra, *The Dinner Guest*, 131 ("He encontrado en Facebook a Kepa, un amigo del colegio de Getxo. He googleado a sus contactos y he descubierto que varios han estado presos. He visto una foto suya abrazado a dos chicos que han pertenecido a ETA. Kepa era cojo. Un día en su casa que no podía ser mi amigo. Me contó que tenía dos primos en la cárcel. Conseguí convencerle que no hablarnos era una tontería y seguimos charlando hasta que me mudé a Madrid. A veces pienso si se habrá vuelto a acordar de mí: [...] Miro fotos de etarras y investigo sus vidas. Me cuesta aceptarles, porque asumir su humanidad significa reconocer que yo también podría llegar a hacer algo así. Mi conciencia estaba más tranquila cuando imaginaba que eran locos o que no eran personas. Marcianos. Ficción,") 158, 159.
96 Portela, *El eco de los disparos*, 146.
97 McCann, "Contested Realities in the Biographical Novel," 149.
98 Ruth Franklin, "Olga Tokarczuk's Novels against Nationalism," *The New Yorker* (July 29, 2019), https://www.newyorker.com/magazine/2019/08/05/olga-tokarczuks-novels-against-nationalism.
99 Muñoz Molina, *Like a Fading Shadow*, 270–1 ("los objetos sobre los que he leído tanto y visto en fotografías, imaginándolos con tanta precisión que

ahora me sorprende que existan de verdad; [...] todo ordenado, etiquetado, como los objetos fragmentarios de remotas vidas cotidianas en las vitrinas de un museo, las huellas materiales de un mundo perdido"), 450.

100 Ibid., 267 ("La intensidad de la injuria, la vehemencia del odio y su mezlca de vulgaridad e ignorancia, no puede ser traducida"), 443.

101 Ibid., 268 ("El pasado es un parque temático; [...] Uno puede entrar en la celda que ocupó Luther King en la cárcel de Birmingham, Alabama, sentarse en un catre idéntico al suyo, leer, proyectada en la pared, la carta que escribió allí, en hojas sueltas, en los márgenes de un periódico, a la luz que se colaba por una rendija [...] Pero quién sabrá cómo era esa oscuridad hedionda, cómo resonarían cerrojos y portillos metálicos y gritos de presos [...] cómo sería la duda insidiosa, en mitad de la noche, la sospecha de la inutilidad de todo aquel sacrificio, el abatamiento anticipado de sufrir en balde y arrastrar a otros el sufrimiento, la sequedad del alma, la cobardía secreta"), 445.

102 Ibid., 281 ("Levantaban a un hombre hacia una santidad que él no había deseado ni solicitado y luego renegaban de él por no estar a la altura imposible que le habían atribuido. Lo convertían contra su voluntad en una estatua heróica y a continuación le apedraban y la derribaban, lo lapidaban a él. La vergüenza era una de sus aflicciones secretas más asiduas, latiendo siempre en él a una mayor profundidad que la angustia de las obligaciones [...] el desequilibrio entre quien los demás veían o querían ver y quién era realmente. No hay figura publica que no sea la de un impostor"), 471.

103 Emma Donoghue, "Voicing the Nobodies in the Biographical Novel," Interview by Michael Lackey, in *Conversations with Biographical Novelists: Truthful Fictions across the Globe*, ed. Michael Lackey (New York and London: Bloomsbury, 2019), 90.

Chapter 3

1 Rosa Montero, "Speculative Subjectivities and the Biofictional Surge," Interview by Virginia N. Rademacher, in *Conversations with Biographical Novelists: Truthful Fictions across the Globe*, ed. Michael Lackey (London and New York: Bloomsbury, 2019), 167. I interviewed Rosa Montero in October 2016. This interview includes various references from that interview.

2 Rosa Montero, *La loca de la casa* (Madrid: Alfaguara, 2003), 264. The English translation of this title is *The Madwoman of the House*. ("Tal vez cada uno de los acontecimientos de nuestra existencia se haya podido dar de diez maneras distintas. [...] Al jugar con los 'y si', el novelista experimenta con estas vidas potenciales.") For readability, the English translations are included in all in-text references, with the original Spanish in parentheses in the endnotes. All English translations are mine, unless otherwise noted.

3 Jens Beckert, "Imagined Futures: Fictional Expectations in the Economy," *Theory and Society* 42 (2013): 234. Beckert references the work of L. Karpik, *Valuing the Unique: The Economics of Singularities* (Princeton: Princeton University Press, 2010) and G. Möllering, *Trust, Reason, Routine, Reflexivity* (Oxford: Elsevier, 2006).

4 Sherryl Vint, "Promissory Futures: Reality and Imagination in Finance and Fiction," *CR: The New Centennial Review* 19, No. 1 (Spring 2019): 12.
5 Vint, "Promissory Futures," 12.
6 Alison Gibbons, "Postmodernism Is Dead. What Comes Next?" *Times Literary Supplement* (June 22, 2017), https://www.the-tls.co.uk/articles/public/postmodernism-dead-comes-next/.
7 Peter Bernstein, *Against the Gods: The Remarkable Story of Risk* (New York: John Wiley & Sons, 1996), 305.
8 Dick Bryan and Michael Rafferty, *Capitalism with Derivatives: A Political Economy of Financial Derivatives, Capital and Class* (New York: Palgrave MacMillan, 2006), 213.
9 Ulrich Beck, *World at Risk* (Cambridge and Malden: Polity Press, 2009), 8.
10 Anthony Giddens, *Modernity and Identity: Self and Society in the Late Modern Age* (Stanford: Stanford University Press, 1991), 3.
11 Montero, "Speculative Subjectivities and the Biofictional Surge," 160, 168.
12 Maryanne Leone has observed that Montero's publications "might be read as a barometer of key issues in Spain since the nation's transition to democracy." ("Unorthodox Theories and Beings: Science, Technology, and Women in the Narratives of Rosa Montero," in *A Laboratory of her Own: Women and Science in Spanish Culture*, eds. Victoria L. Ketz, Dawn Smith-Sherwood, and Debra Faszer-McMahon [Nashville: Vanderbilt University Press, 2021], 235.) The influence of much of Montero's work, translated into more than twenty languages, extends beyond Spain to more universal concerns.
13 For readability, as with other Spanish-language texts in this book, I have used English translations in the in-text citations. *La ridícula idea de no volver a verte* (translated as *The Ridiculous Idea of Never Seeing You Again*) was published in 2013 (Barcelona: Seix Barral). The original Spanish is cited in parentheses in the endnotes, followed by the page numbers from the referenced Spanish edition. All English translations are mine, unless otherwise noted. The interview I conducted with Montero is included in *Conversations with Biographical Novelists*, referenced in note 1.
14 Hereafter, referred to by the abbreviated title, *The Ridiculous Idea.*
15 Montero, "Speculative Subjectivities and the Biofictional Surge," 166. Notably, Laura Cernat has referred to works which incorporate, but are not exclusively biofictions, as "borderline biofictions." See Cernat, "Review: *Truthful Fictions: Conversations with Biographical Novelists across the Globe*," *Biography* 43, No. 2 (Spring 2020): 485.
16 Rosa Montero, *La ridícula idea de no volver a verte* (Barcelona: Seix Barral, 2013) ("he utilizado a la gran Madame Curie como un paradigma, un arquetipo de referencia con el que poder reflexionar sobre los temas que últimatemente me rondan insistentemente por la cabeza"), 209.
17 Paul DiMaggio, "Endogenizing 'Animal Spirits': Toward a Sociology of Collective Response to Uncertainty and Risk," in *The New Economic Sociology: Developments in an Emerging Field,* eds. M.F. Guillén et al. (New York: Russell Sage, 2002), 90.
18 Montero, *Speculative Subjectivities and the Biofictional Surge,* 158, 164.
19 Ibid., 164.

20 Rosa Montero, "Entrevista a Rosa Montero, autora de *La ridícula idea de no volver a verte*," Interview by Javier Velasco Oliaga for *Todo Literatura* (October 23, 2014), https://www.todoliteratura.es/noticia/6977/entrevistas/entrevista-a-rosa-montero-autora-de-la-ridicula-idea-de-no-volver-a-verte.html.

21 Lauren Berlant and Dana Luciano, "Conversation: Lauren Berlant with Dana Luciano," *Social Text Online* (January 13, 2013), https://socialtextjournal.org/periscope_article/conversation-lauren-berlant-with-dana-luciano/.

22 Laura Cernat, "Review of Conversations with Biographical Novelists: Truthful Fictions across the Globe," *Biography* 43, No.2 (2021): 486–7.

23 Bernstein, *Against the Gods*, 329.

24 Mark Taylor, *Confidence Games: Money and Markets in a World without Redemption* (Chicago: University of Chicago Press, 2004), 301.

25 Montero, "Speculative Subjectivities and the Biofictional Surge,"162.

26 Montero, *La ridícula idea* ("Incluso escondí durante décadas mi parte más imaginativa y fomenté la lógica, porque las discusiones intelectuales y racionales eran el ámbito del varón, el territorio de combate en donde te ganabas el respeto del contrario, mientras que las fantasías eran vagorosas tontunillas de mujer. Por eso mis primeras novelas son todas más realistas y sólo pude comenzar a liberarme de esa represión o mutilación mental con mi quinto libro"), 44–5.

27 Ibid. ("Mucho más libre"), 45.

28 Montero, *Historias de mujeres* ("se pasó la vida ocultando cosas, disimulando defectos, alterando virtudes, construyendo de sí misma un conmovedor personaje. De hecho fue un gran farsante, una sutilísima impostora. Fingía, por ejemplo, un aspecto de completo y sereno dominio sobre la existencia, incluso de la fríaldad y despego, cuando en realidad era una mujer llena de fuegos y terrores"), 48–9.

29 Ibid. ("le debía de asustar demasiado"), 47.

30 Rosa Montero, *Historias de mujeres* (Madrid: Punto de Lectura, 1995) ("ese enternecedor afán que tenemos los humanos de retocar nuestras biografías para darles una apariencia de orden al absolute caos de la existencia"), 203.

31 Montero, "Speculative Subjectivities and the Biofictional Surge," 161, 164.

32 Montero, *La ridícula idea* ("Ganas de usar su vida como vara de medir para entender la mía"), 18.

33 Montero, *Historias de mujeres* ("necesitamos un mapa de emergencia que señale el camino entre tanto vacío"), 282.

34 Montero, Rosa. Personal interview by Virginia N. Rademacher in Madrid, July 2006.

35 Montero, *La loca de la casa* ("A los pocos meses, el tema de la desaparición de mi hermana se había convertido en uno de esos tabúes que tanto abundan en las familias, lugares acotados y secretos por los que nadie transita [...]"), 108.

36 Ibid. ("Por ejemplo, supongamos por un momento que he mentido y que no tengo ninguna hermana. Y que, por consiguiente, jamás ha sucedido ese extraño incidente de nuestra infancia, esa desaparición inexplicable de Martina, mi oscura hermana gemela, como dice Faulkner. [...] Pues bien, aun así ese capítulo de la ausencia de mi hermana y del silencio familiar sería el más importante para mí de todo este libro, el que más me habría enseñado, informándome de la existencia de otros silencios abismales de mi infancia,

callados agujeros que sé que están ahí pero a los que no habría conseguido acceder con mis recuerdos reales, los cuales, por otra parte, tampoco son del todo fiables"), 266.

37 Rebecca Solnit, *A Field Guide to Getting Lost* (New York: Penguin, 2005), 7, 22.

38 Montero, "Speculative Subjectivities and the Biofictional Surge," 165.

39 Beckert, "Imagined Futures," 231.

40 Roberta Patalano, "Beyond Rationality: Images as Guide-Lines to Choice," Working Paper 05/2003 (Torino: Università di Torino, 2013).

41 Joshua Rothman, "What If You Could Do It All Over? The Uncanny Allure of Our Unlived Lives," *The New Yorker* (December 14, 2020), https://www.newyorker.com/magazine/2020/12/21/what-if-you-could-do-it-all-over.

42 Montero, *La loca de la casa* ("la Torre de Madrid, un rascacielos de unos treinta pisos que era por entonces el edificio más alto de la ciudad. La Torre, construida en los años cincuenta, había sido el orgullo de franquismo, un ensueño fálico y algo papanatas de modernidad"), 130. Montero alters a similar reference on page 33.

43 Ibid. ("los temibles *grises* del franquismo"), 35.

44 Ibid. ("Si antes me había inventado un M. despreciable, a partir de aquella noche me dediqué a imaginar un M. extraordinario"), 41.

45 Ibid. ("porque ninguno de aquellos yoes remotos formaba ya parte de nuestra narración actual"), 45.

46 Montero, "Speculative Subjectivities and the Biofictional Surge," 159.

47 Montero. Personal interview by Virginia N. Rademacher, 2006.

48 Jens Beckert, *Imagined Futures: Fictional Expectations and Capitalist Dynamics* (Cambridge, MA: Harvard University Press, 2016), 61.

49 Ibid., 10.

50 Beckert, "Imagined Futures: Fictional Expectations in the Economy," 236.

51 Montero, *La loca de la casa* ("Lo que hace el novelista es desarrollar estas múltiples alteraciones, estas irisaciones de la realidad, de la misma manera que el músico compone diversas variaciones sobre la melodía orginal. El escritor toma un grumo auténtico de la existencia, un nombre, una cara, una pequeña anécdota, y comienza a modificarlo una y mil veces, reemplazando los ingredientes o dándolos otra forma, como si hubiera aplicado un caleidoscopo sobre su vida y estuviera haciendo rotar indefinidamente los mismas fragmentos para construir mil figuras distintas"), 265–6.

52 Berlant and Luciano, "Conversation: Lauren Berlant with Dana Luciano."

53 Jose Ovejero, "Interpretamos demasiado el arte y demasiado poco la realidad," Interview by Fernando Díaz de Quijano, *El Cultural* (January 14, 2021), https://elcultural.com/jose-ovejero-interpretamos-demasiado-el-arte-y-demasiado-poco-la-realidad.

54 Martin Fridson, "Exactly What Do You Mean by Speculation,"*Journal of Portfolio Management* 20, No. 1 (fall 1993): 35.

55 Montero, "Speculative Subjectivities and the Biofictional Surge," 162.

56 Montero, *La ridícula idea* ("Sé otro tipo de mujer. Sé una #Mutante. Esa hembra sin lugar, o en busca de otro #Lugar"), 40.

57 Montero, "Speculative Subjectivities and the Biofictional Surge," 167.

58 Leone, "Unorthodox Theories and Beings," 243.

59 Rosa Montero, *Historias de mujeres* (Madrid: Punto de Lectura, 1995), 34 ("propia de ese tipo de mirada tan especial con la que a veces [una noche ante de dormirnos, un atardecer mientras conducimos de regreso a casa] creemos atisbar, por un instante, la sustancia misma del vivir, el corazón del caos.")
60 Montero, *La ridícula idea* ("Pero lo más vergonzoso es que ni Watson ni Crick mencionaron a Franklin ni reconocieron su aportación. [..] Aunque, por lo menos, se conoce. Me pregunto cuántos otros casos de espionaje, apropriación indebida y parasitismo ha podido haber en la historia de ciencia sin que hayan llegado a hacerse públicos"), 13.
61 Montero, "Speculative Subjectivities and the Biofictional Surge," 167.
62 Beckert, "Imagined Futures," 236.
63 Ibid., 231.
64 Montero, "Speculative Subjectivities and the Biofictional Surge,"166.
65 Ibid., 162.
66 Montero, *La ridícula idea* ("'Ya estás en posesión de sales de radio puro. Si pensamos en todo lo que has hecho para obtenerlas, sería desde luego el elemento químico más caro de todos. ¡Qué pena que este trabajo sólo tenga un interés teórico.' Ah, esos progenitores que nunca están satisfechos y para los que nada es bastante ...#HonrarAlPadre. [...] Aunque, ahora que lo pienso, probablemente habría encontrado alguna cosita desagradable que decir"), 107.
67 Max Haiven, *Cultures of Financialization: Fictitious Capital in Popular Culture and Everyday Life* (New York and London: Palgrave, 2014), 23.
68 Shankar Vedantam (Host), *Hidden Brain,* "The Story of Stories: Interview with Tania Lambrozo," (March 15, 2021), https://hiddenbrain.org/podcast/the-story-of-stories/.
69 Beckert, "Imagined Futures," 229.
70 Montero, *La ridícula idea* ("Un ejemplo de vuelo: ¿era el padre de Marie tan fastidioso como insinúo? Yo creo que sí, pero el lector tiene los mismos datos como yo y puede decidir si está de acuerdo o no con lo que digo"), 209.
71 Beckert, *Imagined Futures,* 10.
72 Ibid., 71.
73 Montero, "Speculative Subjectivities and the Biofictional Surge," 169.
74 Ibid., 166.
75 Montero, *La ridícula idea* ("Marie descubrió y midió la radiactividiad [...] fulgurantes rayos sobrehumanos que curan y que matan, que achicharran tumores cancerosos en la radioterapía o calcinan cuerpos tras una deflagración atómica"), 11.
76 Ibid. ("No es fácil saber dónde pararse, hasta dónde es lícito contar y hasta dónde no, cómo manejar la sustancia siempre radioactiva de lo real"), 194.
77 María Fernández-Lamarque, "Review of *La ridícula idea de no volver a verte,*" *Hispania* 98, No. 1 (March 2015): 186.
78 Montero, *La loca de la casa* ("mejor dicho, sólo fragmentos de ese lomo, retazos de esa ballena, pizcas de belleza que te dejan intuir de la belleza insoportable del animal entero; pero luego, antes de haber sido capaz de calcular su volumen y su forma, antes de haber comprendido el sentido de su mirada taladradora, la prodigiosa bestia se sumerge y el mundo queda quieto y sordo y tan vacío"), 54.

Chapter 4

1 Cercas, *Conversations with Biographical Novelists: Truthful Fictions across the Globe*, 59, Javier, "Resisting the 'Dictatorship of the Present,'," Interview by Virginia Newhall Rademacher (New York and London: Bloomsbury, 2019). Cercas has frequently described this novel as a "non-fiction novel saturated with fiction."

2 Javier Cercas, *El impostor* (Barcelona: Random House, 2014); *The Impostor*, trans. Frank Wynne (New York: Vintage Press, 2019). For readability, I use this English translation for all of the in-text citations. All citations in the original Spanish are included in the Endnotes and derive from the edition cited above. English text page numbers are cited first, followed by the original Spanish in parentheses and page number.

3 Adolfo García Ortega, *El comprador de aniversarios* (Barcelona: Seix Barral, 2008); *The Birthday Buyer,* trans. Peter Bush (Madrid: Hispabooks, 2013). For readability, I use this English translation for all of the in-text citations. All citations in the original Spanish are included in the Endnotes and derive from the edition cited above. English text page numbers are cited first, followed by the original Spanish in parentheses and page number.

4 Lucia Boldrini, "Biofiction, Heterobiography, and the Ethics of Speaking of, for, and as another," *Interdisciplinary Studies of Literature* 5, No. 4 (2021), forthcoming.

5 Boldrini, "Biofiction, Heterobiography, and the Ethics of Speaking of, for, and as another."

6 Adolfo García Ortega, *The Birthday Buyer,* 15 ("Y una cualquiera de esas víctimas, quizá la mayor de todas, era Hurbinek. […] Cuando más tarde quise escribir sobre Hurbinek, sabía que un sentimiento de justicia me legitimaba, pero no hallé las palabras"), 15.

7 Mario Vargas Llosa, "Espantoso y genial," *El País* (May 15, 2005) ("Todo lo que cuento lo he vivido, pero en otro sitio; sólo cambié el lugar, para dar a conocer mejor el dolor de las víctimas"). Vargas Llosa quotes Marco in this editorial, "What is most extraordinary is that he was able to deceive those who were best equipped of anyone to expose him: the Spanish men and women that in fact had lived the horror of the concentration camps and managed miraculously to have survived." ("Lo más extraordinario es que engañara a quienes estaban mejor equipados que nadie para desenmascararlo: las españolas y españoles que sí habían vivido el horror concentracionario escapado poco menos que de milagro a la muerte"), https://elpais.com/diario/2005/05/15/opinion/1116108006_850215.html. English translation mine.

8 See Sara J. Brenneis, "The Death of Historical Memory? Javier Cercas's *El impostor* versus the Legacy of Spaniards Deported to Nazi Camps," *Journal of Spanish Cultural Studies* 19, No. 3 (2018): 365–81; Sebastiaan Faber, "Javier Cercas y 'El impostor,' o el triunfo de kitsch," *Fronterad* (February 12, 2015).

9 Colum McCann, "Contested Realities in the Biographical Novel," Interview by Michael Lackey, in *Conversations with Biographical Novelists: Truthful Fictions across the Globe*, ed. Michael Lackey (New York and London: Bloomsbury, 2019), 138.

10 Javier Cercas, "Resisting the 'Dictatorship of the Present' in the Biographical Novel," Interview by Virginia Rademacher, in *Conversations with Biographical Novelists: Truthful Fictions across the Globe*, ed. Michael Lackey (New York and London: Bloomsbury, 2019), 54–5.
11 Cercas, "Resisting the 'Dictatorship of the Present' in the Biographical Novel," 65.
12 Michael Lackey, "Introduction: The Agency Aesthetics of Biofiction in the Age of Postmodern Confusion," *Conversations with Biographical Novelists*, ed. Michael Lackey (New York and London: Bloomsbury, 2019), 6.
13 Javier Cercas, *The Impostor,* 36 ("el miedo a que me acusasen de estar haciéndolo el juego a Marco, de estar intentado entenderle y por tanto disculparle, de ser cómplice de un hombre que se había burlado de las víctimas del peor crimen de la humanidad"), 53.
14 Cercas, "Resisting the 'Dictatorship of the Present' in the Biographical Novel," 59–60.
15 Matthew Fishbane, "Javier Cercas' *The Impostor* and the Lies We Tell," *Tablet Magazine* (September 6, 2008), https://www.tabletmag.com/sections/arts-letters/articles/the-impostor.
16 Cercas, *The Impostor,* 342–3 ("Las mentiras puras no se las cree nadie – continué -. Las buenas mentiras son las mentiras mezcladas, las que contienen una parte de verdad. Y las mentiras de Marco eran buenas"), 405.
17 Ibid., 328–9 (Marco: "No sé, yo creo que, sin tener concienca de que era huérfano, Enric Marco sufrió mucho." […] "Tuve una mala vida. No me acompañó la suerte"), 391–2.
18 See Sara Brenneis, "The Death of Historical Memory? Javier Cercas's *El impostor* versus the Legacy of Spaniards Deported to Nazi Camps," *Journal of Spanish Cultural Studies* 19, No. 3 (2018): 365–81.
19 Javier Cercas, "The Freedom of the Novel," Interviewed by Ag Apolloni, *Symbol* (February 21, 2019), https://www.eurozine.com/the-freedom-of-the-novel/.
20 Javier Cercas, *The Impostor*, 221–2 and 267–9, as listed ("hay que entender que, en cierto modo, no fingía que era un deportado; o que al menos no lo fingió a partir de determinado momento […] Si no supiera que no es uno de ellos, nadie diría que no es uno de ellos. En realidad, es uno de ellos"), 267, 269.
21 "I'm an Impostor but not a Fraud," *El País* (June 30, 2011), https://english.elpais.com/elpais/2011/06/30/inenglish/1309411245_850210.html.
22 Laurent Binet, "Reflections on Truth, Veracity, Fictionalization, and Falsification," Interview by Monica Latham, in *Conversations with Biographical Novelists: Truthful Fictions across the Globe*, ed. Michael Lackey (New York and London: Bloomsbury, 2019), 33, 42.
23 Cercas, "Resisting the 'Dictatorship of the Present' in the Biographical Novel," 60.
24 Cercas, *The Impostor,* 295 ("fantaseé durante todo el día con un diálogo imaginario entre Marco y yo; tal y como lo fantaseé lo transcribe, literalmente. Por una vez, en este libro la ficción no la pone Marco; la pongo yo"), 353.
25 Ibid., 191 ("la mayoría se limitó a maquillar o adornar su pasado (o a desvelar por fin una intimidad miedosamente velada u oportunamente oculta hasta entonces"), 233.

26 Ibid., 254 ("un discurso sin matices ni ambigüedad, sin las complejidades y vacios y espantos y contradicciones y vértigos y asperezas y claroscuros morales de la memoria real y de la verdadera historia y el arte verdadero"), 306.

27 Cercas, *The Impostor*, 298 ("¿No me estará diciendo que la apoteosis de la memoria histórica ocurrió por culpa de mi novela? Soy vanidoso, pero no tanto." – "Ocurrió por culpa de la novela y de otras cosas, pero por culpa de su novela también. […] ¿Por qué cree que tanta gente la leyó? ¿Porque era buena? No me haga reír. La leyó porque la necesitaba, porque el país la necesitaba, necesitaba recordar su pasado republicano como si lo estuviese desenterrando, necesitaba revivivirlo, llorar por aquel viejo republicano olvidado en el asilo en Dijon y por sus amigos muertos en la Guerra, igual que necesitaba llorar por las cosas que yo contaba en mis charlas sobre Flossenbürg, sobre la guerra y sobre mis amigos de la guerra"), 356–7.

28 Ibid., 299 ("¿Y qué hice yo? Lo mismo que usted; no: yo lo hice mucho mejor que usted. Yo me inventé a un tipo como Miralles, sólo que este Miralles estaba vivo y visitaba los colegios y les hablaba a los chicos del horror de los campos nazis y de los españoles encerrados allí y de la justicia y la libertad y la solidaridad, este hombre levantó la Amical de Mauthausen, gracias a él se empezó a hablar del Holocausto en las escuelas españolas, gracias a él se supo que existía el campo de Flossenbürg y que catorce españoles habían muerto allí"), 357.

29 As Sara Brenneis has observed, soon after he was exposed, Marco continued to defend his approach, claiming "People listened to me more and my educational work was more effective" ("La gente me escuchaba más y mi trabajo divulgativo era más eficaz." Quoted in "El ex president de Amical de Mautthahusen [sic] dice que mintió porque así la gente escuchaba más"), *El País* (May 11, 2005). Brenneis notes further that Marco cast "his fictional tale as a more 'efficient' means of communicating the underlying truths of the Spanish deportation to the Nazi camps, and by extension, the Holocaust." See Brenneis, "The Death of Historical Memory?" 68.

30 Brenneis, "The Death of Historical Memory," 372.

31 Cercas, *The Impostor*, 223 ("cuando estalló el caso Marco, mucha gente se preguntó cómo pudo nuestro hombre engañar a tanta gente durante tanto tiempo con una mentira tan monstruosa"), 270.

32 Christopher Taylor, "Enrique of the Silver Tongue," *London Review of Books* 40, No. 6 (March 22, 2018): 36.

33 Cercas, *The Impostor,* 303 ("¿O cree usted que, si hubieran sabido algo de ella y les hubiese importado de veras, mi mentira hubiese pasado por verdad y mi farsa hubiese colado? Mire, con su novela usted les demostró a muchas personas que se habían olvidado de la guerra y sobretodo los perdedores de la guerra, o por lo menos les hizo creer que se habían olvidado, pero con mi impostura yo demostré que en nuestro país no existía el Holocausto, o que a nadie le importaba. […] La diferencia es que a usted lo celebraron por hacerlo y a mí me convirtieron en un apestado"), 362.

34 Louis Menard, "Literary Hoaxes and the Ethics of Authorship," *The New Yorker* (December 3, 2018), https://www.newyorker.com/magazine/2018/12/10/literary-hoaxes-and-the-ethics-of-authorship. Menard

observes a number of defenses for "cheating on the pact." These include the "surrogacy defense," the "theory that, although a particular event recounted in the book may not have happened to the author, it happened to someone." Another is the "higher truth defense"—that "fabrications and exaggerations in books like these are at the service of more fully conveying what it is really like to be Guatemalan or in recovery or whatever the theme of the life story happens to be."

35 Lackey, "Contested Realities in the Biographical Novel," 132.

36 Cercas, *The Impostor,* 299 ("Porque todo el mundo sabe que el novelista engaña, pero nadie sabía que lo hacía usted. Porque el engaño del novelista es un engaño consentido y el suyo no. Porque el novelista tiene la obligación de engañar, y usted tenía la obligación de decir la verdad. Ésas son las reglas del juego, y usted las saltó"), 358.

37 Cited in Menard, "Literary Hoaxes and the Ethics of Authorship."

38 Mario Vargas Llosa, "*The Impostor* Review: The Man Who Wasn't There," *The Wall Street Journal* (August 23, 2018), https://www.wsj.com/articles/the-impostor-review-the-man-who-wasnt-there-1535060707.

39 Cercas, "Resisting the Dictatorship of the Present," 53.

40 Cercas, *The Impostor*, 308 ("Y una mierda: lo tituló así porque supo desde el principio, que igual que yo, usted es un farsante y un mentiroso [...] que yo soy su reflejo en su sueño, o en un espejo. [...] Ésa es la verdad, Javier. La verdad es que usted so yo"), 368.

41 As Cercas described in my interview with him (in *Conversations with Biographical Novelist: Truthful Fictions across the Globe*), "In fact the book is a struggle between fiction and reality, but it's also a struggle between Marco and me, I mean, between two impostors. It's just the writer is authorized to be an impostor and regular people are not," 60.

42 Milan Kundera, *The Art of the Novel*, trans. Linda Asher (New York: Harper Collins, 2003), 42.

43 García Ortega, *The Birthday Buyer,* 10 ("Quiero que Hurbinek exista. Que exista otra vez. Que exista por más tiempo. Que dure su existencia. Que tenga una vida inventada, posible. Fabricada por mi"), 10.

44 Chika Unigwe, "Biographical Fiction and the Creation of Possible Lives," Interview by Michael Lackey, in *Conversations with Biographical Novelists: Truthful Fictions across the Globe* (New York and London: Bloomsbury, 2019), 255. In this conversation, Unigwe says, "readers don't come to biographical fiction for truth. They come to biographical fiction for possibilities [...] alternate possibilities."

45 Roi Bet Levi, "Telling the Truth with Imagination," *Haaretz* (February 26, 2009), https://www.haaretz.com/1.5080880.

46 Primo Levi, *The Reawakening*, trans. Stuart Woolf (New York: Touchstone, 1995), 25. First published in Italian as *La Tregua* (The Truce) in 1963.

47 Levi, *The Reawakening*, 26. As with all memoirs, there is the element of uncertainty of memory. For discussion of "fictionalizing elements" in *The Reawakening,* see Nancy Harrowitz, *Primo Levi: And the Identity of a Survivor* (Toronto: University of Toronto Press, 2017), 87.

48 Cited in Levi, "Telling the Truth with Imagination."

49 García Ortega, *The Birthday Buyer,* 15: "I felt I was Jewish, Russian or any of the victims of persecution, humiliation, and elimination, human beings crushed and erased simply because they existed. Murdered because they existed. I felt like a victim, any one of those victims. And of those victims, Hurbinek was the most victim of them all."

50 Ibid., 15 ("he querido saber más y más acerca de las razones de esa masacre, de esa aniquilación, saber quiénes fueron los culpable y quiénes las víctimas, saber la verdad de la Historia. He querido conocer los *detalles*"), 15.

51 Antonio Muñoz Molina, "La novela del desaparecido," *Letra Internacional* 81 (Winter 2003): 77. "[...] la novela no juega a reconstruir, a la manera ortopédica de las novelas históricas. La reconstrucción del pasado es tarea del historiador, no del novelista. En *El comprador de aniversarios*, está también la distancia en el tiempo, la delimitación necesaria y explícita del *lugar* desde que se escribe: no trata de Auschwitz, sino de nuestra conciencia e imaginación de Auschwitz sesenta años después." As cited here, the more expansive passage also includes the following "[...] the novel does not try to reconstruct, in the orthopedic style of the historical novel. The reconstruction of the past is the task of the historian, not the novelist. In *The Birthday Buyer,* there is the influencing presence of the distance in time, the explicit and necessary delimitation of *place* from which the novel is being written."

52 García Ortega, *The Birthday Buyer,* 18 ("Insisto de nuevo, ¿qué sabemos de Hurbinek? Nada en verdad. [...] Qué sabemos los unos de los otros. Nada. [...] Y si no las conocemos en su grado extremo, como los millones que perdieron a manos de los nazis, al menos las conocemos como para comprender el dolor, la angustia, la soledad y el miedo ajenos. Tenemos compasión, somos humanos. ¿Pero lo somos?"), 18.

53 Ibid., 15. See note 6.

54 Ibid., 10 ("¿Y de qué le vale a él una vida inventada? [...] Pero a mí sí me vale, y de mucho, inventar su vida. Sólo así podremos ser redimidos los dos, él y yo"), 10–11.

55 Cited in Levi, "Telling the Truth with Imagination."

56 García Ortega, *The Birthday Buyer*: "I am, as it were, giving life to Hurbinek," 11; "The range of possibilities ever broadens," 17 ("Soy una especie de progenitor de Hurbinek"; [...] "El abanico de las posibilidades se despliega más y más"), 10, 17.

57 Ibid., 29 ("Pienso que Hurbinek vivió justamente el tiempo en que nadie es capaz de tener recuerdos [...] Todos los recuerdos, salvo raras excepciones, son *a partir* de los tres años, pero no antes. Por eso me espeluzna pensar que Hurbinek, con toda su fuerza y todas sus ganas de vivir, sólo vivió una pre-vida, sólo vivió una extensión foránea del útero materno. Y sin embargo, todo lo que vivió en aquel tiempo sin memoria posible fue un sufrimiento permanente. Dolor y miedo fueron su alimento, su juguete, su aire"), 29.

58 Ibid., 33 ("Es el amor de Henek por Hurbinek encuentro lo que me une a él, por eso le quiero, porque hace de mí mismo ante Hurbinek. [...] Quiero a Henek porque quiero ser Henek. Qué parte de la humanidad es Henek, no lo sé, pero sé que sin él, sin Henek, sí que sería absolutamente cierta la frase de Adorno de que no se habría podido escribir poesía después de Auschwitz. Ni ninguna otra cosa"), 33.

59 Ibid., 80 ("Sabemos que Henek se llamaba en realidad Belo König—lo dice Primo Levi, quien cuenta que le cambiaron el König por el Henek aquellas mismas enfermeras que no sabía cómo cuidar a Hurbinek—y de nuevo como Belo König regresó al norte de Transilvania en julio de 1945"), 78, 26. In *The Reawakening,* Levi describes, Henek's "name too, like that of Hurbinek's, was artificial; his real name, which was König, had been changed into Henek, a Polish derivative of Henry, by the two Polish girls," 26.

60 Ibid., 81, 82 ("Sabemos que Claricia Novaceanu nunca le oyó hablar del verdadero Hurbinek [...] Por eso recordaba Claricia que sus hijos, cuando eran niños iban de árbol en árbol poniendo su carita en los troncos y tratando de escuchar, mientras Belo les decía, 'Estad atentos, muy atentos, y lo oiréis.' [...] Pero desconocía el origen del aquel cuento, como desconocía que un árbol con el espíritu de Hurbinek en su interior crecía en un lugar de Polonia que os alemanes una vez llamaron Auschwitz"), 79, 80.

61 Levi, *The Reawakening,* 27. As Nancy Harrowitz has written in *Primo Levi and the Identity of a Survivor*, with the "gray zone," Primo Levi maintains that "readers can never really understand what it was like in the camps, because of the complexity of the moral situation and the desperate drive to survive that drove the inmates," 114.

62 Ibid., 52, 53 ("los que lo conocieron íntimamente saben que muchas veces le torturaba la idea de no haber recordado el número que Hurbinek llevaba tatuado en el brazo"), 53. While García Ortega starts this section with the statement that "He [Primo Levi] committed suicide on April 11, 1987" a few paragraphs later, he imagines challenges to this claim, echoing the uncertainty around his suicide: "Others say it was an accident: a particular medication that he was taking that made him dizzy."

63 Cited in Levi, "Telling the Truth with Imagination."

64 García Ortega, *The Birthday Buyer,* 75 ("Pero no se preguntara nunca por el alma de Hurbinek, su nieto, porque ni siquiera sabe que ha existido. La vida se lo ha ocultado"), 73.

65 Joshua Rothman, "What If You Could Do It All Over? The Uncanny Allure of Our Unlived Lives," *The New Yorker* (December 14, 2020), https://www.newyorker.com/magazine/2020/12/21/what-if-you-could-do-it-all-over.

66 Cited in Luis María Romeu Guallart, "'Yo iba a Auschwitz pero ya no'. *El Comprador de aniversarios de Adolfo García Ortega y las posibilidades de acercarnos a la Historia desde la* (meta)ficción," *Confluenze* 2, No. 1 (2010): 168. He quotes García Ortega: "Sobre esto de las atrocidades he sido criticado en mi país, incluso personas cercanas a mí me pidieron que rebajara el tono 'cruel' del libro, pero yo no quise. Les dije, 'los crueles fueron los nazis y sus cómplices, no yo. *Yo sólo imagino lo que la realidad ha hecho.*'" (I have been criticized in my country for my narration of these atrocities, even people close to me have requested that I soften the "cruel" tone of the book, but I didn't want to. I said to them, "The Nazis and their accomplices were the cruel ones, not me. I'm only imagining what reality has carried out"). Translation mine.

67 García Ortega, *The Birthday Buyer*, 119 ("La responsabilidad de darle un futuro me llevó en cierta ocasión a descubrir a Hurbineck oculto en la personalidad de un hombre llevado Pavel Farin. [...] Tal vez la vida de Hurbinek sea de verdad la vida de ese individuo, de ese tal Farin, de nacionalidad rusa; una vida vivida de manera interpuesta, decidida por mí, creador de su future. ¿Por qué no? ¿Y por qué no más vidas? ¿Por qué no otras vidas posibles?"), 117.

68 Anthony Dunne and Fiona Raby, *Speculative Everything: Design, Fiction, and Social Dreaming* (Cambridge, MA, and London, England: MIT Press, 2013), 3.

69 Stephen R.L. Clark, *Philosophical Futures* (Frankfurt am Main: Peter Lang, 2011), 17. Cited in Dunne and Raby, 88.

70 Sherryl Vint, "Promissory Futures: Reality and Imagination in Finance and Fiction," *The New Centennial Review*, 19, No. 1 (Spring 2019): 28.

71 Vint, "Promissory Futures," 32.

72 Uncertain Commons, *Speculate This!* (Durham: Duke University Press, 2013), 14. The [anonymous] academic authors state further that "the concept of affirmative speculation directly engages what risk brackets: uncertainty. In the history of classical probability calculations and the emergence of risk discourses, uncertainty has been perennially figured as the site of pathology, that which must be enumerated, managed, and contained. Might a focus on uncertainty, whose potentials we *multiply* rather than harness, provide an antidote to the narrow instrumentality of risk?" 13.

73 Vint, "Promissory Futures," 16.

74 Philip Wegner, *Shockwaves of Possibility: Essays on Science Fiction, Globalization, and Utopia* (Dublin, Ireland: Ralahine Utopian Studies, 2014), 18. Cited in Vint, "Promissory Futures," 16.

75 García Ortega, *The Birthday Buyer,* 124 ("y con ellos llegaron el prestigio y el mito. [...] O bien Hurbinek se metamorfesea en el empleado de la Red de Tranvías de Budapest, József Kulunga"), 122.

76 Einat Talmon, "Interview with Adolfo García Ortega," www.adolfogarciaortega.com.

77 García Ortega, *The Birthday Buyer*, 126–7 ("nos cruzamos con un hombre con uniforme de tranviario que caminaba con unos bastones. No recuerdo su cara, porque solo lo vi de espaldas y por unos segundos tan sólo, mientras se perdía tras una puerta que daba a la zona restringida del personal autorizado. Entonces, empecé imaginar que Hurbinek había sobrevido"), 124.

78 Ibid., 125 ("las piernas del pequeño Józesf [pues con ese nombre lo bautizó como católico en la Iglesia Parroquial del Centro] se fortalecieron, y cuando pudo caminar, su padre empezó llevarlo por la Red de Tranvías"), 123.

79 Ibid., 130 ("Viajará sin problemas, ya que esa cojera, que sólo se despista a la hora de disimularla más presente, no le ha impedido nunca hacer la vida que se la ha antojado"), 127.

80 Ibid., 122–3 ("Mundos nuevos, juegos y caprichos que podía crear a voluntad, incluso crear como únicos sobre la faz de la tierra"), 120.

81 Ibid., 132 ("Paul tiene algunos problemas con sus piernas, en las que ha perdido parte de su sensibilidad, no sabe cómo ni cúando"), 130.

82 Jacob Paul, "Slouching Past Totality; Or, What a Post-Postmodern Holocaust Novel Might Be," *Fiction Writers Review* (November 21, 2013), https://fictionwritersreview.com/essay/slouching-past-totality-or-what-a-post-postmodern-holocaust-novel-might-be/.

83 Rothman, "What If You Could Do It All Over Again?"
84 García Ortega, *The Birthday Buyer*, 137–8 ("Lo ha sabido por sus hermanastros, quienes llevaban various años, a expensas del propio Gus, investigando su verdadera identidad. La larga carta que tiene en sus manos de John, el hermano mayor, y en ella le habla de Auschwitz, un lugar que él, Gus, jamás habría imaginado que podría asociarse a su vida (o a su muerte, en realidad, dispongo yo"); [...] 'Mírate el brazo y saca tus propias conclusiones,' termina la carta de John Hubbard. Lo que a Gus simpere le parecieron rasgos incomprensibles de un tatuaje caprichoso, terminaron siendo números que aun estirando mucho la piel apenas llegaban a ser legibles. Se hace de noche en Bangkok y de pronto él ha dejado ya de ser Augustus Hubbard, tasador artístico"), 134–5.
85 Ibid., 140 ("El eligió este ultimo porque sabía que era el lugar donde había nacido dos veces. [...] No recuerda nada de ninguno de los dos [...] ¿Su madre? ¿Su padre? ¿Sus abuelos? ¿Sus hermanos, tíos, primos? ¿Existieron una vez? [...] Hurbinek volvía a Auschwitz y volvía solo"), 137–8.
86 Ibid., 140 ("Hurbinek iba a Auschwitz, pero ya no"), 138.
87 Ibid., 143 ("Hurbinek no llegará nunca a Auschwitz. Al menos por segunda vez. Y sin embargo, hay algo que es posible aún, una absurda esperanza: que Walter Hanna, el periodista cuya voz es tan famosa en Grecia como la de Melina Mercouri, esté *de verdad* en el mismo presente que yo, el mismo día, a la misma hora en que lo imagino [...] Y podría ser absolutamente real, podría ser verdad que, en el mismo momento en que yo rescato a Hurbinek de los muertos y le doy una vida, el verdadero Walter Hanna, o como se llame, esté ahí, en ese hospital, porque *de verdad* nació en Auschwitz y *de verdad* ha hecho hasta allí el último viaje de su vida. Entonces Hurbinek sí que habría vivido, *über alles,* por encimo de todo, como dice el himno"), 140.
88 Vint, "Promissory Futures," 17.
89 Jo Labanyi, "Introduction: Engaging with Ghosts; or Theorizing Culture in Modern Spain," *Constructing Identity in Contemporary Spain: Theoretical Debates and Cultural Practice*, ed. Jo Labanyi (Oxford: Oxford University Press, 2002), 1.
90 Jose Colmeiro, "Tracing Ghost Stories: Phantasmal Memories and Hauntology in Manuel Rivas' *O lapis do carpintheiro*," in *Approaches to Iberian Cultural Studies*, ed. José Ignacio Álvarez (New York and Bern: Peter Lang, 2019), 41, 42.
91 Marianne Hirsch, *The Generation of Postmemory: Writing and Visual Culture after the Holocaust* (New York: Columbia University Press, 2012), 5.
92 García Ortega, *The Birthday Buyer*, 225 ("por eso quiero nombrar cada detalle, cada insignificante detalle de esos objetos, porque son lo que existió *con* Hurbinek, lo que dio entidad a su vida. Y al ver o imaginar esas ropas que una vez cubrieron el diminuto cuerpo de Hurbinek o los objetos que cruzaron su existencia con la del niño, imagino igualmente cuál sería la historia que tuvieron esa ropa y esos objetos. ¿De dónde procedían, quién los tocó, quién los poseyó, amó o usó antes y después que él?"), 219.
93 Ibid., 238 ("Primo Levi empezó a escribir de Hurbinek a partir de aquí. No sabía el pasado de ese niño ni quiso aventurarle un future imposible. Sin embargo, el sucio pañuelo del dragon habitó su memoria para siempre"), 232.
94 Ibid., 81 ("Belo, alias Henek, solía contarle al propio Stanislazh, cuando este era muy pequeño, la historia de un árboljk en cuyo tronco vivía un ser muy

pálido con cara y cuerpo de niño, pero a quien le faltaban las piernas. Le había puesto a a ese inaudito ser el nombre de Hurbinek y llamaba al cuento 'El árbol de Hurbinek'"), 79.

95 Ibid., 247–8 ("En el árbol de las fotos de este mundo que soñó Hurbinek hay dos fotos en las que ahora reparo mi atención [...] Una de las fotos es de Sofía de pie en un parque de Rzeszów, junto al castillo. [...] Es una foto de la felicidad, que ella ha llevado simpre consigo [...] perdida entre los cascotes del edificio cuando poco después los nazis lo demolieron. [...] Es una foto que nunca vería Hurbinek. [...] No hay esperanza, podría titularse la foto. [...] Tal vez nací de nuevo ese día, tal vez Hurbinek nació conmigo de nuevo, tambien"), 242.

96 Ibid., 248–9 ("Yo no he cambiado en estas semanas y a Fanny y a las niñas no les será difícil reconocerme, estoy seguro, pero en el fondo sí he cambiado. [...] He recorrido el siglo, me he adentrado en el horror del siglo, y he imaginado su gris epicentro en la corta vida del pequeño judío Hurbinek, de tres años. Pensarlo, saberlo, decirlo me ha cambiado, claro que me ha cambiado. Ahora lo sé; yo iba a Auschwitz, pero ya no"), 242–3.

97 Javier Cercas, *El Punto Ciego* ("The Blind Spot") (Barcelona: Penguin Random House, 2016), 47 ("sobre todo [las novelas] sirven para cambiar la forma de percepción del lector; es decir, sirven para cambiar el mundo. La novela necesita ser nueva para decir cosas nuevas; necesita cambiar para cambiarnos: para hacernos como nunca hemos sido").

98 Christopher Schaberg, *The Work of Literature in Age of Post-Truth* (New York: Bloomsbury, 2018), 2.

99 Emma Donoghue, "Voicing the Nobodies in the Biographical Novel," Interviewed by Michael Lackey, in *Conversations with Biographical Novelists: Truthful Fictions across the Globe*, ed. Michael Lackey (New York and London: Bloomsbury, 2019), 85.

Chapter 5

1 Patrick Jagoda, *Experimental Games: Critique, Play, and Design in the Age of Gamification* (Chicago: University of Chicago Press, 2020), vi.

2 Christine Henseler, *Contemporary Spanish Women's Narrative and the Publishing Industry* (Urbana/Chicago: University of Illinois Press, 2003), 109.

3 Lucía Etxebarria, *Courtney y yo* (Madrid: Espasa Calpe, 2004). For readability, the English translations are included as all in-text citations. The Notes reference the page number(s) in the Spanish text, followed by the original Spanish citations in parentheses. All translations are mine, unless otherwise noted.

4 Lucía Etxebarria, *Lo verdadero es un momento de lo falso* (Mexico City, Mexico: Santillana, 2010). For readability, the English translations are included as all in-text citations. The Notes reference the page number(s) in the Spanish text, followed by the original Spanish citations in parentheses. All translations are mine, unless otherwise noted. Versions of small portions of this chapter have appeared in two of my prior publications, the publishers of which

have kindly granted me permission. See Virginia Newhall Rademacher, "The Art of Seduction: Truth or Fanfiction in the World of Lucía Etxebarria's Online 'Friends' and the Blogosphere," in *Hybrid Storyspaces,* eds. Christine Henseler and Debra Castillo, *Hispanic Issues Online* 9 (2012); Virginia Newhall Rademacher, "Playing for Real: Simulated Games of Identity in Spain's Gen X Narrative," in *Gen X Goes Global: Mapping a Youth Culture in Motion*, ed. Christine Henseler (New York and London: Routledge, 2012), 193–221.

5 Fernando Morales, "Luciá Etxebarría: 'Fui tonta porque me metí en algo que no podia controlar,'" *El País,* July 30, 2013.

6 Jan Simons, "Narratives, Games, and Theory," *Game Studies* 7, No. 1 (August 2007), http://gamestudies.org/0701/articles/simons.

7 Jagoda, *Experimental Games,* 47.

8 Ibid., 8.

9 Jose Ovejero, "Ser viral o no ser," *La Marea,* (June 8, 2021), https://www.lamarea.com/2021/06/08/boser-viral-o-no-ser/: "Esa pulsión de multiplicarme a través de seguidores y amigos que, a su vez, difunden mis intervenciones; esa necesidad de intervenir con frecuencia para que no me olviden; intervenir, actuar, responder, dar el 'me gusta,' comentar, subir imágenes."

10 Lucía Etxebarria, *La historia de Kurt y Courtney: ¡Aguanto esto!* (Valencia: Editorial Midens, 1996).

11 Etxebarria, *Courtney y yo* ("el texto de ¡*Aguanto esto*!, escrito cuando yo tenía 27, 28, o 29 años […] Pero lo cierto es que yo había reconstruido el itinerario de Courtney a través de las propias declaraciones del cantante, y es evidente que Courtney era la primera en idealizar su vida. Sin embargo, ahora que existe Internet y que han salido a la luz la varias biografías y ensayos sobre Courtney, veo las cosas de manera muy distinta"), 52.

12 Ibid. ("Es y por eso que la historia de Courtney, o del personaje de Courtney, me llama tanto la atención. Porque, salvando las lógicas distancias, me resulta fácil identificarme con ella. Quizá yo sea o no eidética, pero desde luego me puedo poner en su piel"), 55.

13 Ibid. ("puesto que debe tener una gran imaginación y una gran capacidad para abrirse a espacios e historias nuevas. […] para mí una histora narrada debe convertirse, debe *ser*, una experiencia viva, en constante evolución, desafiante incluso"), 54–5.

14 Ibid. ("no me interesa tanto quién es Courtney como quién creemos que es"), 56. Courtney herself never speaks or is consulted, except for the reprinted inclusion of a brief interview Etxebarria conducted with Courtney in 1996. She prefaces this interview with complaints regarding the long list of conditions and rules that impeded any real discoveries—"and as if these were not enough, they required that the interview take place in the presence of her manager and publicist, who would be there to guard against any tricky questions that the contract hadn't foreseen," *Courtney y yo,* 153.

15 Ibid. ("Pero yo no he hablado de personas. De lo que yo he hablado ha sido de íconos, de representaciones, de mitos. Y es por eso por lo que intencionadamente le he propuesto un juego y les he hecho llegar hasta aquí de la mano de un personaje que en su día vestía pantalones de Zara y una camiseta Psychobitch"), 141.

16 Jagoda, *Experimental Games,* xi, 38.

17 Etxebarria, *Courtney y yo* ("Courtney nos interesa únicamente como mito"), 56.
18 Ibid. ("Entra en la *hiperreal* [que diría Baudrillard] y pasa a convertirse en pantalla en la que una sociedad y, por supuesto, un público, proyecta sus ilusiones, deseos y carencias"), 33.
19 Ibid. ("Me he hecho famosa—'famosa,' léase entre comillas"), 23.
20 Ibid. ("Una celebridad consigue serlo sólo cuando trasciende su propia vida, cuando su biografía se integra en otro metarrelato, el mítico"), 57.
21 Jagoda, *Experimental Games*, 15.
22 Etxebarria, *Courtney y yo* ("Estas palabras las recoge Poppy Z. Brite, en su libro *Courtney, the Real Story*, la biografía—o hagiografía, según se mire—de Courtney, la más fiable de todas las escritas puesto que la autora es íntima amiga de la la diva [...] también la menos fiable, pues constantemente justifica cada metedura de pata y cada salida de tono de la biografiada"), 56.
23 Ibid., 92.
24 Ibid. ("Nick Broomfield, un controvertido cineaste británico especialista en destripar famosos, no se limitó a acusar a la nena de arribista y manipuladora, sino, de paso, de *asesina*, de estar implicada directamente en la muerte de su mitificado marido"), 62.
25 Cited in "Kurt and Courtney: Nick Broomfield on His Controversial Cobain Doc," *Rolling Stone* (April 8, 2015), https://www.rollingstone.com/movies/movie-news/kurt-courtney-nick-broomfield-on-his-controversial-cobain-doc-164700/.
26 Etxebarria, *Courtney y yo* ("la periodista [...] había optado por transcribir las frases que en aquel momento concordaban con su estado de ánimo, las que más relevantes le parecían de todo mi discurso. Pero, aunque transcribía mis palabras, no transmitía mi mensaje, sino el suyo"), 35.
27 Marie-Laure Ryan, "Beyond Myth and Metaphor—The Case of Narrative in Digital Media," *Game Studies* 1, No. 1 (July 2001), http://www.gamestudieIssues.org/0101/ryan/.
28 Etxebarria, *Courtney y yo* ("la mujer fatal, la devoradora de hombres"), 59.
29 Ibid. ("El concepto de la mujer-mantis o vagina dentata aplicado a la música cristaliza en la leyenda según la cual son las novias las que destruyen los grupos"), 61.
30 Ibid. ("la transformación de Courtney de *kinderwhore* a musa de Versace"; "la llegada de un nueva Barbie: Barbie Versace, *Courtney Maquillaje*. (Y recuerdo los dos sentidos de la palabra 'maquillar' según el diccionario: 1. Aplicar cosméticos en el rostro para embellecerlo o caracterizarlo, y 2. Encubrir, falsificar o alterar el aspecto de una cosa"), 39, 107.
31 Ibid. ("El look kinderwhore, por ejemplo, reconocía que se podía ser feminista a la vez que coqueta, e incluso cursi"), 106.
32 Ibid. ("La Lolita es pasiva, la kinderwhore es agresiva. La Lolita provoca sin saberlo [o fingiendo no saberlo] y la kinderwhore es muy consciente de lo que hace"), 105.
33 Ibid. ("y no puedo evitar preguntarme hasta qué punto Courtney no es víctima de su propio personaje"), 157.
34 Winston Manrique Sabogal, "Lucía Etxebarria, Novelist: My Public Persona Creates Problems, No Matter What I Do," *El País* English edition

(February 20, 2010): 8. The original article appeared as "Cuanto más socializados estamos, más mentimos," *El Pais* (February 5, 2010), https://elpais.com/diario/2010/02/05/cultura/1265324405_850215.html.

35 Etxebarria, *Courtney y yo* ("Era *kitsch* (la diferencia entre el kitsch y lo cursi es que lo kitsch tiene conciencia de sí. Lo cursi no sabe lo que es, y pretende ser elegante, mientras que lo kitsch transgrede conscientemente las normas del buen gusto con una clara intención irónica y autorreferencial"), 97.

36 Henry Jenkins, "Transmedia Storytelling, 101," in Henry Jenkins, "Confessions of an Aca-Fan," March 21, 2007, http://henryjenkins.org/blog/2007/03/transmedia_storytelling_101.html.

37 Henry Jenkins, "Quentin Tarantino's Star Wars?: Digital Cinema, Media Convergence and Participatory Culture," in *Rethinking Media Change: The Aesthetics of Transition*, eds. David Thorburn and Henry Jenkins (Cambridge and London: MIT Press, 2003), 281–314. https://mitpress.mit.edu/books/rethinking-media-change MIT Web Publications, http://web.mit.edu/~21fms/People/henry3/starwars.html.

38 Lucía Etxebarria, cited in "Lucía Etxebarria: Mis personajes tienen vida propia," RTVE, https://www.rtve.es/noticias/20100213/lucia-etxebarria-personajes-tienen-vida-propia/317814.shtml.

39 Lucía Etxebarria, reposted from Facebook (February 2, 2010), translation mine, https://www.facebook.com/notes/luc%C3%ADa-etxebarria/la-tragedia-de-pumuky/283983704642.

40 Ibid.

41 Amanda Haas, "What Do Our Online Avatars Reveal About Us?" *The New York Times Magazine* (May 10, 2016), https://www.nytimes.com/2016/05/15/magazine/what-do-our-online-avatars-reveal-about-us.html.

42 Etxebarria, reposted from Facebook (February 2, 2010), translation mine, https://www.facebook.com/notes/luc%C3%ADa-etxebarria/la-tragedia-de-pumuky/283983704642.

43 Lucía Etxebarria "Los espejos de la realidad," Interview in *Shangay Magazine* (February 22, 2010), https://shangay.com/.

44 Jenkins, "Transmedia Storytelling."

45 Ibid.

46 Jenkins, "Quentin Tarantino's Star Wars?"

47 Ibid.

48 Etxebarria, *Lo verdadero es un momento de lo falso* ("no quiero jugar a demostrar el mecanismo del juguete, para acabar entendiendo cómo funciona pero no poder volver a jugar con él"), 17.

49 McKenzie Wark, *Gamer Theory* (Cambridge: Harvard University Press, 2007), 40.

50 Jenkins "Transmedia Storytelling."

51 Lucía Etxebarria, Interview, "La realidad no existe," *Qué Leer*, April 28, 2010, http://www.que-leer.com/6742/lucia-etxebarria-la-realidad-no-existe.html.

52 Paula Carroto, "Lucía Etxebarria: 'Descargar ilegalmente es putear a mucha gente,'" *El Público* (February 4, 2010), https://www.publico.es/actualidad/lucia-etxebarria-descargar-ilegalmente-putear.html. ("Yo he tenido la experiencia de tener un avatar, otra persona que vive en la hiperrealidad y que ha hecho cosas que yo nunca he dicho o hecho. [...] Cuando vives con un avatar te come. Yo he vivido muy mal con todo eso").

53 Lucía Etxebarria, reposted from Facebook (February 2, 2010), translation mine.

54 Etxebarria, *Lo verdadero es un momento de lo falso* ("Pumuky no era más que … algo así como una pantalla sobre la que tanta gente proyectó su propio sueño romántico"), 289.

55 Lucía Etxebarria, *Una historia de amor como otra cualquiera* (Madrid: Espasa Calpe, 2004).

56 Lucía Etxebarria, "Un corazón en el techo," in *Una historia de amor como otra cualquiera* (Madrid: Espasa Calpe, 2004), 183–212. https://www.amazon.com/-/es/Luc%C3%ADa-Etxebarria/dp/8467031735.

57 Eduardo Fernández, "Facebook cierre los pérfiles de Etxebarria," *El Mundo* (November 24, 2010), https://www.elmundo.es/elmundo/2010/11/19/comunicacion/1290166624.html.

58 Alison Gibbons, Thomas Vermeulen, and Robin van den Akker, "Reality Beckons: Metamodernist Depth beyond Panfictionality," *European Journal of English Studies* 23, No. 2 (2019): 174.

59 Thomas Malaby, "Beyond Play: A New Approach to Games," *Games and Culture* 2, No. 2 (2007): 102.

60 Sophie Gilbert, "The Writer Who Saw All of This Coming," *The Atlantic* (September 7, 2021), https://www.theatlantic.com/books/archive/2021/09/lauren-groff-matrix/619998/.

Chapter 6

1 Elvira Navarro, *Los últimos días de Adelaida García Morales* (Barcelona: Penguin Random House, 2016). For readability, the English translations are included as all in-text citations. The original Spanish citations are included in the Endnotes in parentheses. All translations are mine, unless otherwise noted. From this point on, I reference the abbreviated title, *The Last Days* (*Los últimos días*).

2 Antonio Orejudo, *Los cinco y yo* (Barcelona: Tusquets, 2017). For readability, the English translations are included as all in-text citations. The original Spanish citations are included in the Endnotes in parentheses. All translations are mine, unless otherwise noted. Within the text, I reference the English translation of this title, *The Famous Five and Me*.

3 See Beverly Lyon Clark, "From Babylit to Lusty *Little Women*: Age, Race, and Sexuality in Recent *Little Women* Spinoffs," *Women's Studies: An Interdisciplinary Journal* 48, No. 4 (2019): 433–45. See also Birgit Spengler, *Literary Spinoffs, Rewriting the Classics- Reimagining the Community* (Frankfurt; New York: Campus Verlag, 2015).

4 Gérard Genette, *Paratexts: Thresholds of Interpretation*, trans. Jane E. Lewin (Cambridge: Cambridge University Press, 1997), 2.

5 Jan Švelch, "Paratextuality in Game Studies: A Theoretical Review and Citation Analysis," *Game Studies* 20, No. 2 (June 2020), http://gamestudies.org/2002/articles/jan_svelch.

6 Steven E. Jones, "Dickens On 'Lost': Text, Paratext, Fan-based Media," *Wordsworth Circle* 38, Nos. 1–2 (Winter–Spring 2007): 74. Notably, Jones

refers to the impact of new media on the exponential growth of paratextual games that cross "thresholds in pursuit of meanings for the pleasure of taking make-believe into the everyday world," operating "across the borders of their own receptions."

7 Švelch, "Paratextuality in Game Studies: A Theoretical Review and Citation Analysis."

8 John Kay and Mervyn King, *Radical Uncertainty: Decision-Making beyond the Numbers* (New York: W. W. Norton, 2020), 249.

9 Kay and King, *Radical Uncertainty,* 252–3.

10 Patrick Jagoda, *Critique, Play, and Design in the Age of Gamification* (Chicago: University of Chicago Press, 2020), 25.

11 J. Ángel Montañes, "Adelaida García Morales no protagoniza mi libro: Elvira Navarro presenta su novela en Barcelona tras las acusaciones de Erice," *El País* (October 2, 2016), https://elpais.com/cultura/2016/10/01/actualidad/1475344637_671002.html.

12 "Elvira Navarro presenta en Objetivo Bizkaia su libro, *Los últimos días de Adelaida García Morales*" (October 17, 2016), https://www.youtube.com/watch?v=BeoFWbPOqfY.

13 Nuria Azancot, "Elvira Navarro sueña el final de Adelaida García Morales" (Elvira Navarro imagines the final days of Adelaida García Morales), *El Cultural* (September 9, 2016), https://elcultural.com/elvira-navarro-suena-el-final-de-adelaida-garcia-morales. I reference her following comments in my translation: "No he investigado la vida de la autora. No era ése el objetivo que yo perseguía, sino ser fiel a la impresión de extrañeza y miedo que me produjo siempre su desaparición, así como a la sensación de injusticia que me acomete cuando veo el desamor hacia el patrimonio y la memoria que hay en este país."

14 For the prior mention, see Chapter 4, 125, referencing Lucia Boldrini, "Biofiction, Heterobiography, and the Ethics of Speaking of, for, and as Another," forthcoming in *Interdisciplinary Studies of Literature* 5, No. 4 (2022). See also Lucia Boldrini, *Autobiographies of Others: Historical Subjects and Literary Fiction* (New York and Abingdon, UK: Routledge, 2012). As Boldrini observes in this text, "What happens to the name and its authority when it claimed by someone else who can say 'I' under false pretences? (Or, as there is no intention to cheat, under *true pretences*?"), 2–3.

15 Maribel Marín Yarza, "La ficción también duele" (Fiction Also Hurts), *El Pais* (October 19, 2016), https://elpais.com/cultura/2016/10/06/babelia/1475769163_593446.html.

16 Elvira Navarro, *Los últimos días*, 82 ("la idea de hacer el homenaje, vista la escasa repercusión de la muerte de la escritora, pasa de ser una obligación y un remedio para la falta en la que se ha pillado a convertirse en un proyecto romántico, en una causa noble en la que siente orgulloso de militar, pero en la que no invirtirá más sudores. Además, tampoco tiene sentido gastarse el escaso presupuesto en un acto al que no acudirá nadie. Muy pocos en el pueblo saben que allí vivía Adelaida García Morales. Muy pocos, de hecho, la conocen siquiera de oídas").

17 Navarro, *Los últimos días*, 66–7 ("Diás después, cuando monte la parte final de esa conversación, la realizadora no cabrá en sí de gozo por el resultado. […] ¿No se planteó siempre su documental como una suerte de recreación

libre o de continuación atmosférica de las narraciones de García Morales y del personaje y no de la persona, que la escritora era? ¿No resultará entonces conveniente virar cuanto antes hacia la ficción? Se reafirmará en esta idea diciéndose que se confunde demasiado a menudo lo verosímil con lo veraz, y que será mejor para su película deshacer ese entuerto desde el principio, dejar claro que su montaje no pretende ilustrar sobre la vida y obra de nadie").

18 Steven E. Jones, "Dickens on Lost," 73.

19 Jan Švelch, "Paratextuality in Game Studies."

20 Ibid.

21 Víctor Erice, "Una vida robada" (A Stolen Life), *El País* (October 3, 2016), https://elpais.com/cultura/2016/09/29/babelia/1475153443_790435.html.

22 Víctor Erice, "Una vida robada."

23 Ibid.

24 Navarro, *Los últimos días*, 106 ("Y por el médico sabe que Víctor Erice había roto toda relación con ella").

25 Bethany Layne, "Introduction," in *Biofiction and Writers' Afterlives,* ed. Bethany Layne (Newcastle upon Tyne: Cambridge Scholars Publishing, 2020, 1).

26 Layne, "Introduction," 1.

27 Ibid., 2.

28 Michael Lackey and Todd Avery, "To the Readers," *Virginia Woolf Miscellany* 93 (Spring/Summer 2018), https://virginiawoolfmiscellany.files.wordpress.com/2018/12/VWM93Spring-Summer2018_final_version.pdf.

29 J. Ángel Montañes, "Adelaida García Morales no protagoniza mi libro."

30 Javier Rodríguez Marcos, "Erice-Navarro: novelas retocadas con photoshop,"*El País* (October 4, 2016), https://elpais.com/elpais/2016/10/03/opinion/1475514699_917948.html.

31 José María Cuenca, "Ficciones tóxicas," *La Vanguardia* (October 14, 2016), https://www.lavanguardia.com/edicion-impresa/20161014/411010826767/ficciones-toxicas.html.

32 José María Cuenca, "Ficciones tóxicas."

33 Javier Rodríguez Marcos, "Erice-Navarro: novelas retocadas con photoshop."

34 Maribel Marín Yarza, "La ficción también duele."

35 Cristina García Morales, "Elvira Navarro: Cuestíon de autoridad" (Elvira Navarro: A Question of Authority), *Paralelo* (October 10, 2016), http://blog.edicionesparalelo.com/tag/elvira-navarro/.

36 Navarro, *Los últimos días,* 78 ("para ella Adelaida García Morales no podia ser de este mundo, no era real"), 71.

37 Ibid. ("pero finalmente ni siquiera esta desviación minima le resultará tolerable. La idea de transitar por una vía tan correcta la acabará paralizando de esa forma radical en la que prefiere un error, un fracaso propio, a una renuncia. ¿Por qué ha de ofrecer la mirada de los expertos cuando lo poderoso de su relación con García Morales no tiene nada que ver con el valor de su obra, sino con intuiciones, con una materia aún amorfa que el proceso creativo habrá que moldear?")

38 Gary Bortolotti and Linda Hutcheon, "On the Origin of Adaptations: Rethinking Fidelity Discourse and 'Success,'" *New Literary History* 38, No. 3 (Summer 2007): 444–5.

39 Navarro, *Los últimos días,* 83 ("hay informaciones contradictorias, y seguramente se ha colado más de un detalle falso o impreciso. Asimismo, se incluyen algunos testimonios").
40 Antonio Orejudo, *Los Cinco y yo*, 22 ("La primera aventura de Los Cinco se publicó, como he dicho, en 1942 y la última en 1963, el año en que nacimos Reig y yo").
41 Patrick Jagoda, *Critique, Play, and Design in the Age of Gamification,* xiii.
42 Andrew Fleshman, "The Game of Critique," *Los Angeles Review of Books* (April 4, 2021), https://www.lareviewofbooks.org/article/the-game-of-critique/.
43 Fleshman, "The Game of Critique."
44 Henry Jenkins, "Quentin Tarantino's Star Wars?: Digital Cinema, Media Convergence, and Participatory Culture," http://web.mit.edu/~21fms/People/henry3/starwars.html.
45 Mary Pappalardo, "The Network Imaginary," *The Los Angeles Review of Books* (November 1, 2016), https://lareviewofbooks.org/article/the-network-imaginary/.
46 Wolfgang Reißmann, Moritz Stock et.al, "Fan(fiction): Acting on Media and the Politics of Appropriation," *Media and Communications* 5, No. 3 (2017): 15.
47 Peter Lunenfeld, "Unfinished Business," in *The Digital Dialectic: New Essays on New Media,* ed. Peter Lunenfeld (Cambridge: MIT Press, 1999), 14.
48 Orejudo, *Los cinco y yo,* 42 ("Otra cosa que no advertí de niño fue la agobiante presencia de dinero en este libro").
49 Ibid. ("no le perdonaron a la sexista, racista y fascista Enid Blyton que los haya fascinado durante la infancia, así que ahora ajustan cuentas con ella. [...] la Blyton Foundation se llenó de fans que se acercaban a él para felicitarlo y para decirle que había conseguido mirar las cosas con sus ojos, con los ojos de Reig; que su voz, la de él, se había fundido con la de Enid Blyton"), 212, 209.
50 Ibid. ("Y cada vez que abría aquellas cubiertas ilustradas por el gran José Correas—cuyos dibujos no me parecían añadidos de los que se pudiera prescindir, sino prolongaciones naturales del texto—no me sentía lector de una ficción, ese vendría después; me sentía un personaje de la misma. Y las cerraba tan exhausto como Julian, Dick, Ana, Jorge, y *Tim*; como si yo también hubiese remado, como si yo también hubiese zambullido en el mar y buceado para inspeccionar el barco hundido [...] en una experiencia tan intensa y real como la que proporcionan hoy los videojuegos. Mi hijo también sale de su cuarto agotado después de pasarse la tarde escondiéndose con soldados enemigos, urdiendo emboscadas, tomando objetivos y disparando un sofisticado armamento").
51 Guillermo Rodríguez, "Mi generación es de chichinabo," *Huffington Post* (July 4, 2017), https://www.huffingtonpost.es/2017/04/07/antonio-orejudo-mi-generacion-es-de-chichinabo_a_22030557/.
52 Jagoda, *Critique, Play, and Design in the Age of Gamification*, 12.
53 Antonio Orejudo, *Los cinco y yo* ("le costó cara. [...] He visto a mi hijo al modo campaña de una edición limitada del UK Wars 3, donde hay una recreación de la batalla de Mount Longdon, que dio la Victoria final a las tropas británicas en la guerra de las Malvinas. La batalla virtual ha sido supervisada personalmente por Richard, que participó en el episodio real con diecienueve años recién cumplidos"), 181.

54 Ibid. ("Dice Reig en *After Five* que a Richard le sorprendió la naturalidad 'con que la hipótesis descabellada de entrar en combate se convirtió en una realidad irremediable'").
55 Jagoda, *Critique, Play, and Design in the Age of Gamification,* 41.
56 Andrew Fleshman, "The Game of Critique."
57 Thomas M. Malaby, "Beyond Play: A New Approach to Games," *Games and Culture* 2, No. 2 (April 2007): 102.
58 Malaby, "Beyond Play," 107.
59 Ibid., 109.
60 Orejudo, *Los Cinco y yo*, 207 ("Si una empresa necesitaba algo, lo que fuse, donde fuese, MULTIPLE CHOICE™ lo conseguía. Hicieron mucho dinero. Trabajaban sobre todo con productoras cinematográficas, que necesitaban recursos insospechados en lugares inhóspitos; y con laboratorios farmaceúticos, a las que suminstraban material humano, sujetos para la experimentación, que no siempre eran fáciles de conseguir").
61 Ibid., 232 ("Una cosa es perder la fe en el ser humano y otra muy distinta perder una oportunidad de negocio").
62 Ibid., 226–7 ("moviéndose de un lado a otra de las tablas como lo haría una estrella del rock. Poco antes de morir, su amigo Freddie Mercury—dice Reig—le había enseñado a llenarlo todo de electricidad y sinergía. [...] Yo os lo diré: hay un intento de recuperar la inocencia, un intento de hacer compatible el servicio público con el beneficio empresarial. [...] GOOD THINGS no es un ONG, sino un negocio; [...] la decencia y la justicia son rentables").
63 Jagoda, *Critique, Play, and Design in the Age of Gamification*, 10.
64 Fleshman, "The Game of Critique."
65 Rodríguez, "Antonio Orejudo: 'Mi generación es de chinchinabo.'"
66 Orejudo, *Los Cinco y yo*, 250, 251, 249 ("Mazen se mostró aliviado de que finalmente no fuera a hacerlo. [...]—Si hubieras hecho ese reportaje—le dijo a Georgina—, y a consecuencia de ello hubiesen desmantelado todos los Hogares que como el de Jim hay repartidos por todo el mundo, no habrías hecho una buena obra, sino que habrías producido una catástrofe en la vida de muchas personas. Y no se volvió a hablar del asunto. Abrieron las cestas con la comida [...] *organic, fresh,* y sobre todo *fair trade*").
67 Jagoda, *Critique, Play, and Design in the Age of Gamification,* ix.

Coda

1 Oscar Wilde, "A Few Maxims for the Instruction of the Over-Educated," *Saturday Review* (November 17, 1894). First published anonymously.
2 Shane Hegerty, "Losing the War but Winning the Literature," Interview with Javier Cercas, *Irish Times* 71, No. 4 (June 2003), https://www.irishtimes.com/news/losing-the-war-but-winning-the-literature-1.361789.
3 Javier Cercas, "Resisting the 'Dictatorship of the Present' in the Biographical Novel," Interview by Virginia N. Rademacher, in *Conversations with Biographical Novelists: Truthful Fictions across the Globe*, ed. Michael Lackey (London and New York: Bloomsbury, 2019), 51.

4 Colum McCann, "Contested Realities in the Biographical Novel," Interview by Michael Lackey, in *Conversations with Biographical Novelists: Truthful Fictions across the Globe*, ed. Michael Lackey (London and New York: Bloomsbury, 2019), 139.
5 Emma Donoghue, "Voicing the Nobodies in the Biographical Novel," Interview by Michael Lackey, in *Conversations with Biographical Novelists: Truthful Fictions across the Globe*, ed. Michael Lackey (London and New York: Bloomsbury, 2019), 90.
6 Mary K. Holland, *The Moral Worlds of Contemporary Realism* (London and New York: Bloomsbury, 2020), 12.
7 Robin James Smith and Sara Delamont, "Editorial Introduction," in *The Lost Ethnographies: Methodological Insights from Projects That Never Were*, eds. Robin James Smith and Sara Delamont (Bingley, UK: Emerald Publishing, 2019), 8. The authors refer to Meno's Paradox. This same quote is also discussed by Rebecca Solnit, *A Field Guide to Getting Lost* (New York: Penguin, 2005), 6.

BIBLIOGRAPHY

Amago, Samuel. *True Lies: Narrative Self-Consciousness in the Contemporary Spanish Novel*. Lewisberg, PA: Bucknell University Press, 2006.

Avery, Todd. "Pseudo-Quotations and Alternative Facts: Lytton Strachey and the Ethics of Biofiction in the Post-Truth Moment," In *Biofiction and Writers' Afterlives*, edited by Bethany Layne, 26–39. Newcastle upon Tyne: Cambridge Scholars Publishing, 2020.

Azancot, Nuria. "Elvira Navarro sueña el final de Adelaida García Morales." *El Cultural*, September 9, 2016. https://elcultural.com/elvira-navarro-suena-el-final-de-adelaida-garcia-morales.

Baggini, Julian. "Truth? It's Not Just about the Facts." *Times Literary Supplement*, September 21, 2017. https://www.the-tls.co.uk/articles/post-truth-philosophers.

Baggini, Julian. "Consolations for a Post-Truth World." Interview by Hugh D. Reynolds. *3 AM Magazine*, November 2017. https://www.3ammagazine.com/3am/bagginis-consolations-post-truth-world/.

Barry, Peter. *Beginning Theory: An Introduction to Literary and Cultural Theory*. Manchester: Manchester University Press, 2002.

Bauman, Zygmunt. *Life in Fragments: Essays on Postmodern Morality*. Oxford and Cambridge: Blackwell, 1995.

Bauman, Zygmunt. *Liquid Modernity*. Cambridge: Polity Press, 2000.

Bauman, Zygmunt. *Liquid Times: Living in an Age of Uncertainty*. Cambridge: Polity Press, 2007.

Beck, Ulrich. *World at Risk*. Cambridge: Polity Press, 2009.

Beck, Ulrich and Mark Ritter. *Risk Society: Towards a New Modernity*. London: Sage Publications, 1992.

Beckert, Jens. "Imagined Futures: Fictional Expectations in the Economy." *Theory and Society* 42 (2013): 219–40.

Beckert, Jens. *Imagined Futures: Fictional Expectations and Capitalist Dynamics*. Cambridge: Harvard University Press, 2016.

Berlant, Lauren and Dana Luciano. "Conversation: Lauren Berlant with Dana Luciano." *Social Text Online*, January 2013. https://socialtextjournal.org/periscope_article/conversation-lauren-berlant-with-dana-luciano/.

Bernstein, Peter. *Against the Gods: The Remarkable Story of Risk*. New York: John Wiley & Sons, 1996.

Binet, Laurent. "Reflections on Truth, Veracity, Fictionalization, and Falsification." Interview by Monica Latham. In *Conversations with Biographical Novelists: Truthful Fictions across the Globe*, edited by Michael Lackey, 33–48. New York and London: Bloomsbury, 2019.

Boldrini, Lucia. *Autobiographies of Others: Historical Subjects and Literary Fiction*. New York and Abingdon, UK: Routledge, 2012.
Boldrini, Lucia. "Biofiction, Heterobiography, and the Ethics of Speaking of, for, and as Another." *Interdisciplinary Studies of Literature* 6, no. 1 (2022): 581–600.
Bolaño, Jesus. "Overcoming Postmodernism: David Foster Wallace and a New Writing of Honesty." *U.S. Studies Online*, July 10, 2017. http://www.baas.ac.uk/usso/overcoming-postmodernism/.
Bortolotti, Gary and Linda Hutcheon. "On the Origins of Adaptations: Rethinking Fidelity Discourse and 'Success.'" *New Literary History* 38, no. 3 (Summer 2007): 443–58.
Brenneis, Sara. "The Death of Historical Memory? Javier Cercas's *El impostor* versus the Legacy of Spaniards Deported to Nazi Camps." *Journal of Spanish Cultural Studies* 19, no. 3 (2018): 365–81.
Bryan, Dick and Michael Rafferty. *Capitalism with Derivatives a Political Economy of Financial Derivatives, Capital and Class*. New York: Palgrave Macmillan, 2006.
Carroto, Paula. "Lucía Etxebarria: 'Descargar ilegalmente es putear a mucha gente.'" *El Público*, February 4, 2010.
Cercas, Javier. *Soldados de Salamina*. Barcelona: Tusquets, 2001.
Cercas, Javier. *Soldiers of Salamis*. Translated by Anne Mclean. New York and London: Bloomsbury, 2003.
Cercas, Javier. "Javier Cercas: The Perils of War and Fame." Interview by Carlos Rodríguez Martorell. *Críticas*, August 1, 2005.
Cercas, Javier. "The Third Truth." *El País* (English Edition). July 6, 2011. https://english.elpais/2011/07/06/inenglish/1309929650_850210.html.
Cercas, Javier. *El impostor*. Barcelona: Literatura Random House, 2014.
Cercas, Javier. *El Punto Ciego*. Barcelona: Penguin Random House, 2016.
Cercas, Javier. *The Impostor*. Translated by Frank Wynne. New York: Knopf, 2018.
Cercas, Javier. "Resisting the 'Dictatorship of the Present' in the Biographical Novel." Interview by Virginia Rademacher. In *Conversations with Biographical Novelists: Truthful Fictions across the Globe*, edited by Michael Lackey, 49–67. New York and London: Bloomsbury, 2019.
Cercas, Javier. "The Freedom of the Novel." Interview by Ag Apolloni. *Symbol*, February 21, 2019. https://www.eurozine.com/the-freedom-of-the-novel/.
Cernat, Laura. "Review of *Conversations with Biographical Novelists: Truthful Fictions across the Globe*." *Biography: An Interdisciplinary Quarterly* 43, no. 2 (2021): 484–9.
Clark, Beverly Lyon. "From Babylit to *Lusty Little Women*: Age, Race, and Sexuality in Recent *Little Women* Spinoffs." *Women's Studies: An Interdisciplinary Journal* 48, no. 4 (2019): 433–5.
Clark, Stephen. *Philosophical Futures*. Frankfurt am Main: Peter Lang, 2011.
Colmeiro, Jose. "Tracing Ghost Stories: Phantasmal Memories and Hauntology in Manuel Rivas' *O lapis do carpintheiro*," In *Approaches to Iberian Cultural Studies,* edited by José Ignacio Álvarez Fernandez, 40–54. New York and Bern: Peter Lang, 2019.
Craft, Gretchen. "The Persistence of Dread in Law and Literature." *Yale Law Journal* 102 (1992): 521–46.

Cuenca, José María. "Ficciones Tóxicas." *La Vanguardia*. October 14, 2016. https://www.lavanguardia.com/edicion-impresa/20161014/411010826767/ficciones-toxicas.html.

Dimaggio, Paul. "Endogenizing 'Animal Spirits': Toward a Sociology of Collective Response to Uncertainty and Risk," In *The New Economic Sociology: Developments in and Emerging Field*, edited by M.F. Guillén et al., 79–100. New York: Russell Sage, 2002.

Donoghue, Emma. "Voicing the Nobodies in the Biographical Novel." Interview by Michael Lackey. In *Conversations with Biographical Novelists: Truthful Fictions across the Globe*, 81–92. New York and London: Bloomsbury, 2019.

Dunne, Anthony and Fiona Raby. *Speculative Everything: Design, Fiction, and Social Dreaming*. Cambridge, MA, and London, UK: MIT Press, 2013.

Erice, Víctor. "Una vida robada." *El Pais*. October 3, 2016. https://elpais.com/cultura/2016/09/29/babelia/1475153443_790435.html.

Etxebarria, Lucía. *La historia de Kurt y Courtney: ¡Aguanta esto!*. Valencia: Editorial Midens, 1996.

Etxebarria, Lucía. *Courtney y yo*. Madrid: Espasa Calpe, 2004.

Etxebarria, Lucía. *Lo verdadero es un momento de lo falso*. Mexico: Suma de Letras, 2010.

Etxebarria, Lucia. "Lucía Etxebarria: Mis personajes tienen vida propia." *RTVE*, February 13, 2010. https://www.rtve.es/noticias/20100213/lucia-etxebarria-personajes-tienen-vida-propia/317814.shtml.

Etxebarria, Lucía. "Los espejos de la realidad." Interview in Shangay, February 22, 2010.

Etxebarria, Lucía. "La realidad no existe." *Qué Leer*, April 28, 2010. http://www.que-leer.com/6742/lucia-etxebarria-la-realidad-no-existe.html.

Faber, Sebastiaan. "Javier Cercas y *El impostor*, o el triunfo de kitsch." *Fronterad*, February 12, 2015.

Fernández, Eduardo. "Facebook cierre los pérfiles de Etxebarria," November 24, 2010, *El Mundo*.

Fernández-Lamarque, Maria. "Review of *La ridícula idea de no volver a verte*," by Rosa Montero. *Hispania* 98, no. 1 (2015): 185–6.

Fishbane, Matthew. "*The Impostor* and the Lies We Tell." *Tablet Magazine*, September 6, 2008. https://www.tabletmag.com/sections/arts-letters/articles/the-impostor.

Fisher, George. "The Jury's Rise as Lie Detector." *Yale Law Journal* 107, no. 3 (1997): 573–713.

Fleshman, Andrew. "The Game of Critique." *Los Angeles Review of Books*. April 4, 2021. https://www.lareviewofbooks.org/article/the-game-of-critique/.

Franklin, James. *The Science of Conjecture: Evidence and Probability before Pascal*. Baltimore: Johns Hopkins University Press, 2005.

Franklin, Ruth. "Olga Tokarczuk's Novels against Nationalism." *The New Yorker*, July 29, 2019.

García Ortega, Adolfo. *El comprador de aniversarios*. Barcelona: Seix Barral, 2008.

García Ortega, Adolfo. *The Birthday Buyer*. Translated by Peter Bush. Madrid: Hispabooks, 2013.

Genette, Gérard. *Paratexts: Thresholds of Interpretation*. Translated by Jane E. Lewin. Cambridge: Cambridge University Press, 1997.

Gibbons, Alison. "Postmodernism Is Dead. What Comes Next?" *Times Literary Supplement Online*, June 22, 2017. https://www.the-tls.co.uk/articles/public/postmodernism-dead-comes-next/.

Gibbons, Alison, Thomas Vermeulen, and Robin van den Akker. "Reality Beckons: Metamodernist Depth beyond Panfictionality." *European Journal of English Studies* 23, no. 2 (2019): 172–89.

Giddens, Anthony. *Modernity and Identity: Self and Society in the Late Modern Age*. Stanford: Stanford University Press, 1991.

Greenstein, Richard. "Determining Facts: The Myth of Direct Evidence," *Houston Law Review* 45, no. 5 (Winter 2009): 1801–30.

Guallart, Luis, "'Yo iba a Auschwitz, pero ya no." *El Comprador de aniversarios* de Adolfo García Ortega y las posibilidades de acercarnos a la Historia desde la (meta) ficción," *Confluenze* 2, no. 1 (May 2010): 165–84.

Haas, Amanda. "What Do Our Online Avatars Reveal About Us?" *The New York Times Magazine*, May 10, 2016. https://www.nytimes.com/2016/05/15/magazine/what-do-our-online-avatars-reveal-about-us.html.

Haiven, Max. *Cultures of Financialization: Fictitious Capital in Popular Culture and Everyday Life*. London, UK: Palgrave, 2014.

Hansen, Hans. "Modes of Remembering in the Contemporary Spanish Novel." *Orbis Litterarum* 71, no. 4 (2016): 265–88.

Harrowitz, Nancy. *Primo Levi and the Identity of a Survivor*. Toronto: University of Toronto Press, 2017.

Hegerty, Shane. "Losing the War, but Winning the Literature." *Irish Times*, June 7, 2003. https://www.irishtimes.com/news/losing-the-war-but-winning-the-literature-1.361789.

Heller, Kevin Jon. "The Cognitive Psychology of Circumstantial Evidence." *Michigan Law Review* 105, no. 2 (2006). https://repository.law.umich.edu/mlr/vol105/iss2/1.

Henseler, Christine. *Contemporary Spanish Women's Narrative and the Publishing Industry*. Urbana/Chicago: University of Illinois Press, 2003.

Hirsch, Marianne. *The Generation of Postmemory: Writing and Visual Culture after the Holocaust*. New York: Columbia University Press, 2012.

Holland, Mary. *Succeeding Postmodernism: Language and Humanism in Contemporary American Literature*. New York and London: Bloomsbury, 2013.

Holland, Mary. *The Moral Worlds of Contemporary Realism*. New York and London: Bloomsbury, 2020.

Huber, Imtraud. *Literature after Postmodernism: Reconstructive Fantasies*. London and New York: Palgrave Macmillan, 2014.

Hutcheon, Linda. *A Poetics of Postmodernism: History, Fiction, Theory*. New York and London: Routledge, 1988.

Jagoda, Patrick. *Experimental Games: Critique, Play, and Design in the Age of Gamification*. Chicago: University of Chicago Press, 2020.

Jenkins, Henry. "Quentin Tarantino's Star Wars?: Digital Cinema, Media Convergence and Participatory Culture." In *Rethinking Media Change: The Aesthetics of Transition*, edited by David Thorburn and Henry Jenkins, 281–314. Cambridge and London: MIT Press, 2003.

Jenkins, Henry. "Transmedia Storytelling, 101" in Henry Jenkins "Confessions of an Aca-Fan," March 21, 2017. http://henryjenkins.org/blog/2007/03/transmedia_storytelling_101.html.

Jiménez Torres, David. "El espacio de las heridas: violencia, afectos, y context en *Patria* y *El Comensal*." *Bulletin of Spanish Studies* 96, no. 7 (2019): 1077–94.

Jones, Steven E. "Dickens on 'Lost': Text, Paratext, Fan-based Media." *The Wordsworth Circle* 38, no. 1/2 (Winter/Spring 2007): 71–7. https://www.journals.uchicago.edu/doi/10.1086/TWC24043960

Kay, John and Mervyn King. *Radical Uncertainty: Decision-Making Beyond the Numbers*. New York: W. W. Norton, 2020. https://wwnorton.com/books/9781324004776

Kraus, Carolyn. "Proof of Life: Memoir, Truth, and Documentary Evidence." *Biography* 31, no. 2 (Spring 2008): 245–68.

Kundera, Milan. *The Art of the Novel*. Translated by Linda Asher. New York: HarperCollins, 2003.

Kurvet-Kaössar, Leena. "The Archive." *a/b:Auto/Biography Studies* 32, no. 2 (2017): 355–8.

Kurvet-Kaössar, Leena. Paper presented at the American Comparative Literature Association (ACLA) annual conference in Utrecht, The Netherlands, 2017.

Lackey, Michael. *Truthful Fictions: Conversations with American Biographical Novelists*, edited by Michael Lackey. New York and London: Bloomsbury, 2014.

Lackey, Michael. *The American Biographical Novel*. New York and London: Bloomsbury, 2016a.

Lackey, Michael. "The Rise of the Biographical Novel and the Fall of the Historical Novel." *a/b:Auto/Biography Studies* 31, no. 1 (2016b): 33–58.

Lackey, Michael. *Conversations with Biographical Novelists: Truthful Fictions across the Globe*. Editor and Contributing Interviewer. New York: Bloomsbury, 2019.

Lackey, Michael and Todd Avery. "To the Readers." *Virginia Woolf Miscellany* 93 (Spring/Summer 2018). https://virginiawoolfmiscellany.files.wordpress.com/2018/12/VWM93Spring-Summer2018_final_version.pdf.

Landon, Brooks. "Extrapolation and Speculation." In *Oxford Handbook of Science Fiction*, edited by Rob Latham, 23–34. Oxford and New York: Oxford University Press, 2014.

Lasch, Christopher. *The Minimal Self: Psychic Survival in Troubled Times*. New York: W. W. Norton, 1984.

Lash, Scott and Jonathan Friedman. *Modernity and Identity*. Edited by Rob Latham. Oxford: Blackwell, 1992.

Laure-Ryan, Marie. "Beyond Myth and Metaphor—The Case of Narrative in Digital Media." *Game Studies* 1, no. 1 (July 2001). http://www.gamestudies.org/0101/ryan/.

Layne, Bethany. "Introduction." In *Biofiction and Writers' Afterlives,* edited by Bethany Layne, 1–10. Newcastle upon Tyne: Cambridge Scholars Publishing (2020).

Lea, Daniel. *Twenty-first Century Fiction: Contemporary British Voices*. Manchester: Manchester University Press, 2017.

Leone, Maranne. "Unorthodox Theories and Beings; Science, Technology, and Women in the Narratives of Rosa Montero." In *A Laboratory of Her*

Own: Women and Science in Spanish Culture, edited by Victoria L. Ketz, Dawn Smith-Sherwood, and Debra Faszer-McMahon, 235–62. Nashville: Vanderbilt University Press, 2021.

Lepore, Jill. "After the Fact: In the History of Truth, a New Chapter Begins," *The New Yorker*, March 14, 2016.

Lerner, Ben. "This Week in Fiction." *The New Yorker*, June 10, 2012. https://www.newyorker.com/books/page-turner/this-week-in-fiction-ben-lerner.

Lerner, Ben. "An Interview with *The Believer*," Interview by Tao Lin, *The Believer*, no. 110 (2014). https://believermag.com/an-interview-with-ben-lerner/.

Levi, Primo. *The Reawakening*. Translated by Stuart Woolf. New York: Touchstone, 1995.

Levi, Roi Bet. "Telling the Truth with Imagination." *Haaretz*, February 26, 2009. https://www.haaretz.com/1.5080880.

Lillquist, Eric. "Recasting Reasonable Doubt: Decision Theory and the Virtues of Variability." *UC Davis Law Review* 36, no. 1 (2002): 85–197.

Loftis, John. "Review of *Strong Representations: Narrative and Circumstantial Evidence in England*." *Rocky Mountain Revew of Language and Literature* 47, no. 1–2 (1933): 115–17.

Lunenfeld, Peter. "Unfinished Business." In *The Digital Dialectic: New Essays on New Media,* edited by Peter Lunenfeld, 6–22. Cambridge: MIT Press, 1999.

Lynch, Michael Patrick. "The Value of Truth." *Boston Review*, March 1, 2021. https://bostonreview.net/philosophy-religion/michael-patrick-lynch-value-truth.

Lyon, Annabel. "Irony-Free TV." *Geist* 53 (Summer 2004). https://www.geist.com/fact/columns/irony-free-reality-tv/.

Malaby, Thomas. "Beyond Play: A New Approach to Games." *Games and Culture* 2, no. 2 (2014): 95–113.

Manrique Sabogal, Winston. "Lucía Etxebarria, Novelist: My Public Persona Creates Problems No Matter What I Do." *El País* English edition, February 8, 2010.

Marco, Enric. "I'm an Impostor, but not a Fraud." Interview, *El País*, June 30, 2011. https://english.elpais.com/elpais/2011/06/30/inenglish/1309411245_850210.html.

Marín Yarza, Maribel. "La ficción también duele." *El Pais*, October 19, 2016. https://elpais.com/cultura/2016/10/06/babelia/1475769163_593446.html.

McCann, Colum. "Contested Realities in the Biographical Novel." Interview by Michael Lackey. In *Conversations with Biographical Novelists: Truthful Fictions across the Globe*, edited by Michael Lackey, 131–44. New York: Bloomsbury, 2019.

McGowan, Kat. "Numbers Are Failing Us." *Boston Sunday Globe*, April 26, 2020, K1.

Menard, Louis. "Literary Hoaxes and the Ethics of Authorship." *The New Yorker*, December 3, 2018. https://www.newyorker.com/magazine/2018/12/10/literary-hoaxes-and-the-ethics-of-authorship.

Méndez, Rafael. "Cercas pide que se desconfíe del narrador de *Soldados de Salamina*." *El Pais*, July 2, 2002. https://elpais.com/diario/2002/07/03/cultura/1025647206_850215.html.

Merril, Judith. "What Do You Mean: Science? Fiction?." In *The Other Side of Realism*, edited by T. Clareson, 53–95. Madison:University of Wisconsin Press, 1971.

Meyer, Lily. "Breaking Down the Doors to the Past in *The Dinner Guest*." *National Public Radio* (NPR), May 29, 2019. https://www.npr.org/2019/05/29/726346251/breaking-down-the-doors-to-the-past-in-the-dinner-guest.

Miller, Nancy. *What They Saved: Pieces of a Jewish Past*. Lincoln: University of Nebraska Press, 2011.

Montañes, Jose Ángel. "Adelaida García Morales no protagoniza mi libro: Elvira Navarro presenta su novela en Barcelona tras las acusaciones de Erice." *El País*, October 2, 2016.

Montero, Rosa. *Historias de mujeres*. Madrid: Punto de Lectura, 1995.

Montero, Rosa. *La loca de la casa*. Madrid: Alfaguara, 2003.

Montero, Rosa. *La ridícula idea de no volver a verte*. Barcelona: Seix Barral, 2013.

Montero, Rosa. "Speculative Subjectivities and the Biofictional Surge." Interview by Virginia N. Rademacher. In *Conversations with Biographical Novelists: Truthful Fictions across the Globe*, edited by Michael Lackey, 157–68. New York and London: Bloomsbury, 2019.

Morales, Cristina. "Elvira Navarro: Cuestíon de autoridad." *Paralelo*, October 10, 2016. http://blog.edicionesparalelo.com/tag/elvira-navarro/.

Morales, Fernando. "Fui tonta porque me metí en algo que no podía controlar." *El País*, July 30, 2013.

Muñoz Molina, Antonio. "La novela del desaparecido." *Letra Internacional* 81 (Winter 2003): 77.

Muñoz Molina, Antonio. *Como la sombra que se va*. Barcelona: Seix Barral, 2014.

Muñoz Molina, Antonio. Interview by Óscar López, *Página* 2, December 1, 2014. https://www.youtube.com/watch?v=8ySR6pM_uRA.

Muñoz Molina, Antonio. "La literatura tiene la responsabilidad de comprender." *El Periódico*, December 13, 2014. https://www.elperiodico.com/es/ocio-y-cultura/20141213/antonio-munoz-molina-literatura-tiene-obligacion-comprender–3769649.

Muñoz Molina, Antonio. "On the Experience of Fiction," *Hudson Review* LXVIII, no. 1 (Spring 2015). https://hudsonreview.com/issue/spring–2015/.

Muñoz Molina, Antonio. *Like a Fading Shadow*. Translated by Camilo A. Ramirez. New York: Farrar, Straus & Giroux, 2017.

Navarro, Elvira. *Los últimos días de Adelaida García Morales*. Barcelona: Literatura Random House, 2016.

Nelson, Stephen C. and Peter J. Katzenstein. "Uncertainty, Risk, and the Financial Crisis of 2008." *International Organization* 68, no. 2 (2008): 361–92.

Novak, Julia. "Introduction." In *Experiments in Life Writing*, edited by Lucia Boldrini and Julia Novak, 1–38. Champlain, IL: Palgrave Studies in Life Writing, Palgrave, 2017.

O'Grady, Megan. "Why Are We Living in a Golden Age of Historical Fiction?" *New York Times*, May 7, 2019. https://www.nytimes.com/2019/05/07/t-magazine/historical-fiction-books.html

Olson, Lance. "The Biographical Process of Not-Knowing. Interview by Michael Lackey." In *Truthful Fictions: Conversations with American Biogaphical*

Novelists, edited by Michael Lackey, 193–203. New York and London: Bloomsbury, 2014.

Orejudo, Antonio. *Los cinco y yo*. Barcelona: Tusquets, 2017.

Ovejero, Jose. "Toda la verdad sobre mi adicción al sexo." *Esto no es un blog*, April 26, 2017. https://joseovejero.com/2017/04/26/toda-la-verdad-sobre-mi-adiccion-al-sexo/.

Ovejero, Jose. "Interpretamos demasiado el arte y demasiado poco la realidad." Interview by Fernando Quijano. *El Cultural*, January 14, 2021. https://elcultural.com/jose-ovejero-interpretamos-demasiado-el-arte-y-demasiado-poco-la-realidad.

Ovejero, Jose. "Ser viral o no ser." *La Marea*, June 8, 2021. https://www.lamarea.com/2021/06/08/boser-viral-o-no-ser/.

Pappalardo, Mary. "The Network Imaginary." *The Los Angeles Review of Books*, November 1, 2016. https://lareviewofbooks.org/article/the-network-imaginary/.

Parini, Jay. "Fact or Fiction: Writing Biographies versus Writing Novels" from "*Some Necessary Angels: Essays on Writing and Politics* (1997)". In *Biographical Fiction: A Reader*, edited by Michael Lackey, 299–312. New York and London: Bloomsbury, 2017.

Patalano, Roberta. "Beyond Rationality: Images as Guide-lines to Choice." *CESMEP Working Papers* 5 (2003), University of Turin, np.

Paul, Jacob. "Slouching Past Totality; or, What a Post-Postmodern Holocaust Novel Might Be." *Fiction Writers Review*, November 21, 2013. https://fictionwritersreview.com/essay/slouching-past-totality-or-what-a-post-postmodern-holocaust-novel-might-be/.

Pinard, Mary. Personal interview with Virginia Rademacher. August 2020.

Polasik, Karolina. "Historian an Investigating Magistrate. Carlo Ginzberg's Circumstantial Paradigm." *Sensus Historiae* II (2011): 43–50.

Portela, Edurne. *El eco de los disparos. Cultura y memoria de la violencia.* Barcelona: Galaxia Gutenburg, 2016.

Portela, Edurne. Interview with Xandru Fernández. *El Cuaderno*, June 2017. https://elcuadernodigital.com/2017/06/05/edurne-portela/.

Rademacher, Virginia. "Truth and Circumstantiality in Javier Cercas' Biofictions." *American Book Review* 39, no. 1 (November/December 2017): 6, 27.

Rademacher, Virginia Newhall. "Postmodern Quest and the Role of Distance in Antonio Muñoz Molina's *El invierno en Lisboa*." *Contemporary Literary Criticism*, edited by Jeffrey W. Hunter, vol. 289, Gale, 2010. *Gale Literature Resource Center*, link.gale.com/apps/doc/H1100100333/LitRC?u=mlin_m_babson&sid=summon&xid=33ffe1cd. Accessed 10 March 2022. Originally published in *CiberLetras*, no. 18, Dec. 2007.

Rademacher, Virginia Newhall. "The Art of Seduction: Truth or Fanfiction in the World of Online 'Friends' and the Blogosphere." In *Hybrid Storyspaces: Redefining the Critical Enterprise in 21st Century Hispanic Literature,* edited by Christine Henseler and Debra Castillo, 97–122. *Hispanic Issues Online* 9 (Spring 2012). https://conservancy.umn.edu/bitstream/handle/11299/182965/hiol_09_08_rademacher_the_art_of_seduction.pdf?sequence=1&isAllowed=y.

Rademacher, Virginia Newhall. "Playing for Real: Simulated Games of Identity in Spain's Gen X Narrative." In *Gen X Goes Global: Mapping a Youth Culture in Motion*, edited by Christine Henseler, 193–221. New York and London: Routledge, 2013.

Reßmann, Wolfgang, Moritz Stock et al. "Fan(fiction): Acting on Media and the Politics of Appropriation." *Media and Communication* 5, no. 3 (2017): 15–27.

Restrepo, Sergio. "Pos-simulacro e hipermodernidad en *Como la sombra que se va*, de Antonio Muñoz Molina," *Nomenclatura: aproximaciones a los estudios hispánicos* 5 (2017): Article 6.

Richardson, Nathan. "No Pensar', or Does the Contemporary Novel of Memory Really Want to Know? *Tiempo de silencio, Corazón tan blanco, Soldados de Salamina* and Beyond." *Letras Hispanas* 7 (2010): 2–16.

Rodríguez, Guillermo. "Antonio Orejudo: Mi generación es de chinchinabo." *Huffington Post*, July 4, 2017. https://www.huffingtonpost.es/2017/04/07/antonio-orejudo-mi-generacion-es-de-chichinabo_a_22030557/.

Rodríguez Marcos, Javier. "Erice-Navarro: novelas retocadas con photoshop." *El País*. October 4, 2016. https://elpais.com/elpais/2016/10/03/opinion/1475514699_917948.html.

Rothman, Joshua. "What If You Could Do It All Over? The Uncanny Allure of Our Unlived Lives." *The New Yorker*, December 14, 2020. https://www.newyorker.com/magazine/2020/12/21/what-if-you-could-do-it-all-over.

Rüeggemeier, Anne. "Beyond the Subject – towards the Object? Nancy K. Miller's What They Saved: Pieces of a Jewish Past (2011) and the Materiality of Life Writing." *European Journal of Life Writing* 5 (2016): 36–54.

Schaberg, Christopher. *The Work of Literature in an Age of Post-Truth*. New York and London: Bloomsbury, 2018.

Shapiro, Barbara. "Circumstantial Evidence: Of Law, Literature, Culture," *Yale Journal of Law and Humanities* 5, no. 1 (1993): 219–41.

Shapiro, Barbara. "Beyond Reasonable Doubt: The Evolution of a Concept." In *Fictions of Knowledge: Fact, Evidence, Doubt*, edited by Yota Batsaki et al., 19–39. New York: Palgrave Macmillan, 2012.

Simons, Jan. "Narratives, Games, and Theory." *Game Studies* 7, no. 1 (August 2007). http://gamestudies.org/0701/articles/simons.

Smith, Ali. *There but for the*. London: Penguin Press, 2006.

Solnit, Rebecca. *A Field Guide to Getting Lost*. New York: Penguin Press, 2005.

Spires, Robert. "Depolarization and the New Spanish Fiction at the Millennium." *Anales de la Literatura Española Contemporánea* 30, nos 1–2 (2005): 485–512.

Stavris, Nicholas. "The Anxieties of the Present." In *Supplanting the Postmodern: An Anthology of Writings on the Arts and Culture of the Early 21st Century*, edited by David Rudrum and Nicholas Stavris, 349–64. New York and London: Bloomsbury, 2015.

Sturgeon, Jonathan. "The Death of the Postmodern Novel and the Rise of Autofiction," *Flavorwire*, December 31, 2014. https://www.flavorwire.com/496570/2014-the-death-of-the-postmodern-novel-and-the-rise-of-autofiction.

Švelch, Jan. "Paratextuality in Game Studies: A Theoretical Review and Citation Analysis." *Game Studies* 20, no. 2 (June 2020). http://gamestudies.org/2002/articles/jan_svelch.

Tally, Robert. "Meta-Capital: Culture and Financial Derivatives." *Cultural Logic* Vol 17 (2010), Special Issue on Culture and Crisis. Edited by Joseph G. Ramsey. https://ojs.library.ubc.ca/index.php/clogic/article/view/191529.

Taylor, Christopher. "Enrique of the Silver Tongue." *London Review of Books* 40, no. 6 (March 22, 2018). https://www.lrb.co.uk/the-paper/v40/n06/christopher-tayler/enrique-of-the-silver-tongue.

Taylor, Mark. *Confidence Games: Money and Markets in a World without Redemption*. Chicago: University of Chicago Press, 2004.

Thurston, Angie, Casper ter Kulle, and Sue Phillips. *Care of Souls*. Report. https://sacred.design/wp-content/uploads/2019/10/CareofSouls.pdf.

Timmer, Nicoline. *Do You Feel It Too? The Post-Postmodern Syndrome in American Fiction*. Amsterdam and New York: Rodopi, 2010.

Tóibín, Colm, "Colm Tóibín: The Anchored Imagination of the Biographical Novel." Interview by Bethany Layne. In *Conversations with Biographical Novelists: Truthful Fictions across the Globe*, edited by Michael Lackey, 223–34. New York: Bloomsbury, 2019.

Tonkin, Boyd. "Javier Cercas Interview: Picking Over the Wounds of Spain's Recent Past." *The Independent*, June 8, 2014. https://www.independent.co.uk/arts-entertainment/books/features/javier-cercas-interview-picking-over-the-wounds-of-spain-s-recent-past-9500996.html.

Toth, Josh. *Truth and Metafiction: Plasticity and Renewal in American Narrative*. New York and London: Bloomsbury, 2021.

Uncertain Commons. *Speculate This*! Durham: Duke University Press, 2013.

Unigwe, Chika. "Biographical Fiction and the Creation of Possible Lives." Interview by Michael Lackey. In *Conversations with Biographical Novelists: Truthful Fictions across the Globe*, 247–58. New York and London: Bloomsbury, 2019.

van Den Akker, Robin and Timotheus Vermeulen. "Periodizing the 2000s, or the Emergence of Metamodernism." In *Metamodernism: Historicity, Affect and Depth after Postmodernism,* edited by Robin van den Akker, Alison Gibbons and Timotheus Vermeulen, 1–19. London:Rowman and Littlefield, 2017.

Vargas Llosa, Mario. "Espantoso y genial." *El País*, May 15, 2005. https://elpais.com/diario/2005/05/15/opinion/1116108006_850215.html.

Vargas Llosa. "Review of *The Impostor*: The Man Who Wasn't There." *The Wall Street Journal*, August 13, 2018. https://www.wsj.com/articles/the-impostor-review-the-man-who-wasnt-there–1535060707.

Velasco Oliaga, Javier. "Entrevista a Rosa Montero, autora de *La ridícula idea de no volver a verte*." Interview in *Toda Literatura*, October 23, 2014. Online.

Vint, Sherryl. "Promissory Futures: Reality and Imagination in Finance and Fiction." *CR: The New Centennial Review* 19, no. 1 (Spring 2019): 11–36.

Wark, McKenzie. *Gamer Theory*. Cambridge: Harvard University Press, 2007.

Wegner, Philip. *Shockwaves of Possibility: Essays on Science Fiction, Globalization, and Utopia*. Dublin, Ireland: Ralahine Utopian Studies, 2014.

Welsh, Alexander. *Strong Representations: Narrative and Circumstantial Evidence in England*. Baltimore: Johns Hopkins University Press, 1992.

White, Bryony. "The Gaze of Others." *Times Literary Supplement*, April 30, 2021. https://www.the-tls.co.uk/articles/open-water-caleb-azumah-nelson-review-bryony-white/.

White, James Boyd. *From Expectation to Experience: Essays on Law and Legal Education*. Ann Arbor: University of Michigan Press, 1999.

Whitman, James. "The Origins of Reasonable Doubt." *Yale Law School Faculty Scholarship*, March 2005.

Wood, Michael. "Afterward." In *Fictions of Knowledge: Fact, Evidence, Doubt*, edited by Yota Batsaik et al. 213–19. New York: Palgrave Macmillan, 2012.

Ybarra, Gabriela. *El comensal*. Barcelona: Caballo de Troya (Penguin Random House), 2015.

Ybarra, Gabriela. *The Dinner Guest*. Translated by Natasha Wimmer. London: UK. Harvell Secker (Vintage Press), 2018.

Ybarra, Gabriela. Interview (Podcast), *Vostok Seis*, July 30, 2018. https://www.vostokseis.com/episodios/gabriela-ybarra.

Ybarra, Gabriela. "Imagining Truths: In Conversation with Gabriela Ybarra." Interview by Sarah Timmer Harvey. *Asymptote*, June 20, 2019. https://www.asymptotejournal.com/blog/2019/06/20/imagining-truths-in-conversation-with-gabriela-ybarra/.

INDEX

www.ingramcontent.com/pod-product-compliance
Lightning Source LLC
Chambersburg PA
CBHW070526100726
47907CB00004B/995

* 9 7 8 1 5 0 1 3 8 6 9 4 7 *